Empire's Bard

Marian L Thorpe

Empire's Bard
Copyright © 2022 Marian L Thorpe
Arboretum Press
Guelph, ON, Canada

ISBN (print): 978-1-7771783-9-0
ISBN (e-book): 978-1-990711-00-8

www.arboretumpress.com

ALL RIGHTS RESERVED

Oraiáphon
Copyright © 2020 Marian L Thorpe
ISBN (print): 978-1-9992101-2-0
ISBN (e-book): 978-1-9992101-3-7

Empire's Reckoning
Copyright © 2020 Marian L Thorpe
ISBN (print): 978-1-9992101-4-4
ISBN (e-book): 978-1-9992101-5-1

MARIAN L THORPE

This book contains material protected under International and Federal Copyright Laws and Treaties. Any unauthorized reprint or use of this material is prohibited. No part of this book may be reproduced or transmitted in any form or by any means, electronic or mechanical, including photocopying, recording, or by any information storage and retrieval system without express written permission from the author, except for brief excerpts used in reviews.

A catalogue record for this book is available from Libraries and Archives Canada

Cover Design by Anthony O'Brien
www.bookcoverdesign.store

ORAIÁPHON

This one's for you, Brian.

———◆◆◆———

Author's Note

The events of *Oraiáphon* begin almost immediately after the Battle of the Taiva, the penultimate scene of *Empire's Exile*. I hope it will please readers who asked for more of this part of the story, and provide context to the central conflicts of *Empire's Reckoning*, the next book in Sorley's duology.

'Oraiáphon' is pronounced *or **eye** ah phon*, the emphasis on the second syllable. In this world, we know the same mythological character as Orpheus.

———◆◆◆———

Orpheus with his lute made trees,
And the mountain tops that freeze,
Bow themselves when he did sing:
To his music plants and flowers
Ever sprung; as sun and showers
There had made a lasting spring.
Every thing that heard him play,
Even the billows of the sea,
Hung their heads, and then lay by.

Shakespeare; Henry VIII

<h1 style="text-align:center">Chapter 1</h1>

"THE SCOUTS REPORT NO Marai within Linrathe," the soldier said. "There are still skirmishes along the Sterre, but those are diminishing, and appear to be mostly defiance and bluster, *Teannas'óg*."

"Thank you," Ruar said, dismissing him. *Teannas'óg*, they called him, young leader, after his calm and thoughtful leadership during the fighting against the Marai. Hard to believe, I mused, that he was not yet fourteen. Donnalch had taught him well.

His regent, his great-uncle Liam, grunted. "You need to ride north, Ruar. Be seen by your people," he said.

Ruar turned to me. "Will you accompany me, Lord Sorley?"

I should. This was my country's leader asking me. He hadn't been formally recognized as *Teannasach*, but there was little doubt that would happen. The Marai were in retreat, so we must have won, but the rumours from the Empire were confused and contradictory; nothing official had reached us yet, here in the camp hidden among the hills and valleys of Linrathe. Almost everyone I loved was somewhere in the Empire, and I did not know if they were safe.

"You do not need me, Ruar," I prevaricated. "I cannot even play for you, just now." I had taken a sword wound to my left arm; nothing serious, and already healing, but it did prevent me from holding a *ladhar* comfortably.

"But you are my friend, Sorley," he protested. His great-uncle scowled. The *Raséair* did not approve of me, although he had grudgingly praised my efforts in bringing Ruar north, and in the fighting. Talk of my choice of men as my bedmates had reached Liam's ears, I assumed. I wondered, sometimes, if it was one of the reasons my father had supported the Marai, knowing we would be on opposite sides, and ensuring our family's lands went to my younger brother Roghan, and not to his *channàdarra* oldest.

Distant shouts reached my ears. I looked up, frowning, just as the tent flaps parted and a soldier entered. "My pardon, *Teannas'óg*," he said, "but there is a rider come from the south, looking for the Lord Sorley. He has dark skin, and speaks no Linrathan, nor much of the Empire's tongue. He is very agitated."

Druisius? Fear rose. "Excuse me, Ruar," I said, following the soldier toward the perimeter of the camp. I saw Druisius with the guard, pacing impatiently, and broke into a run. "Druise!" I shouted. "What has happened?"

"Cillian," he called. "He is badly wounded. Lena needs you. Why are you still here, Sorley? Did not the messenger sent from the Taiva reach you?"

Cillian. He should have been safe. If he was wounded— "No messenger," I said. "What of the Emperor?" I'd reached Druise now.

"The Emperor Callan is dead," Druise said, frowning at the bandage on my arm. "Traitors, within his own army. Cillian would be dead too, except the Emperor blocked some arrows with his own body. But not all. Come, Sorley. There is no time to waste. You are hurt?"

"Just a cut," I answered. "But what happened?" A twisting, inside: I'd liked Callan.

"I will tell you as we ride," he said. "Gnaius says he will die from infection. Lena will not sleep, barely eats, will not leave him. She is making herself ill."

"Dear gods," I said. Cillian, dying? No, my mind said. No. "She is pregnant, Druise."

He swore. "She will lose the baby," he said bluntly. "We must ride, Sorley."

"Find us fresh horses," I told the guard. "Now. And food and water, enough to get us to the Wall. Ten minutes. Druise, come with me. I must tell Ruar what has happened."

Fifteen minutes later we were riding south, at speed. Ruar had given me leave, immediately. As I turned to go, he stopped me, a hand on my arm.

"Lord Sorley," he said, his young face serious. "I swear to you I will do all I can to regain Sorham and your lands. Believe me in this. I will right the wrong my uncle did."

I didn't really care, at this moment, but a response was needed. "I do believe you, Ruar," I said. "I wish you success."

"There may be a place for you in that fight, some day," he replied.

"If I can be of use, I will be," I said, rote words. My mind was not in this wind-shaken tent, but long hours south and west, at Wall's End. I would have said almost anything to speed my leaving.

Druisius shouted the story at me as we rode: Kebhan's treachery, the Lestian archers within the Empire's army swayed by his promises, the betrayal of the drum codes to the Marai. "Lena killed Fritjof," he told me. "Her arrow, in his neck. Junia had killed his son, minutes before. It was all that saved us, those two deaths."

"Is Cillian really dying?" I asked. I could not bring myself to believe it.

"He is not in this world, and his skin burns to the touch," Druise answered. "Gnaius says only the gods can save him."

Cold fear battled with dull resignation for the rest of the long ride. We switched horses at the first guard post we reached on the Wall, and twice or three times again. I half-slept in the saddle, once we were on the road that paralleled the Wall, rousing only when my horse slowed.

We rode into Wall's End not long after dawn. I slid off my horse, my injured arm aching. I could barely stand. I realized that Druisius must be in agony: he was a foot-soldier, not cavalry, but he had been riding at speed for over three days.

I turned to Druise. "Go," he said.

"Where?"

"The sick rooms. " I turned to the guard who had opened the gate.

"Where?" I asked again. He pointed, explaining. I tried to run, forcing my legs to move.

More questions, inside the building, and then I was in the room. Lena slumped in a chair, her hand holding Cillian's. His chest rose and fell shallowly. She did not look up. "Lena," I said.

She raised her head. Huge dark shadows swallowed her eyes, and her face was thin, far too thin. Her hair spiked and clumped on her head. "Sorley," she whispered.

I knelt beside her, trying to hold her. She shook her head. "Talk to him," she rasped.

"Help me hold on to him, please, Sorley. Please." I put my hand over hers, and Cillian's. His fingers were white and his flesh cold, but the flush of fever stained his cheeks.

"Cillian," I said, my voice catching. "Cillian, it's Sorley. I'm here. Can you hear me?" Tears pricked at my eyes. Oh, gods, Cillian, I thought. Don't die. Please don't die. I felt Lena's hand clench mine, and heard a deep, racking sob.

"Sorley," she moaned, turning suddenly to hide her face against my shoulder, sobs tearing through her. I pulled her close with one arm, the other still holding Cillian's hand.

"I will fetch Gnaius," I heard Druisius say. I hadn't heard him come in. He and the doctor returned in a few minutes. Lena still wept.

"How have you let her get to this state?" I growled at Gnaius in Casilan. "She is pregnant. Did you not know?"

"I did," he replied gravely. "But she has refused whatever I have offered, and even an order from her *Princip* was ignored." He bent to her. "Tell her," he said, "that she must think of the child. His child. She must sleep, or risk losing it."

I translated. She shook her head. "Lena," I murmured. "I will stay with him. I promise. Druise will find an instrument, somewhere, and I will play music for him, and talk to him. But you must sleep."

She shook her head again, but less vehemently. "You promise?"

"I do. Let Gnaius give you a sleeping draught." There was a cot against the wall. "You do not even have to leave the room."

"See if she will let someone take her to the baths," Gnaius whispered. "I will give her a mild dose of poppy now, and a bit more after, to make her sleep."

"No," Lena said, when I suggested it.

"Tell her I will take her," Druisius said. Highly irregular, I thought, but what did it matter? I relayed his offer. She looked up.

"Just for a few minutes," I said. "You do need the baths, Lena." She stank of sweat and fear.

"Oh," she said. "All right. No one but Druisius, though."

"Who is here that can permit this?" I asked Druise. "The baths will have to be closed to all others." I kept glancing at Cillian, watching for each breath.

"I will find someone," he said. Gnaius, at a side table, prepared the first dose of poppy.

"She is to drink this." He held it out. Lena took it, her hand trembling. She swallowed it, making a face. Druisius came back, with, of all people, Casyn.

"General!" I said in surprise.

"I was on my way here to see how Cillian did, and Lena, this morning," he said gravely. "What is it Druisius is asking?" I explained. He turned to Gnaius, making writing motions. The physician gestured him to the table. Casyn wrote a note, quickly. "Take her," he said to Druisius, holding out the note. "He is in good hands, Lena," he said to her softly, as Druise led her to the door.

Casyn's eyes went to Cillian. "The hands of the gods, the physician says," he murmured. I turned to Gnaius.

"How is he, truly?" I asked.

"If the gods love him, he might live, but I doubt it," he said. "I can do little." My heart clenched.

I told Casyn what Gnaius had said. He nodded, reaching out to touch Cillian gently. "I will pray," he said simply. "He is a soldier, too. I am glad you are here, Lord Sorley. I must work, now."

Work. I remembered something Druise told me as we rode. "*Princip*," I said. "I apologize, for how I greeted you earlier." He was Callan's heir, and now the *Princip* of the Western Empire.

"No matter," he replied.

I had barely slept for over a day, but I kept my promise to Lena. I sat beside Cillian, holding his hand when I wasn't playing the *cithar* Druise had found me. I played, and I talked and sang in Linrathan: if anything would reach him, I thought, it would be his own tongue. When I had to leave, for the minutes it took to relieve myself, Druise took over. Even when Gnaius or the fort's medics came to wash and turn him, and to drip liquids or poppy juice mixed with wine into his mouth, I stayed. I saw the terrible wounds on his back and thigh, and the red streaks of infection. I made myself endure it all, although the moans of pain Cillian made tested my self-control to its limits.

"His eyes may open," Gnaius told me. "He may speak. It will not make sense. He may see things that are not here, but not that which is. But if he begins to thrash about, or tries to rise, do not let him, and send someone for me, immediately."

More than a day passed before Lena reappeared. She had slept the entire time, exhaustion assisted by the sleeping draught. Clean and rested, she looked marginally better than the day before. I stood up, swaying with my own fatigue, when she came in. She knelt, unspeaking, to kiss Cillian on his chapped lips, murmuring to him.

"Thank you," she said, looking up at me. "You should sleep now."

"Baths first," Druise said from the cot where he had been dozing. "Then some sleep, and then the two of you take turns, yes?"

"Yes." Her hand went to her belly. "Yes, all right. The cadet is outside the door, if I need someone to go for Gnaius?"

Druisius checked. The boy was there. I bent to kiss Cillian's forehead, feeling the heat of his skin. "Stay with us, *mo gràhadh*," I whispered. As I turned to leave, Lena put her hand on my arm.

"It is all right, Sorley," she said. "I need you to love him, and to tell him that you do. Maybe with two of us loving him so much, we can keep him in this world. Maybe the gods will see, and take pity on us."

I put a hand on her shoulder, and bent to kiss her cheek, fighting dizziness as I straightened. "Maybe they will." I couldn't find anything else to offer hope. I couldn't see any hope.

"Come," Druise said. I followed him to the baths, stumbling more than once. In the antechamber, he undressed me and sponged me down before leading me into the steaming water. Had he done this for Lena, yesterday? I supposed he had.

A wine flask and cups had appeared on the table in my room. From where? Wine must be in short supply; did I rate it because I was the lord Sorley, or because I was thought to need it? Did I care? I poured two cups, not watering mine at all. I drank it, quickly, and poured more.

"Sorley," Druise said, concern in his voice. We had been lovers in Casil, for a few weeks. I had told him the first night that I loved Cillian, but in our casual, temporary pairing, what had it mattered?

"Don't tell me not to," I said bluntly. "I need it, Druise. He is going to die, and there is nothing I can do, or Lena, or even Gnaius, it seems."

"Maybe not."

I drained my wine cup and threw the cup against the wall. It shattered, the sound clear and sharp in the still air of the room. It didn't help. I took a deep, shuddering breath. "I can't even be there all the time. Gods, Druise, I still love him—and I'm sorry, I know I shouldn't say that to you—and I can't take it. I must leave—Lena stays, sleeps there, eats there—and I've only been here a day. Why am I so weak?"

"You are not weak," he said, putting an arm around me. "Lena believes she can keep him alive by her will, her love. That is why she will not leave. You do not think that, in your heart."

I leaned against his solid strength. "No," I admitted. "I don't. Perhaps the music eases him, and it cannot hurt to talk to him, but will it save him? I don't think so."

"Sleep now," he urged.

"You must be exhausted too. Don't you need to sleep?" I yawned, hugely.

"I have slept more than you might think, this last day." A ghost of his grin came and went. "Maybe I stay?"

Fatigue and wine fogged my thoughts. "Stay?"

"The bed is wide. Better than the barracks."

"But…" I had just reminded him I loved Cillian. Why was he offering to stay? "Can you?"

"No one cares where I sleep."

"If you want." I couldn't work this out right now. I sat on the bed, pulling off first my shirt, and then the soft indoor shoes. That was enough. I lay back. Sleep claimed me before I had finished pulling up the blanket.

When I woke some hours later, the blanket was fully over me. In the blackness of the room I could hear soft snores. Where—? Memory asserted itself, and with it fear. I stifled a whimper with my hand. A moment later I felt fingers on my back.

"Sorley," Druise whispered. His hand moved, his lips nibbling at my neck. I felt the pulse of response. But I shouldn't, not now, not with—

Druise bit my shoulder, not quite gently, and I whimpered in a different way and rolled over.

I couldn't call what we did making love. I gave into a need to extinguish fear and death in the demands of hands and tongue and sex, and there was nothing gentle or loving about it. I didn't recognize myself, not in what I did or what I allowed—anything not to think—and when it was done and I lay limp and breathless, hollowed out, Druise put one hand on my belly and kissed me on my lips.

"Did that help?" he asked. He ran his fingers down my cheek, a gesture that spoke of tenderness. Only a few minutes earlier that same big hand had held both my wrists in a trap-like grip. "Better to use anger," he said. "Even as we just did."

"I'm not angry." He chuckled, drily.

"You are," he said. "Sleep again, *amané*."

"I can't," I said, but I was slipping towards a welcome darkness. His hand still rubbed my back. "Druise," I murmured, "Why…?" I didn't hear an answer.

CHAPTER 2

I WOKE MANY HOURS later, alone, to find an older man quietly placing a tray of soup and bread on the table. "Sergeant Birel, isn't it?" I asked. Casyn's soldier-servant.

"Yes, my lord." I looked around. My clothes had been draped over a chair, the breeches on top. I hoped Druise had done that, and not Birel.

"Do you know where Druisius is?" I asked.

"In the infirmary, sir, with the Casilani physician. He acts as translator. The *Princip* asks if, once you have eaten, you would speak with him briefly. He said to tell you that he will not keep you from the Major's side longer than necessary."

The Major. Cillian's rank. He was still alive. "I will return shortly," Birel said. I ate the food—I was hungry, I discovered—and drank a little wine, well-watered. Then I dressed in the clean clothes I found on a stool, combed my hair, and waited, trying to think about what Casyn might want, and not what I had done in the night. Birel returned promptly. He led me through passages to a tall door, knocked once, and opened it. Casyn and Turlo were bent over maps. "Lord Sorley, sir," Birel said, ushering me in.

"Sorley," Turlo said. "Good to see you, *mo charaidh*, even though—" He didn't finish the thought, just shook his head helplessly. No one expects Cillian to live, I thought. And regardless, the work of the *Princip* and his advisors must go on.

"My lord Sorley," Casyn said gravely. "I will be brief. There is work that would have fallen to Cillian that I wish you to take on. I cannot command you, as you are Linrathan; I ask as your *Teannasach's* ally. There are letters to write, to Casil, before the ships sail home; that is the first thing. I also would appreciate your thoughts on some questions I have about the Marai, but that can wait. The letters are more urgent, as the Casilani ships prepare to return home before the winter gales prevent them."

"I will do my best for you, *Princip,*" I said. "But I have not the fluency in Casilan that Cillian has, nor the diplomatic turn of phrase."

"Aye, well," Turlo said. "You can begin with a letter, in Casyn's name, telling the Empress why it is you that is writing. She will forgive any awkwardness of phrase or fluency under the circumstances, I believe."

"Eudekia will be distressed," I answered. I thought she would be; for all her playing of diplomatic games, she had genuinely liked Cillian, had enjoyed his learning and wit and the agility of his mind.

"Aye," Turlo said. "Perhaps."

"When would you like me to write these letters, sir?" I asked Casyn.

"Could you relieve Lena at Cillian's bedside for a few hours, then return to us once she has eaten and rested? Two or three hours should see them done, and then you can go back to the infirmary. I understand she has agreed to take better care of herself, if you are with Cillian," Casyn added. He eyed me, assessing. "My brother told me of the child," he said quietly. "It brought him great joy. It will be, in part, why he tried to protect Cillian from the arrows."

In the sickroom, nothing had changed. Druise wasn't there, and I was relieved by that: I didn't know what I'd say to him.

Lena agreed to a few hours rest, but she went no further than the cot against the wall. I sang and played more than I talked. Somewhere in those hours my fingers strayed to the melody of *An dithës braithréan.* "Not that one," Lena said, from the cot.

"No?" I answered. "Has not war separated us?" There were tears on my cheeks again. I put the *cithar* down, burying my face in my hands.

"Sorley," Lena said softly, coming to me. She leaned against my back, her arms around me.

"It is so unfair," I said. "He was truly happy, for the first time in his life."

"I was wrong in Casil," she said, "thinking what he did there was his descent to the underworld. This is, Sorley, and the god will want to keep him. We have to keep calling to him, to remind him he is loved and must return."

"Do you really believe that, Lena?"

She shook her head. "I don't know. Gnaius does, and perhaps he is right. I am willing to believe anything, if it makes him live."

Dagney, I thought, would say that the story is about the strength of love, and its power to change people. Cillian moaned softly, his head moving from side to side. "Shhh," Lena murmured, taking his hand. "He told me once that his best memory was of his grandmother singing to him, when he was very small," she said to me. "Sing the songs she would have, Sorley. I cannot."

I sang Linrathan lullabies, and they did seem to soothe him. When Gnaius came in with the next dose of poppy, he raised an eyebrow in surprise. "He is very calm," he said to me. "He should be more distressed, from pain. What have you done?" When I told him, he nodded. "Very good," he said. He paused. "That tells me he hears, sometimes. Music and speech are not the same, but be careful of what you say near him. Nothing that will trouble him."

Lena put a hand on my shoulder. "Go to Casyn now."

"You will send for me, if he becomes restless, and music might help?"

"I will," she said. A cadet stood outside the infirmary door, half-drowsing, but there to run for the physician if needed. Or for me.

"A moment." I kissed Cillian's forehead, ran a finger along his jaw, thick with stubble. I glanced at Lena. She nodded, almost imperceptibly. I crouched, my lips close to his ear. *"Thà mi gràh agäthe,* Cillian," I murmured. "We both do," I added, still in Linrathan. "Come back to us."

I wrote the letters Casyn requested, first the one of explanation, then the ones of thanks and appreciation, ending with an estimate of the threat the Marai still posed and the measures being put in place to counter it. There would be Empire's troops on the Sterre, with the Linrathan ones, I learned, and ships on the coast, too. When had Ruar—or Liam—agreed to this?

"They haven't, yet," Turlo said, when I asked. "I ride north soon to make the proposal. I trust Ruar will see the sense in it. I would ask you to come, Sorley, were there not other demands on your time."

"I would have sent Cillian," Casyn said, quietly.

"Neither of us should have been sent," I told them. "Ruar trusts Cillian, but Liam does not. None of that house did, I believe, because his father was thought to be from the Empire. Now it is known that he is Callan's son, Liam would trust him even less, I believe."

"And you?"

I tried to find words to explain. Turlo rescued me. "The southern vice, I believe is the term, in Linrathe and Sorham."

"By the god," Casyn said, "as if whom you bed matters. But it ties my hands, Lord Sorley, if your own countrymen will not respect you. I had hoped you could be an envoy for us."

"I am Linrathan," I reminded him. "I could not be your envoy. But perhaps you could request of Ruar that I be Linrathe's envoy to the Empire?"

He frowned. "Would they do that? If they have no liking for you?"

"Ruar calls me friend," I told Casyn. "It is Liam who wants nothing to do with me, and more importantly, wants me to have no influence on Ruar. But he also, grudgingly, respects what leadership I provided against the Marai, and that I kept Ruar safe. I think he might see the position as a way both to reward my efforts and keep me away from Ruar and out of Linrathe for much of the time."

"Excellent," Turlo said. "I will make that argument, with your leave, Casyn?"

"Perhaps," the *Princip* said. "I have other questions yet." He paused, studying me. "One thing, Lord Sorley. There will be much to talk about, between Linrathe and ourselves, if we are to present a united front against the Marai, assuming Casil allows that. You may have to be away from here, some of the time. Can you do that?"

"Not yet," I said. I had to be honest from the start, if I were to work with this man for the good of both our lands. "I would leave Cillian only under protest, just now. My presence, or rather my ability to sing the songs of his childhood to him, cradle tunes, calms him, it appears. Relieves his pain, perhaps. Nor would I leave Lena, by choice. She needs a friend, and I am one."

"Aye," Turlo said. "That you are, and more, to both of them. But the hard truth, Sorley, is that it cannot be long before we know. Cillian must begin to recover soon or die. By the time I return, I should think."

I returned to the sickroom to let Lena go to the baths and rest. I watched Cillian's chest rise and fall; he'd been dosed with poppy, Lena had told me, and should sleep for some hours. He'd be too deeply unconscious for music.

The wound on my arm hurt, but it was only a tight itchiness, a sign that it was healing. I rubbed it gently.

The door opened. I looked up. Druise. Well, I had to face him sometime. He came over, unspeaking, to lay fingers on Cillian's skin. "Not much fever," he said.

"Gnaius gave him poppy and willowbark, an hour ago," I told him. He nodded, and touched my shoulder, gently.

"Wine?"

"A little," I said. He poured and watered the cups, handed me mine. "So," he said, sitting. "My story. I am from the *subura*, the second son of a minor merchant. I have three sisters, one brother; those who lived, anyhow. I did not want to be a trader, so I joined the army." He drank some of his wine. "I was a pretty boy. I caught the eye of an officer. This happens, you understand? But I did not mind. He was kind, and the food better and the room warmer."

Why was he telling me this now? I didn't know what to say, but he didn't seem to expect a response. "He was killed fighting the Boranoi. I fought and lived. Then another officer, and then another. The last gave me my post at the palace as a present, when he retired to his villa. To keep me safe, he said."

"So he cared about you."

"Yes. All did, I think."

"Did you love any of them?"

"Love? No. I liked the first man best. He could play the *cithar*. He taught me about music and bed." He stood to fetch more wine. "We have things to learn together, yes?"

Heat rose in my face. "What can I teach you?"

He chuckled. "About music, much. The other, when you have learned more about yourself, perhaps much there, too. But your question last night? I do not know. Why does any man like what he likes?"

"Oh, gods," I said. "I wasn't—I didn't—" I took a breath. "That wasn't what I meant, Druise."

"No?" He held out the wine flask. I shook my head. "What, then?"

"Why are you here? Shouldn't you be with your regiment?"

"My captain at the Taiva did not come north. I came with Lena, without permission. No one questioned it."

In the chaos after the Taiva, that did not surprise me. A missing soldier would be presumed to be dead, I supposed. "It is a good thing you did," I said. "But Casyn and Turlo know you are here, surely?"

"Of course. The General Turlo sent me to find you."

"Then I think you are his to command," I said. "Perhaps this should be straightened out? Cillian needs you. Lena needs you."

The next day I listened as Casyn elaborated on his thoughts about the Marai. In his letter to the Empress, he had said he thought that they would be disorganized for some time; with both Fritjof and Leik dead, it would take some time for a new leader to emerge. He hoped, he told me, to take advantage of that, but that he needed me to help him.

"How?" I asked. I could pass as Marai, just, my pale hair and blue eyes indicative of northern ancestors, but I might be known to some who had traded with my father. I said as much.

"No," Casyn said, "not that sort of help. I simply need you to be my translator." He stopped, grimacing. "This will sound harsh, Lord Sorley, and I do not mean it that way, but Cillian's loss will have repercussions beyond personal grief. We need his skills, with language and diplomacy, and if by some miracle he lives, it will still be long months before he might be capable of the work. Turlo speaks your tongue, but not that of the Marai or Casil. It is why I need you, do you see?"

"I do," I said. "I will do what I can, *Princip*. My Marái'sta is good; my Casilan adequate, I suppose."

"That will be enough," he said. "Can you go down to the harbour later today? The Casilani captains have questions that we cannot understand."

I agreed. Birel came in, quietly, but without knocking. "Will the Lord Sorley be joining you for the midday meal?" he asked.

"Yes," Casyn said, "if he likes. My lord?"

"Thank you," I said. *"Princip,* could we dispense with my title? I am unused to being addressed this way."

He grinned. "Certainly, Sorley, except when protocol requires, but only if you too call me by my name. Agreed?"

"Agreed," I said. "I will be pleased to eat with you, Casyn, if you will excuse me afterwards. I should let Lena rest, and play for Cillian while his noon dose of poppy takes effect."

"Anything you can do to ease my nephew's pain, or the strain on Lena, must be a priority."

<hr>

"TELL ME, SORLEY. WHAT is the man who is regent for Ruar like? I know little of him," Turlo asked, as we ate the simple meal. "Did he support Lorcann?" I thought back to the months I has spent travelling through Linrathe, gathering information, carrying messages, letting those whom I believed I could trust know that the *Ti'acha* would provide shelter and food to anyone opposing Lorcann and the Marai. Liam's name had come up once or twice, but never with anything definite to be said about him, or his allegiances.

"Liam did not publicly support Lorcann," I said. "The *Teannasach* is chosen from within the family, by all the men of blood or marriage over eighteen. When Donnalch was murdered, there was no time for that; Lorcann simply announced he was now *Teannasach*. He may have been the second choice when Donnalch was proclaimed; I do not know. But Liam is conservative in his thinking. He may truly not have approved, or he may not have thought it appropriate to voice that support without the formal acclamation."

"Think, Sorley," Casyn urged. "Did Cillian ever say anything that might tell if we can rely upon him to be our ally?"

Had we ever spoken about Liam? A memory played around the edge of my mind...the ship, on the way to Casil. "Turlo," I said, "you were there. Did he not just say that Liam would be the likely regent, for either boy?"

"Aye," Turlo said. "Not much help."

"If he agrees to me being envoy, I will be required to go to them, to receive their instructions. I could gather more information, on the way. Do you trust me with this, *Princip*?" I murmured.

"I think I must," Casyn said. "But I will ask some hard questions now, Sorley. You will forgive me for quizzing Turlo yesterday about your character: I must know the man I am entrusting with our secrets." I nodded. Of course he must, and Turlo would have been honest. "Cillian called you his dear friend, but he is more than that to you." Not a question. "Were I not *Princip*, but only regent for Cillian, where would your loyalties lie? To Ruar, or to him?"

I had come to Cillian from Ruar's side without thought or hesitation. Did not my actions tell the story? "My heart tells me Cillian," I said. "But I made Ruar a promise." *If I can be of use, I will be.* I had made one to Lena, too, that I would always be by Cillian's side. I couldn't think about that right now.

"You will have to swear an oath to him if he appoints you as envoy, will you not?" Casyn asked.

"No. Linrathe has a long tradition of neutral envoys, serving the country and not the man leading it. It is the exception to the oaths we swear. That is why Cillian was not sworn to Donnalch: I did not understand that, until he explained it to me. *Toscairen* are supposed to be detached, observers and recorders only; one of their roles is to gather opinion from all the *torps*, and that will not be given freely if the *toscaire* is known to be loyal to a particular man."

Even as I spoke I knew I was not telling the entire truth. Cillian had not just listened; he had spread ideas in subtle ways, hints and suggestions, I guessed. Whose ideas? I'd never wondered, before.

"And is your…loyalty to Cillian known in Linrathe?" Casyn probed.

"Not by anyone who would use it to cast doubt on me as a *toscaire*," I answered. Perras knew, and I guessed Dagney, but they would never reveal my secrets. There was no one else, unless my father had realized, all those years earlier, why I had been so adamant about going to the *Ti'ach na Perras*. But my reasons—that it was the best school for me to learn music and the *danta*, with the elder *scáeli* of Linrathe as its Lady and teacher— had been credible, and I did not think he had a moment's comprehension of my other motive.

"Then," Casyn said, reaching a decision, "I will trust you to make the judgement regarding Liam. All this, of course, depends on Turlo's skills of persuasion in convincing the man to appoint you *toscaire* to the Empire."

"You are riding to the Sterre?" I asked Turlo.

"Aye. That is where you said they were headed."

"Then the *Ti'ach na Asgaill* will be the closest *Ti'ach*. Asgaill—if he lives—can bear witness to what I did for Linrathe during the Marai occupation, and you, Turlo, can speak to the work we did together for both our lands. They would be further reasons for Ruar to argue for this appointment. Ruar and Liam may even be using that *Ti'ach* as their base."

"Well-reasoned," Turlo said. "I will leave tomorrow. There is much haste to be made, with the year moving toward winter. I would like to be home before the snows."

If he was leaving that quickly— "General, may I ask a question? Druisius—he has no assignment, is that right?"

"Has he not?" He thought about it. "His regiment went back to the Eastern Fort. Did he have his captain's permission to come north?" I hesitated, and he gave me a hard look, before breaking into a grin. "Don't worry, *mo charaidh*. I don't care at this moment. What has he been doing?"

I explained. "He is a very good nurse, it appears. Is there a way to assign him to the medics?"

Turlo shook his head. "I could. But even before the Taiva, was he not translating a little?"

"Some, yes. And he does for Gnaius now."

"Then we need him for more than nursing duties." He tapped a finger on the tabletop. "Would he accept being a soldier-servant? If so, I will assign him to Cillian; a major is entitled to one. He can do what is needed for him, and still be free part of the day for other duties. Send him to me."

I thanked him. He cuffed my shoulder, gently. "An officer's soldier-servant sleeps nearby, to be close if needed. Your room is not so far that he cannot be easily sent for."

My room? I must have looked puzzled. "He is your *consor*, isn't he, lad?" Turlo asked.

"*Consor*?"

"Partner. It is our practice to know when a relationship between men is not just casual, so we consider it in deployment. Isn't that why Cillian asked for him to be released from his palace duties, so he could come west with you?"

"I see," I said. "I suppose it was, yes." But why had Druise agreed? I had some sense now of how poor a lover I must have been in Casil, inexperienced and tentative, and worried about what was being reported back to the palace. Did he really want to be my partner? In music, perhaps.

We talked further of the road north, and what Turlo could expect to find at the Sterre. Then I excused myself and went to sit by Cillian so Lena could rest. Gnaius had dosed Cillian with poppy earlier, Druise told me. "I will turn him now, when he feels little pain," he said. "You will help me?"

I did what Druisius directed me to, settling Cillian on his uninjured side. He moaned, unseeing. I brushed his hair back from his face. "It needs cutting," I said, "to keep it out of his eyes."

"I will cut it, when I wash him later," Druise said, propping pillows on either side of Cillian. How had he learned to be such a good nurse? Cillian moaned again, but it sounded more like a sigh, and less like a cry of pain. I took his hand.

"When Lena comes back, will you accompany me to the docks?" I asked Druise. "The *Princip* has asked me to find out what the Casilani captains want. And Turlo wants to see you, as soon as possible."

Outside, the stones of the fort gleamed in pale sunshine. It had rained earlier. Druise walked beside me as we made our way to the steps that led down to the docks. A commotion at the southern gate caught my attention. A soldier, and from the look of her lathered horse one who had ridden at speed. She ran for the headquarters. I did too, not knowing why: an instinct. We met outside the *Princip*'s workroom, just as the guard opened the door.

"*Princip*," the soldier said, saluting. "I am to tell you a ship has been sighted, sailing north, flying the Casilani flag, sir. There are two smaller ships accompanying it."

"How far away?"

"We were on the headland south of Berge," the scout said, "and the ships were distant. Two hours, perhaps? The winds are favourable."

"Thank you, soldier," Casyn said, dismissing her. "Lord Sorley, who might this be?"

"I have no idea," I said. "But I will find out."

CHAPTER 3

HALF AN HOUR LATER I was back at Casyn's workroom, and not alone. *"Princip,"* I said, indicating the man with me, "this is Rufin, captain of the Casilani fleet. He tells me the approaching ship is almost certainly carrying a Casilani official, the Procurator. His name is Decanius."

"The Procurator?" Casyn replied. "What is his job? And why was I not informed officially?"

"His job is one of great responsibility and great power, *Princip,*" Rufin told him. "He is to ensure Casil's laws are put in place, at least those governing the army, and taxation, and certain resources."

I tried not to look shocked as I translated for Casyn. How had we not known this? But Rufin answered my unspoken question. "Cillian was aware of this man; we spoke of it as we sailed west."

Cillian, I thought, would have seen this as his responsibility, to be discussed with the Emperor and his advisors. But that meant Casyn should have known, and I could tell from his expression he had not.

"What will he expect when he arrives?" Straight to the point, no time wasted in futile questions.

"A formal welcome; the best rooms you can give him, and the best food. He is the Empress's representative, *Princip.*"

"And in terms of my time?"

"Much of it, I am afraid. I am only a ship's captain, *Princip,* and this is beyond my experience."

"And mine," Casyn murmured. "Ask him what Cillian thought, please, Sorley."

"It is not what they spoke of," I relayed, "except that Cillian said he would want access to records here, to prepare for the discussions."

"Why is Rufin telling us this?" Casyn asked. "What is his motive?"

I asked. Rufin smiled. "Tell the *Princip*," he said, "I like it here in these western lands. There is space, and so much sea, and if this coast is to be patrolled and protected against the threat from the north, a fleet will be needed. It will need a commanding officer, and I would like to be that man. A recommendation from the *Princip* might help, and," he paused, "the man appointed as Procurator likes to promote his friends. He does not count me among them."

Casyn grimaced. "Tell us about him."

Decanius, Rufin told us, had been second to the procurator of another province east of Casil. Competent enough, from all he had heard. "He is well-connected," Rufin commented. "His mother's brother is Quintus, advisor to the Empress."

Quintus, who had advised Eudekia not to support our plea for help; who had tried to bribe Cillian with citizenship and lands and was possibly the mind behind the attempt to kidnap Lena. Whose opposition had led Cillian to offer himself to Eudekia as her consort, if that was what was needed to seal the alliance. Even I could make these sums add up.

I explained, quickly, to Casyn. "Eudekia must have agreed to give him this position to allay Quintus's opposition," I told him. "He will be reporting back to his uncle, I would think."

"You are almost certainly right on both counts," Casyn said. "Tell the captain he has our thanks. Ask the guard to find someone to escort him back to the docks. I need you to stay with me, Lord Sorley."

The *Princip*, I discovered, could swear creatively and at length—and some of his invective was directed at his dead brother. "Callan's mind was on defeating the Marai," he muttered. "He would have planned to deal with this man and the terms of the treaty once the war was over. And yet again I am left to clean up the aftermath of his thoughtlessness." He grimaced. "But to the task at hand. This man wants to catch us unawares, I would say. Birel!"

"A formal meal," he told his aide, when he appeared a minute later, "the best we can produce, for this evening. For perhaps ten or twelve. The best wine. See to it." He turned to me. "And now you must teach me to greet the Procurator properly in Casilan."

I went over Casyn's words of formal greeting with him one last time, correcting his pronunciation. Then I left him, going first to the infirmary. I told Lena and Druisius the news. Druise eyed me critically. "You need a shave."

I felt my chin. "I suppose I do," I said. "I better do that now."

"I will," he said unexpectedly. He shaved Cillian, I knew. "This man will notice."

I hoped Birel thought the same. Casyn's chin had shown grey stubble, this morning. I touched Cillian's hand. Cold, as always. But his nails were neatly trimmed, and the skin as smooth as the unguents Lena applied could make it. The small attentions of love.

In my room I sat with a towel draped around my shoulders as Druise shaved me, competently and closely, the scrape of the blade against my throat making me shiver. When my jaw and upper lip were smooth, I took fresh clothes from the chest, shaking them to remove the creases before changing. Druise watched, half amused, half appreciative, I thought. He clicked his tongue. Bending, he picked up my boots, scuffed and worn. I had no others. "I can fix these," he said.

"Druise," I protested. "You are not my servant."

"Friends help each other, yes?" He put the boots down and left the room, returning in a few minutes with something in his hands. As I combed my hair and shrugged on the cloak, managing not to stab myself with the pin of the brooch, I watched him working at the leather of my boots with grease and a flattish piece of bone. I could see the scratches and scuffs disappearing as he worked. Did all soldiers know this trick? By the time he was done, the boots shone.

I pulled them on and stood up. "Lord Sorley," Druise said, grinning.

"Will I impress the Procurator?"

He snorted. "Decanius? Certainly not."

Casyn too was freshly shaven. Dressed in the grey-and-white of his office, his silver pendent catching the sunlight, he appeared to me completely calm as we waited on the jetty. The rowers brought the ship in; ropes were thrown, commands shouted. We stayed well back, out of the way, watching. Its captain disembarked, with a man of middle height, balding, stocky. Rufin, who had been overseeing the ship's docking, joined them.

"Come," Casyn said to me. We approached the captain and his companion.

"*Princip*," Rufin said, "may I present the Procurator Decanius."

"Procurator," Casyn replied, his Casilan pronunciation acceptable, "be welcome. I am Casyn, *Princip* of the Western Empire, by the grace of the Empress Eudekia."

"Lord Sorley of Linrathe," I said, as we had agreed. "I act as translator for the *Princip*, Procurator. May I too welcome you to Wall's End?"

Decanius inclined his head. "*Princip*. Lord Sorley. May I extend my sympathies, *Princip*, at the death of your brother, the last Emperor. And his son?" Something in his voice, the tone of it, told me these questions were formalities. He didn't care.

"Is gravely ill, Procurator. The prognosis is poor. I thank you for your sympathy and your concern," Casyn replied, through me.

"Shall we proceed to the fort, Procurator?" I asked. "You might wish the baths, after your voyage?"

"Baths!" he said, "Baths and wine would be most welcome." As we climbed the steps to the fort, I noticed Decanius stopped more than once to catch his breath, although he claimed to be looking at the view. "Well-situated," he noted. "What is the village I can see?"

"Berge," I told him. "A women's fishing village."

"Women?" he said. "So close? How interesting." He puffed his way to the top. The guards at the gate, their weapons gleaming, saluted. He ignored them.

"I will have the baths to myself?" he asked, but it wasn't a question. I assured him he would.

"Ask the *Princip* to join me," he said, "and you, of course, Lord Sorley, as we cannot communicate without you."

"Of course," Casyn said. "Will you show the Procurator his room, and then we will meet at the baths?

Decanius said nothing about his rooms, situated on the floor above the workrooms and lesser bedrooms. He was happy to see the wine jug. I poured him a cup; he did not offer me one. He went to the window, nodding appreciatively at the view over the training fields and the glimpse of the jetties, and the sea beyond. Shedding his cloak, he tossed it on the bed. If he expected me to hang it up, he was disappointed. I already didn't like him, although I could not have said exactly why. He had been polite enough, but he looked *through* people, I thought, unless he believed them to be of some use. In Sorham and Linrathe, every man and woman had value, their own worth to the estate, and Casyn treated all his soldiers in the same way. Perhaps, I mused, it is because there are so few of us, on both sides of the Wall. Could you value everyone, in a city as crowded as Casil?

But this was not Casil. Birel—I supposed it was Birel—had ensured the Procurator's arrival was known to all the troops, including the cadets, and he was saluted respectfully by all ranks. I acknowledged everyone with a nod or a word, purposefully. If I appeared a barbarian in the Procurator's eyes, I thought, better that than Casilani indifference.

At the baths Decanius behaved no differently, accepting the assistance of the attendant without a word. In the hot pool, he looked around him. The pool and walls were unadorned, unlike Casil's baths. "It serves its purpose," he said. "A modicum of comfort in this northern land."

"Tell him," Casyn said, after my translation, "Wall's End, like the Eastern Fort, is a military complex, and that I am sorry if he is not as comfortable as he would have liked. We will attempt to rectify that, as best we can."

"There is one thing," Decanius said in response. "I am in need of a woman. Or a boy, I suppose."

I am just the translator, I reminded myself. Casyn's face remained impassive, although I could hear the control in his voice when he spoke.

"Procurator," I said. "You must understand that both men and women in the Western Empire choose their own bed partners, and that cadets—male or female—are not permitted to consort with adults. If a woman of Wall's End decides to be your lover, that is her choice, and cannot be coerced."

Decanius looked decidedly put out. In Sorham, I thought, a man of his rank would have been offered a serving woman as a matter of course. It was part of their duties, although they could refuse, and children born of a night with a visiting *Harr* were accepted into the *torp* without question. But this was not Sorham, either.

"I see," he said. "How uncivilized. What about the women from the fishing village?"

"Casyn," I said, "he must know what the Marai did to the women here. Should I remind him?"

"Please."

"My lord Decanius," I said, "the women of Berge, and all the villages, have the same freedoms. But you are unlikely to meet with a welcome there; you will recall the violence they have endured at the hand of the enemy Casil helped us defeat."

"But there are Casilani troops who have chosen to remain?"

"A very few, yes," I told him.

"And as they are Casilani, I may—interact—with them as I wish," he said. The muscles of Casyn's neck tightened.

"Of course," he said.

"We should also discuss the composition of the army," Decanius went on. "There are irregularities in your command structure that must be remedied. I have asked one or two of the officers who came to remain, and I have sent for others."

"Perhaps," Casyn said, "that discussion should wait, Procurator, until the General Turlo, who was in Casil, and my other advisors can be present? We are not accustomed to deliberating matters of policy in the baths. We prefer to speak of lighter things. Do you play *xache*, Decanius?"

"I have been known to," the Procurator said, "with an opponent of sufficient skill. Is there a library here?"

"A small one." On my own initiative, I added, "If it is books you wish, Procurator, I can request some to be sent from the school I attended. Some of Casil's philosophers, and Heræcria's too, although in translation to Casilan."

"Do so," he said. "I must say I am grieved to know the Emperor's son is so unwell. From what my uncle told me of him, I was hoping to discuss philosophy with him. Although he does not speak Heræcrian, of course."

"We too grieve his health," I said, not waiting for Casyn's reply. "He has been my friend for nearly a decade, and his *quincala* is pregnant. I pray the child will know its father." I had been abrupt. "We are grateful for the expertise of the physician Gnaius in attending to Cillian," I added.

"Gnaius." Decanius brightened. "Is he still here? I expected he would have returned home. I look forward to his company."

Somehow both Casyn and I remained calm and polite for the rest of the time in the baths. After I had shown Decanius back to his rooms and assured him someone would fetch him shortly for the meal, I went back to Casyn's workroom.

"If," he said, "we did not need all our wits, I would be drinking unwatered wine just now, and offering you a cup too. Have you ever met anyone so self-interested, Sorley?"

"It fits with what Rufin told us."

"You had better have Druisius warn the Casilani troops of the Procurator's interest." The Princip spoke briskly. "I am surprised, to be honest, he does not have his own servant with him, or a slave to cater to his wants. Or is that not done in Casil?"

"I am not sure," I said. "Should I ask Druise?"

"It would be useful to know," Casyn said. "Such a relationship between an officer and his soldier-servant is not uncommon here, although it is of course by mutual agreement."

I opened my mouth to ask, closed it again. It was none of my business. "So if a Casilani soldier agrees?"

"If so, and the Casilani officer raises no objection, then I suppose the soldier can be assigned to the Procurator as an assistant. Even one of the women, although that will certainly raise eyebrows." Whereas, I thought, a man would not. Still almost incomprehensible, to me.

Casyn had been pouring wine as he spoke, although he made liberal use of the water jug. Handing me mine, he took a sip. "I wonder what Birel has instructed the kitchen to prepare?" But my thoughts were not on food.

"Casyn? Does Decanius have any authority over Druisius?"

He put his wine cup down. "Druisius is under Turlo's command, at this moment. But in truth, Sorley, he could be considered guilty of desertion from the field. It is unlikely to be discovered; the officer who commanded his regiment has returned to Casil. We can simply say a verbal secondment was made, that there was no time to write an order in the aftermath of the battle, if Decanius ever asks. But I doubt he will care about a simple soldier."

Nor did I, upon consideration. Druise was one of the men the Procurator would not even see.

Chapter 4

"I WISH TURLO HAD not ridden north." Casyn exhaled, loudly. "I know nothing of how Callan might have responded, or what Cillian thought," he said, pacing the room. "I have only you, Sorley."

"I am no diplomat," I protested. "Only a musician, trained for little else except managing an estate."

"You spent almost five years at the school where Cillian learned his skills, did you not? Are you being modest?"

"No." How to make him understand? "The same school, but not the same learning. I came to the *Ti'ach* to learn more about music and story. Some history, yes, and the languages were mandatory for us all, but I was not taught the skills to be a *toscaire*—an envoy—as Cillian was. I meant to be a *scáeli*, a bard, I think you would say."

"And your lover? The Casilani? Can he help us understand the intricacies of Casilan politics?"

"I am afraid not, *Princip*. He was only a palace guard. But," I added, the idea coming to me, "the physician, Gnaius, might have more insight. He has been highly placed, both in the Casilani army and in the palace, I believe."

"Then we must speak to him. Bring him to me later this afternoon, if you will."

I should go to Cillian. But my head ached, and I needed time alone, to consider all that had happened, and all that was being asked of me. I found Gnaius, who told me he would be pleased to speak to Casyn after he had seen his patients. An hour, he said, maybe a little more. I had time for the baths.

Several other men were in the hot pool, but after polite greetings they left me to my thoughts. I closed my eyes, leaning back against the side of the pool. Slowly my mind stopped flitting from idea to idea, and settled on one concern. Druisius.

I didn't know what I wanted—or rather I did, at least in one way—but was it fair to him? How could I sort out my feelings for him just now? Cillian was going to die. I was trying to help Casyn understand a treaty I knew too little about, and comfort Lena, and now I had to translate for this unpleasant Procurator.

Turlo had taken it for granted Druise was my partner; he knew we'd been lovers in Casil. I'd thought then I was learning to love Cillian differently, as a friend, an illusion shattered the moment Druise had told me he was dying.

But it had been Cillian who had asked if it would please me if Druise came west with us. He had thought our shared love of music would overcome the differences of upbringing and language…and experiences, I knew now. He'd liked Druise, and he had wanted me to be happy. Wasn't that all the answer I needed?

I collected Gnaius from the infirmary and took him to Casyn. The wine, I noted, was of better quality than earlier.

"Before we begin," Casyn said, sitting across from us, "is there any change in Cillian?"

"None," I said, listening to Gnaius. "The fever does not abate."

"What are the treatments?"

"Poppy to make him sleep, anash against the infection, other drugs for the fever," I relayed. Casyn nodded. He asked about a few other injured men—a shock to me, the reminder that Cillian was not the only man Gnaius was treating—before turning the conversation to politics.

Gnaius stroked his beard with one finger. "The *Princip* wishes to know what a Procurator does?" he clarified. "He is responsible for taxes and rents and pay to the army." Casyn wrote that down. "He will bring surveyors, and they will be sent out immediately to do a census and map the roads and villages. And to find the deposits of metal ore, and where salt could be made, and grapes grown."

"This falls under his jurisdiction?" Casyn asked.

"Yes. As does pay to the army, and therefore its organization, *Princip*." Gnaius sipped his wine. "This was not made here," he commented.

"No doubt it is from Casil," I said. "You are being honoured by it."

"Decanius is the man who will implement almost all the details of the treaty with the Eastern Empire, then," Casyn said.

"Exactly so," Gnaius agreed. "May I say more? I have lived in many of Casil's provinces over the years. A physician travels with the army, if he wishes to become a skilled surgeon. And from my days at the palace I know somewhat of Decanius's family, and what they strive for. I believe Decanius will be looking for opportunities to enrich himself and his friends." The physician raised a groomed eyebrow. "There is nothing unusual in this, you understand. It is what most men want, including myself."

Casyn put his pen down. "Is Gnaius asking for money?" he asked bluntly.

"The *Princip* wishes to know if you require further compensation for your work."

Gnaius looked genuinely surprised. "No," he said. "The Empress pays me well. My enrichment here comes from the challenges of healing, and what—when the men I tend can safely be left—I will learn from the healers of this land, and what I can teach them. But," he added, smiling, "if the *Princip* is offering, more of this wine would be welcomed."

I laughed, as did Casyn when I told him Gnaius's answers. "Tell him I will have Birel send him a supply, in appreciation of his skill."

Gnaius bowed to Casyn, and waving aside my offer to escort him, left me alone with the *Princip*. "What do you remember of the details of the treaty?" he asked immediately.

"Some," I said. "I read Cillian's translation on the ship, and I was there when he and Turlo explained it to you and the Emperor. But I paid more attention to the details affecting Linrathe, *Princip*."

"Understandable." He leaned back. His face, lined by fatigue, was troubled. "I have been concerning myself with all that a general must after losses such as we took in the last year. Our army is in considerable disarray; we have too few officers, and not enough men—people, now some women wish to remain as soldiers—for the regiments. We need horses, and feed and fodder for the coming winter, and food for ourselves, and the women's villages that supplied these are mostly gone."

"But is that not what Gnaius said Decanius will also be concerned with? The reorganization of the army, and a survey of the land? Surely your concerns are not so different, *Princip*?"

He pursed his lips. "Perhaps not. When we conquered Leste we sent officers to do the same there and made their king a nominal governor. Is that what I will be, Sorley, a voice for this Procurator, and nothing more?"

"I don't know," I said helplessly. "Cillian did. Does. What he and the Empress discussed privately—only he knows that. Maybe he told his father. He did not tell me."

"Did he tell Lena?"

"I don't know," I repeated.

"She is with Cillian? Then let us go and ask her. I need to move, and I have not seen him for a few days."

In the infirmary Lena sat holding Cillian's hand. He lay motionless, pale, breathing shallowly, his hair—Druise had cut it, I noted—lank and lifeless. Lena looked little better.

Casyn put a hand on her shoulder. "May I speak to you?"

"Do I need to leave him?"

"No. We will not disturb him, I think," he said gently. I pulled a stool close to the opposite side of the bed, reaching for Cillian's other hand.

"I'm here, Lena. Talk to Casyn."

I stroked Cillian's hand, forcing myself to listen to what Casyn and Lena were saying. "No," she replied, in answer to his question, "he did not tell me. I am sorry, Casyn, but I know nothing of the treaty beyond what is written."

"It was a hope," he said simply, but I heard the disappointment. "I wish," he said, "my brothers were not dead. We need Colm's knowledge, not just Callan's ability to make connections, and his subtle thinking." For a moment he stared past us, his eyes hollow, unfocused. "But we cannot change the circumstances," he murmured. He took a deep breath, squaring his shoulders. He looked down at his nephew. "May the god bring you back to us," he said. "You are needed. Stay here if you wish, Sorley, but come to me in the morning."

"He never wanted to be anything more than a blacksmith," Lena said, after Casyn had left us.

"What?"

"Casyn. He told me that once himself, and Turlo did too. He felt he had to be at Callan's side, to advise and guide him, and Callan wanted to lead. Was meant to, Turlo said. He said the same about Cillian." Her voice held no emotion at all.

"The men from the ship do not like this Procurator," Druise told me as I played quiet music for Cillian, in the hour before midnight.

"I'm not surprised," I said.

"I did not either, in Casil. Be careful. He has power, *amané*."

"He wanted a woman. It was almost the first thing he asked for. A woman, or a boy." I remembered what Casyn had wanted to know. "Would he not typically have a servant, or a slave, to meet his needs?"

"Yes. Perhaps he thought a barbarian would be interesting," Druise said. I caught the slightest hint of a grin.

I gave him the expected response. "And am I?"

"Very," he said, his teeth flashing in the dim room. I remembered, with a sharp twinge of desire, the blade near my throat as he'd shaved me, earlier. "I saw the General."

"And?"

"Soldier-servant," he said, "That is amusing."

"Why?"

"You were not to know. It is what I was called, in Casil. To my officers. So I could share their tents."

"You didn't tell the General that?"

"Of course not. Am I an *idióta*?" He adjusted Cillian's pillow. "Even if he recovers, it will not be me he wants in his bed. Maybe you and I, we need to talk. Before I move my things to your room, as the General thinks I will."

Be careful what you speak of near Cillian, Gnaius had said. I motioned Druise away. "What do want to say?" I asked, when we stood against the far wall.

"I like you," he said. "We are good together, yes? The music, and in bed. I will be your *consor*, if you want."

I glanced over at Cillian. "Even—?"

"My first officer, the one I liked the most? His marriage was not political. He loved his wife. So this is not new to me, Sorley. But I want an agreement."

"What sort of an agreement?"

"About what I see and hear. Do not kiss him, not on the lips, or tell him you love him, if I am there." He smiled, wryly. "For him, you do this already. That is why we moved away from the bed, yes? In case he could understand what we talked about?"

I spread my hands helplessly. He was right, of course. "Are you sure?"

"If you wish. If you can do what I ask." All I saw on his face was patience, like a man waiting for an answer in a business transaction he knew was favourable.

We made good music together, and I wanted him in my bed; he made me feel things no man before had. Cillian was dying. Druise would help me forget.

"I can," I said.

On the bed, Cillian moaned, his head moving on the pillow. His eyes opened, but there was no recognition behind them. Druise went to the sideboard, unlocking a drawer. He brought the poppy syrup over to the bed, and expertly propping Cillian up, spooned the dose into his mouth.

"Play," he told me. I had stopped, watching in concern. I chose a cradle tune, one of the first melodies I had learned. When Cillian was quiet again, Druise arranged the pillows. "Go and sleep," he said.

"I promised Lena."

"I will be here. She trusts me with him now. You have important work to do in the morning." He spoke matter-of-factly. "This is my job, Sorley. When Lena returns, I will give him more poppy. Then I will come to bed. And awaken you, *amané*."

"All right. Do you want the *ladhar*?"

"Why not?" He grinned. "A good time to practice, while the poppy takes Cillian to oblivion." I touched his shoulder in farewell, smiling, but inside I was unsettled. The word Druise had used did mean oblivion in Casilan, but it also meant a river of the underworld, a river the dead drank from to forget their earthly lives.

———◆○◆———

"The Procurator," Casyn told me, the next morning, "has no wish to meet with me for at least a week. He must confer with the Casilani officers first, it appears."

"About what?" I asked.

"Army matters, no doubt. But it does not displease me, as it gives me time to read the treaty, line by line, and discuss the meaning and the interpretations that can be made of each point, and prepare arguments. It is what Colm would have suggested. But he also taught me that one point of view is not enough. Will you spend a few hours with me each day doing this? Not more than two or three: I have other matters that must be dealt with."

"I will," I said. "But am I the right person? I know little of your laws and customs, *Princip*."

"I am sending for Jereme: he is—was—at Casilla, with the youngest cadets. I do not even know if he is still alive: he was already old, before the war. But he was Colm's teacher, although the student quickly surpassed the master. Even so, it will be some weeks before he arrives. I must review the treaty before then. I had a mind to include my daughter Talyn as well; much of the treaty will affect the women's villages."

"It is her son who will be *Princip* after you?"

"Faolyn, yes. He is nine this year."

"Perhaps his father, then, as well?"

Casyn laughed. "I don't know who his father is; Talyn does, of course, but she has never told me. And he is more likely—if he is alive—to be an unranked soldier than an officer."

I flushed. "Forgive me, *Princip*. This is new to me."

"Different customs. Ways of thinking." He gave me a considered look. "Other aspects of life here must also be new to you, and welcome, I should think?"

I understood him immediately. "Does no one think it wrong? What I am?"

"Wrong?" He was genuinely puzzled, I saw. "Sorley, in this land men and women lived separately for all but two weeks a year, with no Festival for the men until they were eighteen. If you can find me a man here who tells you he has not taken pleasure with another man, whether for a night or two or in a longer relationship, he is either a liar or an ascetic. For some men it is casual, for some it is their nature, as I understand it is yours. But wrong? How could it be?"

Was he telling me he had—? I tried to assimilate this. "My father," I said, "would have disinherited me. Would still, if he knew."

"I am sorry for that," he said after a moment. "There is a parallel here, you know, with our sons who will not or cannot fight. Colm suffered that fate."

Turlo had told me—not about Colm, but about the practice—on our travels. "It might be a good thing," I said, "that Cillian grew up in Linrathe."

"Callan said the same," Casyn said. "He did not see Cillian as a soldier. And yet Colm died protecting the Emperor, and Cillian may die from wounds suffered on a battlefield. Courage comes in many forms, Sorley, and only men blinded by prejudice and thoughtlessness think otherwise." He smiled, sadly. "Can we begin analysing the treaty?"

I was glad to escape to the infirmary. Gnaius was there, dripping drugs into Cillian's mouth. He nodded at me but didn't speak. I picked up the *ladhar* and began to play.

Gnaius straightened. "Go," he told Lena, who obeyed him, to my surprise. To me, he said, "Keep playing." I looked away as the physician undid the bandages. I heard him click his tongue.

"I will prepare poultices," he said to Druise. "Wash him. I will not be long."

I could not watch Druise's hands touching the man I loved so intimately. It confused me. I walked to the small window, concentrating on the instrument. I heard Druise moving, the splash of a cloth in water, his tuneful humming of the melody I played. He murmured to Cillian occasionally, his tone calm, reassuring.

Gnaius, true to his word, was back quickly. "Good," he said to Druise. "We will turn him onto his stomach now. Remove these poultices when they cool. Come with me: I will teach you to make them. Apply them four times a day and tell me when the wounds begin to drain."

Druise was gone for perhaps half an hour. He checked the poultices first when he came back, before coming to pull a stool up beside mine.

"He is very ill," he said.

"The wounds fester?" I knew they did.

"Deep inside, Gnaius says. Maybe the poultices will draw it out. Maybe not."

"Does Lena know?"

"Yes. Gnaius tells her the truth. But she will not leave his side, except while the wounds are treated, and that only because Gnaius insists. Or if you are here, or sometimes me, now."

If I was going to do everything Casyn wanted of me, I wouldn't be able to be at Cillian's side as often. "It is because of her vow to him," I said. "He was alone, for so long, Druise. She told me he had never known, before her, what it was to wake with someone beside him." I swallowed. "She swore he would never wake alone again. So she, or someone else who loves him, has to be here."

"There is no one else? From his land?"

"Dagney," I said, and an idea came to me. "Maybe she would come. She and Perras, and Perras could assist Casyn: he knows as much as Cillian about Casil and its laws. I will write to them." Even as I spoke I realized I didn't know if they were alive, they or anyone associated with the *Ti'ach*. My mind recoiled at the thought of more loss.

"Do not tell Lena," Druise said, "until you know this woman will come. She cannot take more disappointment."

CHAPTER 5

IF YOU CAN FIND me a man here who tells you he has not taken pleasure with another man, I will show you a liar. I couldn't stop thinking about Casyn's casual words, the implication—no, the admission—that he had had male lovers. That nearly every man in this fort, this army, this land had. The shameful secret I had hidden for so long in Sorham was just a normal part of life here. My mind felt dislocated, untethered.

Every pair of soldiers I saw laughing together, every casual touch I witnessed made me wonder. I was embarrassing myself, acting like a boy newly aware. Which is what I was, I supposed. I'd told Druise what Casyn had said, swearing him not to repeat it. "So?" he'd said. "Most armies, I think. But more so here, because the boys are together from so young." He'd kissed me, then. "Better than hiding, yes?" he'd said, and we'd stopped talking.

We hadn't repeated the desperate, furious coupling of that first night at the fort, but he was teaching me things I hadn't known about myself. I'd had little experience, before Druise: a few men, mostly musicians. Brief encounters, furtive and frightened. Now for the first time in my life I felt no judgement, real or imagined, and no fear, although what I was learning about what gave Druise—and me—pleasure did shock me, a little.

Still, I hated myself, sometimes. Watching Cillian slowly die was shattering my heart, and my nights with Druise were an escape. Guilt wracked me, too: what solace was there for Lena? Nor was Cillian the only anguish in my life. Dagney's reply to my letter had added to my grief.

Perras had been days from death when she wrote, a lung infection slowly choking him.

'But he understood what I told him: that you and Cillian had returned safely from Casil,' she had written. 'Knowing that, and about Cillian and Lena and the expected child brought him peace. He had worried for you terribly. I did not tell him of Cillian's wounds. He does not need to know.

'When he is gone, and we have mourned him and buried him, perhaps I will come. I might be some comfort to Lena. There have been no students at the *Ti'ach* for some time, and until there is a new *Comiádh*, I may choose not to teach. It will be difficult without Perras.'

I had to stop reading at that point, blinded by tears. Only later did I pick up the letter again, to read the rest.

'You asked for help with understanding Casil's history, and with the language. You must know Cillian was Perras's best pupil in many years in those disciplines, but there were others. But who is alive, and who Ruar and his advisors might allow to be sent is unknown to me. I will enquire.'

The letter had contained a separate note, addressed to Lena, and a postscript.

'Sorley, on consideration, I will come south when I can, if the *Princip* will allow it. I cannot teach Casilan, but I can teach Linrathan, and Marái'sta, if those are of use. It will be better for all of us if we who loved and honoured Perras and Cillian are together, I believe, and the approaching birth will bring us hope.'

I took the note to Lena. She read it, smiling briefly. "She asks me to tell Cillian she loves him," she said. "I already have, long ago, but I will again."

I beckoned her away from Cillian's bed. At the far side of the room, in a whisper, I told her about Perras. She closed her eyes in pain. "Both his real father, and his foster father," she murmured. "I liked Perras, so much."

"Dagney says she will come, to be with us," I said. "As soon as she feels able. She says the child will give her hope."

"She is a reason to live," Lena said. "When he dies, Sorley, she will be the only one I have."

I had never heard Lena admit that Cillian was going to die. I put my arms around her. "I will be here," I said. My own acknowledgment of the truth. She sobbed, once, then took a deep breath and pulled away.

"I shouldn't leave him." She went to the bedside to pick up his limp hand. "Cillian," she began, "there is a letter from Dagney."

———————◄O►———————

WE HAD SPENT THE last week reviewing the treaty, Casyn and Talyn and I, making notes and a list of questions for Turlo when he returned from the north. Then we had compared the structure of the Empire's army with that of Casil's, with help from Druise, at least for the land army. The differences seemed minor to me: the size of cohorts and regiments, the rank at which one was considered a senior officer, rather than a junior. Titles that would need redefining, as they meant different things in each army.

"One other," Druisius said. He was remarkably comfortable in the presence of the *Princip*, I noticed; respectful, but not overawed or obsequious. Then again, I reflected, he had been a palace guard. What was the western Empire's *Princip* when compared to Casil's Empress?

"And that is?" Casyn enquired.

"In Casil, women are archers only. Their own cohorts, foot and horse. They do not mix with the men. In any way," he added.

"I hadn't realized that," I said. I remembered Lena telling me of Junia's surprise when she had learned Lena was partnered with a man. This would explain it. I would have to tell her, someday.

"We need the women throughout the troops," Casyn said. "We do not have the numbers, without them."

Druise shrugged. "The Procurator will argue, I think."

"What do you know of him?"

"I was part of an escort for him, once or twice. He does not thank his guards or consider them in any way. Other officials had us sent water, or allowed us shade, if we had to wait at midday. Not Decanius."

"That," Casyn said, "tells me quite a lot. Thank you, Druisius." Druise saluted and left.

"It will be interesting," Casyn said to the room, "to hear if the Casilani officers tell me the same as Druisius has."

"A bright man," Talyn commented. "I suppose—and forgive me for this, Sorley; I know he is your lover—that we can trust him?"

I bristled, instinctively, but it was a question that had to be asked. "Yes," I said. "But not for that reason. His appointment as Cillian's soldier-servant is not the first time he has held such a post." In some form, at least. "He has always been completely loyal to his officer, and he will be now."

"Birel," Casyn said, "tells me the same, that he is protective of Cillian, and Lena, and not, I am assured, just because of the circumstances. Birel has been with me for a long time, and I trust his judgement in this."

"I will not argue with your sergeant," Talyn said. "I was only wondering where Druisius can best be used, when—when Cillian no longer needs him."

"As a liaison with the Casilani men," Casyn said. "We have Sorley to translate for the officers, but if we have no one to hear the men's thoughts and complaints, we will have a dangerous situation."

"He will need a minor promotion, for that."

"When it is appropriate, yes," Casyn said. "But promoting him too quickly will breed discontent among our own troops. You may tell him that, unofficially, Sorley, if you think it worries him."

"Druise," I said, "worries about very little. But you have reminded me: I have had a letter from my *Ti'ach*." I explained who Dagney was, and what she had written, accepting their words of sympathy regarding Perras. "May she come?"

"Of course," Casyn said. "If for nothing but to comfort Lena, she would be welcome. But lessons in both Linrathan and Marai'ista are a good idea; it is a pity she cannot teach Casilan. But I am less happy with the thought of other Linrathan men teaching our officers: to echo Talyn, can we trust them?"

"Why could you not?" I asked.

"There was significant support for Fritjof within Linrathe, was there not? Has your *Teannasach* demanded an oath from all who survived the war? And even if he has, men have given such oaths falsely."

"Before I joined Turlo," I said, "I was part of those who worked against Fritjof. All the *Ti'acha* were involved, so if the man—or woman— suggested is someone I or Dagney know also did that work, will that ease your concern?"

He rubbed his chin, considering. "It will," he decided. "As a teacher only, though, although a second translator would be useful. But I will need to judge them for myself. You must continue to translate in our meetings with the Procurator."

"Translate, not negotiate," I countered. He nodded.

"Translate only. I do not expect you to argue our cause, Lord Sorley. Now, shall we look at the implications of separating the women into separate cohorts? This was our original practice, before the war with the Marai, after all. We must have all the arguments in place to counter the Procurator's."

CHAPTER 6

IMPORTANT WORK IT MIGHT be, but translating was also incredibly tedious. For days we discussed in minute detail the composition of the Empire's army, land and sea; then in the same detail how Casilani troops were organized, armed, and led. Turlo grew so impatient and testy Casyn sent him away, back to the Sterre. Talyn, newly promoted to a captain's rank to give her sufficient seniority to be Casyn's advisor, joined the talks, along with the *Princip*'s adjutant, Michan. Michan was quick with languages, picking up Casilan rapidly, at least the military terms. A good thing, too, as I did not always know the right words.

Decanius had found a soldier to be his scribe—and perhaps more—and at the end of each day I checked his notes, then ours, looking for discrepancies. When I found one, as I almost always did, it engendered more discussion. Decanius had claimed the baths for himself and his invited guests for an hour in the late afternoons, so Birel served us wine after the Casilani had left us. The water jug remained full, most days.

We compared sizes of cohorts: twelve in Casil, ten here. It became twelve, plus the cohort-leader, no longer a junior officer but a rank below that of sergeant. A *capora* for every two cohorts; a sergeant for every four. A new rank, subaltern, below lieutenant, and together these were the only junior officers. Captains became senior officers.

"This is necessary, you see," Decanius told us, "so that the pay is correct."

"Pay is one thing," Casyn said, "but I do not see how we have the men and women to do this, even if we collapse some of the cohorts, as we must."

"A temporary situation," Decanius said. "In the spring Casilani troops will fill the vacancies, especially among the officers."

Would they? Quintus had been opposed to sending any troops to our aid, given the aggression on the Eastern Empire's borders. I must remember to tell Casyn this, I thought.

"While we are discussing the troops, there is another irregularity to be addressed," Decanius said. "Women have only one role in the army: that of archers, horse or foot. Not mixed among the troops as you have them."

"That may be true in the Eastern Empire," Casyn said carefully, "but here our women have different skills: blacksmithing, carpentry, masonry. All needed, to maintain the fortifications, and the roads, and to shoe our horses and repair our harness and weapons. We cannot waste that expertise, Procurator, and nor can we afford to remove men with the same skills from their work, to ask them to ride patrol or guard the gates when women can do that equally well."

"It is not protocol."

"It is here," Casyn said. I translated his words; his tone of voice would be understood. "The women of our Western Empire have earned their places in this army. Without their defence of the villages three years ago, we would have fallen to Leste. Without their willingness to join our troops, Linrathe, when it was our enemy, would have overrun us. Their numbers too were essential in keeping the Marai from total victory as we awaited Casil's aid. Three times we have needed them, Procurator, and we have a saying here: the third decides. Our women will do the work our officers assign. Not what you think is appropriate."

Decanius's bald head flushed. His toe tapped. "Very well," he said. "I see the need to consider skills, for expediency. Until the spring."

I finished reading the transcripts, marking the passages that did not agree. I rubbed my neck: my shoulders ached. I needed the baths, but that was not possible until later. Or maybe Druise would work the knots out with his strong fingers.

"*Princip*," I said, "I am doubtful that the Eastern Empire will send many troops, or officers, in the spring." I told him why.

"Turlo said the same." He exhaled, loudly. "Decanius is posturing, I believe. My fear is that he will convince Casil of the need, and what they will send will be the dregs of their army: bad soldiers and worse officers."

"Especially if Quintus wishes to show Eudekia that she was wrong in supporting us."

He looked up. "An interesting thought," he said. "You are thinking like a diplomat, Sorley."

I laughed. "Treachery is a frequent theme in the *danta*," I told him. I rolled the transcripts, tying them closed. "Not too much to argue over in the morning. Do you need me for anything else?"

"No. Are you going to see Cillian? I will come with you."

Gnaius was in the sickroom, bent over Cillian, probing the inflamed wounds. I thought he looked relieved to see me come in. Fear prickled. The physician straightened.

"I must open the wounds," he said. "There is infection, deep inside. The poultices have not been enough. I must drain it. It is the only chance, and it is very small." I went to Lena, putting an arm around her. Gnaius's grave tone had told her enough.

"Is he strong enough to survive this?" she asked, her face white, when I had given her the news.

"He is certain to die, unless it is done." I touched Lena's belly with two fingers. "Do it," I urged. "For her, Lena. He swore he would leave no child fatherless. He would want to have the chance to keep that vow."

She nodded, slowly. "All right," she whispered. "When?" I asked.

"Now," Gnaius said. "I will give him poppy, and then I and Druisius will do what is needed. Everyone else must leave, Lord Sorley."

"A minute," Lena said. She turned back to the bed, to kiss Cillian gently. "*Thà mi gràh agàthe*," she murmured. She looked up. "Sorley?"

I took Cillian's hand. "Stay with us, *kärestan*," I whispered, and not caring if Druise was watching, bent to kiss his lips. Then I led Lena away.

She refused to go far, but Casyn convinced her to drink a little wine. "It will calm you," he said. "I must go, but you will send word. I am to be disturbed, regardless of what I am doing, and I will tell the door guard that."

A long time—or what felt like a long time—passed before Gnaius found us. "It is done," he said. "He is alive. Druisius is with him. I drained much poison and washed the wounds with wine and certain herbs. I will not sew them shut for a few days. But it may not be enough, you understand?"

I would not leave Lena's side, or Cillian's. "Tell Decanius I am ill, or whatever you need to," I said to Casyn, when he came himself to speak to me. "My first loyalty is here, *Princip*, and you knew that." He glanced down at Cillian, unmoving, breathing shallowly, then at Lena.

"Stay," he said. "Lena, I will petition the soldier's god, I promise. Sorley, a minute in the corridor?"

Outside the room, he faced me. "How long?"

"Gnaius will make no prognosis, either way," I told him. "There is still some fever, but he says the surgery may account for that. But if it worsens…"

"If Cillian dies," he said, "I have come to realize that the lives of all my people will change. Not just Lena's, and not just yours, Sorley." He sighed. "None of us can fight the battles of intellect and learning against Decanius that Cillian would be able to, and so we will have to submit to laws that I believe unjust, but that I have no defence against. Wars are not all fought with sword and bow. Send to me, if there is news."

Decanius, I was told, was furious at the delay. But while Michan was learning some of the language rapidly, he was not fluent enough to allow the talks to continue. I didn't really care. Cillian grew no better, and even I, who wanted to pretend it was not so, saw he could not live much longer. Every rib stood out, and the flesh of his face had fallen away, leaving the shape of the skull beneath starkly obvious. The hours by his side had become a death watch, for all I prayed—to any god who might listen—that it might be otherwise.

Lena never cried now, and rarely spoke to anyone except Cillian. She grew steadily thinner, drawn with exhaustion, but she sat holding his hand, dripping water into his mouth, rubbing salve into his hands and lips. I played, or took her place when she finally gave into fatigue, and Druise, grim and taciturn, made us both try to sleep for at least part of the night. Someone was always awake, our reason for that unspoken, but understood.

I was playing cradle tunes one afternoon—I was always playing cradle tunes, it seemed—when Talyn came in. "Sorley," she said, "You are needed. A man has arrived from Linrathe; sent by the Lady Dagney and the *Teannasach*, he says. Randall, his name is. The *Princip* asks if you could join them, for a short while."

"Go," Lena said. I hesitated.

"Half an hour," Talyn said. "If you would, Lord Sorley." I nodded, and stood, stiff from sitting. Handing my *ladhar* to Druise, I followed Talyn to Casyn's workroom. She touched my back as we walked; when I glanced at her, she shook her head, slowly, sadly.

"Randall na Asgaill." I greeted the man sitting with Casyn. I remembered him: younger than me, by several years, from a *torp* somewhere in the north of Linrathe. Not a *torpari*, but not a lord's son, either. My numbed mind refused to place him. Educated at the *Ti'ach na Asgaill*, where the focus was on mathematics, astronomy. How good was his Casilan?

"Lord Sorley." He stood, offering a hand.

"Forgive me, Randall, if I come to the point, but I have other duties," I said. "You were asked to come to Wall's End to teach Casilan to the officers here. Do not be offended, but I did not think it was much studied, at your *Ti'ach*."

"A common misunderstanding," he said. "It was, but perhaps with a different emphasis than at the *Ti'ach na Perras*. You learned to read the histories; we learned the mathematical texts, and some of the sciences." He smiled, his blue eyes crinkling. "But I assure you I know it well enough to teach the basics."

"You think you do," I said, and in Casilan, added, "but the spoken language does not sound the way we were taught." He frowned, and I repeated it, much more slowly. A faint comprehension rose on his face.

"Again?'

The third time, he answered me in a poor approximation of my pronunciation. "Closer," I said, reverting to our common language. "You will need some time to correct what you have learned. But it should not take you long. Reading it, of course, remains the same."

We arranged a time to meet. Birel appeared, to show Randall to his room, and explain meals and the baths. Casyn indicated I should stay.

"What do you know of him?"

I told him what I had recalled. "I can't remember just now who his father is, or which *torp* he is from. But that is easy to bring up, in conversation."

"Are you sure of his allegiance?"

"Not personally, no. But I cannot imagine Dagney would have agreed he should come, if she had doubts."

"How long before he can translate for us?" The rapid questions told me Casyn was worried about something.

"A few days, providing Decanius is reasonably patient with him. But that is not why he is here, *Princip*."

"It is not why he was sent. But if you believe he is trustworthy, it is what I need him to do, until you are free to return."

"But Lena will still need me, Casyn. I will not leave her to grieve alone."

"Nor will I ask you to, or diminish your own grief," he said. "But the Procurator demands a return to the talks. I have little choice but to use Randall."

"I can see that." I stood. "I will give him what time I can."

I ate with Randall that evening, although I had little appetite these days. Bluntly, to explain my preoccupation and lack of time, I explained about Cillian.

"I was told," he said. "A terrible loss. I knew him: he taught at my *Ti'ach* for a season, about six or seven years ago? It is in part why my Casilan is as good as it is. Or as I thought it was."

"We all thought that," I assured him. "Cillian was astounded at what we had forgotten, and changed, over the centuries."

"Tell me about Casil?" he asked.

"It is magnificent. But another time, Randall. What were you doing, before you were asked to come south?"

"Teaching, and some other work. My father is factor for the young *Teannasach's* great-uncle, Liam. I taught the children of Dun Ceànnar, and sometimes even Ruar himself, because he too had wished to learn Casilan."

"I am surprised they could spare you, then," I said. If he had been Ruar's teacher, I thought, he could be trusted. "But I am glad you are here. Shall we begin?"

After that first meal I refused to speak Linrathan to him. We met for the three meals of the day, and by the third day I deemed his pronunciation, and comprehension, adequate. He still had to think about some words, and his translation was slower than mine, but he would do. Winter approached, and there was much work to complete.

I took him to Casyn, after our evening meal, for a briefing on the courtesies and protocols when the Procurator was present, and the details of what his duties would be. It took a little time. Walking back to the infirmary, I could hear the wind outside; it had shifted, blowing hard off the sea. Rain lashed against shutters. I shivered in the unheated corridor, the torches guttering in the drafts.

A fire burned in Cillian's sickroom, with braziers set near the bed. I closed the door quickly to keep out the cold. Lena turned to me, her face pale.

"Touch him," she said, fear in her voice. I put a hand on his forehead.

"Dear gods," I said. Against my cold hand, his skin burned.

"He was warm, earlier, but I thought…" Her voice trailed off.

I wrenched the door open again. "Cadet!" I snapped. "Fetch the doctor." I heard running feet. Lena pulled the blankets down.

"Water," she said. I brought it, and a bowl and sponge. She began to bathe his face and neck. He did not move, his breath rasping. I felt the clench of fear at my heart, mixed with the dull acceptance of inevitability.

Gnaius came, Druisius with him. The physician felt Cillian's skin, took his pulse, listened to his heart. At his workbench, he mixed something, and carefully, using a tube, dripped it into Cillian's mouth. None of us spoke to him; his face was closed, concentrating. When the liquid was gone, he looked up.

"The fever has returned," he said. "He will die tonight, in the early hours."

"No," I whispered. Lena said nothing. She sat on the stool beside him, taking his hand. NO, I screamed silently. Blindly I picked up the *ladhar* to play the lullabies that soothed him. What else could I offer?

Hours passed. Gnaius fed Cillian more drugs. Druisius brought us soup, and wine, but it went untouched. Cillian's hands were cold, and his feet. I tried to rub warmth into them. I watched his chest rise and fall, and the flicker of movement under his closed eyelids. Druisius kept the fires burning. Gnaius sat, silently.

In the darkest part of the night I began to pace, grief and a desperate desire to do something warring inside me. "Cillian," I said, too loudly, "I faced down an Empress for you." My voice rose. "Must I now be Oraiáphon, and take my *ladhar* to the underworld to appeal to the god to give you back? I will, if I must." Druise got up. Without speaking he stopped my agonised movement, holding me tightly. He wouldn't have known what I said; I had spoken in Linrathan. With one arm he reached for the *ladhar*.

"Play," he said. "Better than shouting. Use your anger, *amané*. He may hear the music yet." I took the instrument. My fingers began *An dithës braithréan,* and this time Lena did not stop me. The notes of the lament for brothers separated forever by war rose into the dark. Did they fall, to charm the darkest god?

The night wore on. Gnaius still sat, watchful now, his eyes reflecting firelight. I went to Lena, wrapping my arms around her from behind. Her hand was on Cillian's; mine covered hers, my thumb tracing a line on his cold wrist. I rested my lips against her hair. Almost silently, she began to cry. "*Kärestan,*" she begged. "Please do not leave me. Do not leave us." The anguish in her voice was unbearable.

There was one thing I must do. Even as I went to the shutters,I thought Cillian would have laughed at my superstition, but in Sorham and Linrathe, a dying spirit needed a window open, an escape. When the room was open to the night air—the rain had stopped, I half-noticed—I returned to his bedside. Gnaius watched what I did, but made no demur, perhaps understanding.

I took a deep breath. Nothing more now, except to ease his passing. I began to sing, a soothing tune, gentle. I put an arm around Lena, but my other hand stroked Cillian's forehead, and his hair. I wanted, fiercely, for him to feel himself a child again, safely falling asleep, secure and loved.

A dank smell, of wet soil and stone, of the depths of caves and dark places drifted into the room. I did not stop singing, sipping water when Druise insisted. My voice grew raw, hoarse, but still I sang. A shutter rattled on its hook, and the lamps guttered in a sudden warm breeze, carrying with it a faint scent of flowers. The sky beyond the window glowed pink in the first rays of the sun. Behind me, I heard Gnaius say something, low and incredulous.

Lena reached out to touch Cillian's face, still now and so pale. "Sorley," she whispered. I put my fingers beside hers. Cillian's skin was cool. Cool, but not cold.

"Gnaius?" I rasped. The physician placed his hand on Cillian's forehead, then took his wrist. Then he bent to place an ear to his chest and sniffed his skin. He straightened, raising an expressive eyebrow. "What god did you pray to?" he asked. "There is no fever, and his heart beats more strongly. He may yet live."

Chapter 7

DRUISE MADE GNAIUS GIVE Lena and me poppy in wine, and we fell quickly into a drugged sleep, somehow sharing the narrow cot. I woke to the music of Linrathan lullabies, but they didn't quite sound right. Druise, I thought foggily, his *cithar*. If he's playing, then Cillian is still alive. I slipped off the cot, careful not to disturb Lena, and went to crouch beside him.

"No fever still," Druise whispered. "The gods intervened, I think, last night." He put his *cithar* down. "You will sit with him now? I will bring you some food."

"Yes. Thank you, Druise. For everything, last night, and for taking care of us. All of us."

"My job," he said briefly. He glanced down at Cillian. "A brave man," he said. "Maybe easier to die, than face what might be now."

I couldn't think about that. He was alive, and that was enough. "When," I said, attempting lightness, "did Cillian make the easier choice?"

"Not ever, that I know," Druise said seriously. "Soup, Sorley? Or something more?"

"Soup," I told him. "Get some sleep yourself, Druise. Has Casyn been told?"

"Yes. He will come, he said, when you are awake. I will let him know."

Casyn took a long look at Cillian, and at Lena, who still slept. Silently he motioned me to the corridor, sending the cadet to where she could not hear us.

"Gnaius says he will live?"

"May. He is a cautious man."

He nodded. "Keep me informed. Do not worry about leaving him. Your *consor*," he smiled, "is most adamant that you are needed here. An interesting man, Druisius. Respectful enough, but sure of his own worth. He reminds me in that way of Lena's father."

What had Druise said? "Thank you," I said. "How go the talks?"

"Randall's work is adequate. We move more slowly, perhaps, but that is not necessarily a bad thing. We are discussing weapons, and their manufacture. The Procurator wishes our troops to be taught the short sword, a necessity, he says. But we have very few, of course, and making more will take time. A different shield is needed, as well. The conversations are tedious, to say the least."

"And who will do the training?"

"Exactly. You can guess his suggestion. I wonder how many of his friends will arrive next summer?"

———◆◇◆———

A MESSENGER ARRIVED FROM the south, with a letter for Decanius, and shortly after, he announced he must return to the Eastern Fort. He demanded a translator, one who could read, not just speak the language.

"I cannot go," I said to Casyn. "I cannot leave Lena, or Cillian."

"Druisius?"

"He cannot read your language." I didn't know if Druise could read at all. "Nor do I think Decanius would find him suitable, even if he could. He is a man conscious of rank and position." I didn't want Druise to go; Cillian needed him. So did I.

"Randall, then," he said. "Although he may refuse, and I have no power to compel him."

"What will Decanius be doing at the Eastern Fort?"

"He has not deigned to tell me," Casyn said, "but if he needs someone to read documents, then I would guess he wants to look at records. I wish I knew what his message said."

"Now there Druise might be useful," I said. "Is the messenger still here?"

"To the best of my knowledge, yes."

"I can ask," Druise said, "after enough wine. But he is unlikely to know."

"Try." I offered him some coins. "For better wine, or ale, or whatever he wants," I said.

"No," he said. "If I do that, he will suspect." He grinned. "You think this is the first time I have had such a task? I was not just a bedpet to my officers."

I went with him to check on Cillian. Lena was nearby, sewing and looking unhappy about it. "I hate this as much as my aunt Tali did," she said. "But this baby will need clothes."

"If neither Druise nor I are here this evening, will you be all right?" I asked. I explained why.

"Of course, providing someone comes to give Cillian his last dose of poppy."

"Gnaius, tonight," Druise said. "I will ensure it." To me, as we left the room, he added, "Do not wait up for me, Sorley. I will be late, and not sober."

"I may be little better," I said. Out of the building, he turned left, I right, towards the officers' commons. Wall's End had no provision for civilians; I ate mostly with Lena, or with Casyn if he required me to translate. If Randall was not with Decanius, he was most likely in the junior commons.

I found him sitting with a couple of young officers, ones whose names I could not bring to mind. He moved to a table with me without demur. We'd barely spoken since I'd given him his remedial instruction in spoken Casilan. The steward brought us wine.

"Have you eaten?" I asked Randall.

"Yes."

I requested food. When the steward had left us, I picked up my cup. "How is the work?"

"Not very interesting, if I am honest." He gave me a wry smile. "I am good with numbers, and the Procurator is pleased by that."

"Is that what you studied, at the *Ti'ach na Asgaill*?" I asked. The steward put a plate of stew in front of me, and some bread. I picked up my spoon. Mutton and barley, as familiar as the cries of seabirds.

"My *Mathàir* makes better," Randall said, indicating the plate, "but it was not bad. I studied mathematics, yes, and how to build structures using mathematical principles. But my *Athàir* taught me my numbers, and how to calculate, before I went there."

"As did mine," I said.

"Aye," he replied. "But a *Harr's* son learns so you can keep an eye on your factor's books."

"Is that what you think? You're as bad as Druisius. He doesn't believe I can shear sheep." I had made a mistake, and I knew it instantly. I had grown complacent, freely and familiarly speaking of Druise. But I had just equated Randall with my lover, reminding him of what I was, and perhaps insinuating he was the same. "I was overseeing the sales of those fleeces at sixteen," I went on, trying to make the conversation proceed naturally. "Things are likely different in the *Teannasach's* family, Randall, but on a Sorham estate, there is no factor. Believe me, we all worked."

"Plenty of time to make music, though, and the freedom to spend five years at a *Ti'ach* as a grown man."

A hard-won freedom, but I wasn't going to tell Randall that. "My father had a new wife," I said. "I think he was glad to have me gone, so he was not reminded he had an adult son waiting for him to die." I forced a grin. "And music stops us going mad in the winter, when there's nearly no light."

"Aye," he said, non-committal. "What did you want to see me about? It wasn't to reminisce about home, I have no doubt."

I told him of Decanius's demand. "The *Princip* will ask you formally tomorrow," I concluded, "but I thought you might want time to think about it. It is not what you were sent here to do."

He nodded. "I might go. I like the Procurator well enough, and I understand his job somewhat. He is but a factor in a larger way. It was good of you to mention it to me, Lord Sorley."

"I am not Lord Sorley to you, Randall," I said, not for the first time. The rules of the *Ti'acha*: no titles except the ones earned there, the right after five years of study to add the *Comiádh's* name to yours to tell the world who had taught you. I hadn't quite finished my requisite time, but under the circumstances, I thought it would be forgiven.

"Not easy to remember," he said. Inwardly I sighed. He was too conscious of his status, or lack of it. Was it harder for a factor's son, neither one thing nor the other, not a landholder but not quite a *torpari* either? Still, five years with Asgaill should have changed his perceptions. Really? I asked myself. Did all his time with Perras change Cillian's?

"It is a courtesy title," I reminded him. "The lands I were to inherit one day are in Marai hands now."

"But has not our *Teannasach* pledged to regain them? Might not these Casilani be useful in that?" He downed his wine before standing up. "I should ask: how is Cillian?"

"Still very ill," I told him, "but the physician says he will live."

"The Procurator was asking, you see." Was he? I tucked that piece of information away. Randall went back to the men he had been sitting with earlier. I sat, sipping the poor wine. *Might not these Casilani be useful?* Very possibly.

Druise woke me, coming in very late. The noise he made told me he was far from sober. "Tomorrow," he muttered, to my sleepy query. I fell asleep again to his rhythmic snoring.

Somehow, he roused himself at dawn, going to Cillian to administer the morning poppy. He came back a little later, to wake me again pouring water at the washstand.

"How's your head?" I asked from the bed.

He splashed about before answering. "Sore. I will live. At least I am not expected on the parade ground."

"Did you learn anything?"

"The letter is from a *mensore*, one whose responsibility was to identify sources of ore, iron and copper and lead. That is all. Except that the messenger hates it here and wishes he had returned to Casil." He dried his face. "Your head is not sore."

"No. Randall preferred other company. But he told me he likes Decanius, which worries me." I sat up, yawning. "Casyn will be interested in what you learned, Druise. Thank you."

"Iron and copper and lead?" Casyn said. "There are maps, I remember, and records of yields. I knew more, once: it befitted a blacksmith to know where his metal came from."

"Who mines the ore?" I couldn't see women doing it.

"The army or retired officers, in the past, overseeing slaves and captives along the Durrains. But sometimes too the mines belong to a women's village, although only a few, and almost all copper deposits on headlands."

I discarded my presumptions. Women didn't take fishing boats out in Sorham, either. "There could be many reasons Decanius is interested. Did he not say all mines belong to the Empire? So he will want to claim the ones belonging to the villages."

"Likely. Perhaps not a bad thing, if there is not the labour to work them. We will need all the metals, with swords and shields to make. You say Randall will agree to go south?"

"I believe so. He likes Decanius, he says."

"Does he?" Casyn gave a mirthless chuckle. "I wonder why. However, that is one less thing I need to worry about. And I will welcome a break from these endless talks."

———————◆———————

CILLIAN'S SKIN REMAINED COOL, and his breathing no longer rasped. He was occasionally vocal, if incoherent, his eyes open but unseeing, and he moved more, too. Or had he just become very still in the days after the surgery, before the fever raged through him the second time?

"Be prepared," Gnaius told us. "He should return to us soon, but it may be with the mind of a small child. I cannot tell. The gods are capricious."

That will not happen, I told myself. Please not. That would be cruelty beyond comprehension. Better he had died. *Sometimes even to live is an act of bravery*, Catilius had written.

No, I said firmly, but the thought would not go away, although I could sometimes push it to the back of my mind. Lena and I had not spoken of what Gnaius had told us; she had held me, tightly, for a long moment afterwards, but that was all. She was so strong. I had to be, too.

———————◆———————

I PLAYED A MEDLEY of lullabies and children's teaching songs, watching Lena bathe Cillian's face. She dried his skin gently, patting with a soft cloth, and began to salve his dry lips. He had been restless earlier,

Druise had told me. *"Kärestan,"* she murmured, her finger spreading the balm along his lower lip, chapped and red. "Your daughter moved this morning, for the first time. Or maybe your son, but I think she's a girl." His eyelids flickered, as if in response to her words, and suddenly his eyes opened. I held my breath. He blinked, several times. Against the light? Hope surged, and with it, fear.

"Lena," he whispered, barely making the sounds. *"Käresta."* I felt tears begin.

"Hello, my love," she murmured. "You have been asleep a long time. Let me give you some water." She dripped a spoonful between his lips, then another. His eyes never left her face. She kissed him, her lips barely brushing his. Behind me, I heard Druise leave the room.

I should leave them to each other, I thought. Cillian closed his eyes, then opened them again. "Sorley?"

"He is here too." I put the *ladhar* down, unbelieving. Kneeling, I took his hand. His fingers grasped mine loosely.

"Music," he whispered. *"Meas."*

Tears and laughter fought for ascendancy. *"Mo duíne gràhadh,"* I replied. "I am so heartily tired of Linrathan cradle songs. Can I play something else now?"

Chapter 8

DRUISE HAD GONE FOR Gnaius and Casyn, who arrived almost together. Casyn, pulled from talks with Decanius, wore the colours of office. The light was low in the room, but there was no mistaking the pale tunic, or the pendant.

"I am…sorry, *Princip*," Cillian murmured. Words took effort. He lay still. Lena gave him more water. "I didn't see," he managed.

"No more did Callan," Casyn said gently. "Do not worry, Cillian. There is no blame. We won. Fritjof is dead, and the Marai gone."

"Enough," Gnaius said firmly.

"Linrathe?" Cillian whispered.

"Is safe. Ruar is at Dun Ceànnar," I answered. "All is well, *mo charaidh*."

"You will all leave, please," Gnaius said. "Except Druisius. Wait in the corridor."

"He knows us," Lena said, leaning against me. She was allowing herself to cry now, tears of relief and fear assuaged. I wrapped my arms tighter around her, rocking her a little. My own eyes were still wet.

"More than that," Casyn said. "To understand so quickly what I wear means…remarkable."

Gnaius came out of the sickroom, closing the door quietly. "You must listen," he began. "He is sleeping. He will sleep and wake and sleep again, for many days. His mind, from what I saw, appears undamaged. But his body? There is much inflammation, and until that subsides, I cannot know how much permanent damage has been done.

"His pain is intense. He will need poppy syrup for many weeks. He is too weak to withstand the pain without it; he would not be able to sleep, and without sleep he will succumb again to fever. This is a long recovery, you understand? Many months, and it may never be complete."

Lena frowned, looking worried. "He hates drugs," she said. "He would barely accept willow-bark, before. He will argue against the poppy syrup." The physician shook his head.

"He must take it," he said. "I will explain, if he begins to baulk. He must be kept quiet, too. His *quincala*, of course, and you, Lord Sorley, for the music which so soothes him, but even the two of you should not be together, when he is awake. One other person, for a minute or two, each day, perhaps." He cleared his throat. "I believed he would die. It is not my skill that has saved him, but the gods. For what reason, I do not know."

⸺◆O◆⸺

LENA SLEPT, DEEPLY, CURLED on the cot in the sickroom. I returned to the stool beside Cillian, not playing, just sitting. Thinking, about many things. Cillian moaned slightly, moving his head. He opened his eyes.

"*Mo duíne gràhadh*," I said softly. "Lena is sleeping." Druise wasn't in the room. I bent to kiss him, allowing myself the gesture, the affirmation.

He smiled, just a brief curve of his lips. I gave him a little water.

"When?" he asked.

"Five weeks to midwinter," I said. "We are at Wall's End."

"Casil?"

"Casil?" I repeated, puzzled. "They came, yes." Did he not remember?

"No. The treaty."

"There are talks. I translate for Casyn. They go well enough." Not quite the truth, but all he needed to know. He smiled again and drifted back into sleep. I picked up his hand, stroking his fingers. His nails needed cutting. I could do that, I thought, and went to Gnaius's worktable to find clippers. Cillian did not wake while I trimmed his fingernails. I watched him sleep, hearing Lena's regular breathing from the cot behind me.

I had a responsibility now. To Cillian and to Lena, and the unborn child, and perhaps to Druisius as well. I must try to be, for an unknown time, what Cillian had been among the four of us: the guiding presence, the leader. I am taking on his roles, I thought. The idea made me uncomfortable, as if I were usurping him, somehow. But not forever, I told myself. He will recover. He must.

———◆O◆———

I HEARD CILLIAN'S SCREAM of pain from the hallway. I started to run, but the cadet stepped in front of the door. "No entry," he said. "My orders, Lord Sorley."

Lena appeared from further down the corridor. "Gnaius and Druise are with him. They are moving his leg; Gnaius says it is necessary. They told me to go away."

Another scream. She winced. I put my arms around her. The cadet's face was crumpled, the boy barely controlling himself. "Then we should," I said. "We have to trust Gnaius. Come."

I took her back to the room I had claimed as a workroom. She shook her head at the offer of wine, so I added wood to the fire and made tea instead.

"How are the talks?" she asked, her hands wrapped around the cup.

"Decanius has broken them off until he returns from the south," I reminded her. "He leaves in a few days. Casyn and his advisors are working on the reorganization of the army. Which cohorts to keep, and which to combine, and who might be promoted. That sort of thing. I'm not involved."

She sipped the tea. "I wonder if Casyn would let me help."

"Do you want to?"

"I have to do something, at least for part of the day. Druise—" She took a breath. "He will say this to you too. He said when they are doing these exercises in the mornings, and at night, Cillian needs to be free to scream or cry, and if he thinks you or I are near, he won't."

I swore. "Catilius," I said, "has a lot to answer for." She nodded, smiling a little.

"My thought too. But Druise is right, isn't he? They will dose him with poppy after, so he will sleep. I must be there when he is awake, afterwards, or you, but in the mornings at least I need employment. I am," she added, "still a lieutenant, after all."

"On leave," I said, "officially." I wondered if Casyn would let her be part of the talks; she hadn't the necessary rank to advise him. "And you need to rest, Lena. You're recovering too, in a different way, and you're pregnant."

"I know," she said. "I get tired easily. But I can sleep all night now, and sitting with Cillian is no longer a strain. And as for being pregnant, Sorley, when has that ever stopped a woman from working?"

I laughed. "Not at Gundarstorp," I admitted.

"Nor at Tirvan. I will talk to Casyn. What about you? What will you do?"

What could I do? I searched my mind. When the answer came to me, it was so obvious I wondered just how tired I was too, not to have seen it sooner. "What Randall was meant to," I said. "Teach the officers Casilan."

We talked for a while longer, about the changes Decanius was demanding, about Druise's surprising competency as a nurse, about the name—Gwenna—that Lena was considering for the baby. "For my mother, and his," she told me. "Gwen and Hafwen, but his father called her Wenna."

"And if it's a boy?"

"Colm. If Cillian agrees, of course," she added.

"Have you told him?"

"Not yet. I will, soon. When he's a little stronger."

"Wouldn't knowing buoy him?" I asked. "Give him something to look forward to?"

"Perhaps." She put down her cup. "Or something to worry about. This baby is a possible heir to the title of *Princip*, and I do not want the implications of that concerning him yet."

"I thought Cillian renounced his right to inherit," I said.

"He did, for himself. We did not believe we had the right to make that choice for our children, although for Cillian that was only an intellectual decision. I wonder now if he would have felt the same, had he known of her." She touched her belly, only slightly swollen. "But that cannot be changed." She stood. "Nor can certain effects of pregnancy. The tea was welcome, but I had better leave you now."

How did you teach a language? I tried to remember what Perras had done, but it didn't help: he had been primarily teaching us to read Casilan, not speak it, and speaking was the priority here. I had come to the *Ti'ach* fluent in Marái'sta, having learned it from earliest childhood. How had

Dagney taught me the language of the Western—or Southern, as we had called it— Empire? In the classroom, I remembered: basic vocabulary, the phrasing of common sentences. But then at meals, and while playing music, or just in simple requests. I'd have to mimic that, as best I could. And what, in the interactions between officers and men, and officers and Casilani officers, were the words they needed to know?

I asked Druise that night, when he'd finally come to our room. He smelt of beer, and he wasn't quite sober. "I will write you a list," he said, "tomorrow." A question answered, I thought: if he can write, he can read. "Time to sleep now." He sounded tired, and out of sorts.

"What's wrong?" I asked.

He grunted. I ran my hand over his back. "Druise?"

"Mostly I like my work," he said. "Not this part."

"Which part?"

"The exercises. Cillian screaming. It is hard." I rubbed his neck, feeling the tension there.

"Can't you ask Gnaius to use one of the medics to help?"

"No. Cillian is my officer. There will be enough talk, from the cadets on the door. He does not need others to hear, or see his tears."

"Music wouldn't help? I could—"

"No. After, yes, when he has had the poppy. Enough, *amané*. I need to sleep, and I do not want talk of Cillian in our bed."

I couldn't argue with that; it was only fair, and he'd said it gently. "There won't be," I said. "I promise."

"Linrathan men," he said. "Everything a promise." He stood, wearily. "Better not to make them. They tempt the gods."

He stripped off his clothes and lay down, pulling the blankets over him. He'd be asleep in seconds, I knew. "Druise?" He muttered my name. "You said it's better to use anger. Can't I—can't we—?"

He opened one eye. "Tonight, no. But yes. If you want."

Even his words aroused me. "I want," I said, hoarsely. He flashed a sleepy grin.

"Good. Tomorrow."

——————◆○◆——————

"GET OUT OF MY way, girl!" Angry words, spoken in a heavily accented voice. Druise swore and began to run. I followed. At the door to the infirmary, Phaulius, Decanius's aide, pushed the cadet aside. He reached for the handle, just as Druise's big fist smashed upward into his jaw.

The man stumbled, recoiling off the stone wall. Druise grabbed him, wrenching both arms behind his back. "His knife," he ordered. I pulled Phaulius's knife from his belt, avoiding a kick. The man was a head taller than Druise, but nowhere near as strong.

"You all right?" Druise said to the cadet. She nodded. "Then go for help." He pushed Phaulius up against the wall, face forward. Blood was dripping onto the flagstones. I undid my belt and wound it around the man's wrists, and by the time other guards arrived he was on his knees, Druise's foot on one ankle, breathing in gasps and snuffles.

"What happened?" the senior of the two guards asked. Druise told him, succinctly. He turned to the cadet, who confirmed what Druise had said. "And you, Lord Sorley?"

"Exactly what you have heard," I said. "I have his belt knife; I took it from him after Druisius had restrained him. And I'd like my belt back, please."

"Wait," Druise said to them. He went into the infirmary, returning with small pieces of cloth. He twisted them, pushing one into each of Phaulius's nostrils. The man gasped, trying to jerk his head away, but Druise had a hand firmly on his jaw. "Stop him trailing blood all down the halls," he said. One of the guards grinned.

"Come on, Phaulius, it's the cells for you." They helped him up, none too gently. "What sort of idiot are you? The cadet's orders come from the physician Gnaius, and he outranks you."

"He doesn't outrank the Procurator," Phaulius said thickly. He spat blood.

"Did you tell her that?"

"She should have known who I was."

"Would that have been enough in Casil? And I thought we were being told how superior your discipline is to ours. Get moving." The second guard led him away. The *capora* turned to the girl. "Well done, Cadet. Now get the floor washed." He held out a hand to me. "I'll take the knife. You'll get your belt back."

"What did he say to you?" Druise asked the cadet, when the guard had left.

"He wanted to see Major Cillian."

"That was all?"

"Yes, sir. I said he could not, that I had no orders to allow him. I was polite, sir."

"And you are not hurt?"

"No, sir."

Druise grinned. "Then do as the *capora* ordered and wash the floor. The Major will be safe. I will be with him, and Lord Sorley with me."

———◆○◆———

UNSURPRISINGLY, THE NEXT DAY we were called to Casyn's workroom, to face a furious Procurator. Phaulius was not present.

"Who is this soldier?" Decanius demanded. "He attacked my aide."

"My guards report your aide was assaulting a cadet following her orders," Casyn said. "Druisius did what I would expect any soldier in my army to do, and defended her."

"Phaulius was there as my representative, enquiring as to the health of the Emperor's son. The girl had no right to deny him entry to the infirmary."

"The cadet," Casyn emphasized the rank, "had every right. The Major's physician has been specific about who may see him. Even I must request permission to have someone accompany me, Procurator, and the Major is my nephew, I will remind you."

Decanius glared at Casyn, his balding head gleaming red. "Druisius, you say? That is not a name from this land."

"No," Casyn said. "Druisius joined my army, Procurator, after the Taiva, with several other men from Casil who had a liking for this land. He is Major Cillian's soldier-servant."

"Who was your commander?" Decanius snapped at Druisius.

Druise waited for Casyn's nod before he answered. Decanius frowned. "And why did you stay?"

"I like adventure, Procurator." Decanius studied him, eyes narrowed. Druise stared at the wall.

"Why does your nephew have a Casilani soldier-servant?" At the *Princip's* hesitation, Druise answered.

"I have skills in nursing, Procurator. Learned when I was assigned to an injured officer in Casil."

"I see. *Princip,* I am displeased. This man should be punished."

"Punished?" Casyn said coldly. "For protecting the officer to whom he is assigned? I think not, Procurator. Ensure your aide follows protocol in the future, and I will seek no further punishment for him, for his mistreatment of a cadet. Are we agreed?"

"It will do," Decanius said, after a moment.

"Good," Casyn said. "And as you were so determined to discover, Procurator, my nephew is expected now to live, although his recovery will be long and difficult."

"So we will not see him at our discussions? Not even when I return from the south?"

"It is unlikely, unless you are gone for many weeks."

"A regret," the Procurator said, but I was sure he meant the opposite.

"Sit, Druisius," the Princip said, once Decanius had left. I, as the translator, had already been seated. "What did you make of that? Sorley?"

"It seemed too easy. Unless he knows Phaulius is at fault."

"He is at fault. Regardless, it is out of character for Decanius, in my experience. Do you have any other thoughts?"

"Perhaps one." I paused, trying to think of a way to explain. "You know I am a musician. I sing only adequately, but I can hear when a voice is being constrained by fear or tension. There is a tightness in the expression. Every time Decanius has spoken of Cillian, I have heard that tightness."

"Interesting. You think he is afraid of Cillian?"

"Afraid of what he can do in negotiations, given what his uncle, Quintus, might have told him?"

"Was Phaulius searched?" Druisius asked.

"Not that I know of. What are you thinking?"

"Poison. Easy enough to put in a water flask." He sounded very sure of that.

Casyn leaned back in his chair, arms crossed. "Are you speaking from experience, Druisius? Don't answer that," he added. "A cadet is not a sufficient guard, then. I will assign soldiers, day and night. From our own troops. Druisius, thank you. Lord Sorley, please stay."

"Do you think Decanius would seriously try to poison Cillian?" I asked. Even for the Procurator, that would be extreme. Casyn tapped his fingers on the table.

"I think it is possible. Decanius knows I have not the knowledge to counter his arguments, nor always the skill. The man I knew Cillian to be would. If, as I pray, his mind is undamaged by his illness and the drugs he must take, and he recovers in time, we might salvage some rights to our own traditions and laws. Without Cillian, I have no doubt we will be subsumed into the ways of the Eastern Empire."

He had spoken starkly; not resigned, quite, but a man telling an unpalatable truth.

"Turlo could not help?" I asked.

"I doubt it, Sorley," he said. "I feel like a man trying to hold back the tide, knowing it will sweep over us no matter what I do."

—◇—

GNAIUS HAD TOLD LENA to go out into the fresh air, good for her and the baby, he said. Mostly she went alone: mornings, when Cillian's treatments and exercises occurred, conflicted with my teaching and the duties Casyn had found for her. Officially, she transcribed, suitable work for a junior officer. But some days we were both free to walk down to the harbour, or ride along the road that ran beside the Wall, talking usually of little things. On this cloudy, cool morning, we'd chosen to ride. Perhaps half-way to the first guardpost east of Wall's End, Lena pointed ahead. "Riders."

The distance between us lessened. Sun broke free of the clouds, shining on the right-hand rider's red hair. "Turlo!" Lena urged her horse forward into a canter. I kicked my gelding's flanks and followed.

She slid off the horse and into Turlo's outstretched arms. He hugged her, hard, then stepped back a little, looking at her face, and mine. "There is good news?"

"Yes," Lena said. "He is awake, and alert. In much pain, but he will live."

"Oh, lassie," Turlo said, enveloping her again in his arms. "I barely dared ask. But seeing you smiling—" He looked up at the other man. "Get off that horse, Galen, and greet your daughter."

Galen dismounted, offering Lena the soldier's embrace. "You have done great things, I am told," he said.

"What I was trained for."

"Killing Fritjof, yes," he replied. "But crossing the Durrains, and beyond?"

"I brought him," Turlo said, "so you can tell him exactly what you did. He keeps asking and I cannot supply the details." He sounded amused, a friend indulging another's fancy.

"It could be useful to know," Galen said. He turned to me. "Lord Sorley."

"It is good to see you again, Galen."

"At least this time I am not taking you prisoner." He grinned, remembering, and so did I.

"Why are we standing here?" Turlo asked. "I've a friend to see." He put a hand on Lena's arm. "Lassie, may I say…I feared for the child, in your anguish. I am glad to see I need not have worried."

Lena smiled. "She is strong, this one. But, Turlo, Cillian does not know. Do not mention it."

It puzzled me that Lena had still not told Cillian and that he had not noticed. Her belly had only begun to visibly swell in the past week or two, and without the strong breeze pushing her tunic tight, I doubted Turlo would have been sure. But she would have to tell Cillian soon.

"Turlo," I asked, as we rode west, "when were you at Dun Ceànnar last? I wrote to Ruar, telling him Cillian would live, more than two weeks ago."

"We'd left by then," Turlo said. "We rode east, to the track below the Durrains, and came south that way."

"Why?"

"I had an idea that if any of Fritjof's men had escaped, they might go east again."

"And attack over the Durrains?" Lena asked. "I doubt it, Turlo. It took us months to cross them on foot. To bring an army, pack animals, equipment? No."

"I wish there was a map," Galen said.

"There is," I said. "I've seen it."

"So has Cillian," Lena remembered. "He alluded to it once, and an older one. He said they didn't agree on how wide the mountains were."

"Where is this map?" Turlo demanded.

"At the *Ti'ach*. I can have it sent, I would think," I answered. "Maybe now you've crossed them, Lena, the map will make sense to you?"

"Maybe," she said. "Maybe to Cillian, too. He kept notes, the entire journey. But I don't know where his books are."

"I will wager, lassie," Turlo said, "that Birel has them."

Lena grinned, her face alight in a way I had not seen in so very long. "Would you now?" she said. "And what are you prepared to bet, General?"

Turlo sighed in relief when I told him Decanius was in the south. "Officious man," he muttered. We rode into the fort, leaving the horses at the stables. Galen and Turlo spoke quietly for a moment before Galen left us, heading to the soldiers' commons for the midday meal.

"When can I see Cillian?" Turlo asked.

"Late afternoon," Lena told him. "He will not be awake until then. And only for ten minutes."

"Understood," he said. "I'd best report to Casyn." He strode off, then turned on his heel. "I almost forgot. I've a letter for you, Sorley, from Dun Ceànnar. It's in my saddlebags. Where will you be, later?"

"Teaching," I said, "for most of the afternoon. With Lena in the infirmary, after that."

"I'll send a cadet with it." Lena watched Turlo for a moment, smiling.

"He cheers you up," I observed.

"I've always liked him," she said. "But it's the first time I've told anyone Cillian will live; anyone who wasn't here, I mean. It made it real, somehow."

I gave her a quick hug. "Shall we eat?" As we walked towards the junior officers' commons, I remembered my earlier confusion. "Lena, why have you still not told Cillian about the baby? He is stronger, and you can't put it off much longer."

"Because there are complications I cannot solve."

I frowned. "What complications, Lena?"

"For all Cillian's oath to this Empire, Sorley, he is Linrathan. The night before the Taiva, we talked about where home was, after. Home for all of us, including you; he was very clear on that, you know. You had to be there too. There is only one place that can be that home, isn't there? The *Ti'ach*?"

"In what could have been your last hour together, he was thinking of me?"

"Of course he was," Lena said, a bit impatiently. "Sorley, love and responsibility are inseparable in Cillian's mind. You know his vow to me, that he will shelter me all my life. He has not told me what he has vowed regarding you, but since he wants you with him always, it will be something similar."

"Wants me with him always?" I repeated. Words I had dreamed of hearing for almost a decade.

"Have you not realized that yet?" Lena said. "I need your help, Sorley. If we are to go home to Linrathe, this child must be legitimate. We need to marry, but I don't know how to go about it. Marriage does not exist, in this land. Who can perform the ceremony, in Linrathe?"

"*Scáeli'en*," I said, "or at least, those who are senior enough. After seven years, I think. Not that it matters. Dagney is the senior *scáeli* of Linrathe, in rank if not in years. And there is no one else who should preside over Cillian's marriage."

Lena laughed, delighted. "No one else indeed," she said. "She will be pleased, won't she?"

"Very," I assured her.

"Then I can tell him now," she said. "Thank you. He'll be awake, I think. I'll eat later."

I stared after her. Go home to Linrathe. Lena was letting herself think of the future again, a future with Cillian—and me. Unexpected anger, sudden and intense, flared. Cillian would recover, and I would be caught between him and Druisius, loving the man I could not have; not loving the man I should. If he had told me what he had told Lena before the Taiva, that he wanted me by his side, wanted me at the *Ti'ach* with him…maybe I wouldn't have asked Druise to be my partner. Because, of course, Druise was a soldier. He couldn't just come to Linrathe, and we couldn't be lovers there anyway.

I swore. At the gods. At fate. At Cillian. My stomach clenched, bile rising in my throat. Grow up, I told myself. You can't be angry.

Not at him.

———◆O◆———

I WAS WALKING DOWN the corridor after teaching, still chatting to the officer with me in Casilan, when a cadet brought me the letter. I read it quickly, swearing softly. I was summoned to Dun Ceànnar, to be formally made *toscaire* to the Western Empire, and I needed to be there for midwinter, which was not all that far away. I would be gone several weeks, perhaps a little longer, and I didn't want to go. But I had little choice. My country's leader had given me an order I was bound to obey.

I entered the infirmary room quietly, thinking Cillian might still be sleeping. He was, and so was Lena, on the cot near his bed, but my entrance woke her. She yawned. "I was only dozing. But I'll leave him with you. He was awake, earlier, so he might sleep longer than usual." She stopped to watch him for a moment before she left. I sat by Cillian's bedside, thinking about riding north, and what I might expect at Dun Ceànnar.

Cillian woke an hour later. Druise, knowing the schedule, appeared, to wash and reposition him. I played, sitting under the window: I still didn't like watching this. Druise made Cillian as comfortable as possible, before coming over to me. "Do not stay long," he said quietly.

When he'd left, I put the *ladhar* down. "How are you?" I asked Cillian.

"Overwhelmed," he said. His voice was stronger, but there was a note of something new this afternoon. Disbelief? Wonder?

"Why, *mo charaidh*?"

He pushed himself up just slightly and smiled, a brilliant, joyous smile that lit his thin face. "You knew, of course, but I did not, until earlier today."

"Lena told you about the child," I said, smiling. "Is it not the best news, Cillian?" My earlier anger had dissolved. Druise and I—well, it had never been serious, had it?

"Not ever an expectation, in my life," he said softly. "But nor was Lena. Sorley," he added, seriously, "you will take care of her—of them—if I die?"

"You won't," I told him, "but of course, *mo duíne gràhadh*. As if you had been born my brother. I promise."

"*Meas*," he murmured. "How long to the spring equinox?"

"Midwinter is in two weeks, so, just over three months."

"Not long," he said thoughtfully. "I would like to be free of the poppy, when the child is born."

"Gnaius must guide you in that," I said. "Are you strong enough for other news?"

"I think so. Is it bad?"

"Not very. Only that I will be gone, for a month or so, over midwinter."

He took this in. "Why?"

"You may find this amusing," I told him. "I am Linrathe's new *toscaire* to the Empire, as of midwinter, by Ruar's bidding, and his great-uncle's approval. I must ride to Dun Ceànnar for my instructions."

"I wish you joy of Liam," he said. "A reward for your service, but one that keeps you a safe distance from Ruar?"

"How can you do that?" I demanded, smiling. He had sounded almost like himself. "Even drugged and in pain, you are more perceptive than I."

"Long practice," he replied, with an echo of a grin. "And the pain is not so bad, just now. Will you go to the *Ti'ach*?"

"On my way back." I would tell him of Perras's death when I returned.

"Good. They will be relieved to see you." He frowned. "When do you leave?"

"The day after tomorrow."

"Then perhaps I can write a letter, before you go. There is nothing wrong with my hands."

"I will send it from Heurlstorp. I won't make them wait several more weeks to hear from you," I said.

Lena returned, her hair damp. She'd been at the baths, I realized. I gave her a hug. "He is very happy," I murmured.

"Yes," she said. "Unbelieving at first, but the evidence," she touched her belly, "cannot be denied." She sat down beside the bed. "Our daughter was kind enough earlier to kick several times, so that her father could feel her move." Cillian reached for her hand, his long fingers tangling in hers. She bent to kiss him, not the brief brush of her lips from the weeks of vigil, but a longer kiss. Her free hand cupped his cheek. A rush of emotions caught me unawares: joy, hope, and envy mixed together, but stronger than those, overwhelming relief, and gratitude.

Before this last year I had only ever desperately wanted two things: to be a *scáeli*, and Cillian. The first would never happen now: it required years of travel and song-gathering. I had dreamt, once, of riding by his side as he travelled, he the *toscaire*, I the musician. But...*he wants you with him always*. We would still be together. There is very little I would not do, I thought, for this privilege.

CHAPTER 9

HEAVY GREY CLOUDS HUNG over the hills, the horizon blending into the sky. Snow, I thought, at least on higher ground. The vagaries of Linrathe's weather meant I had needed to leave well in advance of midwinter: I could find myself snowed in at any point in the ride. I would travel from *torp* to *torp*, hospitality automatically offered to any traveller, but especially to someone who was both a *toscaire* and a musician. And a lord, truth be told. I would have the best bed available, and the best food, and someone else would rub down and feed my horse and clean my tack and boots. I wondered how Cillian, ascetic and self-sufficient, had dealt with all that. He had probably refused most of it, I thought, accepting only what etiquette required. I couldn't remember, from the few days he had stayed with us when I was sixteen.

I rode east, along the Wall's road. There was no defined track in Linrathe between Wall's End and the road from the Wall to the Sterre, and with snow threatening I would not risk riding cross-country. I wore a fur-lined cloak, slung open over a woollen tunic and breeches, and there were matching gloves and a cap in my saddlebags. I didn't need them, yet. An identical cloak, and gloves, would be delivered to Druisius on Midwinter's Day, my present to him.

Druise. I thought about the previous night; my increased confidence, his deep, delighted laughter. I touched my shoulder, just where it met my neck. I'd need to keep my shirts laced, or explain the bite marks.

Cillian wants you with him, always, Lena had said. Could I have a life that was both with him and not with him? I didn't feel bereft because he loved Lena, but wasn't that because of Druise? Who I was with him was someone Cillian didn't know, or Lena. I barely did myself, in truth, but I was learning.

What would Cillian think? I didn't know, and I didn't think I cared. The idea irritated me, somehow. What he and Lena shared wasn't for me to know, and neither did he have any right to know what my relationship with Druise entailed.

But you always had a life without him, my mind said. Music.

A solitary life, I argued, but no longer. I can make music with Druise; we have that, too. Music and bed, in Druise's words, and much to learn about both. Something separate and private, not crossing into Cillian and Lena's life together. Which was fine, at Wall's End, but what would happen when it was time to return to the *Ti'ach*?

Write some songs, I told myself. Truth could be found in wine, but for me, it was also found in the melodies and the words that flowed when my fingers touched the strings of my *ladhar*. Music would give me answers.

———◄O►———

AT EVERY *torp* where I stopped, I was questioned about Cillian. Somehow, the news of his injuries and illness had spread across Linrathe. I reassured the *Eirënnen* and their wives, and I saw nothing but relief from them all. A tear or two from a *Konë*, and a surprising gentleness from her husband, at one *torp*. "She was fond of him," he said to me gruffly, later, "and what harm was there in it? We all knew what was said."

I'd heard the stories too, and Lena had told me they were true. That Cillian had vowed never to father a child because he had been fatherless himself—but the beds of women were another source of information and opinion. So he had given—and taken, no doubt—pleasure without risking conception. "I became adept at holding a civilized conversation with an *Eirën*, after I had spent part of the previous night with his wife," he'd said to me once, his voice reflecting his revulsion at what he'd done. He'd turned away from that life the year I'd come to the *Ti'ach*, resigning his position as *toscaire*.

I brought the talk around to Ruar and his great-uncle. From every *Eirën*, I heard respect for Liam, if not always liking. By the time I rode into Dun

Ceànnar's long valley, I had a picture of a cautious, conservative man, but one who was loyal to Linrathe, its customs and its people.

Alone among the estates of Linrathe, Dun Ceànnar was more stronghold than *torp*, the associated village sitting some half-mile down its valley, with the massive stone house commanding a position on the hillside. Attack from above was just about impossible, and its long view down the glen meant invaders would be seen early in their approach. Ruar's family had been the leaders of Linrathe for more generations than I could remember, and their importance was reflected in the house's construction and position.

Men waited for me outside the house as I rode up the track. I was expected, and I rode bareheaded and with my cloak swept back, revealing that I carried no sword. I tolerated the assessing gazes. Well, I thought, I am fair-haired. But would any Marai approach the house so brazenly?

"My lord Sorley," one of the men said when I was close enough. "I will take your horse to the stables. Please go with my companion."

I dismounted and began to unfasten my saddlebags. "I can do that, my lord," the first guard said. "I will bring them to your room."

"You will forgive me," I said firmly, "but as you may know I am a musician, and no musician will trust his instrument to another man, however well-meaning. I will take my bags."

"As you wish," he said. He led my horse away, and I followed the second guard up the steps and into the house. I stopped inside the door, letting my eyes adjust to the dimness. Stone flags on the floor; stone walls, high rafters: this would have been the original hall, back when this was just another *Eirën's* house, a long structure of hall and ancillary rooms. It was little different, if a bit larger, than the hall at the *Ti'ach*. But as the family's importance had grown, so had the house, and now this was just a space between the outdoors and the fastnesses beyond.

I shed my cloak, hanging it on a peg on the wall, and let the guard guide me along a passage and to a closed door. He knocked, and at a word from inside, opened the door. "The Lord Sorley," he announced.

I stepped inside. Ruar was on his feet, a smile of welcome on his face; his great-uncle Liam did not rise, nor smile. The guard closed the door. "Sorley!" Ruar said. "I hoped you might come today. Was it a difficult ride? Would you like refreshment?"

"Ruar," I acknowledged him. "You look well. As do you, *Raséair*," I added, turning to Liam.

"I am well enough," Liam grunted. We exchanged the necessary pleasantries, and a brief description of my travels north. Tea and oatcakes were brought. Ruar might be the *Teannas'óg*, but he was also a growing boy, and most of the oatcakes went to him.

Liam finished his tea. "We'd best do the oath," he said, "so that we can talk of what we expect of you, Sorley. A few questions, first."

"Before that," Ruar said, interrupting his great-uncle, "tell me how Cillian does. He lives? The General Turlo told us it was unlikely."

"He does," I told him, "although it was not expected. He is awake now, but still very weak, and in much pain. He sends his greetings to you both."

"I am glad to hear it," Ruar said. "I liked Cillian, when I met him at the Eastern Fort. He explained the treaty and what it meant for Linrathe and my people extremely well. I would have liked more opportunity to learn from him."

"We will think more of your schooling in the spring," Liam said. "To our business, now. Before you swear this oath, there are questions I must ask. Questions that should have been asked before, and not just of a boy not affirmed by his family to succeed."

"It was Ruar's name the men of Linrathe rallied around," I said. "Perhaps not affirmed by his family, but chosen by his people, surely? In their eyes, and from what I heard on the road, he is *Teannasach* already."

"Yes," Liam said, "and we have accepted their choice. It would be unwise on our part to ignore it, after Lorcann. But he is not *Teannasach* yet, and as his regent I will have questions and challenges from the *Eirënnen* who advise us, and I must be able to answer."

I had expected this. Even at the *torps*, there had been some talk of the treaty, and how it had been decided, and not everyone had been pleased that a distant, foreign Empress now had influence over Linrathe. But the details were not known, nor my role in it, and I had pleaded that I had no right to speak of it as *toscaire* until my appointment had been confirmed. But if there was a council of the *Teannasach's* advisors in the spring, as traditionally there was, Liam—and perhaps Ruar—would indeed face some hard questions.

"Please ask what you need to," I said. I glanced at Ruar. He sat quietly, slightly frowning, but in concentration, I thought. He looked a bit like his father.

"Then answer me this," Liam said, and his voice was suddenly colder, "what right had you to give away the independence of Linrathe? Deciding our country's fate is the prerogative of its people. Even the *Teannasach* is responsible to them."

"I was as much the voice of our people as anyone, *Raséair*. My instructions came from Perras, who had long advised Donnalch and knew his mind. I left a country on the edge of defeat and found a chance for support against the Marai. I took it, after much long thought and deliberation." My argument sounded weak to my own ears. I was not Cillian, trained to the precision of diplomatic talks.

I was a musician, and I had wanted to be a *scáeli*. "*Raséair*, my own lands are forfeit." I dropped my voice, slowing my speech. "I have lost the sound of waves on the sea-coast, and the fog lying low over the water, and the barking of seals on the shingle. I have lost the eagle above the mountains, and the purple of the heather on the hill, and the grave of my mother. All those I gave willingly. Perhaps I had no authority, except that of love for Linrathe, to see it not subject to Fritjof's brutality." I paused. "But what would you have done, in my place?"

Silence. Liam studied me, thoughtfully. "I may recall you, in the spring, to say those words again to the council," he said finally. "If the *scáeli* plays *An dithës braithréan* quietly as you speak, you will have them in the palm of your hand. You have a brother, do you not?"

"I do," I said. "Two, actually. Roghan is three years younger than I. The little one, who is a half-brother, I have never met; he is five." He nodded.

"And what of the fact that the treaty was negotiated by agents of the southern Empire, and not by you at all? You agreed to terms, nothing more."

"Cillian na Perras negotiated the terms for Linrathe. Sworn to his father's country he may now be, and nearly gave his life for it, but compare the treaties, *Raséair*. The southern Empire is now no more; Casyn is not the Emperor, nor will there be another. Their laws are now Casil's laws, and Casil's Empress theirs. Ruar will be *Teannasach*, and our laws and independence are mostly untouched. There is tribute to pay, admittedly, but we were paying Varsland, before. Is this a treaty negotiated by a man who does not love the land of his birth?"

"But one who Donnalch never trusted," Liam said bluntly.

"Donnalch was mistaken in that," I answered firmly.

"I agree," Ruar said. "My father was a wise man, and his judgement fair and thoughtful, but in this he was wrong, great-uncle."

"Perhaps," Liam said. "You do not know all of it. Now, Sorley, there is an oath to be sworn, and for that we must be outside. You have a cloak? And after that is done, will you explain to Ruar exactly what you just did here, how you used words and the pitch and tone of your voice to convince? A *scáeli's* trick, and you did it well. Ruar, you must learn to recognize this, and guard against it."

We went out, into the thin sunshine, and across the cobbles of the forecourt. When there was soil under our feet, Liam stopped.

"Ruar, go for Bhradaín, will you? We need the *scáeli* as witness." The boy didn't seem to mind running the errand, although I wondered for a moment why Liam had not sent him earlier.

"What is it you have to say to me that is not for Ruar's ears?" I asked calmly.

"Only this. I know you to be *channàdarra*. You will not lay a hand on the boy, or you will die."

"I have no interest in boys," I told him, "nor in any man who is uninterested in me. You need not worry, Liam."

He gave a sharp nod, an unpleasant business dealt with. A wind blew off the hills, cold and biting. I wished I had my gloves; chapped fingers fared badly on *ladhar* strings. Ruar returned, with an older man, grey-haired and slightly stooped. Bhradaín, *scáeli* to Dun Ceànnar: if he had been here seven years ago, I would have heard him play. Perhaps even spoken to him. I didn't remember.

"Lord Sorley," Liam said. "As *Raséair* for Ruar, the presumptive *Teannasach* of Linrathe, you will give this oath to me. Do you swear that as a *toscaire* of Linrathe, no man, no prince, no foreign power holds sway over you, and that your loyalty is to the people of Linrathe, and to the land beneath your feet?"

"I so swear," I said. I hoped I spoke the truth.

"Done," Liam said. "Bhradaín, you will record it."

As we returned to the house, Liam told me we would not speak of my instructions as *toscaire* until after Midwinter; until then, I was to think of myself simply as a guest, although if I chose to further Ruar's education regarding Casil and the Eastern Empire, he would be grateful.

"It would give me great pleasure," I replied, as I had to. During the meal, Liam was as relaxed and pleasant as I had known him. He ate his soup and bread, and then pushed his chair back.

"Stay and talk to Ruar about the East," he said to me. "I have a short sleep after the mid-day meal, when I can. And if you would play for us tonight, we would be honoured. Bhradaín spoke highly of your music. I will see you at dinner."

What did Bhradaín know of my music? Dagney, I supposed. I would have, in the normal course of things, spent part of each year after I left the *Ti'ach* travelling, singing and gathering songs, a requirement for those who aspired to be a *scáeli*. She had likely been writing letters on my behalf. I wondered, idly, what my father would have said: he had expected me to help run the estate. I'd planned on bargaining with him for a few months travelling each year only once I'd arrived home.

But Fritjof had killed his brother and assumed the kingship, and I had never gone home. I never would, now. A sorrow, that. I had spoken to Liam of what I had lost, and I had done it in a way to evoke emotion and compassion. *All those I gave willingly*, I had said. That part was not quite the truth. I had not wanted to give up Sorham, but I had done it because Cillian had told me I should, and Turlo had agreed. I wondered once again if my brother had thought like my father and sided with the Marai. I wondered if he were even alive. I hadn't seen him since he was fifteen.

Not so much older than Ruar. I pulled myself from my reverie. "Is there a map of Linrathe and Sorham?" I asked. "If so, I will show you where we started for the east."

Chapter 10

FOR THREE DAYS I was treated exactly as Liam had implied: as the lord Sorley, musician and guest, and nothing more. Other men and a few women arrived: *Eirënnen* and their wives from close *torps*, a few officers from the Sterre. Dun Ceànnar's hospitality at Midwinter was legendary. I played every evening, at Bhradaín's invitation, even tuning my *ladhar* for Casilani melodies, introducing a different music to the audience.

Midwinter's Eve itself, the fire burning high in the huge hearth, I alternated between dancing and conversation, both required of me as lord and *toscaire*, and being a musician. When Bhradaín rested his voice, I played traditional songs, and watched as others danced. Food and ale and *fuisce* were in generous supply, but I wanted a clear head: it would not do for a musician to forget his fingering or the words. I had another reason, too, or a possibility of one. Bhradaín had an apprentice, Kester, and the boy had been just a little too attentive.

That alone I could have dealt with, but my last conversation with Cillian before I left had been instructive. "*Mo charaidh*, be careful," he had said. "The oath you will swear demands that no man has sway over you. Some —including Liam—may try."

"But on what grounds?"

"You are vulnerable," he said. "Sleep alone, Sorley, even if an overture to you seems freely made." I had said nothing. Cillian had pushed himself a little more upright. "It was not just disgust at my own behaviour that led me to choose a solitary life," he said quietly. "I will tell you, someday. Just be careful."

"I will," I promised. I hadn't needed to be, on the ride north, but this boy worried me. I had noted Kester's occasional covert glance towards Liam after he had helped carry my instrument, or arrange a stool. I had learned to look for certain behaviours, sitting with Cillian over the long days of negotiation in Casil, and I thought it just possible that the boy glanced at Liam to look for approval, not to check if his behaviour towards me had been noticed. I truly hoped the interest was at least in part feigned, or being channelled for his lord's use. Blood would run high tonight, after the music and dancing and the *fuisce*.

Liam shouted for silence, and when the noise died down, offered a toast to the new year. Bhradaín stepped forward on the low dais, waiting again for silence; then, as befitted his status as *scáeli* to the house, he played and sang the traditional last song of the evening. He was, I thought, listening to the modulation of his voice, very skilled.

Kester appeared at my side. "Can I help you carry your music and instrument to your room, my lord?" he asked softly. He touched my arm.

"Thank you, no," I said, my voice at its usual conversational tone. "I can manage. Help Bhradaín, if he needs it. I wish a word with the *Raséair.*" I stepped off the dais and crossed the floor to where Liam stood, talking to another man.

"*Raséair,*" I said, when he turned to me, with a nod of dismissal to his companion. "Am I to receive my instructions tomorrow?"

"Eager to leave us, are you?" he asked.

"Only that the weather looks to be clear for some days, unless the wind changes." I said, shading my voice towards apology. "At this time of year, a traveller needs to take advantage of that."

"I suppose you are right," he said. "But not too early tomorrow. Late morning. If you wish, you can leave after the mid-day meal, and reach the first *torp* south before nightfall. Thank you for your music tonight. I think Bhradaín's apprentice might prefer to be yours."

"I have no need of an apprentice, or anything else the boy might be induced to offer," I said, quietly but very clearly. I saw the flash of surprise —and annoyance?—in his eyes, quickly masked.

"Good night, Lord Sorley," he said brusquely. "I wish you joy in the new year."

I spoke at length with another guest, one of the Linrathan officers from the Sterre who wanted a first-hand account of the battle along the Wall. We were housed in the same corridor, and we walked together once I had satisfied his curiosity. My room was first, and I turned to it, wishing him goodnight. I opened the door.

Kester sat on the bed, half-undressed, a lamp burning on the table. He looked up, his nearly-black hair falling over his forehead, his eyes dark and huge in the lamplight. Desire shot through me, immediate and demanding.

I stepped back into the corridor. "A minute!" I called to the officer, who turned and came to me. "Look," I said. "I want you to witness that this is how I found him."

"I was invited," Kester said, defiantly.

"He was not," I told the officer, "and Bhradaín will stand as witness to that, I believe. Kester here did indeed offer to bring my instrument to my room, but I refused. The *scáeli* will confirm my words." *Scáeli'en* were sworn to speak the truth, even if unpleasant.

"Put your shirt on, boy, and come with me," my companion barked, frowning. "The *Raséair* will still be awake. Lord Sorley, I suggest you remain here. I will deal with this. If you are needed, I will send someone for you."

I sank onto the bed, still shocked at my reaction. I picked up my *ladhar*, for lack of anything else to do, and let my fingers do what they would. A tune began to emerge, mournful, a lament; a song for night and lamplight, of regret and longing. Words began to form into a verse.

An hour passed. I heard a quiet knock at my door. The Linrathan officer stood there.

"The boy is dealt with," he said. "No blame will be attached to your name, Lord Sorley."

"What will happen to him?" I asked.

He shrugged. "I left that to the *Raséair* and the *scáeli*," he said. "In the army, a flogging, for a first offense. It does little good, if the inclination is there."

"Thank you," I said. "I am sorry I kept you from your bed this night." He wished me goodnight and went off to his room. I closed the door, reached for the *ladhar*, began to sing, softly:

My true love's eyes are softly gleaming
In candlelight and music's lure
One night alone, at spring's fair dawning
To keep me longing through the years
To keep my soul bereft and mourning….

I put the *ladhar* down, weeping. The apprentice had looked so much like Cillian.

MOST OF WHAT I discussed with Liam and Ruar the next morning was what I had expected: the considerations for movement across the border; the division of responsibility for troops on the Sterre, locations along the coast where ships of the Empire could take in water or dock for repairs, and a dozen other points. I took notes, explaining that I did not have a memory trained to this. A meeting between Casyn and Liam and Ruar was proposed. Finally, Liam straightened in his chair.

"There is one more thing, Lord Sorley," he said. This would be the most serious, I thought. "There is no action to take on this yet, but the *Princip* and his advisors must be clear on one thing. Linrathe will use whatever means we deem fit to regain Sorham. It is our intent to do so, although it may take many years."

"Noted," I said, keeping my voice neutral.

"And for the tribute we pay to Casil, or will pay, in a year or two, we expect their help."

"Am I to act as your *toscaire* to the Eastern Empire, as well as to the *Princip, Raséair*?" There'd been no mention of this. Negotiate with Decanius? I hadn't the skills.

"For now," he growled. "I will give thought to who might be better suited, but there has been no time. Nor are we planning any attempt to take back Sorham for some years. All you need to do is state our intent. Nothing more. You can do this, I hope?"

"If I must," I said evenly. "Are you thinking of war, *Raséair*?"

"As a last resort," Ruar interjected. "I hope to find peaceful means. My taste of warfare has not whetted my appetite for more, unless there are no other options. I expect I will be fully *Teannasach*, before this plan comes to fruition." I heard a note of rebuke in his voice, directed to his great-uncle.

"If I can be of help, I will be," I said.

"You have promised me that already," Ruar reminded me. "Daylight is short, and you have a distance to ride. You are free to leave, Sorley."

Enough light was left in the day for me to reach a *torp*. I was on the road quickly, riding south.

DUSK AND FALLING SNOW slowed my pace, but I was on the *Ti'ach's* lands now and I knew this path even in full dark. Approaching from the north, I would come through the small *torp* and past the stables. I would leave my horse there and walk to the *Ti'ach* itself.

As I had reached the first of the cottages, a dog barked. I saw the dull glow of firelight as a door opened and closed. "Who is there?" a voice called.

"Anndra?" I called back. "It's Sorley."

"Sorley!" He stepped forward. I reined my horse to a stop. "The Lady Dagney said you were coming, but why are you at the *torp*, and not the house?"

I dismounted. "I thought I would stable my horse first. I wasn't sure if there would be anyone at the house to take it. How are you, Anndra?"

"Well enough," he said. "Isa too. She'll be up at the house just now. We were that glad to know you were well, after the fighting. And Cillian too. A strange business, with him."

"A long story," I told him. "I wrote a *danta* about it all. Perhaps I will sing it for you, one night before I leave." I had never sung it all, the last verses unfinished in the uncertainty of Cillian's fate. I could devise an ending, now.

"That would be grand," Anndra said. "We'll have a sip or two of *fuisce*, by the fire." He played the *ladhar* himself, with fair skill, and I'd spent more than one evening in his cottage, learning songs.

"No word of Niav?" I asked. His niece, with a singing voice fine enough for her to have been taken on as a student at the *Ti'ach*, Dagney—and I— nurturing and training her.

"None," he said bitterly. "If she's alive, she's been taken north, poor girl. Her, and the Lady Jordis, and many others."

"South of the Wall too," I told him. "And the Lady Dagney, Anndra? How is she?"

"Missing the *Comiádh*," he said, "as you would expect. A sad day, that, when we rang the bell of remembrance for his passing. You will cheer her up. Shall I stable your horse, so you can go to her?"

I slipped in through the kitchen door, putting my saddlebags down on the flagged floor. Isa gave a tiny gasp before she recognized me. "Sorley!" she said. "Frightening me like that!" I grinned at her and gave her a hug.

"I saw Anndra," I told her, as much to prevent her from needing to speak of Niav as anything.

"The Lady Dagney is in her teaching room," she told me. "Go through. I will bring tea in a few minutes. Your room is ready; I've had a fire burning the day, thinking you might come."

I walked across the hall, dark except for a couple of candles on the table. I couldn't quite comprehend that Perras wasn't just behind his study's door. Dagney's door was closed, keeping the warmth in. I knocked and opened it.

She was reading by the fire. Cillian's letter, I thought, glancing at what was in her hands. "Sorley," she said. "How wonderful to see you." She stood, holding out her arms.

There were tears in both our eyes after that embrace. She is older, I thought, watching her composing herself; thinner, more fragile. She must be lonely here.

"I don't know where to start," she said. "You have so much to tell me. Sit. How was Cillian, when you left?"

"He is improving," I told her. "Still in much pain, and not able to be out of bed; there is a long physical recovery ahead of him. The Casilani doctor, Gnaius—I doubt Cillian would have survived, without his treatments. Gnaius himself would say it was all up to the gods."

"Casil. It is unbelievable. Perras would have so liked to hear your stories."

"Yes," I said sadly. She took my hand.

"He went peacefully," she told me. "Knowing you were both safely home eased him. Even," she said with a rueful smile, "if I bent my *scáeli's* oath in encouraging that belief."

Isa came in with tea, and Dagney and I spoke of my appointment as *toscaire*, and Ruar and Liam, and the travelling I would need to do between the Empire and Linrathe. "Perhaps," she suggested, "you can collect songs, as you travel; we might make a *scáeli* of you yet." She told me of Perras's last weeks, and where he was buried. I would visit the grave in the morning.

"Now, my dear, before we eat, I have a task for you. Would you go to Cillian's room and choose which books to take back for him?" she asked. "He wants his copy of Catilius, but there may be others as well. And perhaps his clothes?"

"Of course," I said. "I'll do that now." I left her by the fire, and crossed the cold hall to the annex, the added wing of rooms used mostly for guests. I should be housed here, but Isa had given me my old student room, and I had no objections, except that it had meant her aging legs had climbed two flights of stairs to make up the room and tend the fire. I didn't know when Cillian had moved from the boys' floor to his room in the annex: long before I had arrived at the *Ti'ach*. As a journeyman teacher and a *toscaire*, he had certainly been entitled to live separately from the students.

I carried a candle, shielding the flame carefully as I walked. I had never been to Cillian's room; the annex was off-limits to students, even adult ones. Dagney had told me which door. I set the candle on a table against one wall, looking around me. The room was as austere as I might have guessed: a narrow bed with a chest at the foot, a table and chair, the washstand, and a shelf of books. I am trespassing, I thought. But no, Cillian had asked for his book, giving permission for someone to be here.

I found *The Contemplations*, a well-thumbed copy bound in worn leather. It fell open as I took it from the shelf. I glanced down at the text. *In the morning, when you wish to stay asleep, think this*, I read. *I am arising to do a man's work. Is this not my purpose in the world?* I had never heard Cillian quote this line, for all his love of Catilius. I felt slightly embarrassed, as if I had stumbled upon a private note. I closed the book and examined the other titles. There were not many. I would take them all. He might be glad of them in the months of convalescence.

Inside the chest I found a few clothes, neatly folded, and below them, a drawstring bag. I took it out, reluctant to open it. The contents shifted in my hand, and I realized what must be inside. I loosened the drawstring, letting the *xache* pieces spill out onto the bed. They were carved of wood, and small, made for a child's hands. The wood had the patina of long use. Perhaps made for him by his grandfather; perhaps older than that. He would want these, in a few years, for his own son or daughter. But by then, I thought, he and Lena and the child should be here. And I? It was what he wanted. What I wanted. I would leave the game in the chest.

After a simple supper, we retired again to Dagney's teaching rooms. It did not surprise me when she turned the conversation again to Cillian. "Do you know what is in this letter?" she asked.

"No," I answered.

"A request," she said, "that I come to Wall's End, as a *scáeli* of Linrathe, to marry him and Lena. Now tell me, Sorley: is this only to make his child legitimate in this country?"

"What has he said?" I asked, frowning.

"Just that he and Lena had paired, during their exile, and that the child is due at the end of winter, and he wishes it to be legitimate."

I smiled at Dagney, wryly. "He is heavily drugged, and perhaps that was all he could manage, or trust himself to say. Dagney, Cillian loves Lena with all his heart. He is a changed man in many ways, and has been since we met them in the wilds. It is not all her doing; there is a story there, but it should be Cillian's to tell you. But to hear his voice when he calls her *käresta* is a story—no, a song—in itself."

"I am so glad," she said softly. "And she returns his love?"

"Completely."

"You can accept this, my dear? Your own letter was quite brief, too."

"I apologize for that," I said. "It was written at a difficult time. I long ago accepted that he loves Lena. Cillian and I are friends now in a way I would have never thought possible, almost brothers." I had never openly revealed my nature to Dagney, but it was clear she knew. "And I have a companion now, a soldier from Casil who returned with us. He's a musician, too. Druisius, his name is, and in the Empire, we can be together openly. "

"Another joy, then," she murmured.

"Yes." I hesitated. I would need her approval of an idea that I had had, on the ride south, if she were the *scáeli* performing the marriage. "When I turned sixteen," I said, "my father gave me a set of *li'ítho* bracelets, as is the custom. I do not know if he was genuinely blind, or simply hoping that I would give in and marry, to at least father an heir. I will never use them, of course. I was thinking—perhaps—to give them to Cillian and Lena."

She considered. "Cillian will say he is not entitled to them, as they are a custom of the nobility," she pointed out.

"And would not the son of the Emperor be considered noble, by our standards?" I countered.

"True," she said. "But are you sure?" I understood her unspoken question.

"A gift," I said. "Offered in friendship for them both. Nothing more. Should they lie unused in a chest?"

"I suppose not," she said eventually. "If Cillian and Lena will accept the *li'ítho*, I can perform the ceremony that includes them. It is a generous offer, my dear."

"The child is due in under three months," I said. "When will you come?"

"If you will act as my escort, I will ride south to Wall's End with you, in a day or so. Would I be welcome to stay a while, do you think?"

"I imagine the *Princip* will be honoured," I told her. "Your presence can only speed Cillian's recovery."

Walking up the stairs to my old room felt strange. I had been a boy—for all my twenty-three years—when I left. No longer. A peat fire scented the room, glowing red, and the small space was warm enough. My bags sat neatly against the wall. But otherwise the room was as bare as Cillian's had been.

That stark space had disturbed me. When I had lived in this room, I had made it mine, as much as possible. A blanket woven at our *torp* and dyed in our family's colours had covered the bed; a wood carving of a sheepdog, from the hands of one of our *torpari*, sat on the shelves, beside a seal-shaped pebble I had picked up along the strand as a child and kept ever since. My music had littered the table, and often the floor. Cillian had left his room for a short journey north with Donnalch, expecting to return to it in a few weeks, so he had not prepared it to sit empty for a long time. It was simply the way he had lived, and the barrenness of it made me want to weep.

Was my reaction only to the contrast between the detached and unhappy man he had been, and the loving, generous friend he had become? All those years he spent alone looking for meaning in an ancient, ascetic philosophy. I had read Catilius, and while I'd found some good advice in his writing, I'd also found a lot I couldn't accept. Catilius had not approved of love between men, and made that clear, but that was only part of it. He'd disapproved of any pleasure, it seemed to me, and had said nothing at all about music. Life was for work, and personal discipline.

Cillian's room had reflected that: a place to sleep, alone; to read and write, perhaps, and nothing more. But why did that unsettle me? I frowned, trying to analyse my feelings. I looked at Cillian's books, stacked on the table. Catilius had guided his life for twenty years or more: how easily could he let those teachings go, truly? Especially with the book to hand, and the adjustments to pain and disability and loss he had to make. I do not envy you, Lena, I thought.

All the confusion I had felt for the last weeks rose again. *I love you,* Lena had told him in my hearing at Casil, *as difficult and complicated and flawed as you are. And I,* I had added. It had been true, and it was still true. I loved Cillian, but I didn't want a difficult and complicated life. I wanted simple and uncomplicated. I wanted music and a wide bed and a man who was teaching me about who I was. I wanted Druise.

Chapter 11

WE LEFT TWO DAYS later, Dagney on her placid mare and a packhorse carrying baggage being led behind. I had sung the *danta* of our exploits in the east the night before, for the *torpari* and Dagney, in the hall of the *Ti'ach*. They were my first audience, apart from those of us on the ship home.

"Another accomplishment to be put against your name," Dagney had told me afterwards. "Sorley, shall I inform the council that you wish to be examined? Your travel to Casil, and gathering songs from there, and this *danta*, are almost enough now. If you could add songs from the Empire to your repertoire as well, I believe that would tip the balance. If this is something you still want?"

Could I truly be a *scáeli*? Not while I was a *toscaire*: the *scáeli's* requirement to tell the truth conflicted with the necessary deceptions of an envoy. But the title could be conferred in principle, to be granted in full when I was no longer a *toscaire*. "Something I want?" I said, wonder and a disbelieving hope spreading through me. "Dagney, do you have to ask? I hadn't thought it possible."

"There will have to be some change to the requirements," she said, "if travel in Sorham and Varsland are no longer possible. One of many changes, I suppose, that will occur over the next years."

When we reached the Wall and a guard post the next day, I had a messenger sent ahead to alert Wall's End to Dagney's arrival. Riding at speed, he would reach the fort several hours before us.

The western sky glowed in shades of pink and gold as we rode into the fort. Cadets came to take horses and baggage, and I led Dagney into the low infirmary building. She wanted, she had told me, to see Cillian first, before anything else. And, she added, she would take on the sad task of telling him of Perras's death. It was her responsibility.

I hoped he would be awake, and not too heavily drugged. The door was slightly ajar, which I took as a good sign. I knocked, with the triple rap I used to tell him it was me, and gestured Dagney into the room.

"Oh, my dear man," she said. Over her shoulder I could see Cillian sitting—sitting!—in a chair, his left leg on a footstool. Lena sat close to him; they had been talking, I thought.

"Dagney!" he said, smiling slowly, "I am afraid you must come to me. I do apologize."

She crossed the room to him. I caught Lena's eye, smiled, and with a movement of my head indicated I would leave. She held up a hand to ask me to wait.

"I will leave you," she said. "I am so glad you are here, Dagney. I'll come back in a while, and show you to your room, and the baths if you would like. If you are not too tired, the *Princip* will be honoured if you will join him at dinner."

"You do not need to go, Lena," Dagney protested.

"I'll come back," Lena said, "but you should have some private time together right now." She bent to kiss Cillian. "Do not tire yourself," she told him.

"I will try not to. Sorley, *mo charaidh,* come and greet me properly," he called. I went to crouch beside his chair for an embrace and the brief kiss of welcome.

"You are so much better," I murmured.

"A long way to go," he said, "but better, yes." He sounded uncertain, his voice hesitant.

I straightened. "A half hour, *käresta,*" Cillian said to Lena. I glanced at Dagney, seeing both worry and wonder on her face. Worry for his health; wonder at hearing him call Lena *beloved.* She had not, I thought, quite believed me.

"We will bring tea," Lena said.

"Welcome back," she said in the corridor, giving me a hug. Her belly was larger, with only a bit over two months to go. She leaned against me, as if needing the support.

"How is he, really?" I asked.

"Not good," she said bluntly. "He is putting on a brave face for Dagney."

"But he says he is better."

"With help, and the two walking sticks, he can get up and move a few steps, but the left leg drags. Tears rose in her eyes. "Oh, Sorley. He is in so much pain, and dependent on Druise for almost everything. He hates that. Cillian never wanted to ask anyone for anything, and now he is little better than an infant again. And he hates the poppy juice, as you can imagine."

"It will improve," I said, rubbing her back.

"Maybe. Gnaius will only say maybe." She began to cry in earnest. I pulled her closer, letting her lean against my shoulder.

"Tell me."

"He may never walk properly. He may never make love again. And his mind...Gnaius does not know if the dullness and confusion is the poppy and other drugs, or damage. Cillian knows he cannot think properly, and he is angry and frightened."

"And Cillian angry and frightened is Cillian cold and sarcastic?" I asked, as gently as I could.

She shook her head. "No. But detached, distant. I am so afraid for him. Sorley—please stay with us? Cillian needs you, for his own language, and music, and something more."

What did it cost her, to ask me this? I had suggested in Casil that she and I needed each other, to cope with Cillian's brilliance. And his darkness, she had added later. This was a responsibility older than my relationship with Druise. "For as long as you need me, Lena," I told her.

"Thank you," she whispered. "You are my anchor right now. If you left us…" She ran out of words.

"I'm not going to," I told her firmly. "Not more than my *toscaire's* duties require. Absences, not abandonment."

She straightened, wiping her eyes. "Should you not go to find Druise? I can fetch tea. Bring Druise back, if you wish, to share it with us. Unless," she said, sudden concern on her face, "Dagney?"

"I told Dagney about him," I said. "She knows what I am. "

Lena frowned. "What you are?" she said. "Sorley, do you not hear yourself? You are a musician and, right now, an envoy. That is what you are. That you share your bed with men is as natural to you as your blue eyes. Why do you judge yourself on it?"

I felt heat rise in my face. "Why do you think?"

"Linrathe and Sorham are wrong, not you," she said. And yet, I thought, Cillian wanted to return to Linrathe, and he wanted me to go with him. Without Druise, and without the freedom to be myself I had found here. Even at the open-minded *Ti'ach*.

That reminded me. "Lena," I said, "Dagney will be telling Cillian of Perras's death. How will he be?"

"Bereft," she said. "We have been talking, these past days, of how Dagney and Perras were almost foster-parents to him. He has been thinking about being a father; it frightens him, you know."

"Then perhaps Druise and I should not join you for tea? Will he not want just you?"

"You can speak to him of Perras. I can, a little, of course, but not in the same way. Join us. You will know if he wants you there, but, Sorley, since Casil, when has he ever not? He has missed you, these weeks."

Cillian looked tired, and saddened, but he made an effort again in our presence. I introduced Druise to Dagney. She charmed him with a few words in Casilan; he was growing better with the language of the Empire, so as a group, we could converse without too many translations needed.

We'd been talking for ten minutes or so when Druise's attention turned to Cillian. "You need poppy," he said firmly.

"No," Cillian said. "Not yet."

"Yes," Druisius said. He switched to Casilan. "You are over an hour past your time," he said, "and you have been up far too long. Poppy, and bed. Do not argue."

I don't know if Dagney understood the Casilan, or just the tone of Druisius's voice. "I am tired," she said. "Lena, did you mention baths? That would be most welcome. And is there time for a rest, before dinner?" She stood. "Cillian, my dear, I will see you tomorrow." She held out a hand to him. He took it, raising it to his lips.

"I know when I am bested," he said. "The baths for you, then, and poppy and bed for me. I am glad you are here, Dagney."

He dropped the pretence once the women had left. Pain tightened his neck and jaw. "I will need help to stand," he said. I stepped forward, but Druise shook his head. Expertly he held out both arms, letting Cillian grasp them, then pulling him up and, at the same time, towards him, so that Cillian stood straight but supported. Druise waited until Cillian nodded before reaching for the crutches.

"You have them?" he asked, and at Cillian's assent let go of his arms,

It was no more than half a dozen steps to the bed, but watching Cillian walk that distance tore at my heart. His left leg would not bear his weight, and his lower body twisted with each step. He lowered himself to the bed, and Druisius lifted his legs up and slid him towards the centre. "Deep breaths."

Once Cillian was on the bed, Druise mixed poppy syrup with wine and a little water. "Drink," he ordered. "Maybe Sorley will play for you."

"Sorley," Cillian said, haltingly. *"Allech'i… for Perras…"*

Tears glittered in his eyes. Not from the physical pain, I thought, and felt the answering sting in my own. *"Thá,"* I murmured, and, taking the *ladhar* down from where it hung on the wall, I played the ancient lament, the parting song.

Druise stopped what he was doing, listening. The pipes would be played at a grave, but we were not there, and they were not my instrument. I played the last three notes slowly, letting each resonate and fade before the next: one note for forgiveness, one for loss, and one for love.

I put the *ladhar* down and with fingers as gentle as I could make them, I wiped the tears from Cillian's cheeks. *"Meas,"* he whispered. I kissed his forehead, not caring if Druise saw. Then I picked up my instrument again and played lullabies until Cillian's breathing told me he was asleep. Simple and uncomplicated had been a fleeting wish, nothing more, as naïve as the cradle songs I had been playing.

Druise lay on the bed, watching me dress. I had brought my formal clothes from the *Ti'ach*, the breeches and tunic grey, trimmed with green, and the cloak of green-and-grey plaid, the colours of Gundarstorp. "Will you be late?"

"I shouldn't think so. Dagney must be tired. I am not the *toscaire*, tonight, or I don't think I am."

"The *Princip* comes to talk to Cillian now, sometimes. Late mornings, when the poppy has worked but he is not yet asleep."

"About what?"

"The Marai. Casil. He seeks advice, on both."

"Should he be bothering Cillian with this?"

"Why not? It is good for him." He stretched. "I will do his exercises, when you go to dinner."

I remembered something. I went to my bags. "Take this to him, will you?" I asked, holding out Catilius. "He asked for it."

Druise opened it, reading a few words. "I have heard of this book," he said, "Not just from Cillian, I mean, but from before."

"Druise? Does it bother you, that you are left out of these dinners?" It had been nagging at me.

"No," he said, surprised.

"Lena will be there," I pointed out.

"Lena is an officer, and Cillian's *quincala*, and soon his wife, yes? And she has known the *Princip* for many years. I am happy to eat with the soldiers, Sorley. Do not worry."

Dagney was tired, and so while dinner was a formal welcome for her, it was also not a long evening. But after Dagney rose to leave, Lena with her, Casyn spoke to me. "A minute, Lord Sorley?"

"*Princip*?"

He signalled to Birel to pour more wine before dismissing him. Official business, then. I waited. "I will not keep you," he said. "One question only: what did you think of Liam?"

"He can be trusted, *Princip*," I answered. "My judgement, based on both what I learned riding north and my observations there, tell me that." He nodded. "Perhaps there is one message from them I should give you now," I said. "For your consideration, before we address all the other issues which my instructions require me to discuss with you, over the next weeks."

"Certainly, then."

I told him what Liam had vowed: that Linrathe would regain Sorham, by any means necessary. "There will be no immediate action. This is an avowal, not a call to arms. But the *Raséair* expects Casil's assistance, for the tribute paid in future years."

"The regent? Not the young *Teannasach*?"

"At this moment, Ruar considers diplomatic means preferable."

"I am glad to hear that. But who has the real power, Sorley?"

"The *Eirënnen* and the *torpari* speak of Ruar as the *Teannasach*, regardless of his age. He took his sword into battle to defend Linrathe against the Marai, and in their eyes that makes him their leader. Or at least that is how the more southern landholders regard him. In the *torps* around Dun Ceànnar and the Sterre, where Liam is a powerful figure, the opinion may be different. I could not determine that."

"I see." He drank a little wine. "I seek Cillian's opinion sometimes, on various matters, but he is reluctant to give it. He does not trust his memory, or his reasoning, he says; the drugs cloud his mind."

"Have you asked him about Liam?" I asked, recalling our conversation before I had ridden north. "He expressed clear opinions to me."

"I did, yes," Casyn said. "And I agree: he was very certain. A subtle mind, he said, and devious, but with Linrathe's welfare his first consideration. A reluctant admiration, I thought."

"And I must take direction from Liam," I said. "Although direction only; my decisions are my own, as to what is best for my country and my people."

"You can disobey him?"

"Yes. My oath is to the land, and I have sworn that no man holds sway over me. That includes the *Teannasach*, and his regent. In practice *toscairen* are neutral, gathering information, reporting it, delivering responses, but if I believed a decision was contrary to what was best for Linrathe, I could decline to give the message, or counsel against it. I can refuse any task for the same reason, without reprisal."

"Colm told me once that the custom in your land is that all men are equal; that a shepherd considers himself no different from the *Teannasach* in terms of his worth."

"He spoke correctly. One of Ruar's cousins—Liam's daughters' husbands—is an *Eirën's* son, but the other was a bright *torpari* boy, sent to the *Ti'ach na Asgaill* to be educated. Men are judged by their skills and their minds, not by their father's position."

"As long as there is a father."

"Cillian was—is—respected, for his intelligence and insight," I said. "But Linrathe's people, and Sorham's, claim kinship and—" I searched for a translation, but I did not know the word for *dùthcas* in Casyn's language, "belonging, through their fathers. Cillian had no family, and no place to call home."

"For men of the Empire," Casyn said, "home is their regiment, wherever it is sent. A boy is claimed by his father, or his father's regiment. Perhaps it is not so different."

"You see commonalities," I observed, "where others see contrasts."

"Do I? I tend to think men have the same wants and needs, wherever we are from. Perhaps even Decanius," he added with a wry grin. Over the months, I had come to like the *Princip* very much. Endlessly patient in the negotiations, but capable of firmly expressing his disapproval, his sardonic remarks in private revealed an amused understanding of men. I wondered what he said about me.

"Possibly," I said. Casyn laughed.

"You must be tired. Have you things to address with me, now you are officially Linrathe's *toscaire*?"

"Nothing difficult," I told him. "Details of troops on the Sterre, and the like."

"Turlo can deal with that. Begin with him, if you will: he is eager to return north, and I would prefer not to delay him more than necessary. Turlo," he added, "does not like forts."

"Or palaces," I said. "He escaped to the docks in Casil whenever he could."

"We have asked much of him, Callan and I," the *Princip* said. "But who among us can do only what we prefer, in these times? Or any, I suppose."

—◆—

TURLO MIGHT BE EAGER to escape the confines of Wall's End, but he did not stint on discussing the details of patrolling the Sterre. Maps and game pieces, like the ones Callan had used to show the positions of Marai and the Empire's forces in his workroom at the Eastern Fort littered the table, and by the time we were done, I knew more about the landscape on either side of the Sterre than I had ever thought I would. "I worry about the eastern end," he told me, "where the earthworks meet the Durrains. I want more men there. Galen tells me it is not too difficult to move across the slopes above it, well out of sight."

"Linrathe never looked east for its enemies," I said. "Only north."

"Aye, and south, once," Turlo reminded me. "It is strange to see the Wall undefended, except for cohorts at the watchtowers."

"Another thing I must discuss," I said, "the conditions for movement across the border."

"That is for Casyn, not me," Turlo said.

"I suppose it is," I said, "as it is open and permitted travel we will be discussing, and not covert reconnaissance." Turlo had told me quite a few stories on our journey east. He barked with laughter.

"Aye, laddie. But knowing secret ways is useful. Are we done?"

I looked at my notes. "I think so. I will need to send the details to Dun Ceànnar for approval."

"Get it written, and I'll take the report north. Easier now for me to argue the fine points with the Linrathan commander than to go back and forth with messengers and letters," he suggested.

"Not to mention you can leave sooner," I said. He didn't disagree.

Chapter 12

I TOOK MY PAPERS to the room that I had taken over as my study. I needed to clear my mind before attempting the report, and I hadn't seen Cillian since the previous day. Druise had said he'd be at his best in the late morning.

He was out of bed, talking with Casyn. "Shall I come back?" I asked.

"We were talking of the Marai, of the kinship and allegiances among them," Casyn said. "There are links to Sorham, too, are there not?"

"Many," I said, pulling up a seat. "Both through marriages and through trade arrangements. The Marai traded for wool from Gundarstorp and our neighbours, and sometimes for fish as well."

"What did they offer in return?"

"Hides, ivory, sometimes metalwork. And horses."

"Horses?" Casyn asked.

"Ponies, really, but large and strong. Solid. We used them for riding and draught work at Gundarstorp; better than our own hill ponies, and with a good temperament."

"I remember your horse," Cillian said. "Grey, wasn't it?"

"Grey dun, yes," I said, oddly pleased.

"And your brother's was paler."

"They are all shades of dun," I said, surprised he remembered what I had ridden at Gundarstorp, "from nearly white to almost black."

"Fritjof's son rode a white horse at the Taiva," Casyn said, "to fool our troops into thinking he was Callan. Our own symbol, used against us." I remembered Turlo's unabashed tears when he saw the flag of the Empire, the white horse and the Wall, still flying as we sailed into sight of the Eastern Fort, returning from Casil.

"Has the Procurator insisted that Casil's flag be flown?" Cillian asked. His thoughts had reflected mine, I guessed. Making connections.

"Yes," Casyn said heavily. "He has allowed ours to be flown beneath it, until, he says, the troops have learned to identify the eagle as their flag. As if an order to do so is not sufficient."

"He is used to illiterate troops," Cillian said, "and has not bothered to discover that ours are not."

Casyn's eyes narrowed. "And he will not, I wager, exert himself to learn to read our language."

"A way to communicate with our troops, then, openly but secretly?" Cillian said softly. My eyes went from one to the other, these two men discussing how they might deceive their Empress's representative.

"Be very careful," I heard myself say. "Randall speaks and writes both languages."

"You do not trust him?" Casyn asked sharply.

"I think," I said, trying to give substance to instinct, "that he may be easily swayed. We were speaking just the other day, *Princip*, about the worth of men in Linrathe, do you remember? Randall is an exception, it seems to me: he should consider us as equals, as we both spent five years at a *Ti'ach*, but he cannot forget I am Lord Sorley. Decanius is the type who will recognize that in him, and use it."

"Liam's factor's son? He attended the *Ti'ach na Asgaill*?" Cillian asked.

"Yes," I replied. "He was sent here to teach Casilan to our officers, but he has been acting as Decanius's translator, as I could not."

"I taught him, for a winter. Casilan, as it happens. That tendency to resentment was there, certainly, but he was young. You say it has not changed? Then I would concur with Sorley, Casyn: be careful of him."

"Thank you, both of you" Casyn said. "Cillian, do you see that your advice is worth having?"

"On certain things, perhaps," Cillian answered. "Not strategy. Not yet."

When Casyn left, I smiled at Cillian. "You are sounding more like yourself."

"My thoughts are a little clearer. I wonder..." His voice trailed off.

"What?"

"Could you come tomorrow at this time, when I am at my best, and we will attempt a game of *xache*?"

"Certainly." I grinned. "Is it unfair of me to say I look forward to the chance of beating you?" I was rewarded by the flash of a smile.

"Taking pleasure in besting an ill man?"

"Ill you may be, Cillian, but you will still win at *xache*," I told him.

I was wrong, and it was clear after the opening moves. I didn't speak while Cillian studied the game, reaching for a piece, then withdrawing, unsure. His eyes moved over the board. Finally he pushed a piece forward, then immediately shook his head.

I pretended to consider, although my move was obvious. "Don't," he said. "You know what to play: do it." I took his piece. He exhaled, his lips thinning.

"I can't see the pattern," he said. "I know what the pieces do, but I can't hold it in my head."

"It's too soon," I suggested. "Perhaps we should wait a week or two more."

"Or perhaps I will never see the pattern again," he said flatly.

"You cannot know that. Not while you need the poppy."

"How long will that be? All my life?"

"Surely not," I protested.

"It is possible," he said. "What use am I, Sorley, if I cannot think; cannot see patterns in men's thoughts and behaviour?"

"Do you have to be of use, Cillian? Cannot you just let yourself recover? And this," I indicated the *xache* board, "is just a game."

"Is it? Consider how you would feel, if your fingers forgot what to do on your *ladhar's* strings."

Lost and bereft, I admitted to myself. I would not know who I was. "I could not play for some time after the battles," I said, stretching the truth. "I took a swordcut to my arm. I gave it time to heal cleanly. *Mo duíne gràhadh*, put the board aside, with the pieces in place. Study it at your leisure. We will play slowly. Did you not tell me once of two scholars who took years over a game, exchanging moves by letter?"

"Perras told you, not I," he answered. He looked at the board again. "I suppose we can try. Perhaps in solitude I will see what I cannot now. Leave me, *mo charaidh*. I am not fit company."

"Do you want one of your books, before I go?"

"Yes. There is one there by Serventius: Gnaius gave it to me. A translation from the Heræcrian. He influenced Catilius greatly, but I knew of him only by name." I found the small, bound book, handing it to him. He had sounded happier again, speaking of the writing. An idea budded. I bent to kiss his head.

"Don't brood," I said. He didn't smile. I left him, and went to find Gnaius.

"I do not know," the physician said in answer to my first question. "Long fever, and high, can damage the faculties of thought. But poppy clouds and confuses also. Until we can wean him of the drug, we will not have an answer."

"When will that be?"

"Not until he can walk properly, or nearly so. He needs the drug to mask the pain: if he does not have it, his body will contort, finding ways to move that hurt less, do you see? That will become first habit and then fixed, and he will never be anything but crippled, reliant always on two sticks and moving only a few steps. I believe we can better that, but not without poppy."

I would not wish Cillian a crippled body any more than I would a crippled mind. He had been grace itself when I had first met him. I remembered him dancing at Gundarstorp, to the music I'd been playing.

Forcing my mind back to what I had come for, I asked my second question.

"Of course," Gnaius said, sounding just the tiniest bit affronted. "I was a student at the finest school in Casil."

"Then…" I explained my idea. He raised an elegant eyebrow.

"I could," he said. "It might be instructive. An experiment. Will Cillian agree?"

"Almost certainly."

"Then we will begin tomorrow."

◆○◆

THE DAYS OF COLD and snow just before midwinter had given way to a mild spell; mild and dry, an unusual combination. No one objected; less fuel was needed for the fort and barracks, and neither horses nor men broke legs on ice, or became mired in mud. Druisius complained, good-naturedly, and wore the cloak and gloves I had given him, even on days when I went outside only in my tunic and breeches.

Turlo returned north, his tolerance for the restrictions of the fort at its end. "It is not just the fort," Casyn told me one day, after we had concluded our business. "We are too close to Berge, and he cannot forget what happened there. What we let happen to the woman he loved, and to others. He is better on the Sterre."

We had been talking of movement across the border, allowing people from Linrathe to come south, to find employment in the villages or Casilla. "Tell the *Teannasach* not yet," Casyn had said. "This survey of our lands and the census of our people that the Procurator has begun must be completed first. He said a year, before he returned to the Eastern Fort; less if Casil sent more men to work on it in the spring."

"But it will be allowed then?"

"Can I say?" He had sounded tired. "Sorley, increasingly I think *Princip* is a meaningless title, and I will be allowed to make nothing but decisions that do not matter. What is Decanius's phrase—'A modern province of Casil'? What do I know about that?"

"You know your people, *Princip*," I said. "How they will see these changes."

"Perhaps. But if I have no power to gainsay what Decanius imposes, what good is knowing my people? But this is not your concern. What else do we need to decide?"

"Just a list of places deemed appropriate for the ships that patrol the coast to stop to take in water or make repairs. Harbours deep enough or sheltered enough."

"I do not need to see it," he said. "I will ask the commander of the northern fleet to meet with you."

"As you wish, *Princip*."

"Is that all?" I had told him yes, and he'd leaned back in his chair. "I miss Turlo, and his advice, but I could not ask him to stay. I had hoped Cillian would be more willing to counsel me. But he refuses, still."

"He doubts himself," I said.

"Does he blame himself for what happened at the Taiva?" Casyn asked. "I cannot bring myself to ask him."

"If he does, he hasn't told me. But were I to guess, knowing Cillian, yes."

"Callan would have taken the blame, too, had he lived," the *Princip* said. "They are very alike, Sorley, in so many ways, and yet Cillian is like Colm too. The best of both twins, in one man."

"The best man I have ever known."

"He engenders an unusual depth of loyalty, that is certain. Birel tells me that Druisius says he is the finest officer he has served, and that I do find—interesting. Coming as it does from your *consor*."

"Druise," I said, "is a pragmatic man. We are good companions, with the music in common, and our partnership suits us both."

"Regardless of your complex loyalties," Casyn said. "A friend worth having."

⚊⚊⚊⚊◄O►⚊⚊⚊⚊

"SORLEY, WILL YOU STAY, so if I am not back when Cillian returns from his treatments, you are here?" Lena asked late one morning. "He will be in pain, until the poppy begins to work, and you will distract him."

"Of course," I answered. "But where are you going?"

"For a walk. I need to be outside for a while. You don't mind?"

"Don't be foolish," I said. I settled down with my *ladhar*, working on the song I had promised Casyn. I wasn't getting anywhere with it: I simply hadn't known Callan well enough, and I wanted it to be more than a standard tribute. I could write a tune, but would it fit the words?

Perhaps an hour had passed when I heard a knock at the door. "I was looking for Lena," Talyn said to my greeting.

"She's gone for a walk," I told her. "But that was some time ago; I expect her back soon. Come in." I didn't know Talyn well; she'd come a few times, when Cillian was still unconscious, but we'd never exchanged more than a word or two. "Cillian and Druisius are with Gnaius. I'd be glad of the company."

She gave a little shrug. "If you think Lena won't mind."

"Of course not. Wine?"

"Yes. Why not?" She sat down. I handed her the cup, placed the water jug on the table, and sat across from her. "So," she said. "Lord Sorley. How were the horses I gave you, long months ago?"

"The horses?" I asked. I'd been sent to her for mounts to take Ruar and myself and our guide north along the Durrains from the Eastern Fort, a hard ride to reach and rally the men of Linrathe against the Marai there, to keep them from marching south to the Taiva. "I'm still riding the gelding. Did you want him back?"

She laughed. "No. Consider him yours. I wanted to know if the cohort-seconds chose well, that's all."

"They did. Should Linrathe pay for the others? I left them at Ruar's camp."

She shook her head. "Your countrymen are welcome to them. A small thank you, shall we say?"

"I will let Ruar know." I groped for something to say. "You have bred horses all your life?"

"Yes. It's what we do, in the grasslands, horses and cattle, both mostly for the army. Oh, some of us are blacksmiths, or harness-makers, and of course we have midwives and woodworkers and tanners, but the midwife can deliver a baby or a foal, and we all ride. It's what brought my father there originally: at Festival in our villages, the men come for the usual reasons, but also to take the horses we have broken and trained for them away. Casyn was sent as a blacksmith, to help ours shoe the animals for travel. My mother said she fell in love with him when she saw how gentle he was with the horses."

"You know him well? I didn't think that was usual, here."

"It isn't. But he came back, every year, and frequently for both Festivals, even after my mother died. They loved each other, and he loved us, me and my sister. We looked forward to seeing him as children, and as we grew into adulthood, we had the horses and their training in common." She smiled. "I remember my mother's partner Jesa swearing he was trying to make soldiers of us, when he showed us what men needed the horses to be able to do in battle. How little she knew how prophetic her words would be."

"Your mother's partner?" I said. "But did you not just say—"

"That she loved my father? She did. But two weeks a year, and not always that, if he was posted too far away? Would you live that way, Lord Sorley? She loved her partner too, and Jesa her. But when Festival came, Jesa took herself off to sleep in the stables—and not alone, I am sure—and left their big bed to my parents."

"I see," I said. "Forgive me, Talyn. I am still learning. North of the Wall, life is different. Although men—especially those who are noble—do bed women other than their wives. And if I am truthful, those wives who have produced the requisite heirs have their own freedoms." Many a noble wife in Sorham worked every day with women her husband bedded, and the welcome given by *Konë* and *Härra* to certain *scáeli'en* and *toscairen* was known, if rarely openly acknowledged, by their husbands. A different way to spread ideas, and to learn what women thought but might not say in front of their men.

I tore my thoughts away from that path. "Not so different, then," Talyn said, "except that here our freedoms are for everyone, and for all pairings. Which I understand is not true in your land?"

"No. What I am—my nature—is shunned there. Worse than shunned."

"But there are always men who want only men, just as there are women who want only women. What do you do?"

"Live that part of our lives in shadows," I said, hearing the bitterness in my voice. "Shadows and corners, and in fear."

"How terrible." She sounded as if she meant it. "Everywhere?"

"It is a little better, among the *scáeli'en*, and around those who are educated at a *Ti'ach*, like Cillian," I admitted. "But all must be secret, still. Not like Casil, or here."

"You were Cillian's lover, then?"

"Gods, no," I said. "No. He is not—he is my friend, nothing more."

"I have misunderstood, then," she said. "I thought Lena had told me differently. My apologies, Lord Sorley."

"What Lena will have told you is that I love him," I said bluntly. "I do. It is not returned, not in that way. It is not his nature."

"And if it were?"

Puzzlement wrinkled my brow. "He is vowed to Lena. They will marry soon."

"But this is not Linrathe, or Sorham. Freedoms are for everyone, and we do not understand the limitations of marriage."

"Cillian does," I said.

"Lena's ideas may be different," she countered. Then she leaned back, spreading her hands. "And now I must apologize again. I am offending you, without meaning to, aren't I? When I was only trying to show you that you may see things here that are different, but that to us are normal." She grinned. "I should leave diplomacy to my cousin, I think. Shall we talk of something else? Tell me about what a...a *scáeli*, is that the word? does."

I would be churlish if I did not accept the apology. "I wasn't offended," I assured her, "just surprised. These ideas, as I said, are new to me. A *scáeli*, Talyn, is a travelling musician, but much more than that. He or she is a historian, the holders and disseminators of our deeds and stories, in the form of songs." We spoke of music and the teaching of history for some minutes, until Talyn put down her empty wine cup.

"Lena must have gone for a long walk," she said. "The sun is shining, and it isn't cold, so I'd guess she's just enjoying the day. I had best return to my work. Thank you for the wine and conversation, Lord Sorley."

"No title," I said. "Please."

At the door she stopped, turning to look at me. "Only men for you, Sorley?"

I smiled, involuntarily. "Only men, Talyn."

"Pity," she said, returning the smile. "I like you. Tell Lena I was here, will you?"

"I will," I said. When Talyn had gone, I didn't feel like going back to the song. I'd have to get the *Princip* to tell me stories about his brother, I decided. Where was Lena? I walked over to the window, opening the shutters wider to look out. Behind me, the door opened.

I didn't need Lena to speak to tell me she was angry. Every muscle radiated tension. "What's wrong?"

"Berge," she said, her jaw tight. "I went to Berge, a women's village, Sorley. No one wanted to talk to me; they were barely polite."

"Gods, Lena, why? They should be thanking you, for killing Fritjof."

She stalked over to the sideboard to pour herself wine. Without asking she handed me a cup too. "Maybe they should. But what they see is a woman who wasn't brutalized by the Marai, and who carries a child conceived in love. Or so Kyreth told me, when she asked me to leave."

"Kyreth?" She was the midwife, and she came to see Lena weekly. "She thinks that too?"

"No." Lena sighed, sinking into a chair. "She says her concerns are the babies, and the health of the mothers, but that my presence upsets too many pregnant girls—and they are girls, many of them, Sorley—and so I should not come again."

I started to rub her shoulders. She leaned back into my hands. "Maybe after the baby is born?" I suggested."

"No. She is the problem, really, I think. The Marai did not reach the grassland villages, or Casilla, so those women escaped capture and rape as well. But a child born of love reminds the women of Berge of what they have lost. Even my own sister expressed doubt she could love the child she carried, when I saw her in Casilla, months ago."

I had no advice to offer; how could I? I bent to kiss her on the temple. "You have us," I said. "And the *Ti'ach*, someday."

"I know. I'd already realized I couldn't go back to Tirvan, but I wanted it to be my choice. And that isn't why I'm angry. How dare they judge my child on how she was fathered?"

"Because theirs will be," I said gently.

She exhaled, loudly. Her hands were still clenched. "But why should they be? I told Cillian once that if…if Ivor had left me pregnant, I didn't think I could have loved the child. He reminded me it would have been innocent, and he was right." She reached for her wine, draining the cup. "I will not expose our child to hatred, Sorley. I will marry Cillian, and go home with him to the *Ti'ach*. The sooner the better."

Chapter 13

WINE WITH THE *Princip* became part of my day more and more frequently, Casyn sending Birel to find me even on days when we had had no business together. "Who else is there?" Lena said, when I commented on it to her. "His brothers are dead; Turlo is on the Sterre. Bren?"

"Leste," I said, "I believe. Or maybe the Eastern Fort."

"Casyn was always a man for reflection," she said. "At Tirvan, he ended most days with Dern—he was captain of *Skua*, the ship sent to support us —over food and wine. Or with Gille, once they had paired for those few weeks."

"He should be talking to Cillian."

"He tries. Cillian will not talk of the negotiations; only of philosophy and history." She sighed. "He spends more time with his books, paying less attention to what is happening around him, every day. How can I complain? He submits to the exercises and treatments without argument, although they leave him in pain. If he needs to find relief in Catilius, or other ancient writers, then he must be allowed to."

"He is not neglecting you?"

"No. We have a difference of opinion over something right now, and it is causing a certain tension between us. We will resolve it, do not worry," she added. "It is just Cillian being self-sacrificing, once again."

I didn't press her. She'd tell me, if she wanted. Or he would. Some days after our aborted *xache* game, I'd gone to talk to him. He had been reading —Lena was right, books were his occupation and his solace now—but he'd put the volume down to greet me with genuine welcome.

"It is your move," he said. I studied the *xache* board, seeing what he'd done, and that whatever move I made, I was left in a vulnerable position. How long had it taken him to see where to place his piece?

"You've had days to think about this," I complained. "Do I get the same?"

"No. Consider it practice for your work as a *toscaire*, once the Procurator returns. You will need to weigh your moves quickly then." He'd sounded serious. I raised an eyebrow, considered the board again, and made my choice.

Since then we had continued the game, Cillian inviting me to make my move almost daily now. The outcome was still uncertain, and that told me much. In the past, he had usually beaten me in half-a-dozen moves, or even fewer.

Druise came in, carrying a tray with jugs of wine and water. "You needed more," he said.

"I could have done that," Lena said. "You are Cillian's aide, Druise, not mine."

"You both drink the wine," he said. "And so do I, sometimes. Sorley, you are wanted in the *Princip*'s workroom. Bring your list of harbours, I was to tell you."

The commander of the northern fleet must have arrived. The ships had been out, the calm, mild winter allowing them to patrol the coast at a time when it would have been next to impossible, most years. I went to my study, found my papers, and presented myself to Casyn.

He was looking at a map with another man, younger than I had expected, dark haired, lean, with lines around his blue eyes that spoke of hours spent in sea light.

"Lord Sorley," Casyn said, "may I present Dern, commander of our northern fleet? He knows the waters between here and the Sterre well; I will leave the two of you to discuss harbours."

Dern? Where had I heard that name recently? "Captain of *Skua*?" I asked.

"I am. How did you know that?"

"Lena mentioned it, not very long ago," I told him.

"In all that has happened," Casyn said, smiling, "I had almost forgotten those weeks you spent at Tirvan. An oversight. Lord Sorley is a close friend of Lena's, Dern. He will give you news of her, as well as of Linrathe's harbours. Other duties require my attention, but this room is yours."

"How is Lena?" Dern asked, as soon as Casyn had left us. He gestured to the chairs. "Shall we sit, Lord Sorley?"

"Sorley," I said. "Lena is well, now." I hesitated. "I don't know what you last heard of her."

"I knew of her exile, and return, with a new form of archery, and that using it she killed Fritjof," he said, a man used to delivering concise reports. "Beyond that, very little. We have been on patrol almost ever since. Was she injured at the Taiva?"

"Not her," I said. "Her partner. The Emperor's son, Cillian."

"Didn't he die, alongside the Emperor?"

"No. He was very badly wounded, but somehow he survived. His recovery is certain now, but it has been a strain on Lena. In part because their child will be born in a few weeks."

"I remember her as resourceful, and a leader, even at eighteen," he said. "I would like to see her, if possible."

"I imagine she would be glad to," I said. I liked him already, an instinctive reaction. "If you know the waters as well as Casyn says you do, our business won't take long. I'd guess you are using all the harbours the *Teannasach* has suggested already. I could take you to see her, afterwards, if you have time."

"Then shall we get to work?" He eyed me. "May I say, Sorley, you are not what I expected in Linrathe's official envoy?"

"You thought someone older, austere and precise?" I said, grinning. "I am a musician, Dern, not a diplomat. But war and its aftermath ask many things of us we did not expect, and I am in this role because I was party to the treaties signed in Casil. A signatory, for Linrathe. It is a long story," I added, at his look of astonishment.

"One I would like to hear, someday," he said. "Shall we get to work?"

As I had guessed, there was little to discuss. Dern knew the coves, and which harbours could take the ships, and where the fresh water was. He even pointed out two locations where shifting sands made access impossible now. I rolled up my map. "Come and see Lena," I said.

I knocked at their door before opening it. Lena had long ago told me not to wait, but I always let them know it was me by my triple rap. Lena looked up from where she sat with Cillian and Dagney, and for a moment I thought she was irritated by the interruption. Then her eyes moved past me, to Dern, and her face changed.

"Dern?"

"Lena." The moment felt awkward.

"Dern is commander of the northern fleet," I said. "We have been meeting about harbours, and I remembered you had mentioned his name, Lena."

"If I am intruding?" he asked.

"Not at all," Cillian said. "You have simply surprised us. Forgive me for not rising, but it is still difficult for me." He saluted Dern. "Commander, I am Cillian, Major and adjutant to the *Princip*, currently on leave. May I introduce the Lady Dagney of the *Ti'ach na Perras*?" So very formal. Why?

Dern said the appropriate things, and as Dagney asked a polite question Lena almost visibly took command of herself and stood up. "You did take me by surprise," she said. "I am so pleased to see you, Dern. I asked about *Skua*, before the Taiva, but no one knew where you were."

"North," he said, "almost to Varsland, among the islands. We owe you the victory, I understand."

"I killed Fritjof," she said, "but there was more to the victory than that. I did what I was trained for, nothing more."

He heard the unspoken message in her tone, responding only with a nod. "Garth?" she asked.

"On Leste," he said. "Did you not know? He knows their customs and the language so well. He is one of Bren's adjutants." Lena smiled then, relief evident on her face.

"I have not seen him since Karst," she said. "I wonder if Maya knows where he is?"

"Messengers ride to the Eastern Fort, and Casilla is on the way," Cillian said. "A letter can be sent." He had not offered wine. "As one can be to Leste, if you wish."

"Perhaps." She smiled at Dern again. "Thank you for the news, Dern."

"Had I known you were here, and worrying, I would have made sure you knew before," he said. "I must return to the harbour. Lady Dagney, Major. No, Lord Sorley, I know my way," he added, as I made a move to accompany him. Lena did walk with him to the door. They exchanged a few quiet words, Cillian's eyes on them the entire time. I glanced at Dagney. She made a tiny negative movement with her head. What had I brought Dern into? Whatever it was, his presence had not helped.

"Sorley," Dagney said, as soon as Lena had closed the door, "I have the beginnings of a headache. Will you walk with me out-of-doors? The light fades, and I do not see as well as I used to. I would appreciate your arm."

Outside in the dusk, I gave Dagney my arm. Her need for it was not feigned, although I was sure her reasons for taking me from the room were. "Are you going to tell me?" I asked.

"It is not mine to tell," she replied. We walked a few steps.

"Is it serious? Lena said a little while ago they disagreed over something, but it was only Cillian's tendency to self-sacrifice again, and not to worry."

"It will be serious, if Cillian does not see sense within a few weeks."

"Within a few weeks? You mean before the baby is born?"

"Yes," she said. She was bound by her oath to answer any direct question honestly, and both of us knew it. I framed my next words carefully.

"Is he risking their child's legitimacy in Linrathe?"

"I do not understand how he can," she said, frustration breaking through in her voice. "He swore he would not make any child live through what he did, and yet he is baulking now at the marriage he asked me here to perform. He will not tie her to him, he says."

"She is vowed to him, and he to her," I said. "I held those vows for them, Dagney, before they told them to each other. What difference can a ceremony make?"

"He has told her she is free of that vow to him. She says she is not, and never will be. I have tried to mediate, but—" Her hand tightened on my arm. "Sorley, they are breaking my heart. All Perras wanted, all I want, is

Cillian home again, at the *Ti'ach* where he belongs. He is making that impossible."

"It is all he wanted, too," I said slowly. "He told Lena that, before the Taiva. The *Ti'ach*, and her there with him. And me, he said. What has changed?"

"His injuries," she said, and words Lena had spoken weeks before came back to me. *He may never walk again, or make love.*

"Oh, gods," I said. "And I brought Dern to her? There was something between them once, don't you think? And she asked about Garth, and I know they were lovers, and so does Cillian."

"Maya, too, was mentioned. Lena has told me what happened in the Kurzemë camp, and that she cannot ever see herself with another man. Cillian, with precise logic, argues that she does not preclude a woman, and he will not rob her of that comfort. Nor of the chance to have another child, if some day she wishes to."

"What does Gnaius say?"

"That he does not know, and only time will tell. But time we do not have, Sorley."

We walked towards the outer walls. A white owl perched, staring down into the fields beyond. At our approach, it lifted off on silent wings, gliding into the dark. I looked up at the first stars, thinking about a conversation with Talyn. "Can you marry them without vows of physical fidelity?"

She stopped. "What are you suggesting, Sorley?"

"I cannot speak for the *torpari*, Dagney," I began, "but among the *Härren* of Sorham, marriage is about joining lands together, or strengthening trade alliances. Vows of faithfulness are made, but no one really expects those to be kept, certainly not by the man. And not always by the women, once the heirs are safely born. Will you tell me I'm wrong?"

"You are not," she admitted.

"Then why cannot Lena and Cillian be married without making those promises? Is it a requirement of the ceremony?"

"Not that I have ever been told. It is simply the tradition."

"And what is traditional about a Linrathan *scáeli* marrying two citizens of the southern Empire, a land which has not held a wedding in several hundred years?"

"You," she said, "have learned quite a lot in your time with Cillian, haven't you? You were never so devious when you were at the *Ti'ach*."

"There wasn't the need."

"Not that you saw. If they agree, I will do this. Shall I speak to them, or will you?"

"I will," I said.

I escorted Dagney back to her room. Cillian would be expecting me, I thought. He was alone, a book in his hand. "You asked, of course," he said.

"Of course." I poured myself wine. He shook his head when I held up the flask. "Where is Lena?"

"She went for a walk. Gnaius tells her it is good for her and the baby, and we needed time apart."

I sat down across from him. "Cillian, you are being a fool."

"I am not," he said firmly. "How can I tie Lena to me?"

"Is that not her choice?"

"One she will regret."

"You dare say that to me?" I asked, anger flaring. I was angry so often now. "Do you think Lena less constant than I?"

"No," he said. "No, I do not. But you have Druisius. I am not questioning her love, Sorley. But I am—not a man, and may never be again. How can that be fair to her?"

"This is not just about you and Lena," I said. "There is the child."

"Who in this country will be acknowledged as mine by a declaration."

"But not in Linrathe." I held up a hand, forestalling his next utterance. "Cillian, there is a simple solution. You are not arguing that you do not love each other, nor that you are not vowed to each other, only that to swear an oath of bodily fidelity is unreasonable, given the circumstance. Am I right?"

"You are."

"Then don't swear that oath. Dagney will marry you without it." I hesitated. "I expect you can swear fidelity if you like, but not Lena, if that suits you better."

His eyes narrowed. "Dagney will do this?"

"She has told me she will."

I watched him considering the proposal. "Whose idea was this?"

"Mine," I admitted.

"We are making a *toscaire* of you after all," he said. "I need to think about this, Sorley, and there are things I must say to Lena."

"Shall I find her, and ask her to return?"

"If you would. Thank you, *mo charaidh*."

I drained my wine cup. In the corridor, I leaned against the wall. I needed a moment to regain my own composure. Why was I shaking?

I had suggested to Dagney she marry them without an oath of bodily fidelity, to overcome Cillian's reluctance and ensure the child was legitimate. But had that been my only motive? Cillian would never break an oath. Had I hoped not just Lena would forgo that vow, but that he would too, leaving the possibility that, someday, he might—?

I forced my mind away from the thought. What a fool I was. I had to mould what I felt for Cillian back into what I had believed it had become in Casil, and what I had claimed to Dagney: a brotherly love. Unless I did, what future could there be for us?

Chapter 14

A RIDER ARRIVED VERY early the next morning, to announce that Decanius would reach the fort by midday, and expected his rooms warmed, the baths reserved, and that after he was suitably refreshed, he would meet with the *Princip*. Or so Casyn told me, with such a look of intermingled horror and resignation that I could not help laughing.

"Will you join us?" he asked. "After what you and Cillian said about Randall, I want your translation, not just his."

"With pleasure," I said, as drily as I could, which made Casyn laugh too. Accordingly, I cancelled my afternoon language classes and presented myself at the appropriate hour.

"Lord Sorley," Decanius said. "I see no need for your presence."

"But the *Princip* does," I told him. "Randall na Asgaill can return now to the duties he was sent here to perform, and which I had taken over so as not to delay the officers here learning your language, Procurator. I will translate now."

He didn't like it, that was obvious, but Randall was not his to command. He wasn't really mine, either, but I was senior in years, and Linrathe's appointed envoy. "Randall may stay for this meeting," I added, "but after today he must return to teaching."

"Very well," Decanius said. "*Princip*, the *mensores* have completed their surveys in the south. There is much good land for vineyards and grain, and to the west salterns, and closer to the mountains, fine grazing. We will discuss the division of this land into estates, and the management of those estates to feed both this land and to send surpluses to Casil."

"The salterns and much of the land of which you speak are held by the villages," Casyn said. "They manage them, and have fed themselves and our army for generations."

"But now it must feed both villages and armies here and in other parts of the Eastern Empire," Decanius said. "Different techniques are needed. And the product of salterns, by our laws, goes first to the Eastern Empire. Casil alone needs much salt, and our armies as well. I will be overseeing that personally."

"Of course," Casyn said, managing to keep his voice level. "Shall we consult a map about these lands you wish to divide, Procurator?"

By the time the discussion ended, my neck and shoulders ached with tension. Casyn smashed his fist on the table as soon as the door closed behind Decanius. "He cares not at all for how this land has been held for generations," he said. "He will reduce the villages to the equivalent of your *torps*, Sorley, but with his Casilani friends in place of your nobles." Anger roughened his voice. "How did Turlo let this happen? I place no blame on Cillian; I can see such an arrangement would seem normal to him, being Linrathan. But Turlo should have objected."

"It was never discussed," I said, "or not while I was there, at least. But we read Cillian's translations of the treaties, *Princip*, and you know it is not included, not in this detail. But Casil's laws take precedence in your agreement, and that has a broad interpretation."

"We are being treated as a conquered people."

"Forgive me, Casyn," I said hesitantly. "I know very little of your country's history, but this land was a province of Casil once before, wasn't it?"

"Yes. Many generations past."

"And your laws derive from Casil's, assumedly?" A vague memory was stirring, too vague to mention to Casyn.

"Many of them. Those governing the army, certainly. But after the assembly that divided men's lives from women's, and created the women's villages, the laws governing those developed separately. How, I cannot tell you."

"Are there records?" I asked.

"If there are, they are at the Eastern Fort. Old Jereme would have known, and Colm, but they are both dead. Where is Birel, with the wine?" He got up to open the door to the adjoining room, calling his aide's name.

"Will you excuse me, *Princip*?" I asked. "I should speak with Randall about the language classes."

"Yes, certainly," he said, head bent again over a map. "Tell the guard I am not to be disturbed, if you will."

Randall, I was told, was still with Decanius. I left word with the Procurator's guard that I needed to see my countryman, either this evening or tomorrow morning. I walked down the corridor, rotating my shoulders to try to ease the tension in them. I needed the baths.

And why not? I turned into the corridor that led to the bath house. I didn't need a cloak for the brief distance outside, not this winter. Steam escaped from its ventilation shafts: unlike Casil's baths, the water of the hot pool here came naturally from underground.

No one was there but the attendant: with Decanius back, probably the assumption had been made that he would claim this time for himself. I soaked, trying for a while to remember what it was I knew about the laws of this land, and Casil's. The memory eluded me, although I was sure Turlo had been the one who had told me. On Irmgard's ship, maybe?

Inevitably my thoughts took me to finding Cillian and Lena so unexpectedly, so impossibly, in that empty, distant land, the chances of that meeting infinitesimal. But it had been that tiny possibility that had sent me east with Turlo, an admission I had never made—nor would ever make—to anyone. From the moment I had heard, horrified, of Cillian's exile, I had promised myself to search for him. How, I had no idea. Until I met Turlo in the foothills of the Durrains and heard his plans to find the route east to Casil.

I had not done what I had been sent to Sorham to do, to see if there were men who would oppose Fritjof. My loyalty had not been to Linrathe, but to my heart. I had abandoned my land in war for a hopeless dream.

Yet, if I hadn't—could Fritjof have been defeated, otherwise? Without me, to convince Irmgard in Marái'sta of the need, we would never have been on her ship. And without—what? the hand of a god?—that had brought Cillian and Lena to the riverbank at the precise moment our ship passed, we would never have obtained Casil's aid. Perhaps I had been meant to choose to go east, not north.

And perhaps I was justifying what I had done, and nothing more.

I left the baths, my aches barely alleviated, deciding to eat at the senior commons. Someone would claim me as guest; preferably someone who would leave me alone. I scanned the interior of the room, not yet full, finding Talyn. I indicated her to the steward; he went to ask. She turned, nodded to the steward, and beckoned me over.

"I'm leaving shortly," she said.

"That's fine. I'm not in the mood for company, really."

"Decanius? I heard he was back."

"Yes. Full of plans to oversee salt production, among other things."

"Enriching himself in the process, no doubt," she murmured. I moved to a small table, welcoming the wine the steward brought. I was half-way through my meal when he came over to me again.

"You are being asked for, Lord Sorley," he said. "Your countryman, Randall."

"Should I go out to him?" I asked. "Or may he join me?"

"I shouldn't allow it, as you're a guest." I knew him slightly, outside of this role; he diced with Druisius, and sometimes I joined my lover in the soldiers' commons. Musicians were welcome almost everywhere. He gave me a wink. "But seeing it's you, I'll make an exception."

He ushered Randall over. I offered wine, and food; he accepted the first. We chatted for a few minutes about the unseasonable weather, and the ride north. "I have four groups of officers I have been teaching," I told him, bringing the conversation around to business. "Shall we go to my workroom to review the lessons?"

That took nearly an hour. When we had finished, I asked, casually, "Did you find it difficult to translate the old records at the Eastern Fort?"

"Very few of the records the Procurator looked at were old," he said. "He was more interested in maps, and meeting with his surveyors, and the captain newly arrived from Casil. I was rarely needed, so I did what the *Teannasach* sent me to do, and taught Casilan to the officers there."

"He did not consult the tax records, and documents on land ownership?"

"A few. But only when we were first there." Some instinct told me he was being evasive.

"I see. You said a ship arrived from Casil?" I supposed they must now, and their first docking would always be the Eastern Fort.

"Aye. The captain had records from Casil that interested the Procurator. Something to do with the army, but that is all I know."

"Well, thank you, Randall," I said. "I will not keep you, after your long ride today."

He stood. "Good night, Lord Sorley." I turned back to my papers, tidying them.

"Leave the door," I heard Druise say. I looked up. He didn't come in, just stood in the opening. "Cillian wants you," he told me, once Randall had left. The peremptory statement irritated me, even though the words were probably Druise's, not Cillian's.

"I wish," I muttered, regretting the words immediately. I'd promised Druise. But he just grinned.

"Cillian would like your company," he amended. "Although," he added, as I stood to go, "the other could be possible, too."

"When cows fly," I said in my dialect. At Druise's questioning look, I translated.

"We would say 'when a mule foals'. He is in his study."

I was still vaguely out of sorts when I knocked on the study door. Too many meetings, too many problems to solve, too little music. I hadn't brought my *ladhar*, though. Cillian was studying the *xache* board; we were part-way through a game.

He greeted me with a smile, and my irritation receded. "*Mo charaidh*, thank you for coming."

"Did you want to play?"

"Perhaps later. I proposed your idea to Lena."

"And?"

"She sees the sense."

"She isn't the one who needs to," I said. "Do you?"

"You are sure Dagney will do this? Marriage vows that do not speak of fidelity?"

"Haven't you asked her?" He shook his head. I sighed in exasperation. "Yes, I am sure."

"Lena and I talked late into the night," he said, his eyes reflecting candlelight, "of all the reasons I have been reluctant to commit us to the traditional vows." He studied me across the table. "May I ask something?"

"Of course."

"Do you have half-brothers or sisters? Other than by your father's second wife, I mean."

"On other estates, almost certainly. On our own *torp*, no. Gundar has his own code of behaviour. What does this have to do with you and Lena?"

"Something she told me made me realize I need to—rearrange my ideas. A lesson for me in the danger of making assumptions. I have therefore been considering what I know of marriage in Linrathe and Sorham. Very little, it appears."

"Why would you? You grew up at the *Ti'ach*."

"So what is marriage for, in your view?"

"For the landholders? To unite property, create alliances, raise children," I said.

"A form of politics, then?"

"Among the nobles, yes. But also for day-to-day companionship, and shared responsibility. And laughter, and enjoyment and comfort. If the pairing is a good one, it is like true harmony in song."

"Always the musician," he said. "But harmony is not disturbed by the occasional grace note?"

"Dagney," I said, "would be pleased. You did pay attention to her lessons."

He smiled a little at that. "I am decided, Sorley, although there is one barrier yet. I will not marry Lena while the poppy clouds my mind. I have spoken to Gnaius. Tomorrow we will begin to reduce it. Two weeks to free me from it completely, he says."

Two weeks. "The child is due when?"

"She was conceived on midsummer's day," he said. "Of that Lena is sure."

"You may be holding the ceremony in the birthing room," I said.

"First babies are often late," he said, "or so I am told, and choose to believe." He shifted, wincing.

"I hope you are right." I would offer him the *li'ítho* at another time, I thought. "Are you in pain, Cillian?"

"Not more than usual. Druise will bring the drug soon, the last full dose. I have told Lena, and now I tell you: stay away from me, until I am fully free of it."

"Cillian," I protested, "will not music help?"

"It may. But Druisius can play for me. This will be an unpleasant process, I understand. I may do and say things I would regret you witnessing."

"As you wish," I said. What else could I say? "But if you need me, send for me."

"I will. I am afraid I do not have the concentration for *xache, mo charaidh.* Will you leave me to my books?"

Walking back to my room, I thought about my own words: *companionship, and shared responsibility; laughter, and enjoyment and comfort.* Wasn't this what I had with Druise?

"He has told you?" Druise asked, drinking a last cup of wine before bed. "He goes back to the infirmary tomorrow. Stay away, Sorley, until you are told to come. He does not want you to see him as he will be. Neither you, nor Lena."

"So he said," I told him. "You have seen this before?"

"A friend. Another soldier. But no Gnaius, to do this gently. He was put in a cell and left for ten days. Some of us brought water, and food, and tried to help." He shrugged. "He made it through and lived. But the poppy was too easy to get, and his desire too great. He died from it, in a way: stabbed one night in an alley for his money, while searching for an apothecary."

"Druise, thank you. For doing all you have, for Cillian." We did talk of Cillian in our room—almost impossible not to, given Druise's responsibilities. But only for a while, and only as we sat by the fire reviewing the day. The bed was for us alone.

"He wants to be free of it. My friend did not. It is all the difference." He put down the empty cup. "I will not see you, *amané,* for two weeks. Maybe a little less."

"Not at all?"

"Briefly. So perhaps we could leave these chairs? I must sleep, but not yet."

CHAPTER 15

DRUISE, EXHAUSTED AND GRIM, sat with Lena and me in her rooms. Grey with fatigue, he had accepted wine gratefully. "Gnaius is with him," he had told us, when he'd appeared unexpectedly.

"Is he…" Lena's voice trailed off. "There is no danger, is there?"

"No," Druise said, "only it is hard. Harder maybe than Cillian imagined."

I went to stand behind him, massaging his neck and shoulders. I wasn't particularly good at this, but I needed to do something. "Do you have time for the baths?"

"Harder how?" Lena asked, at the same moment. "Is the pain very bad, without the poppy?"

"Maybe the baths," Druise agreed. "Not the pain, Lena. Gnaius gives him other drugs for that. It is what he sees, what comes from his mind. Bad memories. Things he has done, that he does not forgive himself for."

Lena stared at nothing, shaking her head slightly. "I wish I knew what haunts him," she murmured. "He would never tell me. But there is something, isn't there? He said once he didn't believe redemption was possible, not for living people."

We had spoken of this in Casil, I remembered. "How can he have done anything that terrible?"

"Terrible to him," Druise said. "Maybe not to you." In the hall outside the room, I heard voices, and heavy feet. I turned, frowning. The door swung open. Four soldiers—all Casilani—marched in. One was a sergeant.

"Druisius, soldier of Casil," the sergeant said. "You are under arrest for desertion."

"No," I said. "There is some mistake. Druisius is assigned to the Major Cillian, on General Turlo's orders."

"This soldier deserted after the battle at the Taiva," the officer said. "I have my orders."

"Orders from whom?" Lena demanded.

"The Procurator." My hand was still on Druise's shoulder.

"Address me properly, Sergeant," she snapped.

"Lieutenant," he said. "Do not try to stop us. Lord Sorley, move aside."

"Do not argue," Druise said softly. He stood up.

"No," I said, trying to shield him.

"Sorley." Druise's voice was firm. "Tell Gnaius." He pushed past me, allowing two of the soldiers to take his arms, none too gently.

"Your name, Sergeant?" Lena demanded. He told her. "Where are you taking Druisius?"

"The cells, Lieutenant. Take him," he said to his men. They marched out. I took a step to follow, but Lena stopped me.

"No, Sorley. Go to the infirmary, as Druise said. Tell Gnaius. I will find Casyn. But tell me first: did he desert?"

I came with Lena, without permission. "Yes," I said. "But Turlo knew. He said it wouldn't matter, that we would just say the transfer to the Empire's troops was made on the field, without written confirmation."

"Maybe. But think, Sorley. To arrest a senior officer's aide so peremptorily, when that senior officer is signatory to the treaty, and the *Princip*'s nephew? Decanius is making a statement about who has power now, and he is using Druisius to do it."

"Oh, gods," I said. "Is there a message here to Linrathe, too? All Wall's End knows Druise is my partner."

"Very likely. Now go. Gnaius needs to know, and he will not, if you stand there."

She had reached for her officer's insignia as she spoke. Off duty, she didn't wear it; it lay on the sideboard beside Cillian's. "Sorley," she said sharply, pinning it on, "Go."

The cadet at the infirmary door did not want to let me in. "I must," I said, trying not to shout. "I must see Gnaius. I have an important message for him. The *Princip* is aware."

The last might be a lie, but I didn't care. The girl stepped aside. I entered the antechamber, turning left to what had been Cillian's room before. Gnaius was just coming out. "You should not be here," he said.

"Druisius has been arrested," I said.

His eyes widened, but he said nothing, only closed the door quietly behind him. "Cillian is sleeping, but only because I gave him valerian," he murmured. "A light sleep, easily disturbed. Come over here, and keep your voice down."

I told him what had happened, as quickly as I could. "I cannot leave Cillian," he said, his brow furrowed.

"Could I stay with him?"

"No. You do not know what to do, and there is no time to teach you. And…" He hesitated. "What Cillian says to us—you must understand that he has little control, and he tells us things he would not otherwise. Some of it, Lord Sorley, concerns you. As his physician, I cannot allow him to see you; I would fear the effects on the balance of his mind." He turned to a table. "I will write a note to Decanius. Wait outside, please. I will not take long."

I waited silently by the cadet, confusion and fear warring in my mind. Fear for Druise, and confusion at Gnaius's words. What could Cillian be saying? That he had turned my advances down? That wasn't a secret, not among us, and surely we had moved beyond regret.

Staring down the corridor, I let myself remember. He'd taken me aside on the river, one early morning, and we'd walked a long way from the ship before we stopped. 'Sorley,' he'd said, 'I have made many mistakes in my life. One has caused you great pain. I regret that.' I'd interrupted, with some disavowal or dismissal, but he'd gone on. 'Loving Lena has made me understand.' He'd put a hand on my shoulder, then. 'I wish I had known.'

I had begun to cry, trying to hide the tears and failing. The hand on my shoulder had moved to my back, and I had turned to him. He had held me gently, not speaking. I hadn't let it go on for too long; pride made me step away. The glitter of tears in his eyes had surprised me.

'But there is no going back,' he'd said. 'Can you forgive me, and be my friend?'

Of course I had said I would: friendship was preferable to nothing. And in the weeks in Casil and the ship home, we had been friends, and I had thought myself content. Had Cillian sensed my anger and confusion this winter? Had I inadvertently resurrected his guilt and regret?

I couldn't make sense of it. And maybe there was none: maybe the poppy twisted memories and thought, and what Cillian was telling Gnaius and Druise was nonsensical. I'd talk to Druise about it, someday.

If he was here to talk to. Fear surged again. I began to pace. Where was Gnaius? He appeared a minute or two later, a sealed note in his hand. "Take this to the *Princip*. If the Procurator is to be found, ask them both to attend me, if they would."

Casyn, Lena with him, was in his workroom. I handed him Gnaius's note. "I have spoken to Randall," he said. "He believes the captain that Decanius met with at the Eastern Fort had brought records from Casil, names of missing men. I have seen how carefully they keep their lists and tallies, and the god forbid they allot pay improperly. Druisius's name must have been on that list."

"But we can still argue the transfer was made in the field," I said again.

"No," Lena said. "If he is listed as missing, then his commander knows no transfer was made."

I swore. "What is the punishment?"

Casyn looked up. "Surely you know?"

"No."

I saw the answer in his eyes before he spoke. "Death."

Lena reached out to me, but I turned away, staring at the wall. "There must be a solution," I insisted. Fear made my voice sharp.

"A temporary one, yes," Casyn said. "Sergeant!" Birel appeared almost immediately. "My compliments to the Procurator," he said, "with a request from the physician Gnaius that we both join him immediately. Lord Sorley will accompany you to translate, but here is the physician's note, and my signature."

He touched Lena's shoulder. "You must stay here. I can think of no reason to have you join us, and your presence will inflame Decanius."

The Procurator came with bad grace, but Gnaius held a senior rank in the Casilani army, and his note had made it clear, I guessed, that he could not leave the infirmary. Gnaius took us all into an inner room, well away from where Cillian was being treated.

"Physician?" Decanius said. "What requires my presence?" Posturing, I thought. He knows.

"Procurator, *Princip*, you have had a man I need arrested," Gnaius said. His voice was quiet, almost questioning. "Druisius, his name is."

"A deserter," Decanius said.

"That may be," Gnaius replied. "But I have spent many hours training this man, and I need him just now, for another week. I request his return. You may, of course, send guards. I will take responsibility for him, as my rank allows."

"You have many medics."

"But the treatment I need Druisius to assist with is a delicate one. One from which I will learn to the benefit of all Casil's army. I will ensure your cooperation will be made clear to the Empress."

Decanius rubbed his chin. "You will take full responsibility?"

"Of course."

"A week, you say?"

"Or a day or two more. No longer."

"Then—" His eyes flicked to Casyn. "If you agree, *Princip*. I want it clear," he said, turning back to Gnaius, "that if anything goes wrong, the *Princip* and I both agreed to the deserter's stay of execution."

"Of course," Gnaius said again. "*Princip*?"

"I agree, if you believe only he has the skills you require," Casyn said, through me. Gnaius smiled, blandly.

"Thank you both. I would appreciate it if Druisius could return immediately. I will need him very soon."

I sank into a chair in Casyn's workroom. Birel handed me wine, unwatered. "The physician is also a diplomat," Casyn said, sipping his own wine.

"They must be, I should think," Lena said. "But you say Decanius was quick to include you in the decision?"

Casyn laughed, cynically. "Only to ensure any blame would be shared. But we also know now that Decanius curries the Empress's favour, not just his uncle's, which might be useful. At least we have gained some time."

I did not sleep that night, even though Gnaius sent the cadet with a note to tell me Druise was back with him. 'A few bruises, nothing more,' the physician wrote.

Did the argument make sense? I paced, picking up and putting down my *ladhar* a dozen times. The flask of *fuisce* grew lighter, and with it, my remorse. We—Cillian and I—had offered Druise the chance to accompany us west. To war, yes, and so there had always been risk. But somehow death in battle and execution for desertion weren't the same.

But, my muddled mind said, how can he have deserted? He'd fought with his regiment at the Taiva; the battle and the war were won when he left his fellow soldiers to support Lena. And Callan had signed the treaty weeks before. He was still a soldier, assigned his current post by a general of the Empire's army, and the Empire's army now was Casil's.

I didn't know. I wasn't a soldier. But it gave me hope, and it was something to think about, something other than the thing I didn't want to examine, the other reason behind my guilt. As much as I wanted to deny it, when Casyn had told me the punishment, a voice in my mind, insidious and unwelcome, had whispered: *then you would have no choice to make.*

I dozed briefly, sodden with *fuisce*, just as the sky began to lighten. I woke after an hour or so, my head pounding and my stomach roiling. Sitting up was a mistake. I vomited into the chamber pot, several times, and then I sat with my back against the bed, waiting for the room to stop spinning.

Eventually I kept some water down and managed to wash and dress. Shaving was not possible, my hand far too unsteady. I made my way to Cillian and Lena's rooms, and weakly rapped three times.

"Oh, Sorley," Lena said when she opened the door to me. "Sit down. Tea?"

"No. Nothing."

"*Fuisce*," she said, sniffing. "I shouldn't have let you leave."

"There's only one bed."

"So? Have we not shared a cot before?"

"I had a thought," I said.

"I'm surprised you could," she said. "Before the *fuisce*?"

I shook my head and wished I hadn't. "No. During…and so it might not make sense." I told her my thinking, about how Druise couldn't have deserted. She listened, biting her lip.

"Maybe," she said. "Casyn will know. He said to come to him, whenever we were ready. Are you?"

"Yes. As long as there isn't food."

Casyn gave me a sympathetic look, and heard me out, but at the end of my explanation he shook his head. "The argument is not without merit, Sorley. But I doubt Decanius will accept it: Casil's military laws are harsh. But it is worth trying, if he rejects Gnaius's idea. The physician came to see me very early this morning."

"Which is?"

"I bribe him," he said simply.

"With what? Doesn't he think everything is his for the taking?" Lena asked.

"Perhaps bribe is the wrong word," Casyn said. "I agree to certain practices that will enrich him, practices that in truth divert money from Casil's coffers to his own purse."

"Does not that endanger you?" I asked, "if Casil discovers the fraud?"

"It is a possibility," he agreed. "But one that has little chance of detection, because the man who oversees such things in Casil is Decanius's kinsman, Quintus."

"You would do this," I asked, "for Druisius? One soldier, not even of your land?"

"I will do this because Decanius is going to divert taxes to his own use whether I agree or not. Also, it suits me to have the Procurator think he has cowed me into submitting to his authority," Casyn said. "And because Druisius matters to you, and to Cillian and Lena, and too many we love have died." He stood up. "Go to the baths, Sorley. Lieutenant, you will stay with me, please: there are many facets of this plan to work out, and Michan cannot be part of it."

I soaked a long time, and let the attendant shave me. I felt somewhat better, physically. Soup and bread, tentatively approached, stayed in my stomach, and once I was sure of that I went back to see what Lena and Casyn had devised. I stopped at the infirmary first, but a large guardsman at the door told me convincingly I was not allowed inside. I wondered what he'd say if I told him I had come for a remedy for my uncertain stomach, but decided not to try my luck.

"Decanius has agreed to meet with me in an hour, with you to translate," Casyn told me. "I have sent Lena for food and a rest, as she must be our scribe."

He told me the plan, and what he had to offer. "I am taking nothing from the women's villages that the Procurator will not claim as Casil's due," he said, "from what he has informed me of already." He looked at me critically. "I am glad to see you are shaven. May I suggest you change into your formal clothes?"

"Am I not just your translator?"

"It will not hurt to remind Decanius that you are also the ears and voice of Linrathe. Whatever they will ask of your country, Sorley, when they choose to ask it, having even the slightest sway over the Procurator might be to your advantage."

I couldn't argue. I went back my room, both relieved and embarrassed to see it had been cleaned. I'd have to make my appreciation known to the orderly. When I returned to Casyn's workroom, Lena was present, and Birel, the latter laying out writing supplies on a smaller table against the wall.

"Is there anything else, *Princip*?" he asked.

"Not if there is water and wine," Casyn said. "Thank you, Sergeant."

His soldier-servant didn't leave. The two men regarded each other. "Be careful, Casyn," Birel said. "You are needed still."

"I will be."

A smile half-formed on Birel's lips, then disappeared. He saluted and left us. A few minutes later, Decanius's scribe knocked, and the two men came in.

"What is she doing here?" Decanius demanded, looking at Lena. "A pregnant woman?" His lip curled.

"The lieutenant," Casyn said firmly, "is my scribe today. My adjutant has other duties."

Decanius scowled. "At least she is not at this table," he muttered. He chose a chair. "What is it you so urgently need to discuss, *Princip*?"

"I have been giving thought to an appropriate residence for you, Procurator. You cannot wish to reside in the rooms you were assigned here permanently, surely?"

"Well, no," Decanius said, looking both surprised and pleased. "This fort is far from what I am accustomed to."

"I thought as much," Casyn said. "Coming from Casil, you must find these northern lands both cold and damp, do you not?"

"It is damp in Casil in the winter, but not this cold," Decanius said. "And of course our heating is better. What did you have in mind? I did ask the *mensores* to consider this, as they mapped the land."

I handed Casyn the map that, rolled, lay beside me. We spread it out, weighting the corners. "Here," Casyn said, pointing to land between the Eastern Fort and Casilla. Decanius's eyes widened.

"Is not that a residence of a retired officer?"

"It is. But the officer could be persuaded to let you have it. The house is of sufficient quality that you should be comfortable there until you can build something more fitting your position, Procurator." Casyn sat back, letting Decanius study the map.

"There are vineyards?"

"Established ones. The wine is very good, by our standards."

"I would bring a wine-maker from Casil. Are there slaves?"

"Yes. Only male, of course."

"And metals?"

"Copper. The mines are on this headland here." Casyn pointed.

Decanius leaned back in his chair. "I have one concern," he said. "Shall we ask our scribes to stop writing, *Princip*?" When pens were down, he continued. "I would, of course, need to build a villa that honoured myself and my family in Casil. My salary as Procurator, while generous, is insufficient for that purpose."

"Have you a solution?" Casyn inquired neutrally. "I too will have payments to make, to ensure these lands can be yours."

The inner door opened. Casyn looked up, frowning. Birel came in, a wine flask on a tray in his hands. "My apologies, *Princip*. I remembered I had not put out the best wine." He put it down and slipped away, pulling the door closed behind him.

"A cup would be welcome," Decanius said. I rose to pour, something nagging at me. Something missing…a sound I should have heard. I poured two cups, put the flask down. It clicked against the metal tray.

I served the wine cups, then reached for the water jug. As I did, I glanced at the inner door, sure now of what I hadn't heard: the click of its latch. It stood ajar, the tiniest crack.

Decanius began talking again. "The taxation rates on certain commodities are my decision. That I keep a percentage of the rates I set, for the responsibility of managing those commodities, is common practice, *Princip*. An unspoken agreement between Casil and its provincial administrators, you understand."

"Is it?" Casyn said. "What commodities might you consider for this arrangement?"

"Salt, for one," Decanius said. "It is in great demand, and this coastal land has much opportunity for its production. A percentage of its taxes would quickly enrich me, and," he cleared his throat, "perhaps you too, *Princip*, if other arrangements of this sort could be made?"

"You are forgetting something, Procurator." We all turned. In the frame of the inner door, Cillian leaned on a cane, his face drawn, his hands trembling. He wore grey and white, his court clothes from Casil, although they hung on him. Lena made a sound, but she didn't move.

"Cillian!" Casyn said. "Major, what are you doing here?"

Decanius looked at Cillian, his face cold. He said something in a language I did not recognize. It sounded like *zinkolo*.

Cillian replied in what I assumed was the same language. "I can repeat that, if you like," he added, in Casilan, "for all to understand."

The procurator's lips thinned. A faint flush touched his ears.

"I am here," Cillian said to Casyn, "because I believe you have need of your adjutant. An important piece of information is being overlooked in these negotiations."

I got up and pulled out a chair. "Sit, Major." I offered my arm. Close to him, I could see the beads of sweat at his hairline, and the set of his jaw.

"I object to this man's presence," Decanius said. He pushed his chair back to rise.

"As the Empress would object to your usurping of her authority," Cillian said.

Decanius's lip curled again. "Usurping her authority? I am the Procurator here, and the voice of the Empress in this province."

"Procurator, you are mistaken," Cillian said. Gods, I thought, do not be so direct. "This Western Empire is a Royal province, under Eudekia's direct oversight, and as such taxes and laws are the responsibility of the Governor, not a Procurator. The Governor who is not yet here."

The flush on the Procurator's face was spreading to his bald crown. "Until he is, they are mine to administer," Decanius said.

"They are not. They are the *Princip's*, until the Governor arrives. I negotiated the treaty, Procurator. I know what it says." The shaking in Cillian's hands was growing worse. "I must write to Eudekia, very soon. We became," he paused, "not what you implied earlier, but good friends in my time there, and I promised to let her know how we prospered as part of her Empire." His eyes were locked on Decanius's.

"You do not know Casil's laws," the Procurator said, dismissively. "How could you? I stand proxy to the Governor."

"I could also let her know what rumours you are spreading about the ties between the son of an Emperor, and the Empress you purport to serve." Cillian said.

As unobtrusively as I could, I put one hand on Cillian's back. He leaned into it, just a little. He felt hot, feverish. I looked at Lena. She was watching him, her eyes frightened. "Water," I mouthed.

She brought the cup. He didn't look at her, his gaze fixed on Decanius. The Procurator's bald head gleamed red, now. He licked his lips. "All letters go by our ships."

Under my hand, I felt Cillian tense. The Procurator smiled.

"Not necessarily," I said. "There is another route, Procurator. The one I took to reach Casil."

He made no reply. No one spoke for a heartbeat, and then another.

"But of course," Cillian said quietly, "my memory sometimes falters." Tremors were running through his back now.

Decanius blinked. His mouth opened, closed, as if he searched for words. "What might bring on those lapses?"

"The skilled attention of my soldier-servant," Cillian said. "His ministrations so relax me, my mind wanders. My physician concurs, if you would prefer to ask him."

I glanced at Casyn. He was leaning forward, a hand over his mouth. Disguising a smile, I was sure.

Decanius turned to his scribe. "Give me paper." He scribbled a note. "Fetch me the soldier Druisius, from the infirmary. Give this to his guards."

No one spoke for the minutes it took the scribe to do as Decanius had ordered. I could feel Cillian's muscles clenching as he tried to control the tremors. "Water?" I whispered to him. He shook his head slightly. Under the table, his right hand found my knee.

Summoning a memory long suppressed. I had been sixteen, a man in Sorham, not a boy, but young. Cillian, in his role as *toscaire*, had come to see my father. One night we had music, and dancing, and as I played I had watched him dance, desire rising. He'd glanced over at me: our eyes had met. And when the dance was done, he'd come over to me, knelt in front of me to ask about the instrument. He'd reached out to touch my fingers on the neck of the *ladhar* with one hand. The other had rested on my knee, as if for balance.

I forced my mind to the present. Runnels of sweat wet Cillian's face. His hand on my knee tightened, almost to the point of pain.

No, I thought, fighting my body's unwanted reaction. No. Concentrate on why you are here. He has no idea what he is doing to you; it is to control his own desires, which have nothing to do with yours. Nor will they ever.

I put a hand over his. He let me take it, entwining his fingers with mine, squeezing hard. I didn't flinch.

Druisius's eyes went straight to Cillian when he came in, his lips thin and tight. Then he saluted both the Procurator and Casyn, standing rigidly at attention. He did not look at me.

"Soldier," Decanius said. "A mistake has been made, due to records poorly kept in the heat of battle. That you requested and were given permission to transfer your service to the army of the Western Empire was —overlooked."

"And so we must remedy it," Casyn said. "You will swear allegiance to me, in front of these witnesses, Druisius. My scribe will record it, and the Procurator will sign, as will I, so there is no chance of future confusion. If you so wish, that is."

"I do, *Princip*," Druisius said. "Do I kneel?"

"No."

"I am Druisius of Casil," my lover said, following the words Casyn gave him to say. "On this day, released from my service to the Eastern Empire, I freely give my allegiance to Casyn, *Princip* of the Western Empire." Of his own accord, he added, "and to his heirs, born and unborn." I translated, wondering at the last part.

"I, Casyn, *Princip* of the Western Empire, accept your oath, Druisius." He turned to Lena. "Have you recorded that?"

"In our language, *Princip*."

"Lord Sorley?" I wrote the translation and passed it to Decanius's scribe to check. He nodded. Casyn signed, and then Decanius. The Procurator stood, immediately.

"A satisfactory conclusion," he said, not meaning it at all. "I am keeping the lands, of course."

CHAPTER 16

THE MOMENT THE DOOR shut behind him, Druise was at Cillian's side. "Give me that water," he ordered. Cillian had stopped trying to control the tremors. Sweat ran down his face. Gnaius appeared from the other room, holding out a vial. Had he been there the entire time? Druise mixed its contents with the water. "Drink," he ordered, holding it to Cillian's lips. "*Idióta*. Six hours ago you should have had this."

"I needed a clear mind." He swallowed the drug. Druise got up, moving aside for Lena. She put her arms around Cillian, one hand stroking his hair, whispering to him. He pulled her closer, but his hand was still in mine. Gnaius stood, watching him.

Slowly the tremors subsided, and his breathing became steadier. Druise had disappeared into the back room, returning with a damp cloth. He wiped Cillian's face. "*Idióta*," he said again, but this time he was smiling. "Thank you."

Cillian almost grinned. "Don't thank me," he said. "It was your question this morning that made me realize. Druise," he said to the rest of us, "asked me what sort of province we were. Casil has two types of provinces: ones administered by the officials, and Royal provinces which belong to the Empress. In the former case, the Procurator is often also the Governor. But never in Royal provinces, which is what we are."

"Did you know this?" Casyn asked, turning to me.

"I saw the words in the treaty," I said slowly. "I did not know what they meant."

"I knew this was a Royal province," Gnaius said. "The Empress would not have sent me, otherwise. But that you did not understand the implications, no. I am sorry, *Princip*. I could have saved you worry."

Cillian sat up a little straighter, releasing my hand so he could rest his on the curve of Lena's belly. She covered it with one of hers.

"You did know," Casyn said to him, "didn't you? That was why you hadn't told us the Procurator would arrive: he wasn't that important."

"I had told the Emperor," Cillian said, "but, yes. The man should never have taken the power he has; his work was to be counting and mapping. I could not make the connections between what Sorley or you told me, and what was happening, not while the poppy dimmed my mind."

"You couldn't see the game board," I said.

"Exactly."

I got up, touching his shoulder as I walked behind him to put my arms around Druise. *"Amané,"* I murmured, "I was so worried." A surge of something I couldn't name ran through me, something deeper than relief. Could I ever atone for what I had thought?

"I was not," Druise said, stepping back from my embrace. "The gods decide."

"You, my friend," Cillian said, "are a better follower of Catilius than I am, I think. But perhaps I have repaid a tiny portion of the debt I owe to Sorley today."

"You would have," I said, "had there been one owed. *Meas*, Cillian. *Meas, mo charaidh gràhadh.*"

"Kiss your *quincala*," Gnaius told him, "and then we go back to the infirmary. Six or seven more days, if you have not done too much damage today."

"Before you go," Casyn said, "what did Decanius say to you at the beginning? And what language was that?"

Cillian smiled. "He called me, effectively, a *scraptus*. A man who sells his body. He had not expected me to understand, as I had no Heræcrian when I met with his uncle in Casil. Gnaius has remedied that, for which I have Sorley to thank, I believe."

A WEEK LATER DRUISE came to find me, late in the evening. "He has done it," he told me. "Five days now since the last tiny dose, and the sweating and nausea and fever are all gone. Now," he shrugged, "it will be his strength of will, and our help, that will keep him free of it."

I wrapped my arms around him. "You must be exhausted, Druise," I said.

"Not too bad. I could sleep, these last few days, when Cillian did. Lena can see him tomorrow, I think."

"And they can marry, now he is free of the poppy. Are you going to bed now?"

"Yes." He yawned. "Sleep, nothing else. You go to Cillian. I would not wake Lena; the morning is soon enough." Lena, I thought, would not agree. And perhaps I would override Druise's decision, after I had seen Cillian.

He looked thinner even than the week before, and there were dark circles under his eyes, but he was himself. Calm and reflective, clearly in some pain, but wholly Cillian, in a way he had not been since Druisius had come to fetch me, almost five months previously.

"Sorley," he said. "Help me stand. I just need your arm, to steady me." I held it out. He brought himself to his feet, one hand on my forearm. "Come." I stepped into the embrace, tears threatening.

"*Mo duíne gràhadh*," I murmured. "I am so glad to see you well."

"Thank Druisius," he said. "And Gnaius. Without them, I would not be." He released me, studying my face in the low light of the room. "We have much to talk about. I remember most of what you have told me over the months, and what I said to you—or I believe I do—but it feels distant. As if I responded with only part of my mind. Will you forgive me for that?"

"Do not," I said, "be a fool, Cillian. You cannot ask forgiveness for the effects of a drug your physician prescribed and would not allow you to forgo."

He laughed. *Laughed.* "Perhaps not. Gnaius tells me I will want poppy when the pain is bad for a very long time, perhaps years," he added in a graver voice. "That my desire for it will overrule my judgement and control."

"It certainly didn't, the afternoon you bested Decanius," I pointed out.

"I could not have gone on much longer, and not at all without you beside me. It is not in my nature to ask for help, but I believe I may need it, occasionally."

"I will be here," I said, reflexively. Well, I would be, for some time.

"Your constancy, my lord Sorley, is welcomed," he said, a faint smile playing on his lips. My formal title had the sound of an endearment. "Now, tell me your thoughts about Decanius."

"Cillian," I protested, "not now. I thought I would come to see you, then fetch Lena."

"Let her sleep. She needs her rest. Decanius troubles me. I have made an enemy there, and so, I think, have you, for yourself and for Linrathe. I worry for our lands, because I believe this Procurator wants nothing less than complete Casilani control, and that was not what the Empress and I discussed, nor what the treaties were meant to give."

"Won't it depend on who the Governor is, now you've clarified this is a Royal province?" I settled into a chair. If Cillian wanted to talk about politics—before seeing Lena?—then I would concede.

"It may. What concerns me is that the things Eudekia and I spoke of were not recorded, made official. She was intrigued by what I could tell her of how women and men lived here; the separate lives and responsibilities. It was not her intent in ending the Partition agreement to destroy that, only to give more choice to both. Much what my father wanted."

"I wouldn't know."

"He told me of his ideas, in the nights we spent talking at the Eastern Fort. He wanted no more boys castrated for not being able to fight, as his brother had been. He saw Colm in me, he said. I could have suffered the same fate, had he known of my birth while I was still a child, and claimed me."

"Fighting is not that hard, Cillian."

"No? I have only once known the impulse to violence, Sorley, and it was directed towards a man already dead."

"Because you are thinking theoretically," I said. "When a man with a sword or axe is swinging it at you, your impulses change. Believe me."

"Perhaps they do," he said. "I did kill a bear once, when it would not listen to calm words and a reasoned approach." I heard the dry, self-mocking tone, and grinned. "But I felt remorse, even though it would have killed us for no reason except that we were between it and the water it wanted. And Lena—" He shook his head. "Killing did not grow easier for her, Sorley."

"Except Fritjof," I said.

"Has she told you that?"

"No. She has never mentioned it, and I assumed—after everything he or his men did—"

"I wonder," he said softly. "But to return to Decanius. Assuming the Governor—who should arrive very soon—is of like mind, exactly what are they demanding?"

We spoke of the Procurator and his dictatorial approach to what he saw necessary to make the Western Empire a 'modern province of Casil' as he so constantly put it. I told him of the surveys and censuses and maps, and plans for vast estates, and men brought from Casil to oversee them.

"The army, he says, must be completely re-organized: the ranks brought into line with Casil's, and women's cohorts limited to archery, as they are there," I told Cillian. "The *Princip* has agreed to the first, reluctantly, but is rejecting the second." I watched him assimilate the information. "What do you think they will ask of Linrathe?" I asked.

He shook his head. "I do not know. Some subtle way of gaining influence? Or simple military force? The former is my guess, but until we know more of the Governor, it remains a supposition. But there will be much work for me to do here." The lamp flickered and guttered; the oil was running low. "The *Ti'ach* will have to wait, I am afraid."

"Then it waits," I said. I wouldn't mind. Not at all. But what would Lena think? She had been adamant she wanted to bring up their child in Linrathe.

"What will you do in this land?" he asked.

"Teach languages, probably," I said. "And I am still Linrathe's *toscaire*. It's very late. Shouldn't you sleep?"

"I doubt I will," he said. He grimaced, moving his leg.

"You are in pain. What can I do?"

"Nothing more than what you are doing. Talking distracts me."

"Is there willow-bark here? If I make tea, will you drink it?"

He smiled. "If you will play *xache* with me while it steeps, yes." His easy capitulation surprised me. He told me where the supplies were, and I busied myself making tea while he, refusing my assistance, rose to limp to a sideboard to retrieve the game. "I taught Druisius; did he tell you?" he asked as he set up the pieces.

"No. We have not had much time to talk," I said, pouring hot water on the shredded bark. I set the pot beside the brazier. "Is he any good?"

"Not yet. He is prone to taking risks. But teaching him was another distraction."

We played the game. After some time I brought Cillian the tea, but regardless of his pain I was losing badly at that point, and he had me defeated in only a few more moves. His game had been precise and deliberate, and I knew I'd never really had a chance. As he made the final victorious move, I laughed. "I have never been so happy to lose," I said.

"Callan and I played a few times," he said thoughtfully. "He was better than I, or perhaps more truthfully his strategies were not ones I knew. I wish—" He stopped. *Do not wish for a different fate,* Catilius would say. But I do. I wish he had not died, for the sake of his land, and his brother, and because we were beginning to be friends."

"At least you had some time with him," I said, "time to talk, to understand and accept each other."

"Not in all ways. I accepted, and forgave, that his oath to his country had superseded his love for my mother. He had been very young, and the penalty was death. We had not discussed in any detail why I, somewhat older, had betrayed mine. I would like to have had that talk."

"Would you? I can think of nothing worse than having a similar discussion with my father."

"Asking Callan to acknowledge me was not the betrayal," Cillian said, looking away from the fire, into the dark. "No man, nor prince, nor foreign power has sway over me, and my loyalty is to the people of Linrathe, and the land beneath my feet."

"Given the treaty you convinced Eudekia to sign regarding Linrathe," I said, "I'm sure you have atoned for anything you might see as betrayal. In my father's eyes, if he knows, I have betrayed him simply by being who I am. Nothing I can ever make up for, unless I deny my nature, and marry and father children."

"Catilius," Cillian said, "would say then that you loved yourself too little, or you would love what your nature asks of you."

"Cillian," I said, yawning, "It is far too late for philosophy."

"You are taking me to task?" he answered, lightly. "As you should. I am keeping you from your bed, and you have work to do in the morning."

Reluctantly I stood, finishing the last drops of wine in my cup. "You should sleep too." I bent to drop a kiss on his head. He grasped my arm, resting his temple against my cheek for a moment.

"Perhaps I too need to consider Catilius's words," he murmured.

"Cannot we both just be content with what we have, at least for a little while?" I said, straightening. "You are alive, and recovering, and you have Lena, and the baby very soon."

His hand was still on my arm. "And you, *mo duíne gràhadh?*"

My beloved man. A sudden restriction in my throat made my voice hoarse. "I have enough," I managed to say, "being here. With you. And I might be able to be a *scáeli* after all."

He looked up at me, his eyes unreadable in the flickering light. "You are one, in my mind. I know the dark gods well now; they wanted me, and without your music they would have me still. I fear for you, for the price they will demand in return."

"Don't," I said. Something clawed at my heart, stripping away defences and arguments. "Don't fear, Cillian. You are worth any price to me." The inexorable, inevitable truth. How could I have denied it?

"You believe that now," he said. "But a reckoning will come, for all of us, for the choices we have made. You may think differently then. Go and sleep. I will see you in the morning."

In the corridor outside I turned right, away from the direction of my room. I let myself into the sitting room before knocking gently on the bedroom door. When I heard Lena's sleepy question, I opened it and went in. "Sorley?"

"I have just left Cillian," I told her. "He is awake, and free, and himself, Lena."

She slid out of bed, pushing her feet into soft slippers, hurrying from the room. I stood quietly for a few moments, watching her, before I closed the door.

Empire's Reckoning

For Bjørn Larssen. Thank you.

Tis not the many oaths that makes the truth,
but the plain single vow that is vow'd true.

Shakespeare: All's Well That Ends Well

Each one, his own priest, and own sacrifice.

John Donne, The Calm

Only where love and need are one,
And the work is play for mortal stakes
Is the deed ever truly done
For heaven and the future's sakes.

Robert Frost, Two Tramps in Mudtime.

CHAPTER 1

15 YEARS AFTER THE BATTLE OF THE TAIVA

"WHY ARE THERE SO many secrets in this family?" Gwenna's voice wasn't raised; if anything, it was lower, colder than normal, her clenched fists reflecting her anger. "No one tells me anything. My classmates laugh at me, because they know more about you than I do. It's not fair."

"Kitten," Druise began. I shot him a warning glance, too late. Gwenna rounded on him.

"Do not call me Kitten," she snapped. "I hate it!"

"Gwenna," Cillian said firmly, "if you cannot be civil, you must leave. If you are prepared to outline your complaints in a manner both calm and logical, you may join us after dinner for a while, and I," he glanced at Lena, who nodded, "we, will listen. But you may not shout at any of us. Go to your room, please."

She glared at him, but even Gwenna, as angry as she was, would not gainsay Cillian. Both because he was the *Comiádh*, and because he was her adored father. Colm looked up from the book he was reading. "May I go too?" he asked. "I want to finish my drawing."

"Of course," Lena said. "Bring it to show us, later."

"Properly labelled," Cillian added. He held out an arm to embrace his son, kissing him on the temple. Gwenna stood sulkily near the door. She opened it as her brother approached, then turned on her heel to look directly at her father.

"I am not a child. Stop treating me like one," she said fiercely. The door closed, quietly—she was not that defiant—behind her.

"Gwenna has a point," Cillian said quietly. "I did not fully realize our part in the victory over the Marai was taught so early in the officer cadets' education."

"Perhaps it's an extra class, for those who will become diplomats?" Lena suggested.

"Perhaps. In either case, she needs to hear the truth from us. But I worry."

"About what?" I asked.

"She is volatile. More so than usual," he amended, at Lena's raised eyebrow. "I do not quite trust her to differentiate between what she deserves to know, and what she can speak about. When a secret shared must remain a secret."

I stood to pour myself more tea from the pot on the sideboard. I stopped behind Cillian to put a hand on his shoulder. "You'll have to elicit a promise," I said. He looked up at me. I was leaving in two days, for much of the summer. He leaned back, a tiny movement, acknowledging the touch.

"I suppose I will, my lord Sorley," he said. "When she is calmer."

A gentle knock at the door and Apulo slipped in. "Am I early?" he said, seeing that I was pouring tea.

"No," Cillian said. "We had an upset daughter to deal with. Have some tea, Apulo, and tell me if any of the new students has a voice to be cultivated."

I handed Apulo a mug of tea and listened with interest as he spoke intelligently about the three new students' singing voices. "The boy has the most potential," he said, "if his voice remains true. Both girls carry a tune adequately, but nothing more."

"The boy plays, too," I said, "and with some skill. Apulo, he's yours for the summer, although Tamm can give him some instruction on the *ladhar* while I am gone." I was riding north into Sorham, to supervise the beginning of a music program in the newest *Ti'ach*, recently established in my homeland. By tradition, *scáeli'en* travelled alone. I turned to my partner. "And you on the *cithar*, Druise, if you want."

"Why not?" Druise said. "If I am teaching the others anyhow."

"I am ready," Cillian announced. He pushed himself upright, reaching for his walking stick. Apulo stood, going to Cillian to ensure he was steady.

They would go to Cillian's treatment room in the annex, where there was a high bed for massage, and shelves for Apulo's oils and lotions, and from there to the baths Druise and Apulo had built, the first summer here. I might join Cillian in the hot pool later, I thought.

"What is Colm drawing?" I asked Lena idly, finishing my tea.

"A squirrel skeleton he found," she said, rolling her eyes. "It was old, and bleached, so I let him keep it. Cillian found him an anatomy book from somewhere, so he's labelling the teeth and bones as best he can." Colm was as precise and thoughtful over his work as his father, and by nature self-contained, but a loving and generous child. Privately, I thought he was what Cillian might have been, had his childhood been different. Where Gwenna, tall and inherently graceful, looked almost exactly like her father, the strong stamp of Callan's line evident, Colm was a blend of his parents. He had Lena's skin colouring and her hazel eyes, but, like his sister, Cillian's dark hair. He had been born into the peace of the *Ti'ach*, to a calm and ordered life, and I wondered sometimes if this has contributed to his happy, unbothered personality, so unlike Gwenna's. Her first year had been different, and difficult.

"*Amané*," Druise said, "should we review what you expect from the students this summer?"

"I suppose we should," I replied. We made our way to my teaching rooms — ours, really, as Druise taught here too, but by convention they were mine, as I held the appointment as *scáeli* to the *Ti'ach na Cillian*. When they had been Dagney's rooms, she had used one as a bedroom, but Druise and I shared a suite of rooms in the annex, where students were never allowed. So there were two rooms to use for teaching, and the instrument room, so even when Lena was teaching aspects of *danta* interpretation, we all had space.

We went over the students and what I thought they should be learning for much of the next hour. Tamm would work with the younger ones on the *ladhar*, and Apulo on voice with them all. "Gwenna is competent on the *ladhar*, too," I said. "It won't hurt her to start helping the others with tuning and fingering."

"She is angry at the world," Druise said, "and in no mood to help anyone. I will wait to suggest that, yes?"

"Yes," I agreed. "Although you know what Cillian would say."

"That it is her role in life. I know," he said. "But she is fourteen, Sorley."

"Two years an officer cadet, and heir to Faolyn. She doesn't have the luxury of being moody. What were your sisters doing at fourteen, Druise?"

"Marrying," he said with a shrug.

"As was mine," I said, "or at least being betrothed. And I could do a day's work in the *torp*, and you were a soldier."

"A day's work overseeing, you mean," he said. It was an old tease between us. "What does a lord's son know of work?"

"Tell me when you have sheared sheep for a day," I replied. He chuckled.

"I will miss you," he said softly. "It is many years since we have been apart for so long." I glanced at the door; firmly shut, and we were in the rear of the two rooms. He was violating one of our rules, but I saw no harm in it. No one could hear. Or see. I leaned over to kiss him, just lightly.

"I'll miss you, too," I replied. I would have liked to take him with me, to see my homeland, even to take the time to travel to Gundarstorp, my ancestral holding now in the hands of my brother Roghan. But I could not take a guard, and I would have no other way to explain, in Linrathe or Sorham, Druise's presence at my side. Here at the *Ti'ach*, our rooms in the annex gave us privacy, our hours with Cillian and Lena gave us acceptance, and Apulo's care of our rooms and laundry and his responsibilities for the baths meant no servant ever had cause to suspect we were anything but friends. A necessary deception made easier by the traditions of the *Ti'ach*, which also prohibited any signs of affection between Cillian and Lena in front of the students. We had our public lives, and our private ones, and we kept them separate.

"Tomorrow," he said, grinning, "we will say goodnight early, yes?"

"Yes," I assured him.

"But not tonight, though," he said, matter-of-factly.

"No."

"He too will miss you," Druise said. "Lena will have to improve her *xache* game."

"He can play Gwenna," I suggested. "She's better than I am, already, when she concentrates." I stretched. "Baths, Druise?" He shook his head.

"Tomorrow."

"I'll see you at dinner, then," I said.

Apulo was just helping Cillian into the pool when I arrived. "Are you joining us?" I asked.

"Not this time," he replied. I didn't press him. I slipped into the water beside Cillian, luxuriating in its heat. My shoulders and neck, bent too long over my instrument or that of my students, needed relaxing.

"Is Colm coming?" I asked. We maintained the rules of bathhouse use from Wall's End: no mixing of sexes, although that did not extend to Cillian and Lena, alone. The baths were strictly for family, except for the occasional Casilani envoy.

"No," Cillian said. "Druisius?"

"No." We regarded each other. A smile played on his lips.

"Sorley," Apulo said. "Do not let him try to get out without us both." I grinned. Apulo fussed over Cillian more than Lena did.

"I won't," I told him.

"*Mo duíne gràhadh*," Cillian murmured, when Apulo had left us. "You are going home."

"Back to Sorham," I said. "Home is here."

"Will you go to Gundarstorp, though? To see your brother, and your family?"

"Yes, likely. The new *Ti'ach* is only a short ride south, as you know."

"And you believe Roghan will provide for it? I am still not entirely happy that there are no lands to support the school, but asking the lords to give up part of their estates and their people is not reasonable, not yet."

"I wonder," I said idly, feeling the heat of the water beginning to relax my neck and shoulders, "which *Teannasach* ordered the lands given for the first *Ti'acha?*"

Cillian told me, without hesitation, of course. "But our leaders had more authority then," he added. "Ruar cannot do the same, or not without causing discontent."

"You would think," I said, "that after eight years all the *Härren* would have accepted Sorham is part of Linrathe again. They were pleased enough when Ruar married a Marai woman, after all."

"But an earl's daughter, not royal," Cillian said. "Was that a mistake, I wonder?"

"There was no royal daughter," I pointed out. "And the marriage bound powerful earls to Ruar, and to Linrathe." We'd discussed this a hundred times. I wondered why it was on Cillian's mind tonight.

"Going back to the question of food for the *Ti'ach*, my brother's promised fish and wool and mutton," I said, "and I imagine it will be much the same from Pietar and Karl, whose lands are close. Roghan tells me he will send his sons, too, although Hairle is angry with his father about that. He is sixteen, a man, not a schoolboy, he says."

"A sixteen-year old from Gundarstorp?" Cillian said. "Dangerous creatures, they can be, insinuating themselves into a man's heart."

"No more dangerous than a visiting *toscaire*," I said.

He chuckled, lifting his hand out of the water to put an arm around my shoulders. "I am long past being dangerous, at least in that way," he said. I felt the touch of the silver marriage bracelet on his arm. It had been mine, once, it and the one on Lena's wrist. I had given them to Cillian on the eve of their wedding.

"I disagree," I murmured. Grey streaked his hair, and lines of pain never fully alleviated scored his face, but to me he was as beautiful as he had been the night I had fallen in love, watching him dance to the music I was playing. Twenty-three years ago, that had been. Grace unfettered, I had written later, although he couldn't be described as graceful now. I didn't care. That he was alive and that I was here at the *Ti'ach* with him was more than enough.

We sat for some time, not talking, until we heard Apulo clear his throat in the anteroom. With a wry smile, I moved away. Apulo knew everything there was to know about all of us, but his personal history meant we were careful with expressions of affection between men in front of him, regardless of how comfortable he was with us now. I stood in the water, and between Apulo and me we helped Cillian out.

We wrapped towels around our waists and went to dry and dress. "Will you want another massage later?" Apulo asked quietly, drying Cillian's back.

"I think not," Cillian said. "But the baths again in the early morning, please."

Chapter 2

DINNERS AT THE *Ti'ach* meant a topic of discussion chosen by one of the adults, or occasionally by the senior students. If Cillian chose, it was frequently a passage from Catilius he offered for the *daltai's* thoughts, and tonight was no different. "Catilius wrote: *Look back over the past, at the empires that rose and fell, and predict the future.* What is he telling us?" he asked. As always, he began with the youngest students, asking supplemental questions if necessary, to elicit an answer.

"That nothing lasts," Gwenna said, when it was her turn. "But if this is true, *Comiádh,* then why do we work so hard to maintain our governments, and the relationships among our lands?"

"What happens if we do not?" he asked in return.

"War," Tamm said. He was the oldest of the students, although not quite old enough to remember coherently. Images, perhaps, and fear. "Anarchy."

"Indeed," Cillian said. "Look around this table, *daltai.* I, as you know, am Linrathan born, but now a citizen of Ésparias and by extension of the Eastern Empire. The Lady of this house is Ésparian; the lord Sorley was born in Sorham, the Captain in Casil and Apulo from a land even further east. And among you, I count two of Ésparias, five from Linrathe, and two from Sorham. We live together in peace, with common goals. How do we do that?"

"Because there are rules," Colm said.

"Who decides on the rules?" Cillian asked. "Am I free to do what I wish?"

None of the students spoke. "I don't believe so," Tamm said finally. "Even the *Comiádh* has rules, does he not? Expectations? "

"Yes," Cillian said. "I am less bound than Lord Sorley, whose responsibilities as a *scáeli* are set by his council, but still I am not free to do what I wish, either in how I lead this *Ti'ach*, or in my public life."

"*Comiádh*?" Tamm said, "I would like to ask something, but I'm not sure if it is appropriate."

"Is it on topic?" Cillian enquired.

"The question came from your last statement." I smiled to myself. Tamm had been twelve when he came to us, quiet and shy; he was often still quiet, but his confidence now was apparent. He would be an excellent travelling teacher, and, perhaps, a *comiádh* himself one day. He was a competent musician, too, but he lacked the skill, or interest, to be a *scáeli*.

"You said you are not free to do as you might wish, in your public life. But you have two public roles, sir." He hesitated. "Should I go on?"

Cillian looked down the table at Lena. He spread his hands. "There is no reason not to," he said. "One rarely influences the other, but the question is valid."

"Which role constrains you more? "

"Day to day," Cillian said, "the role of *Comiádh* governs my life. The other concerns me only occasionally, when the envoys visit, or the *Princip*. But beyond those times, and my signature on a few letters each year, I am the *Comiádh*, and so its constraints have a greater influence."

"Is that true?" Gwenna asked. A direct rebuttal to the *Comiádh* — whether he was her father or not — was rare from a student of her age. Only when the head of the *Ti'ach* had invited a *dalta* to call him by his name did anyone, traditionally, challenge him.

"Why is it not, in your eyes?" Cillian replied.

"You are *Comiádh* of this *Ti'ach* through an appointment by the *Teannasach*. But your other role," she frowned a little, "comes from the Empress of the Eastern Empire, and Linrathe pays tribute to her. She is therefore the greater power, and the *Teannasach* the lesser, so *Comiádh* is the lesser role."

"That is one way to measure the value of the roles," Cillian said. "Is there another?"

"One title is very new," Tamm said. "The other has been in existence for generations, and is greatly honoured."

"But *Comiádh* means only that you teach us, and while that is important, isn't advising the *Princip* and the Governor of Ésparias more so?" Colm asked.

"There is no correct answer," Cillian said. "What we do in our lives, the roles we take on, will be seen differently by different people, because the value a person gives a role or an action is a reflection of what they believe is important. But I will ask you this: would the leaders of Ésparias seek my advice, had I not been educated at this *Ti'ach*? Would being the last Emperor's son be sufficient?"

"Then you value being *Comiádh* more?" Tamm ventured. "What about you, Lord Sorley? There are parallels between you, aren't there? If I am not presuming?"

"Present your argument," I said.

"Both you and the *Comiádh* advise your leaders. You were both heirs to a position you relinquished, although you retain the titles for diplomatic reasons, I believe. Both of you were important *toscairen*, and both of you chose to give that up to return to this school in Linrathe. Are you happy with your choice too?"

Lena's eyes met mine along the table. There was nothing — other than his family — that Cillian valued more than being Perras's chosen successor at this *Ti'ach*. My appointment as *scáeli* here meant both my lifelong dreams had come true, although that was too personal to speak of to the students. But Tamm had asked me a direct question, and I thought there might just be more than one reason for it.

"I am happy in this life, yes," I said. "It is an honour to be the *scáeli* of this house, and I am a *scáeli* before anything else," Just as Cillian was the *Comiádh*, first. But beyond our official positions, beyond the calm and ordered life of the *Ti'ach*, we had other work, all four of us. Work the *daltai* knew — and could know — nothing about.

"Thank you, Lord Sorley," Tamm said. "May I make one further observation?"

"Go ahead."

"We think, as children, that the adults around us are free," he said. He glanced at all of us, but I thought his eyes lingered on Druise and me. "But you are not. We are not, I must learn to say soon. I appreciate the example you have set me, in my years here."

He will still be here when I return, I thought, so I have time. Time to tell him how to conduct himself as a *channàdarra* man in Linrathe and Sorham. It wouldn't be the first conversation of this sort I had had over my years at the *Ti'ach*. I wished someone had done it for me, when I was a student here. Perras had tried, but he could not speak from experience. Perhaps I would have a word before I left, I decided.

"If we have taught you that, we have taught you much," Cillian said. "Apulo will supervise tonight, *daltai*. Tamm, will you assist until first bedtime?"

"Of course," Tamm said. Cillian stood, indicating the end of the formal dinner.

"Gwenna," he said. "I gave you an assignment. Is it ready for review?"

"Yes, *Comiádh*," she said.

"Then will you accompany us?" In public, Cillian treated his children exactly as he did the other *daltai*, with the same grave courtesy and expectation of obedience. In private, he was very different.

"So, *mo nihéan*," he said, as soon as the door to their rooms closed. "You have catalogued your grievances?" I heard the amusement in his voice, and so did Gwenna. She glared at him. Only in her expressions of frustration or anger could I see Lena in her.

"If you are not going to take me seriously," she said, "I will ask to leave."

"Cillian," Lena warned. He sobered.

"I apologize," he said to Gwenna. "Your complaint of secrecy is valid. We have not told you enough. Sit, *leannan*, and tell us what you want to know. You may have a little watered wine, if you wish."

"Not now," she said, taking a seat. "Could I wait, and have it later?"

"You may." We all sat.

"This is what I have heard," Gwenna began, taking a folded piece of paper from a pocket. "and I want to know what is true, and what isn't." She looked down at the paper. "I'll just give it to you. There is one other thing, but..." She hesitated. "I didn't want to write it down, and I don't want to ask you. Or mother."

"Then ask Sorley, or Druisius," Cillian said. He took the list from Gwenna, scanning it quickly. "This is quite a lot, Gwenna. More than we can talk about tonight. Is one thing more important to you than the others?"

"Yes," she said, a little defiantly. "You have always told us promises are binding and should not be made unless you will keep them. But you broke your oath to Linrathe to save your life, didn't you?"

"No," Cillian said evenly. "I did not, Gwenna. I had resigned as *toscaire* some years earlier, which freed me of my oath to Linrathe and its people."

"Then if not to Linrathe, then to your *Teannasach*," she persisted. "Sorley, when you stopped being a *toscaire*, you swore an oath to Ruar, didn't you?"

"I did," I said.

"Then you would have too," she said, turning back to her father, "to Donnalch." Cillian's eyes met Lena's, a long look.

"At my trial," he said, "who was *Teannasach*?"

"Lorcann," she said. "Donnalch was dead."

"Had I had the opportunity to swear allegiance to him?"

"I suppose not," she admitted. "But allegiance to a new *Teannasach* is assumed until there has been time for the oaths to be made, so it makes no difference."

"Your argument is correct," he said, "but the assumption you have made is not."

Just tell her, I thought. Don't play games. Then I mentally shook my head at my own reaction: this was Gwenna, brought up nearly since she could talk to think about what was hidden by words, about what was not said, as much as what was. Both her father and I used language as tools, but very differently.

Cillian waited. Gwenna's frown deepened, her eyes narrowed and distant, thinking. A hand went to her hair, twisting its almost-black strands. She cocked her head. "You were not sworn to Donnalch?"

"I was not," he said. "Well done, *mo nihéan*."

"Why not?" Curious, more than confused.

"He would not accept it. He had no trust in me; had not since we were children together at this *Ti'ach*," Cillian said, no emotion in his voice at all. Just a fact, to be related. I glanced at Lena. Her eyes were on Cillian, not Gwenna.

"Why not?" she asked again, but this time disbelief coloured her voice.

"Donnalch was twelve when he decided that since my mother had borne me to an Empire's soldier, she was a traitor to Linrathe. Remember that Linrathe and Ésparias were enemies at that time, Gwenna, so that view would have been widely held, and he would have heard it from his own father, no doubt. His thinking was this: since my mother and I had both been brought up by the same people, if they had raised her to be a traitor, then they must have also raised me to be the same."

That conversation had led Perras, then the *Comiádh,* to tell Cillian he would need to be man of utmost integrity, and always keep his word. Dagney had explained it to me, many years later. What might have been different, if that accusation, and Perras's counsel, had never been spoken?

"But that's a fallacy," Gwenna said.

"Perras explained that to him, but he chose to follow his emotions rather than logic. Even when we were both adults, I never had his full trust."

"So you were free to choose Ésparias over Linrathe," she said.

"Not entirely free. I could make that choice only because my father was willing to acknowledge me."

"Can I tell my classmates this?" Her voice trailed off. "But it won't help."

"Kitten," Druise said, "tell us what they are saying."

"All sorts of things," she said, "and sometimes they contradict each other. But — " She straightened her shoulders a little. "I tried not to be upset. I'm sorry I was earlier today, *Athàir.* I analysed what they were saying, as you taught me, and as I have learned to do too at the White Fort."

"And your conclusion?" Cillian asked.

"They think the same as Donnalch, that you cannot be trusted. *Mathàir?*" She turned to Lena, and I thought she looked about ten again for a moment. "Has he ever broken a promise to you?"

"Once," Lena said. Gwenna went very still, her eyes wide. "In Casil, trying to ensure my safety, and that of all of us, by attempting to convince the Empress to support the war against the Marai. He had promised to be constant, and he wasn't. I forgave him, under the circumstances," she added, with a smile.

"And that is the only time?" Apprehension quivered in her voice.

"Yes," Lena replied. "Haven't I just said so?"

"*Mo nihéan gràhadh,* will you listen for a moment?" Cillian asked. "You have heard my loyalty questioned, and especially my reasons for accepting my father's acknowledgment of me. Those questions come from those who only know part of the truth. That both Casyn and Ruar, who know it all, continue to trust me should tell you more, but you must never accept such trust blindly."

"Then you haven't told me all the truth?" Gwenna asked immediately. I swore silently.

"It is not entirely my story to tell, Gwenna," her father answered. I watched her, seeing the confusion, mistrust battling against love. Oh, Gwenna, I thought. I know almost exactly how you feel.

"Shall we have wine now?" I asked.

"A good idea," Druise said. "Kitten, you will share a cup with us, and then you will let us talk, the four of us, yes?"

"All right," she said.

"Gwenna, we have a ritual with wine, of an evening," Cillian said. "Sorley began it, many years ago. Do not drink when you are given your wine, until the toast is made." He pushed himself up and went to the sideboard. I joined him. He poured five cups of wine, watering two — his and Gwenna's — extensively, the others less so. He handed one to me. I gave it to Lena, the first cup of the night always hers, my acknowledgment of the primacy of her bond with Cillian. Then Druise's. Gwenna was next. My own I took from Cillian's hand, feeling even in his daughter's presence the light brush of his fingers.

Cillian raised his cup. "*Seek the truth, by which no one was ever truly harmed.*" Catilius, of course. I wasn't sure I agreed.

Chapter 3

WHEN GWENNA HAD LEFT us, Lena uttered a deep sigh and sank into a chair. "I am not looking forward this summer," she said. "She is going to be confused and angry, and *so* pleasant to live with. Wasn't it enough to explain that you were not sworn to Donnalch, Cillian? Why did you have to imply there was more to it?"

"Because there was, *käresta*."

"I know that. Does she need to?"

"I believe so." Lena didn't reply. She wasn't angry, I knew, just considering the situation.

"Do you truly believe Donnalch never came to trust you?" I asked Cillian. "Not even in his last days at Fritjof's hall?"

Cillian sipped his wine. "At the very end, when he knew he would be killed, I think so," he replied. "What choice had he? But I have wondered, over the years, his reasons for taking me with him."

"To observe, and listen, and remember," Lena said. "That is what I recall him saying."

"And would he not also be observing and listening to see how Fritjof and his men acted towards me?" Cillian ran a hand through his hair. "What had Liam told him?"

"Kitten needs to hear the truth," Druise said bluntly. "What you did, Cillian, and why."

"She's too young," I said.

"She is young," Lena said. "But better she hears it from us than have her mind filled with rumours and half-truths at the cadet school."

"All of it?" I asked. "Even — ?"

"A certain question will follow, I think," Cillian said. "I see no other reason for her asking if I had broken a promise to you, *käresta*."

"Maybe she does need to hear the truth," I said. An idea had appeared, swirled, coalesced. I wasn't sure I liked it, but it made sense. "Or most of it. But not as a lesson, Cillian, the bare facts. Not like you told me."

"What are you suggesting?" Lena asked.

"She needs stories," I said, "to give her perspective."

"Stories told by you, with all your *scáeli's* skills?" Cillian asked. "A tale spun to coerce and convince, my lord Sorley?"

"Yes."

"But you are leaving in two days," Lena said.

"I am," I said. "But why can't I take her with me?"

The immediate objection came, of course, from Druise. "You cannot protect her properly," he growled.

"But you could," Lena said. "Sorley, would it break tradition if Druise went with you to guard Gwenna?" *Scáeli'en* travelled unarmed, except for our belt knives, and usually alone, although there were exceptions to that.

"Not considering who she is," I said.

"Then…" Lena turned to Cillian. "There is wisdom in Sorley's suggestion," she said to him. "In Tirvan, it was other adult women who helped us make sense of our rules and traditions, when we were young and argumentative."

"You, argumentative?" Cillian said. "I cannot imagine it, *käresta*." His eyes were soft, as they always were when he looked at her in their private rooms. Lena pulled the cushion from behind her back and threw it at him. He caught it easily, laughing.

"Such behaviour from the *Comiádh* and the Lady," I said. "And what were you like at fourteen, Cillian?"

"I would ruin Druisius's good opinion of me, were I to say," Cillian answered. He tossed the cushion back to Lena. Druise snorted.

"If I had one, perhaps," he said. "Am I going north?"

"I have no objection," Cillian said. "It is an excellent idea. But it is not my decision. What about the guard, Lena?"

"They can be my responsibility for the summer," Lena said. "But are you completely sure, Sorley?"

"If you are, yes," I said. "I may well be glad Druise is with me, though." Since earliest childhood, it had been Druise Gwenna had gone to when she was upset or confused.

"No doubt," Cillian said, understanding. "And now I am going to make an exception, and have a second cup of wine. Who is joining me?"

We talked no further about it. Druise and I played music, and we drank a bit more wine, Cillian limiting himself to two watered cups. He'd mixed the few drugs he sometimes allowed himself into one, and he was relaxed, free of pain. Not terribly late in the evening, Lena yawned. "Bedtime," she said. She got up from the floor where she had been leaning against Cillian's good leg, her usual place when she listened to music. She bent to kiss him. "Try to get some sleep."

"I will see you in the morning, *käresta*." He smiled up at her. Druise picked his *cithar* up, stretching as he stood.

"Good night," he said. "See you at breakfast."

We let them leave. I stood, holding out a hand to Cillian to help him up. We walked across the silent hall to the annex and his library. The door between it and the adjoining treatment room was open, lamplight flickering in the space beyond. His *xache* set—mine, really: Irmgard has sent it to me, in gratitude for learning her sons were alive—sat on the table, the carved walrus ivory gleaming palely as I lit a lamp. Cillian went to the shelves that lined one wall, pouring me a small amount of *fuisce*.

I picked up the white cat from the chair where he had been sleeping, transferring him to my shoulder. He purred, rubbing his head against mine before jumping down to stalk out into the hall. Sitting, I looked at the gameboard. We were part-way through a game, although we hadn't played for some weeks. The lamp flickered. I deliberated over my move, taking a sip of the peaty spirit. I moved a piece, capturing one of his, eliciting a faint sound from Cillian. I looked up at him, seeing the amusement in his eyes, dark in the lamplight. I had left myself vulnerable.

Reaching out, he took my game piece in one deft move. He might never walk easily again, or dance, but his hands were as graceful and skilled as they had been before that terrible autumn, nearly fifteen years past. "Will you never learn?" he asked.

"Someday, perhaps," I said. "But you don't really want me to, do you? It will always suit you to be the teacher."

"Not always." He smiled, slowly, his true, radiant smile, rarely seen. "Not in all things, *Somhairle*."

<hr>

"GOOD MORNING, SORLEY," APULO said quietly, when I met him in the corridor just before dawn the next morning. "There is a jug of hot water by your door."

"Thank you," I said. I picked up the jug of water, crossing our sitting room to the bedroom that was nominally Druise's, and almost never used. As I washed, I thought about my dream just before waking. Apulo had been in it, as the enslaved, frightened *castrati* he had been, arriving from Casil fourteen summers past. What he had been subjected to at the baths, by men who saw a pretty boy who could not refuse them, made me angry even now. When Druise had told me that Apulo had been a singer before his enslavement — his sentence for stealing a *cithar* — somehow that engendered even deeper anger. He had already paid a terrible price to keep his high, pure voice, and that had not been his choice, either.

Why am I thinking of this? I wondered, as I dressed again. But it wasn't hard to work out. Gwenna's questions would have no easy answers. In offering to tell her the stories, I would have to face my own memories: disillusionment and doubt, uncertainty and discontent, and deep sadness and deeper joy. Much of what I remembered was confused now, events recalled out of sequence. Gwenna's birth was a fixed point, and I knew Cillian and Lena were married just before that, and that the Governor arrived after it. Two other memories were as clear as the day they happened. But others were distorted by time, both the details and the chronology blurred.

I didn't think it mattered. If I wanted Gwenna to truly hear what I had to tell her, I would have to wait for her questions. Even then, I would need every *scáeli's* skill I had to explain her father's actions, to help her understand his reasons. All my skill, all my own hard-won acceptance, and all the love I had for them both.

CHAPTER 4

14 YEARS EARLIER

SPRING CAME EARLY, THAT first year after the Marai defeat. Grass gleamed green in the pastures and coltsfoot flowered a week or more ahead of its time. The strong southerly winds brought swallows back to their mud nests under the eaves of byre and cottage, and they brought a fleet from Casil, too.

We had expected it, but still we barely had time to prepare. A messenger had been sent from the Eastern Fort, but the ships had travelled almost as fast. A flagship, and six ships behind it, bringing the new Governor of the Western Empire and his entourage.

"How convenient for us that Decanius is not here," Cillian said, as we walked out into the sunshine. He leaned heavily on his stick, and our progress was slow, but he didn't need my arm. "First impressions, on both sides, will not be marred by his influence." Professing an interest in horse breeding, the Procurator had decided to visit the grassland villages to see the first foals of the year. Talyn had gone with him, taking Druisius to translate. I wondered now if Decanius had guessed the Governor would arrive soon, and chose to absent himself.

"Accompany me to the docks, if you will, Lord Sorley," Casyn had requested, when the ships had been sighted a little earlier. "The officers you have been teaching can converse adequately, but for this I need your fluency in Casilan." The stairs were still too difficult for Cillian. He would wait at the gate that led to the harbour.

We were at the harbour before the ships were rowed in, the breeze off the water catching cloaks and hair. The first vessel approached. Oars were withdrawn, ropes thrown, and the ship eased in beside the jetty. Rufin escorted a man in middle age off the ship, his hair close-cropped hair, his expression genial. He looked around him in interest. Two other men followed closely behind them.

"Governor," Rufin said, "may I introduce the *Princip* of the Western Empire, Casyn? *Princip*, the Governor of this Royal province, Livius." I translated quietly, although the gist was clear. Livius stepped forward, offering an arm to Casyn.

"*Princip*. I look forward to our work together."

Casyn replied, in the formal words I had taught him. I introduced myself, in both my roles. Livius smiled and made an appropriate reply. His eyes were friendly, I thought. "Where is the Procurator Decanius?" he asked.

"Inspecting our horse breeding locales, some days east," Casyn answered, after I'd explained. Diplomatic, making it sound as if it was an official duty. Livius pursed his lips.

"We had little warning of your arrival, Governor," I said. "Your ships almost outpaced the messenger."

He nodded. "Now a difficult question, one I am commanded to ask immediately so that word can be sent back to the Empress as quickly as possible. The lord Cillian? He was not expected to live, the last we heard."

I glanced at Casyn: he would have heard Cillian's name. With a motion of his fingers he indicated I should speak. "The lord Cillian," I said, the title strange on my lips, "has made nearly a full recovery, and waits for you at the fort. He is lame, and cannot climb the stairs, but otherwise is healthy. And," I said, for my own reasons, "he is married, and newly a father."

Livius smiled. "How fortunate. The Empress will be pleased. Now, *Princip*, may we go to the fort? I have instructions for you, and personal letters to deliver. And Rufin tells me there are baths?"

"*Princip*?" I asked. "Do you wish me to stay here to translate for the ships?"

"No need," Rufin said, in Casyn's language. "Some of your officers came to Casil with us in the autumn." He gestured to two men behind him on the quay. "They have taught me enough. I can manage."

"Excellent," Casyn said. "Thank you, Captain. Please accompany us; Lord Sorley, you too, please."

Cillian had left the gate to stand near the top of the steps, supporting himself with his cane. *Filus Imperium de Westani* had been appended to his signature on the treaty that had made this land a province of the Eastern Empire, and he wore the grey-and-white of his father's office. "Governor," he said in his flawless Casilan, "I welcome you to Wall's End fort. I am Cillian, son of the late Emperor Callan, and the *Princip*'s nephew."

"Lord Cillian," Livius said, offering his hand again. "Your recovery will bring the Empress great relief."

"I am pleased to hear it," Cillian said. "The Empress is well? I have written to her, if that is not too great a presumption."

"The Empress is very well," Livius replied. "And the letter is no presumption at all, my lord."

"Major," Cillian said. "The Western Empire has only military ranks, Governor."

"If you prefer it, yes," Livius said easily. I translated the conversation for Casyn, quietly. We entered the fort, our pace slowed to accommodate Cillian. At Casyn's workroom the door guards saluted. Livius returned their salutes. Wine and pastries waited on the central table, Birel standing against a wall. At Casyn's signal he served both before leaving us.

"Before any other topics are discussed," the Governor said, after an appreciative sip of the wine, "I have a letter for you, *Princip*, from the Empress, written in your language by our most competent official, but you will forgive any errors. He has only had a few months to learn. Although," he tapped his chin with a loose fist, "the presence of the Lord Sorley, as his country's representative, might be inappropriate."

"May the *Princip* read the letter first, and make that judgement?" Cillian asked.

"As you wish." The Governor handed a sealed letter to Casyn. He broke the wax, unrolling the vellum. His eyes scanned the writing. Carefully, he put the letter down.

"I see," he said. "I would prefer the Lord Sorley to stay. Better Linrathe's envoy is aware from the beginning of what has been ordered."

"Certainly," Livius replied, genially. He sat, apparently completely relaxed, looking around.

"Our land has a new name," Casyn said to us, "one that better places it in the Eastern Empire. From today, our country is to be known as

Ésparias."

"The Western Land," Cillian said, "in Heræcrian. Was this our land's name before, Governor?"

"So I am told. Do you speak Heræcrian, Major?"

"I am learning," Cillian said. "The physician Gnaius is teaching me, when we both have a little time."

"Do you approve of the name, *Princip*?" Livius asked. He sounded as if he cared.

"It is appropriate," Casyn said. "I expect it will take a little time for it to become reflexive on the tongue."

"No doubt," the Governor agreed. "Now, as to the second directive, is there child to be sent? Or is the Major's newborn —" He turned to Cillian. "Forgive me. Son or daughter?"

"Daughter," Cillian said.

"Daughter," Livius repeated "Is she the only heir? We would not expect her to be sent to Casil to be educated, not for some years."

Cillian's jaw tightened almost imperceptibly. "I would hope not."

"The presumptive heir, Governor, is my daughter's son, Faolyn." Casyn said. "He is nine."

"Of sufficient age," Livius said. "Can he be ready in ten days, or perhaps less? You may send companions and an escort befitting his rank, of course."

He turned to me. "Lord Sorley, the Empress extends an invitation to Linrathe, if your leaders would like a child of their house to also be educated in Casil."

The only appropriate child was Ruar, and Liam, his great-uncle and regent, would never agree. "I will make the invitation known, Governor."

"Now," Livius said, "we have much to discuss. The Procurator has completed the census and land surveys, I trust?"

"I can answer that, as the *Princip's* adjutant," Cillian said. "The accounting is complete, and the composition of our cohorts, and our ranks, have been aligned with Casil's."

"Very good. Tomorrow will be soon enough to review those figures, I think. *Princip*, I would like to see your fort and your men. Will you show me?"

"Of course," Casyn said.

Cillian made an apologetic grimace. "I will accompany you, but I may not be able to walk as far or stand as long as is needed. The Lord Sorley could also translate, if you wish."

"I think not," the Governor said. "Perhaps one of the officers who returned with me?" No surprise, I thought. Why would he allow me to hear his opinions?

"Major, this is not your area of responsibility," Casyn said to Cillian. "My other adjutant, Michan, has been more concerned with matters concerning the troops," he added, addressing the Governor. "I will request he join us."

Dismissed, Cillian and I stood to leave. "Major," Casyn said, casually, "consider who should accompany Faolyn to Casil. An officer with proficiency in the language, and an appropriate guard, I think."

CHAPTER 5

"MY WORKROOM," CILLIAN SAID to me in the corridor. We didn't speak until we'd reached the room and the door was closed. "Your impressions?"

"A man used to power, and to being obeyed," I said.

"Close to Eudekia, and not a friend of Decanius, I would say." He leaned on his cane. "The Empress gave in to Quintus on the Procurator, but has prevailed in her choice of Governor. If Decanius anticipated this, it more fully explains his attempt to consolidate power and wealth before this man's arrival."

He sat, stretching his bad leg out in front of him. Without asking I moved the footstool into place. "What do you think of this request to send Faolyn to Casil?" I asked.

"Order," he said, "not request. I am unsurprised: Gnaius told me once it was common practice, to bring the heirs of provinces to the palace to be brought up there." He ran a hand through his hair. "Educated, he said, in the manners and ways of Casil, although I think indoctrinated might be better word."

"What will Talyn say?" I sat down.

"Very little, most likely," he said. "In the normal course of things in this land, Sorley, he would have joined the cadets at seven."

At seven I had been learning to control my pony, irritated by a four-year-old brother who wanted to do everything I did. To be sent away from family and familiar things, to a city so far away that even the language was new — I couldn't imagine it. I'd been homesick at eighteen.

"Can Talyn go with him?"

Cillian laughed drily. "I believe the boy would be mortified, Sorley. His mother? His father would be acceptable, and perhaps should be sent, if he is alive. But tell me of the officers in your language classes: who is proficient, not just in language, but in the other qualities he or she will need to navigate the politics of the palace? I would like someone there whom we trust, who will provide us with information that is not also shared with the Governor."

I thought about the officers I taught. One was friend of Lena's.

"Yes," Cillian said, when I offered his name. "He might well be suitable. I have another thought, and not one you will like, *mo charaidh*. Who among us swore loyalty not just to the *Princip*, but to his heirs, and has sources of information within the palace that no one else will have?"

Druisius. I bit back my first instinctive 'no'. Druise was a soldier of the Western Empire — Ésparias — before anything else. "How long will Faolyn be expected to stay in Casil?"

"For several years, I should think. But I was not thinking to send Druisius for so long, Sorley. A few months, to allow him to re-establish friendships, or perhaps even connections with his family. Someone who would write to a soldier in a far province, but unimportant enough that those letters would not be considered of interest to anyone else."

I spread my hands. "He is yours to command, Cillian."

"But you do not like the idea."

"Would you?"

"Were it Lena being deployed away from me for some months? No." He studied me. "Do you care that much for him, Sorley?"

"Does it matter?"

"I must consider it, in ordering a man away from his *consor*."

"Which answer will make you feel better?" I asked, abruptly irritated. "Yes or no? If I say yes, will it relieve your remorse over my feelings for you, but make the decision to send Druise away harder? Or do you prefer no, which makes it easier to have Druise go to Casil, but resolves nothing between us?"

He took a deep breath, and another. Gods, I thought, why had I raised my voice? He was only six weeks free of the poppy, and after standing so long today he'd be in considerable pain. "I'm sorry," I said.

He shook his head, not speaking. I reached out to touch a clenched hand. "The real answer is I don't know, Cillian. Perhaps a summer apart would make that clearer."

He half-smiled. "Not only for you, perhaps."

"Perhaps," I said. His hand relaxed under mine. "But if Druise baulks at leaving someone he loves, he'll be thinking of Gwenna, not me."

That elicited a full smile. "His Kitten. If she were being sent, we could not keep him from going."

"No." I sat back. "But Lena will never let Eudekia have her."

"Nor I," he said. "She is not to be a piece in the Eastern Empire's games. I would agree to her going only if Lena and I went with her, to counteract the indoctrination. But it should never happen: Faolyn has a younger sister."

"But Gwenna is an heir," I said.

"In theory, but unlikely to mean anything. I have met Faolyn; he is a bright boy, and thoughtful, and I see no reason he will not be competent to be *Princip* in time."

Except that children died, or I would have never been heir to Gundarstorp, my older brother lost to fever when I was two or three. I thought better of saying so. The day before I'd gone to see Lena and the baby in a free moment. I'd found Lena trying to calm a screaming Gwenna. "Colic," she'd said, to my question. "Or so Kyreth says. Apparently, she will outgrow it."

"Soon, I hope," I'd replied, the baby's piercing cries making my ears hurt. "You look tired."

"I'm not getting much rest," she'd admitted.

Nor was Gwenna's father, I thought now, looking at the shading of fatigue under his eyes, the skin purple from more than his immediate pain. I wondered if he was taking the valerian that helped him sleep. Probably not.

"Who is doing your exercises and massage, with Druise away?" I asked.

"Gnaius. He would be doing the massage in any case; a new technique, working deeper muscles and nerves, he tells me. The exercises take only a little longer."

"So you wouldn't miss Druise."

"Not for that reason, but, yes, I would miss him. As would Lena, for his cheerfulness and practicality, and his kindness, and he and I are friends, beyond officer and soldier."

An unexpected friendship, and one that confused me a little, this understanding between a Casilani soldier of little learning and Cillian, educated to Linrathe's highest standards — and beyond, now. I was, to my shame, obscurely jealous of their relationship, disturbed in part by the simple fact that Druise would never tell me what he and Cillian talked about. I had the sense that, in the long days of weaning himself from the poppy, Druise had become a confidant for Cillian in a way neither Lena nor I were. *I wish I knew what haunts him,* Lena had said to me once of Cillian. I thought Druisius just might know.

CHAPTER 6

THE NEXT DAY LIVIUS had closeted himself with Casyn and his two adjutants, and I, looking at the steady rain outside, had worked all day on my music, although I ate the midday meal with Lena. Late in the afternoon Birel had brought me a note from the Governor, requesting a meeting with Linrathe's envoy the next morning.

"And the Major asks if you would join him in the baths," Birel added.

Just Cillian? I didn't ask. The baths were kept for Cillian's private use late in the afternoon, Gnaius decreeing that the exercises and massage he required should be performed privately, and immediately after a period in the hot pool. Casyn, and sometimes Michan, joined him frequently now, at least in the pool, the only time they could find to privately discuss strategy. "I have been a soldier all my life," Casyn had told him, in my presence, when Cillian had expressed reluctance. "I have seen scars worse than yours."

He was alone. "Casyn and Michan are still with Livius," he told me. The attendant left us; now I was there, he would stand outside the door, preventing anyone else from entering; it also meant any conversation could not be overheard. I settled into the steaming water beside him. "You are meeting with the Governor tomorrow in your official role," Cillian said.

"Yes. What should I know?" I'd guessed this might be the reason he'd asked me to come.

"I believe he dislikes Decanius; I would like your thoughts on that, afterwards. Otherwise, I would say he is experienced in governance, with very clear ideas of how to — integrate, I think is the right word — this distant land into the Eastern Empire. Perhaps more open to considering its history and traditions than the Procurator, especially as how its laws have evolved from Casil's."

"What does that mean for Linrathe?"

"The most pressing issue will be tribute, I should think." He shifted on the ledge, only the tiniest flicker of muscles around his eyes telling of his discomfort. Under the water, he rubbed his left thigh. "The treaty does not lay out the amount to be paid."

"Liam plans to offer what was paid to Varsland," I said slowly, wondering how much I should tell Cillian. "But I wonder how he can. That amount was taxed from both Linrathe and Sorham in a time of prosperity. Now all the cost must be borne by Linrathe, and from estates that have lost not just men and women, but whose flocks and crops were ravaged by the Marai."

"I hear the *Harr*'s son speaking," Cillian said. He grimaced, stretching his leg, his hand still massaging the muscles.

"Would it help if I did that?" I asked, touching his thigh with my fingertips.

He looked at me in what I thought was surprise. "No," he said after a moment, "no, my lord Sorley. Better leave it to Gnaius, whose hands will give relief without unintended consequences."

"I suppose I could do harm," I said. "But I hate seeing you in pain."

"It will ease. You may wish to think about this: Livius spoke today of building a line of forts along the coast, north from Torrey, to protect against any further raids from the sea. To do that, he will need timber, something Linrathe has in quantity."

That was indisputable. Along the Durrains, and stretching out into the hills and valleys below them, grew an ancient forest of pine. I — and Turlo — had followed tracks through it when we'd travelled north, tracks made by hunters and trappers. But outside the autumn cull of the forest's wildlife, few ventured into it.

"It could be cut in winter," I said. A thought struck me. "Should you have told me about the forts?"

He smiled, wryly. "Most likely not. I forget we are envoys for two separate countries who cannot share all we know. If Livius mentions them to you, I would appreciate it if you would let him believe the information is new. If he doesn't — " He stopped. "I cannot ask you to not tell Liam."

Except he just had, indirectly. To my surprise, he put a hand on my shoulder before leaning over to kiss my temple. "You must do what you believe is right."

"If anyone sees you do that, Cillian, they will think we do share more than is appropriate for our positions." He hadn't moved his hand. I covered it with my own for a moment. I'd sounded judgemental. "Although some may think that already, given the amount of time I spend with you and Lena."

"They may," Cillian said. "But you are right; there are expectations that must be seen to be met. For your sake as much as mine." I heard the door open, and Gnaius's voice calling a greeting. Time for Cillian's treatment, and for me to leave. I'd offered to play music for him while the manipulations to his leg and back were made, but he'd refused. He would allow neither Lena nor me to witness the treatments, whereas Druise —

Stop it, I told myself. It is Druise's job. I climbed out of the pool and went into the antechamber to dry and dress. I was just readying to leave when Cillian called from the massage table in the adjoining space. "Eat with us, Sorley?"

"Not tonight," I called back. "I promised music in the senior commons." It wasn't quite a lie; I had promised, but I hadn't specified this evening. But I would be welcomed; I always was.

I made my way back to my bedroom late in the evening, my *ladhar* in hand. Too late: I should have left earlier, to think about what I needed to say to the Governor in the morning. But I wasn't going to sleep; I was restless, unsettled, frustration I didn't understand simmering. I missed Druise, both for his cheerful company and in my bed. I didn't love him — the last few months had told me that — but music and shared pleasure made us good companions.

Yet Cillian was sending him away, knowing it left me without a bulwark against my feelings. And, I fumed, he'd had the temerity to touch me casually, kiss me, in the baths today. That he was affectionate towards me physically when we were all together was one thing: he was with Druise, too, to a lesser extent. But alone and unclothed?

I knew, because of his reluctance to marry Lena, that his injuries had left him incapable of physical arousal. A temporary situation, Gnaius hoped, but would not promise. But I had no such limitations — and Cillian had acknowledged that, I realized now, in refusing my offer to massage his aching leg: *no unintended consequences.* So why ignore it, a few minutes later?

You are making too much of an unthinking gesture of affection, I told myself. Cillian knew how I felt about him, in an abstract sense, but he didn't truly understand; didn't experience the same physical longing brought on by even a brief touch of hand or lips. I picked up my *ladhar* again. Preparation for Livius could wait.

Chapter 7

SOME INNER SENSE WOKE me early; I would be on time for my meeting with the Governor. I'd worked on the song for some time, but I'd gone to sleep discontented with the music and more. But in the clarity of the first minutes after waking, the cause of at least some of the irritation revealed itself: Cillian had lied to me. *I forget we are envoys for two separate countries who cannot share all we know.* I didn't believe it. Cillian forgot nothing: Perras had taught him to remember what he read, what he heard, what he saw, preparing him for his role, and a decade as a *toscaire* had honed that skill to exquisite precision.

I washed, and shaved again, to be not thought a barbarian. At the appointed time, I presented myself to the Governor of Ésparias in the room assigned to him. He was alone.

"Lord Sorley," he said, "of Gundarstorp." He made a credible attempt at pronouncing the Linrathan word. "Where is that?" A sweep of his hand told me to sit.

"In the far north of our land," I told him. "The Marai hold it now."

"Ah," he said. "Part of the lands too difficult to defend. That was the reasoning, was it not?"

"Yes," I said, resentment and regret at that decision flattening my voice. Cillian's decision. My name on the treaty, though. He'd convinced me, he and Turlo. "Yes," I said again. "Mountains and valleys, a rough and difficult land, and many islands. Too many hiding places, and divided sympathies among the people."

"But yours were to your leader," he said, not quite a question, "the *Teannasach*."

I corrected his pronunciation, and he smiled and tried again.

"I had spent five years in Linrathe, at a *Ti'ach*," I told him. "I had met the *Teannasach* more than once; conversed with him. I chose — " I paused. I'd never articulated this to anyone, not even Cillian. "The Marai would have burned the schools, and destroyed the libraries. Songs and stories going back to our beginnings as a people; books relating our history, and that of Casil and Heræcria, too."

"You chose learning over land."

"In a way." There was more to it than that, but I doubted I could fully explain. Sorham had always looked north, as well as south, for trade and marriage; even the dialect I had spoken as a child owed much to the language of the Marai, and we shared songs and stories and beliefs. From Perras and Dagney — and Cillian — I had learned of other lands and older stories, and a sense of a greater world. Then I had travelled east, lived in Casil for a few weeks, heard history and stories and songs unknown. Life in Sorham would go on nearly as it always had, under Marai rule. Life in Linrathe would have been forever changed, its tiny, tenuous link to that wider world of thought and history lost.

"And you are a musician?" Livius's polite question brought me back to the present.

"Yes. I play an instrument not so different than your *cithar*, although the tuning is different."

"I would like to hear it," he said. "Now, Lord Sorley, there are three things related to the treaty to discuss, and one other. I would like to begin with that other, for my own understanding. Who rules in Linrathe?"

"The *Teannasach* will be Ruar, son of Donnalch," I told him. "Donnalch was *Teannasach* when the Marai began their incursions south: he was killed by their king, Fritjof. Donnalch's brother Lorcann sided with the Marai, although they killed him too: he was a means to an end, not an ally with any value in Fritjof's eyes."

"How did Ruar survive?"

"He and his cousin Kebhan were hostages to the truce between Linrathe and this land, and so were south of the Wall when the invasion began. That kept them safe."

"And why is Ruar the next *Teannasach*, and not Kebhan?"

"Kebhan is dead," I said. "He followed his father: his loyalty was to the Marai. He — or his men — killed the Emperor Callan, and nearly his son. Kebhan died for that. Had not the leader of the horse archers, Lena, put an arrow in Fritjof's throat, we would have lost the battle, even with all the Casilani support, I believe."

"I see," Livius said neutrally. "How old is Ruar?"

"Fourteen," I said. "His great-uncle Liam is regent for him until he comes of age, and his two older cousins advise him as well."

"And when is he of age?" Livius wasn't taking notes. He was sitting back, relaxed, apparently interested.

"By our laws, at sixteen: he could marry then, or inherit land in his own right, or be responsible for trade agreements."

"He rules absolutely, then?"

"No. There is a council of nobles who meet twice a year and from whom the *Teannasach* takes guidance. He leads his people, but not arbitrarily. He is expected to listen and take their opinions into account. They will meet with him soon for the first time."

"Regardless," Livius said, "Ruar will have a regent for at least two years, if I understand correctly. I would like to meet him, and his regent. Can you arrange that?"

"I will request a meeting, certainly," I said. "But Liam is an old man, Governor. I assume you expect them to travel to you?"

"Yes. It would be impolitic of me to leave Ésparias, having so recently arrived." Genially said, but firm.

"Is this an urgent meeting?"

"No. If Liam prefers to wait until the warmth of the summer, that will be soon enough. I like to meet the men I deal with, not just their envoys; that is all." I doubted that, but I wasn't going to say so. The Governor leaned forward, attentive now. "Shall we discuss the other points now, Lord Sorley?"

We spoke of tribute. I reiterated what I had said to Cillian: there were little of Linrathe's usual goods available, after the year of warfare. I did not propose timber. "Some might be paid in labour," he suggested.

"Labour? For what, Governor?"

"I am building forts along the coast," he said. I hoped I kept my face impassive. "We will begin at the river where the last battle with the Marai was, and then more in both directions, until the coast is adequately defended." He paused. "What forts I build within Ésparias are mine to determine. But the threat is from the north, so forts along Linrathe's coast would also be valuable. But I cannot compel those, only ask your *Teannasach* and his regent if they would consider cooperating in their construction."

"And this is where you see our people providing labour, in lieu of tribute?" I asked.

"In Linrathe, or here in Ésparias. Many hands will be needed."

"Who would garrison the forts in Linrathe, Governor?"

"Casilani troops, and your own," he said easily. "Details can be worked out later. But we would supply those forts from the sea, and that leads me to my third request to your Teannasach."

The third decides. The phrase from my childhood ran through my mind. "And that is?" I asked.

"While we must guard against attack and attempted invasion by the Marai," he said, "at the same time we should encourage trade. Many a peace has been built on the back of an economic relationship. To that end, a trading harbour in Linrathe would be advantageous. The Marai would then not need to sail further south, limiting the information about our fortifications their captains can take back."

"The ships that supply the forts would use this harbour to take on goods into their empty holds?" I asked.

"And do any repairs needed. If there is a suitable natural harbour, even ship-building could be possible. Opportunities for your people and your country, as you must see."

A persuasive argument. "Do you wish me to put this to the *Teannasach* in my own words, Governor? Or would you prefer to write to him?"

"Your own words, for now, I think. And," He tapped a finger on the tabletop, "you understand this is for your ears only? The *Princip* — and his advisors — have no need to hear of this yet. I can trust you with this, Lord Sorley?"

I returned his gaze as levelly as I could. "Do you have reason to believe you cannot?"

He didn't react; he was far too experienced for that. "You must know I ask questions. Your close friendship with both the Major Cillian and his wife is no secret in this fort, and your lover has been his aide and nurse. An unusual situation for an envoy from another country, you cannot deny."

"Then," I said, damping down my irritation, "you may also have been told that the only reason I am Linrathe's envoy to the Eastern Empire is that I speak Casilani better than any of my countrymen. I am not trained in diplomacy and its intrigues, Governor, but I am loyal to my *Teannasach* and my country."

"As the Major was once, I understand?"

Anger surged. I controlled it, almost. "You must discuss that with him, Governor."

He smiled approvingly. "A diplomatic answer. I am pleased that you did not leap to his defence. When will you go north to your leader?"

"The landholders meet with the *Teannasach* in a few weeks. I must be there then. Will that suffice?"

"It will. Perhaps a meeting could be arranged for a few weeks after that?"

"I will ask," I said.

CHAPTER 8

GODS, I THOUGHT, WALKING back to my workroom, I do not have the skills for this. I needed to talk to someone, and it couldn't be Cillian. Or Lena. But with Druise away, who was there? My countryman Randall, sent by Dagney to teach languages to the officers here, crossed my mind, briefly, but I rejected the idea: Linrathan or not, I didn't trust him. He liked Decanius, and that was enough to make him suspect. I was on my own.

I wrote notes on the meeting, and ate a solitary meal. Then I crossed the fort to a long, low building, the scent of wood shavings rich in my nostrils as soon as I opened the door. A man looked up from the bench where he was planing a board. "Lord Sorley. I just checked that yew I offered you. It's ready. Do you remember where it is?"

"I do," I said, and went through to the storeroom, where wood dried on racks. Yew was bow-wood, but when I'd come to the carpenter some days before, explaining my need, he'd offered me several pieces.

I hadn't heard, officially, that I would sit my *scáeli's* exams in the late summer or early autumn, but I had to presume I would. As part of demonstrating my skills, I was required to construct a new *ladhar*, beginning with seasoned, uncut boards, a process that took several months.

The carpenter had been happy to make space in the workshop for me and lend me tools as I needed them. He'd been at the soldiers' commons several times when I'd gone with Druise to play of an evening, and he liked music. I took one piece off the rack and carried back to a bench. I'd brought the *ladhar* I used most often with me, as a template. I'd built it, too, at the *Ti'ach*; I'd built several, over the years. I enjoyed the precise work, and the smell and feel of the wood as I cut and shaped it, but it all took a lot of time. My master's instrument — for that was what it would be — should be finished to a very high standard. Often they included ornamentation, in silver or gold or sometimes jewels, but that wasn't possible now. Or was it? I had money; *toscairen* were paid well enough. I would have to talk to the metalworkers, I thought. Then I turned my mind to the measurements: I couldn't get this wrong.

Hours later, I put the pieces I had cut into a chest, and locked it. I couldn't risk them being accidentally lost, or used for another purpose. I cleaned the tools, and returned them to their drawers, and then I picked up the broom. "Leave it, Lord Sorley," the carpenter said.

"Not a chance," I said, and swept up the shavings and sawdust I'd created. The carpenter grinned appreciatively.

"I watched you working," he said. "You can have a job here any time you want." I handed him the record book I had to keep, for him to sign.

"But all I can build is a *ladhar*," I said. "Not much use to you."

"You'd soon learn," he teased. My answer hadn't been true, either, I reflected as I walked back to the headquarters. I could build both barns and barrels, if I had to: my father had ensured both Roghan and I were competent with almost all the tasks required on the estate.

I stopped to see Lena; singing to Gwenna soothed her, sometimes, and the colic hadn't subsided yet. But the baby was quiet, quiet as a sleeping kitten in Druise's arms.

"Sorley!" he said, grinning up at me. Lena took her daughter from him, and he stood to embrace me. I hugged him, hard. He smelled of sweat and horse; he'd come straight to see Gwenna, I thought.

"Where were you?" Druise asked, as I poured myself wine. I explained.

"I would like to see this," he said. We talked about woodworking for a few minutes, Gwenna, remarkably, still sleeping quietly.

Druise drank the last of his wine. "I should go," he said. "Cillian will be at the baths now, yes?"

"Yes," Lena said. "But Gnaius will take care of him. You haven't seen Sorley for some time, and don't you deserve a little time off? You've been on hard duty."

"Not so hard as Captain Talyn," he said. "All I did was translate. She had to be the host, and polite. The man is a *serpens*." He stretched, rolling his shoulders. "The baths would be good. If Cillian does not need me, then I will go to the soldiers' bathhouse." He stood up, rolling his shoulders. "Come with me, Sorley?"

Should I? But Druise knew the boundaries of our relationship. And we'd both been alone for too long.

Baths and wine and a private reunion took us to early evening. We'd eat in the soldiers' commons, later. Druise was not one to linger after lovemaking: either he'd fall asleep immediately, or get up after a minute or two. But today he stayed beside me, stretched out on the bed with his hands behind his head.

"I am glad to be back," he said. "The Procurator is an ass." He added something extremely rude in Casilan. "Talyn had to tell him if he did not stop his behaviour with the women of the village, we were leaving. He touched a woman's buttocks and she nearly punched him. He said it was an accident, that he had been reaching to touch the horse and she had stepped in front of him, but it was a lie. I was there."

"How was he with you?" I'd been surprised when Druise had been sent as the translator. Only a few weeks earlier, Decanius had had him arrested for desertion. Cillian, sick and shaking, had intervened to save him, and now Druise was indisputably sworn to the *Princip*.

"He treated me like a servant." He grinned. "I expected that. The soldier who agreed to be his aide hates him, and he will ask to be sent back to Casil this year. He does not share his bed," he added, "although Decanius offered him gold. So the Procurator is frustrated."

I laughed. "Serves him right. Did he proposition you?"

"Yes. No gold, though. Stupid man."

"You would have said yes, if there had been gold?" I teased. I put a hand on his stomach, the muscles firm, taut.

"No," he said. "I have to like my bedmates. Even if I have been ordered to be with them."

"Have you been?"

"Once or twice. For information, yes?" He stretched, arching his abdomen under my hand. I watched the ripple of muscle in his solid, scarred body. "Who is the new Governor?"

"Livius, his name is." I was growing uninterested in conversation.

"What does he look like?" I told him.

"If is who I think it is, he is decent. He was Governor of a little province to the east; little, but rebellious. But few problems, under him."

I slid my hand lower. "Enough politics."

I woke in the night, Druise snoring lightly beside me. Words he'd spoken had been circling in my sleeping mind; not a dream, quite, but I had almost *seen* the implications. *Ordered to, for information.* Had he been in Casil, with me? I couldn't see how. He'd been assigned to us from the beginning, before anyone reporting to the palace could have known I was a lover of men. And the only *ladhar* had belonged to one of Irmgard's women, so they hadn't even realized I was a musician.

Cillian was sending Druise back to Casil with Faolyn, to set up a conduit of information. I had not thought of how that might happen, or not of all the ways. Surely, though, he would not ask this of Druise? Not after his own experiences.

I couldn't bring myself to believe it. He wouldn't do this. Not to Druise — and not to me. I stared up into the blackness. When Druise knows he is going east, I thought, talk to him. Find out. Don't speculate.

But I was Linrathe's envoy, and Druise would have his orders. Would he tell me?

Chapter 9

DRUISE ACCEPTED THE ASSIGNMENT without question, except to mourn leaving his Kitten. He would leave in a week, or a little more. I couldn't find the courage to ask him what he and Cillian had spoken about regarding how he was to find his informants. I did not want to be told I wasn't allowed to know. Nor did I want to hear my suspicions were correct.

The Governor hadn't asked to meet with me again. I spent time with Lena: Gwenna screamed less, but she wasn't a happy child. Druise, when he wasn't busy, came to carry her, humming to her endlessly, or sat with her sleeping on his lap. I tried to do the same, but she was fractious with me, turning her head away listlessly. Lena was both exhausted and worried. Kyreth, and Talyn, and even Gnaius commiserated, but they all agreed: colic, and it would pass, in time.

Cillian was with the Casilani officials and Casyn or closeted in his workroom far too many hours of the day, in my opinion. But when I mentioned it to Lena she just shook her head. "He isn't neglecting us, Sorley, but there is little he can do. He takes her willingly, when he's here; but if she needs someone to walk with her, he can't do that. And he can't read in our rooms," she said, "with Gwenna crying so much, or just grizzling, and there are so many records he needs to review."

I'd helped with records, in Casil. So had Lena, but she was far too busy with Gwenna — and far too tired. Late in the afternoon, when I thought Cillian would be back from the baths, I returned to their rooms. As I expected, he was there, and so was Druise. Gwenna slept on Druise's lap, and Lena was curled up against Cillian, nearly asleep herself. She opened her eyes long enough to smile at me.

"*Käresta*," Cillian said, "go and sleep properly. Gwenna is fed; she does not need you for a few hours."

"Maybe I will," she murmured. "Except she'll need changing."

"I will do it," Druise said. "You need sleep, Lena." She didn't argue any more, just kissed Cillian and made her way to the bedroom.

"Kyreth was here today," Cillian said. "She has suggested ginger steeped in warm water to soothe Gwenna." He indicated an odd cup, shaped almost like an oil lamp with a long spout, on the table between the chairs. "Small drops in her mouth, using that. It seems to have worked."

"Good," I said. "Maybe Lena will get more sleep. And you."

"I am tired," he admitted.

"Lena told me you're reviewing records. Can I help? I have little to do, for a week or two." I went to the sideboard. "Wine?"

"Water it well," Cillian said. I poured three cups. I put Druise's on the table beside him. He glanced up, smiling his thanks before his eyes returned to the baby. I handed Cillian his. He took it, and as he did his fingers curved around mine. A thumb brushed my wrist. I nearly gasped. "My lord Sorley," he said. "Thank you."

I turned away to take my own cup. What had just happened? It hadn't felt accidental, but it must have been. Had there been a tremor in his hand he couldn't control? Since Casil, he had occasionally touched my fingers in thanks, and he was tired, and in pain — that had to be the reason. I sat down. "The records," I said again. "Can't I help?"

"You cannot." He took a drink of the wine. "Not because I would not welcome your help, but because Decanius had made much of our friendship to the Governor, and I want no doubts about your independence as Linrathe's *toscaire*, nor of your impartiality with regard to the decisions made for Ésparias."

I sat back. "I suppose you're right. But isn't there someone, one of the junior officers, who could help?"

"Yes. Not a junior officer, though. Talyn is going to assist, as soon as she is sure the new officer leading the reorganized regiments understands what is needed there."

"That shouldn't take long," I said, relieved. "He's been doing much of the work anyhow, with her advising Casyn."

A short while later, Druise gently transferred the sleeping Gwenna to Cillian's lap. "I will be back," he said. Cillian gazed down at his daughter, stroking her hair gently with one finger.

"Just think," he said softly, in Linrathan, "had you and Turlo not gone to the ship, that first full day in Casil, and left Lena and me alone, she might never have been."

"So I can claim some responsibility for her?"

"You can," he said, smiling. He looked up. "Just as I can claim some for you and Druisius, can I not? How intertwined our lives all are now, the four of us. "

"Five," I said. "How you can separate Druise from his beloved Kitten for several months, I do not know."

"I am sorry for that. And for separating the two of you, Sorley. Truly."

If I was going to ask my question, it had to be now. "I'll survive," I said. I paused. Had I the courage? Apparently not.

"I wouldn't have seen that much of him, anyhow," I said instead. "I'll be back and forth to Dun Ceànnar, and maybe the *Ti'ach*, depending on when my scáeli's exam is. If there is one."

"Do you truly doubt that?" he asked. "I suppose you will be away a lot, won't you? I will miss you."

"There are other *xache* players."

"No one with whom I can speak my own language, *mo charaidh gràhadh*. And as you said, we have things between us to resolve."

Had I said that? Gwenna made a small noise. He stroked her back, and she settled back into sleep. I remembered his fingers on mine, the brush along my wrist, and desire shot through me, intense and immediate. I looked away.

"Perhaps not the best choice of words," I prevaricated.

"Or perhaps they were," he said. I didn't reply. Where had Druise gone?

To get us food, it transpired. He returned with a kitchen cadet, carrying trays laden with bowls of fish stew, and a loaf of bread and some cheese. With the utmost gentleness he took Gwenna from Cillian. She woke, and blinked at him, and while we ate he fed her more ginger water, and took her through to the nursery to change her. We heard him singing to her, softly. Only after she was sleeping in her cradle did he eat. Lena didn't stir.

I took the empty dishes to the kitchen. My hands full, I left the door ajar. Coming back, I heard their voices, and my name.

"You will be careful with Sorley," Druise said. Not a question, and not the tone of a soldier to his officer.

"When have I not been?" Cillian replied. "Since he was sixteen, Druisius."

"Does he know?"

"I have made certain indications. Nothing more."

"But you will act, while I am gone?"

Cillian laughed, a wry, almost bitter sound. "If it is ever possible, and only if I am entirely sure Lena means what she says."

"She does, I think," Druise replied. "We have talked too, yes? She is angry about many things, but not this."

"She has a right to that anger," Cillian said softly. "I have not been shelter for her, for too long. I am breaking yet another vow."

"A tree can be shelter in a storm," Druise said, "but only if its roots and branches have grown in all directions. Or it will fall when the wind changes."

This time Cillian's laugh was one of amusement. "I had not taken you for a philosopher. But perhaps you are not wrong."

"Cillian." Not Major, I noted. "This is possible, yes? But not without risk."

"The risk is what worries me."

"But what happens, if you do not act? We go on as we are. Maybe we are happy. Content. Maybe not. I think maybe not. Sorley is angry, too, yes? He misses his home. He is confused about me. Something will break, I think."

Silence. I began to step forward, when I heard Cillian's voice. "Are you considering staying in Casil?"

"I am sworn to return."

"Then a different question: might you ask to be posted south?"

Druise chuckled again. "It would be warmer. But no." His voice became grave, and somehow reflective. "I have done many things, good and bad, and here is a new life for me, yes? I am no *idióta*. I wish not to lose all I have here, especially Kitten. An instrument has value to more than one musician in its lifetime, and sometimes to more than one player at a time."

"Thank you, my wise friend," Cillian said quietly. "You have eased my mind." When he spoke again, his tone had changed. "At least you are not angry with me."

"No? You think I want to go to Casil?" I could hear the grin, though. Cillian laughed. My cue, I thought, and scuffed my feet on the flagstones, making enough noise to tell them I was outside the door. Both men were sitting, relaxed and companionable, and I guessed they did not think I had overheard anything.

"Now you are back, I am going to dice," Druise said. "You will stay, so if Kitten cries you can fetch her?"

I agreed, and brought the *xache* set from the sideboard. The baby and Lena slept, and Cillian and I played the game as we had a hundred times before. We were on the second match when Lena appeared, tousle-headed and yawning.

"There is food, *käresta*," Cillian said, indicating the bowl keeping warm on the hearth. "Eat before Gwenna wakes."

She bent to kiss him. I stood up.

"Don't leave," Lena said.

"I'm going to. You have little time together, just the two of you," I said. "Don't argue. I'll see you tomorrow."

Back in my room, I thought about what I had overheard. It nagged at me. I wasn't sure what they'd been talking about — *certain indications*? — but what had shaken me had been the tone of their voices. They had sounded like equals together, regardless of differences of rank and education. Druise was closer to his age, but that wasn't why. Cillian, I thought, was considerate of Druisius's feelings, but not protective, whereas with me… *You will be careful with Sorley.* Anger rose, shocking me: not just at Cillian, but at my lover too.

I am twenty-five, I thought. I am Linrathe's *toscaire* to this land, with Liam's trust, and Casyn's. I did dangerous work in Linrathe during the war, and took on an even more dangerous journey east. Yet even Druise had spoken of me as if I were a child, homesick and confused, needing gentle handling.

Druise returned earlier than I expected. "Unhappy men," he said, at my expression of surprise. "Bad company. I have heard enough."

"What's bothering them now?" I asked, handing him wine.

"Inspections, by the Governor's staff," he said.

"Surely that isn't surprising?" I asked, sitting across from him.

"No. But just one more thing. They need work to do," he said. "Patrols are not enough. Bored men create trouble." He stretched his legs out. "I leave in three days."

"Three?" Sooner than I had thought.

"Rufin says the tides are best then."

"Druise…do you want to go?"

"Want?" Genuine surprise in his voice. "What does it matter, what I want? Soldiers do not choose their assignments."

"But if you could?" I persisted.

"Better not to think that way," he said. "Better to do what is required, enjoy what is good, and not worry about the future."

"You will enjoy what there is in Casil, then, and not just food and wine?" I asked, trying to keep my voice steady.

"Yes." He spoke matter-of-factly. "I have old friends to see." By choice? He put his cup down, leaning back in his chair. "And you should here, too."

"No."

"Why not? You would if Cillian offered."

"But he won't. You're being ridiculous, Druise."

"You think? But if he did, you would not believe you had betrayed me. From the beginning, I have known this, and even when I asked you not to kiss him in my sight, you could not. So we do not belong only to each other. Am I wrong?"

It had only been once, I thought. Only once on the lips, and that was what Druise had asked me not to do. But I had broken the promise. "No," I said.

"Then do not worry about what we do outside this room." He picked up his wine again. "But inside it — we have three days, *amané*."

CHAPTER 10

15 YEARS AFTER THE BATTLE OF THE TAIVA

BREAKFAST WASN'T FOR A few hours, and I wouldn't go back to sleep now. I went to my teaching room, thinking about what the *daltai* would do this summer, with both me and Druisius gone. Lena would take over most of his weaponry lessons, I thought, but there was no one else to teach the *cithar*. As only Tamm was close to leaving us, that wasn't a problem. They'd just get more voice training from Apulo, and perhaps more *danta* interpretation from Lena.

Lena. Her hours teaching would double, at least, and she would also take over the accounts and estate management from me, although old Anndra would assist with the latter, if she needed him. And undoubtedly, she would insist in riding patrol with the guard, more than once: Druise did, she would argue, so she should too. Like Druise, she still held her commission in Ésparias's army, officially seconded to the *Ti'ach* to teach weaponry.

She should probably ask Mhairi to find someone else to work in the kitchen and house, I thought. Then Mhairi could take on more of the oversight of the *daltai* that was the Lady's role, leaving Lena free to teach. I would suggest it.

I heard a light knock at the door. I turned to see Apulo. "Cillian would like a few minutes with everyone before breakfast," Apulo told me. "He is just returned from his treatments."

"I'll be there," I said. I finished the outline I was working on — I would take it with me, for Cillian's approval, as it depended heavily on Tamm, and he was not my student to direct — and went next door. Cillian was standing by the window, looking out. He turned, awkwardly, even after his massage and exercises, but his eyes creased in a smile of welcome. "Good morning," Lena said from across the room. "And do *not* look at each other that way over the breakfast table."

"Have we ever?" Cillian said mildly. "Have you and I ever, *käresta*? We all know our roles."

She laughed. "I was only teasing." She came over to give me a kiss on the cheek. "You need a shave," she told me.

"I know. What are we meeting about?" I went to the sideboard to pour tea.

"Wait for Druise. I am going to talk to Gwenna now," Lena said.

"No second thoughts, overnight?" I asked.

"None, except for your safety," she said with a grin. She turned to leave.

"*Käresta*?" Cillian said. She stopped, turning back to his outstretched arms. They kissed. I watched, amused that she had nearly forgotten their unvarying morning ritual.

Cillian and I talked about inconsequential things until Druise and Apulo joined us. Druise put a hand on my shoulder in greeting; nothing more, with Apulo here.

"Sorley," Cillian said, "do you need to leave tomorrow?"

"Yes," I said. "Ruar expects me, and he was specific about dates."

"Then we had best make today a half rest day, so that we have time to organize ourselves, now both you and Druisius will be gone. The *daltai* will not mind, I am sure," he added. "Now, can we meet again, say perhaps an hour before we normally do this afternoon? Is that enough time to make arrangements?"

We agreed it would be. I gave Cillian the schedule I had worked on, asking him to review it before we met again. "I will announce breakfast," Apulo said. A few minutes later, the gong sounded. We were on duty, as soon as we stepped outside the room.

Breakfast was simple: porridge, tea, bread and cheese, and not formal. The only requirement for the students was to attend, washed and dressed, and eat at least something. "As I take little food in the morning," Cillian had pointed out, "I cannot fairly ask the students for more than that." Gwenna in particular disliked breakfast, eating no more than a spoonful or two of porridge with her tea, another way she took after her father.

"*Comiádh*?" one the boys said, "may I ask something?"

"You may," Cillian said.

"At dinner last night, we were speaking of empires falling, and what happens when they do." He spoke precisely; he had been well-taught, before being sent to us. "When I went to bed, I thought about what my grandfather has said to my father: that while we sell most of our fish and wool to Ésparias, it is always prudent to reserve some for Varsland, so that we have more than one market. Do our leaders do the same? Have other countries in reserve, for alliances if an Empire falls?"

"It is sound advice your grandfather has given your father," Cillian said. "That is a very good question. One which I will not answer directly, but give to you as an assignment to discover yourself. I will suggest to you what to read when we meet later this morning."

Neatly deflected, I thought, and a completely reasonable response from the *Comiádh*. Whose job, after all, was to introduce his students to ideas, to new thoughts and attitudes, with the hope that as the *daltai* left us, they took those ideas with them out into Linrathe and Sorham.

"Now," Cillian said, gaining everyone's attention. "Today will be a half rest day, with free time for everyone after the midday meal. The day looks fine, so if it remains so, perhaps an opportunity for *líathró*, if you would organize it, Tamm?"

The game, which involved kicking a ball made from a sheep's bladder around, was a favourite among the students. It both relieved their excess energy and taught them teamwork. A similar game was played in Casil, Druise had told me.

"Of course, *Comiádh*," Tamm said. He was used to this; in my last years at the *Ti'ach*, Perras had asked as much of me, and Cillian would have experienced the same a decade earlier.

We spent the morning teaching, and after the meal at midday, Druise went to talk to the guard, while I returned to the plans I had been working on earlier. I'd mostly completed them, and until Cillian approved what I had given him, I didn't have much more to do. I had done the accounts just a few days before. I had best go speak to Anndra, I thought, not that he needs me to. It gave me an excuse to go out into the sun and air.

I stopped to watch the game, the students happily chasing the ball around on what was usually our training ground for swordplay and archery.

Gwenna wasn't among them, I noticed; probably with Lena, preparing for travel. "Tamm," I said, seeing the opportunity, "a word?"

"I suppose they won't kill each other if I stop watching for a moment," he said with a grin.

"I'm not so sure. You can watch while we talk."

"Catriona will stop them if it gets too wild," he said. Catriona was the next-oldest student, a redhead who spoke every language we taught fluently. She was a *torpari* girl, from central Linrathe, and more than once I had caught Lena watching her.

"Had Turlo not said he had been true to Arey all his life," she'd said, "I would swear she was his."

"She could be, I suppose," I had replied. "He did travel through Linrathe on his way north to find the route to Casil, and Arey was dead by then."

"We'll never know," she had said. Turlo, and his scout Galen with him, had simply disappeared a year after the Taiva. He'd been commanding the Ésparian troops on the Sterre, and had gone to look for weaknesses in the defences where the earthen dike met the Durrains. No one ever saw either of them again. Lena believed they had attempted to go east across the mountains, following the route she and Cillian had taken in exile: an almost-certainly fatal decision, in autumn.

"Tamm," I began, "last night at dinner, your views on the constraints on us as adults were thoughtful. May I ask if you have learned that equally from all of us, or perhaps in one certain way from me?"

Surprise — or fear? — flashed in his eyes. He looked around, but there was no one in hearing distance. He did not speak for some moments. I too had learned from texts and discussions in my years at the *Ti'ach* that my desire for men as my bedmates was neither unnatural nor universally scorned, but it had made me no less frightened to reveal my nature in Linrathe and Sorham. The *Ti'acha* had made little headway in changing opinions in this area, except among the *scáeli'en*, and Ruar.

"Perhaps," he said finally. "An example set by you and the Captain, I believe."

"Beyond what we have taught you about music?" He nodded. "I'm pleased we have given you guidance," I said. "Tamm, I'll speak a little more freely now, and from experience. You will need to be very careful in

Linrathe and Sorham. Both beatings and blackmail are possible, and not infrequent." His head came up.

"You?"

"The beating, yes," I said calmly. "The extortion was attempted, but I had been warned, and saw what was planned."

"How can I know what — who — is safe?" he whispered.

"A difficult question. Easier for a musician; the *scáeli'en* are more accepting, and you're more likely to find others of similar tastes among them. You're a good enough musician to mix with them, and perhaps that is all you should do, until you are older, and more experienced."

His eyes were turned towards the game, but I didn't think he was seeing it. "Lord Sorley? Thank you."

"I would have benefitted, had someone said this to me, and others I know, when we were young men," I said. "I would save you what we went through, if I can."

I found Anndra, and talked about pastures and sheep and drainage with him for an hour, helped by a nip of *fuisce*. His wife, Isa, still spent her days in the *Ti'ach*'s kitchen, although she mostly drowsed in a chair, waking to give instructions or to occasionally sort a pan of dried beans. Cillian went to speak to her every day. She had lived to see the frightened *torpari* child she had taken under her wing become *Comiádh*, and to hold his children, and she would die content when her time came. I wondered, not for the first time, how the difficult, complex child — and man — had managed to engender such love in so many of us.

Then I walked back through the late spring afternoon, hearing the maa-aa of lambs drifting up from the field beyond the stream, and larksong high above me. Sounds I had known all my life, but suddenly I missed the cry of gulls and the barking of seals, and the ceaseless beat of the waves. I missed Gundarstorp, and I knew deep inside me I always would.

Chapter 11

BEFORE THE CHILDREN JOINED us for tea we had the summer's learning mapped out, with significant roles for Tamm and, to my surprise, Catriona. Language teaching was Cillian's specialty. "Why?" I asked.

"I want some extra time with Colm," Cillian said. "To improve his Heræcrian, in part."

"Heræcrian?" I said. "He is ten. Spoken or written?"

"Both. I believe he may need it, in the future."

"Are you planning to share your reasons why, *kärestan*?" Lena asked.

"Consider what interests him. Anatomy. Lambing. His collection of animal skulls. He has asked Apulo quite a few questions about how massage helps me. What might that suggest to you?"

"A physician?" Druise said.

"Perhaps," Cillian said. "We should let the interest develop or wane as he chooses, but learning Heræcrian will not be a burden to him in either case. And," he said, "I will not object to more time spent with my son, especially as Lena will be busier than usual."

It was Lena, usually, who rode or walked with Colm, encouraging his interest in birds and animals while giving her time out on the moors, under the wide skies, the space and silence she craved. Both would miss that, I thought, if the summer's demands limited it.

"Has he said something to you?" I asked Druise. "You were very quick to see what Cillian was suggesting."

"No," Druise said. "But I wanted to be a doctor, when I was his age, or a little more. Not possible, for a boy from the *subura*. I collected skulls, too.

Mostly rats and pigeons.”

“Why didn't I know that?” I asked. Druise just shrugged. “All that time you took care of Cillian, and you never mentioned it?”

“Gnaius knew,” Druise said. “We talked. He said, no, too late for me to learn, except as an army medic. That would have taken me away, and I did not want that.”

“Oh, Druise,” Lena said. “Surely you could have learned, and stayed at Wall’s End? Casyn would have ordered it, had you told us.”

“Soldiers do not like men who break the rules,” Druise said. “They would know. Either I did it properly, or not at all. Cillian needed me, and then...” He hesitated, rare for Druise. “I did not want to leave my family, not for as long as it would have needed.”

He had been torn, two years ago, when Gwenna had gone back to Ésparias to become a cadet. He had desperately wanted to go with her, to guard her, but Cillian and Lena had talked him out of it. She would be well-protected, they argued, but being their daughter was going to be burden enough without the presence of a personal guard. He had seen the sense, and after her first visit home, mostly stopped worrying.

“Anyhow,” he said, with his characteristic grin, “I like teaching. Maybe I am a better teacher than I would have been a doctor.”

“You were an excellent medic,” Cillian said, “training or not, but for the same reasons you are good teacher, Druisius. You knew when to encourage, and when to challenge. And when discipline was needed. I will be forever in your debt for that.”

The children came in then, Colm’s hair unkempt and with mud still on his face. “Didn't you wash?” Lena said, in fond exasperation.

“My hands are clean,” he said, showing her. “Is there cake, *Mathàir*? I am starving.”

“You are not,” Cillian said. “Be precise, Colm.”

He sighed. “I am very hungry,” he amended. “Tamm made us play two games. But my side won both. Where were you, Gwenna?”

“Getting ready to travel,” she said. “I’m going north with Sorley. And Druise. Tomorrow.”

“Are you?” Colm said. “Will you bring me any skulls you find?”

The kitchen girl arrived with a tray of food — bread and the spring’s first butter, as well as cakes; she knew well what an afternoon’s exercise did to young appetites. We listened to Colm tell us about the game, in between bites of bread and cake. But after a while, he stopped. "Could I go to my room?" he asked.

"Go," Lena said. He needed solitude, as both his parents did, and rarely got. After an afternoon's boisterous play, he would want time to read, or draw, or just to think. He gave both his parents the expected kiss, smiled at his sister, and left.

"Baths?" I said to Druise. Apulo would have them heated; someone always used them, in the late afternoon.

"Yes," he said. "Cillian?"

"Later, perhaps, with Colm."

In the steaming hot pool Druise touched my face. "You need a shave," he said.

"I know," I said once more. "After the baths."

"I will," he offered. He was a skilled barber, careful and precise; he had shaved Cillian, for the weeks of illness and for months afterwards. Occasionally, he shaved me, a gesture I found both tender and arousing. We were not going to be separated for six weeks or more now, but we would likely have no opportunity to make love beyond tonight. I kissed him, not quite gently.

"I look forward to it."

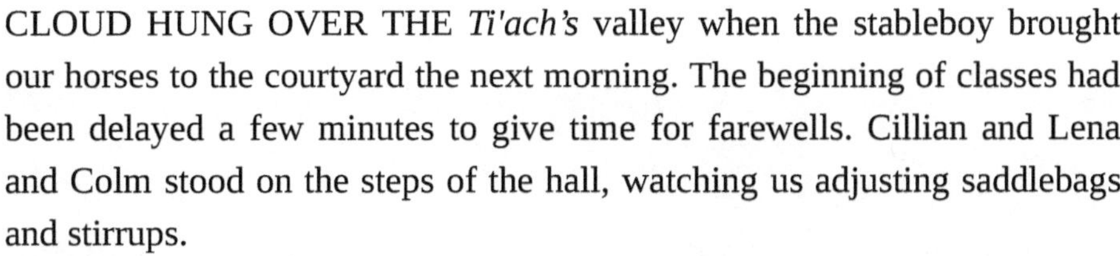

CLOUD HUNG OVER THE *Ti'ach's* valley when the stableboy brought our horses to the courtyard the next morning. The beginning of classes had been delayed a few minutes to give time for farewells. Cillian and Lena and Colm stood on the steps of the hall, watching us adjusting saddlebags and stirrups.

Gwenna gave the huntress statue in the courtyard a quick touch, then went to each of her parents in turn, for an embrace and a kiss. Cillian said something quietly to her, and she nodded. Colm allowed a kiss on his cheek, and a quick hug; he was used to Gwenna being away from the *Ti'ach*. She swung up on her horse, waiting for us.

Ironically, departures and homecomings allowed — no, expected — visible affection between men in Linrathe. Druise saluted Lena, as the senior captain, and laying a hand on Cillian's extended forearm accepted the brief touch of his lips. Then it was my turn. I kissed Lena's cheek before turning to Cillian.

"My lord Sorley," he said gravely, after the kiss. "Do not mislead her, but neither can she be told anything that would endanger her. Take care of my daughter."

"With my life," I promised.

CHAPTER 12

WE RODE NORTH, NOT up the winding path that led to the plateau south of the *Ti'ach*, but along the stream and through the *torp's* collection of cottages and byres, calling farewells to the *torpari* we saw. Our first stop would be at the next *torp*, about an hour further north, to have our horses' shoes checked at the smithy. My horse had been readied for a long journey, but Druise's new gelding and Gwenna's mare had not.

The horses knew this track, and we rode easily, Gwenna leading for this section, although I guessed Druise would insist she rode between us for safety later. But we were still on the *Ti'ach's* lands, somewhere out on the hills was the patrol, and in our thirteen years here nobody had ever threatened us. In earlier days, when Ruar had come to the *Ti'ach* to learn, and Faolyn too, the guard had had a purpose. But was there really anyone who still held a grudge against Cillian? Or any disaffected Marai who would target Lena?

Probably not. But neither the *Princip* of Ésparias nor the *Teannasach* of Linrathe would allow even that small possibility not to be mitigated, and so we were guarded. Beacon fires were always ready to be lit on the hilltops, and bells hung in the *torp* and around the *Ti'ach* to be rung in an emergency. And every *torpari* over the age of twelve knew how to use a bow or secca or sword. Druisius did his job very, very well.

At the smithy, we dismounted to allow the smith to check the horses' feet. I strolled around the smithy and its adjoining cottage, noting the neatness of its garden and the repair of the buildings. This was Hagenstorp, and Hagen was a conscientious *Eirën*, well-liked by his *torpari*. A man carrying a puppy strode towards the stream from behind another cottage.

"Shugo," I called, recognizing him.

"Lord Sorley," he said, coming over to me. The puppy squirmed in his grasp.

"What is that?" I asked. Shugo was one of the shepherds, and his sheepdogs were the best around. We bought young dogs from him, rather than breed our own. But the puppy he was holding was no sheepdog, although its black and white colouring suggested one of its parents was.

He spat. "Hagen came through with his hound just when Meg was in heat," he grumbled. "This is the result. I drowned the others at birth — what good would they be? Left her this one to raise so the bitch wouldn't pine, but I need her back with the sheep. So it's drowning for this one, too."

"How old is he?" I could see from how he held the pup it was male.

"Six weeks."

"Don't drown it," I said. "I'll buy it from you."

"Buy it? What do you want it for?"

"The *Comiádh's* son is ten. Just the right age for a puppy. Will you send it? I'll write a note, if you'll wait a few minutes."

"Aye," he said. "It'll make a boy's dog, I warrant. How is your own son, Lord Sorley?

"Far away," I said. Bjørn was in Varsland, as far as I knew.

I wrote the note and gave him a few coins for the pup and for delivering it. Druise grinned when I told him what I had done.

"Good thing we're leaving," he said. "Lena might take her secca to you, otherwise."

But, I thought, a puppy will give Colm a companion, and a reason to be out of doors, and if Cillian is right and he leaves for the *Ti'ach na Iorlath* in two years, then it can be Lena's justification for her solitary trips up onto the moors. The blacksmith called to me then, telling me no work needed to be done. We remounted and continued north.

"Why did you buy a puppy?" Gwenna asked, after we had been riding for some time.

"For Colm," I told her. "Your mother will worry less about him when he's off exploring if he has a dog with him."

"Maybe," she said. "There's always a guard somewhere, though. I hate that, you know."

"I know," I said. "But you also know why it is necessary."

She made a face. "Because of what *Mathàir* did. Because someone tried to kill my father in the past, because of the treaty. Sorley? The other students — some of them — say if he was a traitor to Linrathe, then he shouldn't have been given so much power in Ésparias. A traitor is always a traitor, they say."

"They are still saying that your father gave up too much to Casil, when he was negotiating the treaties?" I asked, trying to keep the bitterness from my voice.

"Yes. Our instructors say otherwise, but some of the students don't believe it. And I don't know what is true, and what isn't."

"He told you that accepting his father's acknowledgment of him wasn't an act of treason," I reminded her, "but something he was fully entitled to do."

"He still deserted his country, though," she argued.

"Would you have had him die? Your father has faced death more than once, Gwenna. That he is here with us today is a gift from the gods."

"Quiet!" Druise said. His captain's voice. He stared at the track ahead, his light cloak back pushed back for easier access to the short sword on his belt. "Gwenna, behind us," he ordered.

She obeyed, his tone bringing immediate compliance. I threw back my own cloak. "What?" I asked Druise.

"Men, approaching," he said. "I caught a glimpse. Where the track drops into that valley, ahead. They looked like Marai, Sorley."

CHAPTER 13

RUAR HAD GROWN AT least a handspan, and when he spoke his voice was deeper. "Sorley, welcome," he said, more formally than he had even at midwinter. To me, he seemed both more assured, and more subdued. Assured in the way he handled himself, but subdued in his great-uncle's presence. Liam gave me his usual half-grudging greeting.

"We will talk after I rest," he said. I'd arrived just before mid-day. "I want your report first, before we begin to discuss this summer's business."

"Certainly." I gave him the formal letter of greeting from the Governor, and the news of the Southern Empire's new name. Ruar asked about Cillian then, to Liam's scowl. I told him, briefly, that all was well, that Cillian was working again, and a father. He had no need to know about the pain Cillian still lived with, or the yearning for poppy he fought.

"He is not popular, I hear, among the officers and men," Liam said.

"Who told you that?" I asked, although even as I said the words I knew. "Randall?"

"Aye."

I weighed my words. "Changes of the sort taking place within the Ésparias's army will inevitably cause discord. Cillian is a target for that dissent, being largely unknown. Easier to blame him than the *Princip*, I suppose."

"The *Princip* did not negotiate the treaty," Liam said.

"No. But his brother signed it."

"Aye. Unlike ours, not signed by any man with the right to do so. But it is done, and we will abide by it." The steward knocked, then, to tell us the meal was ready. Ruar glanced my way as we followed Liam from the room. His eyebrows flickered. Perhaps, I thought, what I took for deference is just restraint.

Bhradaín ate with us, and Ruar's older cousins, Daoíre and Oisín, whom I had met at mid-winter. We talked of the mild weather, and the hopes for a good crop of lambs this year. The Marai had devastated the flocks to feed their men, but the few ewes left had had an easy winter, and unless the weather turned vicious — as it could — most of the lambs should live.

"We cannot give fleeces in tribute," Oisín said, "not this year."

"This is not the time to talk of that," Liam said. The younger men exchanged looks but said nothing.

"I understand you will be examined by the *scáeli'en* council in the autumn?" Bhradaín said to me, deftly changing the subject. *Scáeli* to Dun Ceànnar cannot be an easy job, I reflected.

"Is that official?" I asked. "I hadn't heard."

"I had a letter from the Lady Dagney just two days ago," he said.

"A *scáeli*?" Liam said. "You cannot be *scáeli* and *toscaire*, Sorley."

"I am aware," I said mildly. "The title can be deferred until I am no longer needed as a *toscaire, Raséair.*"

He nodded, a sharp motion of disapproving agreement. "That may be some time. I am going for my sleep now. There will be no discussion of tribute to Casil until I return; Bhradaín, ensure that it is so. We will meet in two hours."

"More ale?" Daoíre asked, once Liam had gone. The mood in the room had changed.

Bhradaín stood. "I will fetch my *ladhar*," he said. "I may be a little while. You all heard Liam's instructions."

Daoíre waited until the *scáeli* had gone, busying himself pouring ale. "Were we still paying tribute to Varsland," he said, almost idly, "what would we offer this year?"

"It couldn't be food," Ruar said, "or we would force our people to starve. What might be needed, Sorley?"

"Need? Timber," I said. "Timber, and men to build with it." Oisín, I noticed, had stayed silent, listening. His wife was Liam's younger daughter, and he perhaps deferred to Daoíre. I hoped that was the reason, anyhow.

"Timber we have," Daoíre said. "Men, less so."

"Just south of where the Tabha reaches the sea," Oisín said, "the headland curves to make a sheltered harbour. Timber could be floated down the river, and loaded onto ships there. Were there a need to do that, of course."

"Whose land is that?" Daoíre asked. Ruar told him, without hesitation. "He's not an unreasonable man," his cousin said. "He would agree to lease land, if the price was right, I think. Do you agree, Oisín?"

"Aye, I do."

"You must understand, Sorley," Daoíre said, "that Liam is an old man. He grows forgetful, and more dogged that his designs are right, and cannot be overruled. We handle him carefully, feeding him ideas that he then believes are his own. Try to say as little as possible in our talks over the next days. And do not mention Cillian na Perras, if you can avoid it. Liam hates him, although I do not know why."

The feeling might be returned, I thought. "Well," I said, "that precludes me singing the *danta* I have recently finished, about our travels to Casil."

"Sing it now?" Ruar said. "We have time to hear it, before my great-uncle wakes."

"If Bhradaín gives me leave, I would be honoured." Bhradaín's approval was a formality, of course: Ruar's request effectively meant the *scáeli* could not refuse. I went for my *ladhar*, thinking about what I had just heard. That Daoíre and Oisín and Ruar felt the need to plan without Liam, or perhaps for him, spoke of strategy, preparations for when the *Raséair* could no longer guide the boy. The long view, Cillian would have said.

"May I accompany you?" Bhradaín asked. I played the tune, and the refrain, once alone, once with him. It wasn't complex, the key and the timing speaking of dark times, of war and death and doom.

I'd spent countless hours on this *danta*, both on the ship home from Casil and later, after the Marai were defeated, sometimes even at Cillian's bedside. With Bhradaín's *ladhar* blending with mine, I sang of the Marai invasion, and the early battles, and of how Callan had ordered Turlo east. I sang of our meeting, and of Irmgard and her ship, and the long voyage along an unknown river.

I changed the key to tell of Cillian and Lena, from their trial and exile and long journey east; of their winter in the Kurzemë camp, and their walk across the plain, and part way through I brought in a theme of growing joy, using the accepted motifs of an offered hand and a bestowed kiss to indicate their changed relationship. A faster beat for our meeting on the river, and a sweeping run of notes as we sailed into Casil. Then a sombre interlude for the negotiations, blending into martial themes as the Casilani ships arrived at the Eastern Fort.

Bhradaín had kept with me for the entire *danta*, effortlessly. But now I held up a hand to him. I would part from tradition now, to tell the battle of the Taiva almost completely by voice alone.

I sang the betrayals, and the impossible acts of archery that had ended the battle, then Callan's death and Cillian's terrible injuries, my fingers plucking only a simple melodic line. Notes from *An Dithës Braithréan* briefly intermixed with mine before the theme rose in thanksgiving for all the battles won, and fell again, into silence.

Quite a long silence. "Well done," Bhradaín said, breaking it. "A new *danta* to be taught, I would say." High praise; he was nearly as senior a *scáeli* as Dagney. Heat rose in my face. "Ruar," Bhradaín went on, "may I take Sorley away? I would like to counsel him about his examination in a few months."

"Not yet," Ruar said. "Sorley, when you pass your examination, will you be an advisor for me?"

"An advisor?"

"My great-uncle is old. He won't be my *Raséair* much longer: he'll die, or ill-health will mean he can no longer continue. I will not have another. My cousins, and Bhradaín, will be my advisors instead. I would like you to be one of them, too."

I drank some ale, to give me a little time to think. None of the other men spoke. "Why me?"

"For two reasons," he said. "A *scáeli* must tell the truth, and so your voice can be trusted. But more than that, you promised to help me regain Sorham. We need your knowledge of the *Härren*, and their politics and allegiances."

Were these his own thoughts, or those of his advisors? He did not sound fourteen. "Who would replace me as *toscaire*?"

"That will have to be considered carefully."

"Not Randall," I said, and a realization struck. "Ruar, I can't be your advisor."

"Why not?" Now I did hear a frustrated boy, and I had unthinkingly put myself in an awkward place. "Why not, Sorley?" Ruar said again.

"May I speak to the *Teannasach* alone?" I asked, looking at his cousins.

"Daoíre, Oisín, leave us, please," Ruar said immediately. "And you, Bhradaín."

"As you wish," Daoíre said. "But the *scáeli* stays."

Ruar glanced at me. I nodded. Bhradaín's presence would be a buffer, and what I had to tell Ruar I was sure he already knew.

"Well?" Ruar demanded, when his advisors had gone.

"I might be used to discredit you."

He frowned. "How?"

"You're old enough to understand. The truth about me will be widely known, soon if not now. Randall will ensure that. I won't be acceptable in the eyes of many *Eirënnen* whose support you must have." I took a breath. I'd never spoken these words to anyone, never made the overt admission. "I am *channàdarra*, Ruar."

His eyes widened fractionally. "Are you?"

I laughed, drily. "Would I claim it, were I not?"

"No," he said, dropping his eyes. "I suppose not. But I need you, Sorley. Who else can tell us so much about Sorham? You promised me you would help."

"I will," I said. "But not as an advisor."

"Then how?"

"Ruar," Bhradaín said, "do not demand an answer just now. We will think about it, all of us. Sorley and I are going to discuss music for a while." His voice changed, becoming conversational, casual. "You might think about what you say to your cousins, Ruar. Especially Oisín. The *Teannasach* is not required to share everything he knows about the men he leads."

I followed Bhradaín to his music room, *ladhar* in one hand and ale in the other.

"You are how old, Sorley?" the *scáeli* asked once we were alone.

"Twenty-five."

"And your years with Dagney did not begin until you were eighteen?" I nodded. "Remarkable. Who taught you, at Gundarstorp?"

"My mother," I said. "Until I was fourteen, when she died. After that, no one, really, although visiting *scáeli'en* gave me lessons occasionally."

"You must sing that *danta* at your exam, and exactly as you did now, regardless of tradition," Bhradaín said. "Your singing voice is only adequate, as I am sure you know, but your skill in composition and verse more than makes up for it. In my opinion, at least."

His opinion was worth a great deal. "Will you be an examiner?"

"If the Lady Dagney so decides," he said. A neutral answer. I shouldn't have asked, and he was gently reminding me of it. "You're right, I am afraid: you cannot be Ruar's advisor, not officially."

"I would be a flint against which the spark of rebellion could be struck,"

"Poetically put." Bhradaín folded his arms, sitting back. "But Ruar is right too: we need your links to Sorham. An unofficial advisor, then?"

"If he still wants me."

"I doubt he will care whom you choose to bed,"

"Liam does," I said bluntly. "Do his nephews share his revulsion?"

"Daoíre judges the deeds, not the man. Oisín? He is *Ti'ach* educated; he'll have been given a wider view. But I am unsure of his personal beliefs."

I drained my ale. "I would have to visit often. *Toscaire* would be a good cover for that."

Bhradaín raised both eyebrows. "You would defer your *scáeli's* oath?"

"Perhaps. Are Ruar and his advisors planning ways to retake Sorham without war?"

"They are," he said evenly.

"For that, I will defer joining the *scáeli'en*." I had promised Ruar. He was my *Teannasach*, if not yet in full.

"You want your lands back."

"No. I'll never have an heir of my body to leave them to. My brother's son or daughter will inherit, assuming he is still alive, or those of the half-brother I have never met. But I would like the freedom to visit, and to talk to my brothers, and to know the child who will become Gundarstorp's *Harr* or *Härra*." Homesickness swept through me, a wave of longing:

cianalas, in my tongue. I concentrated on the man in front of me. "It will always be my home, even if I never live there again."

"A compromise," he said. "Some might say a half-measure."

"Some might." I sad. "Not me."

Chapter 14

"TIMBER," LIAM SAID. "WE have trees to spare, and the Casilani will need wood, for ships and buildings. Do you not agree, Daoíre, Oisín?"

Twenty minutes earlier, Daoíre had enumerated items he had thought possible for tribute. Timber had been in the middle of the list, mentioned in passing. Oisín frowned. "Do you think so?" he asked. "How would we get it to them?"

"Down a river, man," Liam said. "How is timber ever moved?"

"You expect them to send ships for it?" Oisín said.

"Aye, I do. We cannot transport it south. Now where on the coast would you propose a harbour?"

Neither Oisín nor Daoíre spoke, exchanging worried glances. "Just south of the Tabha? That *Eirën* would not object." Ruar offered. He got up to fetch a map. The entire conversation had been planned, I realized, both to plant ideas in Liam's mind, and to allow Ruar to be seen as a leader, knowledgeable about his land and people.

By the end of the afternoon, I marvelled at the two men's ability to maintain their composure in the face of Liam's scathing remarks to them. Oisín, I judged, was less in control of himself, visibly holding back his anger. But I had my instructions: I was to offer timber and furs to pay the expected tribute over the next year.

"Tomorrow," Liam said, "we will speak of movement across the border. We have done enough for today." Even though he had slept after the midday meal, his skin was grey with fatigue. "Bhradaín, you have recorded this?" he asked.

"I have. I will review my notes with Sorley."

"Then I bid you good evening. I will not see you at dinner."

Very little was said about Liam at the meal: what was there to add? After the food Bhradaín and I played for a while, Liam's daughters joining their husbands, along with other men and women of the household. It was not late when I went to my room.

There was *fuisce* on the sideboard. I poured myself a little. Restlessly I paced the room, wondering what the plans were to regain Sorham without warfare. I doubted they would tell me: my *toscaire's* oath was to the country, and if I thought their plans endangered Linrathe, I could denounce them. If I asked Bhradaín directly, though, he was bound to tell me.

Or was he? There were limits to the *scáeli's* requirement to tell the truth, to prevent them from being captured for information. Only that which they knew first-hand, or had permission to reveal, I thought. If Bhradaín had been excluded from all, or much, of whatever planning Daoíre was leading, he was not obliged to tell me, even if I asked. But neither could he lie. All he could say was that it was not his to divulge.

I hadn't raised the idea of the forts yet, but the conversation about allowing Linrathan people across the Wall would be a starting place: some might wish to go, if there was work to be had. Tomorrow would be soon enough for this. I reached for my *ladhar*. The last time I 'd been in this room, I'd begun a song, a song I'd added to a little, but it wasn't finished. Maybe I needed the clarity of distance. I tightened a couple of strings and played part of it again.

You danced that night with grace unfettered…

It wasn't a beginning. Perhaps a chorus? Then I rolled my eyes at my own lack of insight. Only one opening was possible: the traditional one of so many of our songs. An image coalesced.

My true love's eyes are darkly gleaming
In candlelight and music's lure.
One night alone, at spring's fair dawning
To keep me longing through the years,
To leave my soul bereft and mourning.

Now the already-written lines

You danced that night with grace unfettered
A glance my way, a touch bestowed
Your dark hair swept by supple fingers.
Too soon the day, the calling road,
The shaken head when asked to linger.

Words poured out of me. By the end I was trembling with tiredness and spent emotion. The song was good, but more than that, it had told me what I had needed to know. No, I amended, what I already knew. *You are worth any price to me,* I had said to Cillian not so very long ago. Perhaps Druise accompanying Faolyn to Casil was for the best.

My head spun, from fatigue and *fuisce*. The bed beckoned, and I accepted its invitation.

"THERE IS LITTLE I can tell you about our people's ability to move south of the Wall permanently," I told Liam and the others the next morning. "No declaration will be made until the Procurator's men have finished surveying the land and counting every head in it, and the Governor has seen the numbers."

"Why should it be allowed?" Ruar asked. "And why would we want it to be?"

Good questions, both. "Your father wanted it," Daoíre told him. "Access to better land was most of his reasoning. It was to be considered in any formal treaty between the two lands, or so I was told. But that treaty was never signed, and both Donnalch and Callan are dead."

"We might lose too many of our people," Ruar argued.

"We might," Daoíre agreed. "But I think not. The ties of land and family are strong among our people. Are they not, Lord Sorley?"

So Bhradaín had told him of our conversation yesterday. To be expected. "They are," I said. "But, *Raséair*, Ruar, there is another consideration." I explained about the proposed forts.

"Who is to pay for these forts?" Liam asked sharply.

"The Eastern Empire, as I understood it," I answered.

"And their troops to man them?" Daoíre pushed his chair back.

"Aye, and why not?" Liam said. "We want their help in regaining Sorham. If there are troops stationed here, all the better. But tell me more about the trading harbour, Sorley. I see opportunity there, but Linrathe must control tariffs on what the Marai bring in for trade. Here is what you must say to the Governor." He dictated questions and numbers. I wrote it down."

"The Governor has proposed a meeting," I said, when the long list was done.

"He said so, in his letter," Liam said. "I am too old to travel. Daoíre can go in my stead."

"And I, Great-Uncle," Ruar said.

"You do not need to." Liam's hands, on the arms of his chair, shook. The palsy of age, I thought.

"He should," Daoíre said. "It is our tradition. Donnalch would have taken him, to observe and learn."

Liam shook his head, his characteristic single, terse movement. "We will discuss this later. Preparations for the council meeting take precedence. The *Eirënnen* will begin arriving today, I should think. I want no discussion of the trading harbour, do you hear?"

"Why not?" Ruar asked, giving voice to what I guessed we were all thinking.

"D'ye think I trust the coastal lords not to argue among themselves as to where it should be?" Liam said. "I want no *Eirën* taking advantage of the knowledge, sending messages into Varsland and offering favourable rates. The tariffs from trade with the Marai must be set by this house."

Messages into Varsland? I tucked that piece of information away to be considered later. Was that still happening? And if so, how?

CHAPTER 15

THE *Eirënnen* began arriving in the afternoon, singly and in groups who had travelled together. Old men, their sons killed in the war; one woman, holding her land on her own now her husband was dead; young men barely old enough to take the title, and a handful close to my age, survivors. At dinner the first night, the council not formally begun, the talk was of loss: girls taken, *torpari* killed, granaries emptied and flocks slaughtered. But with the resilience of a people who lived always with the vagaries of a harsh land, they spoke too of lambing and sowing, of marriages and babies born. A night of reunions, of conversations that might lead to betrothals and lands joined, of commiseration and, in some corners, argument.

I sat with the *Eirën* Ingold, and young Hagen, lord now of the *torp* just north of the *Ti'ach na Perras*. Hagen — I was having trouble remembering not to call him Hagi — was a year or two younger than I. I'd known him since I was eighteen. He'd fought beside me at the Wall, watched his father fall to a Marai axe. We talked of Perras's death, and the *daltai* girls taken by the Marai: little Niav, and Jordis. "No news?" he asked.

"None," I told him. "Nor likely to be."

"I suppose not," he said. "I'd asked my father to approach Egan, you know, for Jordis."

"I didn't," I said, surprised. "I'd have thought you betrothed years ago."

"I was, but she died. I liked Jordis. What about you, Sorley? A northern lord, unmarried at your age?"

I broke a piece of bread. "There was a girl waiting for me. My time at the *Ti'ach* was almost over when the war began." I said. Not a lie. I had never worked out what I was going to do about Betis.

"I see," he said. "What will you do now? Find an *Eirën* in Linrathe with no sons to inherit, and marry the oldest daughter?" I couldn't take offense: it was how landholders thought, both sides of the Sterre.

"Possibly," I said. "But probably not. I sit the examination to join the *scáeli'en* in the autumn."

"Do you?" he said. "Aye, well, as good a life as any for you now, I suppose." He leaned over the table to ask Ingold something. I looked around the room. Bhradaín caught my eye, beckoning to me.

"You'll play with me?" he asked.

"Tonight?" A very great honour, to play for the assembled *Eirënnen*. With a tilt of his chin he indicated we should step away from the tables.

"Tonight," he confirmed, his voice quiet. "I've a mood to set, one that will help convince these men that a fourteen-year-old boy should be their *Teannasach*."

We played the songs of battle, of victory and loss, and Bhradaín spoke of Ruar's bravery and valour. The boy had been unflinching, both in the long ride north — sixteen hours a day in the saddle, scant food and scanter sleep — and on the field. I'd fought beside him, and there had been others wielding swords not just to defeat the Marai but to keep the last loyal *Teannasach's* son safe. He'd killed his share of the invaders, and Bhradaín reminded the men before him of that, too.

The *Eirënnen* hoisted drinking cups and cheered; if there were dissenting voices, they were drowned out by the tide of approval. Bhradaín held up his hand for silence. It was late now, time for the last song of the evening.

"Many of you know the musician who accompanies me tonight," he said. "The lord Sorley rode north with our young leader, and never left his side in the fighting. He has done much more, but we will leave that for tomorrow. Only remember this: so that Linrathe had a chance of peace, he relinquished his lands and his family, for Lord Sorley is a man of Sorham. My lord, will you sing *An Dithës Braithréan* for us?

Even as I nodded my assent — I could not refuse, even had I wanted to — part of my mind recognized Bhradaín's ploy: the emphasis on my nobility, the reminder I had protected Ruar, the choice of final song, driving home to the assembled landholders of Linrathe what I had given up to buy them victory. I needed to remember these tactics, both as a *scáeli* and a *toscaire*. Bhradaín gestured me to the higher stool. The hall was silent.

I had sung this song of brothers separated forever by war twice for Cillian, in love and anguish. But tonight I needed a different vision. I closed my eyes, picturing Gundarstorp, its coves and hills, the rhythm of the waves, the screams of gulls. Sheep on the hill and curlew on the moor. Roghan, chasing behind me, fighting me with wooden swords, bundling fleeces as I sheared. I plucked the strings slowly, letting my heart and my fingers suggest the wavering curlew's cry, the susurration of water on rock, a boy's laughter. An entire verse with only the *ladhar,* before I began to sing.

I didn't try for purity: I'd never reach it. I let my voice crack and falter, and by the time I finished, tears gleamed in more than one pair of eyes in my audience. I bowed and stepped aside, unspeaking.

Bhradaín touched my shoulder. "Very well done," he murmured. "Go straight to your room. Speak to none of them tonight, or it will lessen the effect."

⸻⸻◦⸻⸻

A SERVANT BROUGHT BREAKFAST to my room the next morning. "The *scáeli's* orders," he told me. "I will return when the council is ready for you, my lord." I ate my porridge, and thought about what I might be asked about the treaty, and what I would and wouldn't say, in answer.

When I entered the hall, Ruar, seated at the high table between Liam and Daoíre, stood immediately. "Lord Sorley," he said, his voice clear and confident. "I had no chance last night to thank you for your music. You honoured us."

"The honour was mine," I replied, "and I thank Bhradaín for allowing it."

"You play well," Liam said, "but you are not here today as a musician, Lord Sorley. Daoíre will read the treaty to the *Eirënnen,* and then we will talk about its implications, and you will answer questions." I took the seat indicted, at the end of the high table, and Daoíre began to read.

It was Cillian's translation he was reading, and it was as precise as I remembered. Cillian had asked my advice a time or two on the ship home from Casil, weighing the Linrathan words against the Casilan for shades of meaning. I doubted I'd added anything, but I'd appreciated being asked. The *Eirënnen* sat, silent for the most part, except for the occasional murmured comment to a seat-mate. Daoíre read fluently, stopping for a sip of water once or twice. The last words he read were my formal signature: Somhairle of Gundarstorp. My birth name, although only my mother had used the old pronunciation.

"If I heard correctly," Ingold said, "this treaty is favourable. The biggest change in that we pay tribute south rather than north."

"The biggest change," another *Eirën* said, "is that we have lost Sorham, and have less than half the lands to find the tribute from. What right had you, Lord Sorley, to agree to those terms?" I didn't recognize him.

"Who else was there?" I said. "Casil offered help, but only to regain and hold Linrathe. Was I to refuse?"

"Who sent you east?" the man asked.

"No one. Donnalch was dead, Lorcann a prisoner, perhaps already dead when I left. I acted as a man loyal to Linrathe, and with its best interests at heart, nothing more."

"We could not have held Sorham," Daoíre said. "Too many *Härren* saw the Marai favourably. Too many marriages and trade alliances made across the narrow sea."

"Not only is the treaty favourable," Ruar said, "but I will remind you again of Lord Sorley's loyalty to me, your *Teannasach*. He saw the need for me to come north to my people, accompanied me and fought at my side, taking a wound."

"Ruar," Liam said, "you forget yourself. No support from the *Eirënnen* has yet been offered."

"Donnalch's son is your choice, *Raséair*?" Ingold asked. "Yours and the other men of your house?"

"He is," Liam said. A reluctant choice, I knew. "The boy should succeed his father."

"Then let us hold that oath-giving and get on with the council," Ingold said.

"How old are you?" the *Eirën* who had challenged me asked.

"Fourteen," Ruar replied.

"*Na,*" the man said. The northern pronunciation: his lands would be near the Sterre, then. "You're only a youngling. Daoíre, will you not stand?"

"I will not," he said. "I am not of the *Teannasach's* blood."

"But your sons — " The man stopped. "Forgive me, Daoíre. They died early on, did they not?"

"On the Sterre," Daoíre said quietly. I hadn't known. Hadn't asked. "With yours, Utar."

So many men had fallen that day, fighting against a strong Marai force supported by too many men of Sorham. Surrender had come quickly, and shortly afterwards, the quiet organization of the *Ti'acha* and certain *torps* into a network for those who opposed Fritjof's rule.

"Shall we give our oaths?" Ingold said, after a moment's silence.

"No," Utar said. "I want something decided. The lad clearly favours Lord Sorley, and I still don't accept his right to sign the treaty. We should settle that question first."

"What question?" A woman's voice. Birgit, wife to the *Eirën* Sullis; he'd died with only an infant daughter as his heir, and Birgit had declared her intent to run the *torp* on her own.

"The question of consequence," Utar said. "Is he to be allowed such a presumption? He was not an envoy. I say it was almost treasonous."

"If I am a traitor to anyone," I said, "it is Sorham. What would you have had me do, Utar?" I felt a flare of irritation, damped it down.

"Let Cillian na Perras sign it," he said.

A laugh from among the men. "Utar," someone said with an impatient edge, "he is sworn to the southern Empire."

"A traitor long before that, from what I've heard," Utar said.

That first flare of irritation blossomed into anger. "A traitor?" I growled, my chair scraping against flagstones as I stood to lean over the table. "Who do you think negotiated these terms? Could you have done better?"

"Not likely," I heard from among the men. "Utar, shut up. You could barely sell fleeces to the Marai."

Voices rose, in argument and defence. Liam pushed himself to his feet. "Quiet!" he shouted, smashing a fist on the tabletop. The hall fell silent. Blood pulsed in my temple.

"The loyalties of Cillian na Perras are known to me," he said, his old voice quavering a little. "I have no love for the man, and he could not have signed the treaty for Linrathe, but its terms are fair."

"They are," Ingold agreed.

"And Cillian na Perras is no traitor," Hagen said. "I've known him all my life."

A derisive snort from Utar earned him Liam's silencing glare. I took a deep breath. "Were I not a *toscaire*, and sworn to the land and its people," I said, "I would be first to offer my oath to Ruar."

"Then I will be," Ingold said, standing.

"First after his family." Daoíre said.

"Aye," Liam said. He coughed, shook his head for patience as he found his breath. "I cannot kneel, Ruar. You have my oath as your great-uncle and your regent, *Teannasach*."

Daoíre swore next, and Oisín, and then Bhradaín, before the *Eirënnen* came, one by one, to pledge their loyalty to Ruar. Birgit, too: women did not usually make the oath, but as a landholder she was required to. When she and the others arrived home, their *torpari* men would swear too, their lords standing proxy for the *Teannasach*. Men who were not landholders: the army, the *Comiádha*, the travelling teachers and traders, the *scáeli'en;* all would swear the oath too, at different times and places. Unless Ruar refused a man: it was his right. I wondered if he would accept Utar's.

Bhradaín, recording who swore their allegiance this day, bent close to my ear. "See who is last," he murmured. "Utar, and others whose lands abut the coast and the Sterre. They will bear watching, in the years to come."

Ruar took their oaths. Wise, I thought, to not encourage division this early in his leadership. I had not seen Liam or Daoíre offer him advice, although it was quite likely Utar's obstinacy had been known, and the counsel given privately.

"We will stop for food and drink," Daoíre said. "After the meal, it will be time to discuss details of how tribute is to be paid."

"I will go for my rest," Liam said quietly. "*Toscaire*, you may stay for the meal, but the discussion afterwards does not concern you."

I began to nod, before the words of my *toscaire's* oath flashed across my mind. *My loyalty is to the people of Linrathe.* "Liam," I said, "forgive me, but I believe I must remain. How can I know the thoughts of Linrathe's people, and serve their interests, if I am not here to witness?"

His face contorted, colour rising. "Great-Uncle," Ruar said calmly, "Lord Sorley is correct. He is not yours, or mine, to command. What we will speak about this afternoon concerns him directly in his role as *toscaire*. He should be present."

Liam's fist clenched and unclenched. Spittle formed at the edge of his lips. "Witness, then," he said, He struggled to stand. "But keep your mouth shut and learn from your elders. As you must too, Ruar."

|Chapter 16

"YOU'VE EARNED YOUR ALE," Daoíre said, when we were seated again, and the servants were bringing food and drink.

"I shouldn't have lost my temper at Utar." I drank gratefully.

"Why ever not?" he asked. "He's an obstructive idiot, and ridiculous, spreading those old rumours."

"Started by Donnalch's distrust?" I asked. I'd worked it out, once I'd calmed down a bit.

"I've always thought so. Donnalch never said much about why he didn't trust Cillian, and maybe that wasn't for the best: it allowed speculation." He eyed me. Ruar had left with Liam, saying he would see him safely to his room. "May I say something, Sorley? You're too nice. Too much the peacemaker. You'll need to be tougher in these negotiations. You shouting at Utar's the first time I've ever seen a spark of anger from you."

I nodded. "I know." Daoíre turned to speak to someone, leaving me with my thoughts. My mother, sweat soaking the bedclothes, her face flushed and thin. Grasping my hand. "*Somhairle*, do not fight with your brother," she'd whispered. "You are nearly a man; he is a boy. He will need your guidance and comfort, not your anger. Promise me."

I'd promised: what else could I do, knowing she was dying? She'd closed her eyes, breathing heavily. Then she'd opened them again. "Do not neglect your music," she'd said, "and be careful. So careful, my son." They were the last words she spoke to me: she died that night.

In the months following my father had dealt with his grief by working almost every hour of the long northern days, and the task of comforting my younger brother and sister had fallen mostly to me. How could I be angry with them, bereft and confused as they were? And I'd promised. I learned to damp down my own feelings, playing peacemaker between them and sometimes between Roghan and my father; and when I felt frustration and rage begin to rise, I'd turned to my *ladhar*. My ability to play with emotion and depth began that year after my mother's death.

But anger had become a foreign feeling to me, and expressing it almost impossible. That it — or at least something more than mild irritation — had surfaced these past months confused me, making me uncomfortable. That it was engendered mostly by Cillian bewildered me even more. Even today, it had been Utar's comments about him that had raised my ire.

In the early afternoon, when Liam returned, the council reconvened. "We must determine tribute," he told the assembled landholders. "This is our proposal." I listened as he told them of the need for timber, and the proposal to float it down the Tabha to a harbour built at its mouth. "For a fair rent," he said, to the *Eirën* whose land that was. He spoke of the forts planned, and the labour needed, and nothing else.

During one heated discussion on who had *torpari* to spare to harvest the timber, Ruar bent his head to mine. "My great-uncle told us this morning he wants no rumour of trade with the Marai. You are not bound by his wishes, or mine, but in this I think he is correct. It is too soon."

"You think I should say nothing to the *Eirënnen*," I said.

"Not yet. There will come a time when their opinions will be sought." He met my eyes, and he was only a boy again. "Do I overstep, Sorley? Am I trying to sway you?"

"No," I said. "You're just giving me your thoughts. I will consider them, Ruar. And I am pleased I heard them from you, and not Liam."

I listened to the council for two days. I heard a fair amount of argument about details, but little about direction; for the most part, the *Eirënnen* had only minor issues with the treaty. By the third day, when the talk had turned to who might have ewes to sell, or hands to send to a neighbouring *torp* at harvest, I began to listen with only half an ear, and to wonder about returning to Wall's End. Liam had not attended, this third day, and Daoíre and Oisín moved among the men, Ruar with one or the other of them, making suggestions and calming tempers. By mid-morning, I was bored enough to join Hagen: his lands abutted the *Ti'ach's*, and I knew them fairly well. If I could help anyone, it would be him.

"Sorley," he said when I sat down. "Should I put the meadows along the water to the plough, if I can find seed? They've been grazed, but we'll not have sheep in numbers for a few years yet."

"If those meadows are like the *Ti'ach's*, they're wet," I said. "Better leave them to the sheep, and plough better drained land, if you can." He'd be late getting the barley in, but it needed only three months to be ready to harvest. We talked a while longer, before I asked, "You've no factor?"

"Dead," he said succinctly.

"Go see Anndra," I suggested. The *Ti'ach na Perras*, unlike some, had no appointed factor to oversee the farming of its lands. Perras had preferred to work with one of the *torpari* men, husband to the housekeeper Isa. What Anndra did not know about the *Ti'ach's* lands, he'd said to me more than once, wasn't worth knowing, and Dagney had been happy to keep the accounts.

"Aye, I will," he said. "Although you've given me good advice. You know, Sorley, you should be *toscaire* to the landholders, not to the foreigners. You understand us, and our ways and needs."

"If I fail my *scáeli's* exam," I said with a grin, "I just might consider that."

He laughed. "As likely as that is, with the Lady Dagney as your teacher for all those years. I'm riding home in the morning. Join me?"

"If the *Teannasach* and his regent allow it," I said, "I'd be happy to." I liked Hagen, and company on the road would be welcome.

Dinner that night was raucous; there would be sore heads in the morning. But not mine. Liam appeared briefly, long enough for me to request of him and Ruar that I might leave in the morning. "Aye," Liam said, "you have your instructions."

"I was hoping you would stay," Ruar said. "I wanted to learn more about Casil."

"I'll return," I said. "But I should not keep the Governor waiting."

"I suppose," he said, making a face. "I am coming with Daoíre to meet him, in the summer."

"Perhaps," Liam said sharply. Ruar didn't reply. But it reminded me of what else I wanted to do. Excusing myself, I poured myself a cup of ale and found Daoíre. He followed me to a quieter corner of the hall.

"I was thinking about what you said," I told him. "That I am not strong-minded enough to negotiate with Casil. I never thought Liam would ask me to be *toscaire* to the Eastern Empire. Talks with the *Princip* — that I can do. Casyn's nearly a friend. But Decanius was too much for me, and while Livius is friendlier, there's iron behind his smile."

"Are you suggesting you want to resign? You are all we have," Daoíre said. "No one else can speak Casilan properly, and no one else has been there."

"I won't resign, not yet," I said. "But I'm not the right person. I don't think quickly enough, or subtly enough."

He chewed his lip. "You can be little more than an intermediary, I suppose. It will mean more travel, back and forth, and letters. If we recall Randall, can he teach me to pronounce Casilan properly?"

"He's fluent now, so yes."

"Then perhaps I will. And perhaps when I come to meet the Governor, with Ruar," he glanced over to where the boy sat, "and it will be with Ruar, regardless of what Liam says now, I will stay, and you can revert to being only our *toscaire* to — what is the new name?"

"Ésparias."

"Ésparias. Or maybe you can resign then, and become the *scáeli* you are clearly meant to be." He clapped a hand on my shoulder. "But you have seen how carefully we handle the old man. Say nothing to him. I will let you know, in time."

"*Meas*, Daoíre," I said. He turned to go, then swung around.

"Sorley. Say nothing to Cillian, either. I know you and he are friends, but this is Linrathe's business. Remember your oath."

Chapter 17

MUSIC DRIFTED OUT FROM Dagney's workroom when I ran up the steps into the hall a few days later. The door was open, so I didn't knock. She put her *ladhar* down as soon as she saw me, rising to give me a long embrace. "My dear," she said. "Did you get my letter?"

"No, but Bhradaín had received his, and he told me. In the autumn?"

"Or late summer. Have you enough time to build your instrument, if it is early rather than late?"

I grinned. "I anticipated a little, and began it some weeks ago. It will be of yew, but I'm afraid I have little chance of ornamenting it properly."

"It is the sound that matters," she said. "How is Cillian? And Lena and the baby?"

"Cillian," I said, taking the seat she offered, "works too hard. Yes, already. Would you expect anything else? And Gwenna had colic, and screamed endlessly, but it had eased when I left." I told her of the Governor, and the request to send Faolyn to Casil, and that Druise had gone with him.

"Not for all the years the boy will be there, surely?" she said, frowning.

"No. Just the summer, to smooth his way. He'll be home in the autumn." When I would have a difficult truth to tell him. Maybe it would be best if I resigned my *toscaire's* role completely, if I passed the *scáeli's* exam. I could wander then, as so many did.

While Isa prepared a meal, I went to the room she'd given me in the annex. I dressed in fresh clothes, and thought about shaving, deciding against it. In the corridor, I stopped outside Cillian's room. He'd asked me to bring the *xache* set back to Wall's End, and to collect some books for him. I'd take the *xache* set now, I thought, while I was here.

I opened the shutters to let light into the room. Unheated, the air felt damp, and unsurprisingly the wood of the chest had swollen, the lid hard to open. I ran my hand around the edge of the open box to make sure I hadn't damaged it. Perhaps because I had been looking carefully, when I took out the bag with the *xache* pieces, I noticed something. The chest appeared deeper on the outside than on the inside. I lifted out the folded blankets that were all that the chest held now, and when I did a compartment below became obvious, the leather hinges and handle in full view.

You cannot trespass, Cillian had said, when I'd told him I felt uncomfortable rummaging through his things, and yet as I lifted the panel — also with some difficulty — I felt as if I were. Then I knew I was, because neatly arranged in the hidden space were diaries, their covers labelled and the handwriting changing from a child's to Cillian's now-familiar adult hand. I sat back on my heels. Had he forgotten they were here? I closed the compartment's lid, replaced the blanket, and took the *xache* set.

Then I went to Perras's study. The room, empty of Perras's warm, welcoming presence, echoed with silence and loss. I opened shutters and examined the bookshelves. The books had been arranged logically, and I found the three Cillian had wanted without difficulty. The titles meant nothing to me. With a pang of sadness, I closed the shutters again, and took the books to Dagney.

She glanced at them. "Those are all Perras's, and therefore Cillian's. He does not need to return them."

"Cillian told me to be discreet about these books. He said they might be considered subversive, by the Casilani. Do you know why?"

"This one," she touched the smallest of the three, "is an account of the life and death of one of Heræcria's philosophers. He challenged their form of government and was executed as a result. I don't remember much more than that. The others I do not know. But, yes, the first could be considered controversial."

"I wonder why Cillian wants them?" I asked, not expecting an answer. "Have you seen these?" I showed Dagney the *xache* set.

"Not for years," she exclaimed. "They were all Cillian brought with him, other than his clothes. He asked for them?"

"He said he wanted Gwenna to have known them all her life."

She took one of the pieces, turning it in her fingers. "When the *Eirën* whose was lord to Cillian's family wrote to Perras, asking if we would take Cillian so young, he said 'the boy exceeds my own sons at *xache*, and they are twice his age'."

"He exceeds everyone at *xache*. Except his father, the General Turlo once told me."

"I remember the first time he won playing Perras. He was eleven or twelve. Perras was so pleased." She smiled at the memory. "The pupil surpassing the teacher."

"Did he ever disappoint Perras?" I asked impulsively.

"Disappoint? No more than any other student, and never for the same thing twice, if I recall. I had more responsibility for his behaviour — for all the students' behaviour — beyond the classroom, and he could be as thoughtless as any boy, but not excessively."

"And as an adult?" She looked at me sharply.

"What are you asking me, Sorley?"

"Something he said to me more than once. That he doubts he deserves to be loved. I wonder why; what he might have done to think that way. I thought if he had disappointed you or Perras, it might be part of it."

A look of pain crossed her face. "There were choices he made, as a man, that Perras wished he had not. But completely redeemed, by later decisions. I should find a way to tell him that, if it is preying on his mind." She frowned. "Should I have seen this, Sorley? He said nothing to me, nor did Lena, in the months I was there."

"Nor has he to me, since Casil," I told her. "A fear well hidden."

"Nonetheless, a concern," she said.

What had he done? There were the diaries, carefully hidden. They might hold the answer, but telling me I could not trespass did not extend that far.

But later, after I bade Dagney good night, I paused outside the door to Cillian's room. Then I went in. Placing the candle I carried on the desk, I opened the chest again.

I looked at the diaries for a long time before I reached for one. The first one, labelled in a childish hand with Cillian's name, and his age. Slowly, hating myself, I opened it, to the first page.

The Comiádh tells me I play xache *well,* I read in Linrathan. *I have not cried in five days. I will not cry again.*

I closed the book. I could not read this. I had no right.

CHAPTER 18

I LEFT EARLY THE next morning. As I mounted my horse, I looked first up at the track up from the courtyard, then south across the stream and the long valley. Cross-country might be faster. I rolled my eyes at my own folly and turned up the track. Half a day could not make that much difference.

When it began to rain again in the early afternoon, I was glad of my decision. I checked the books and my *ladhar* again, securely wrapped in oiled hide, found my hat, and kept riding. I slept that night at a guardpost on the Wall, reaching the fort in late morning. As I rode through the opened gate I had been holding the thought of the baths and perhaps a massage close for the last hour. Leaving my horse at the stables — it would get a rub-down and food and drink before I did, I thought wryly — and carrying my saddlebags, I entered the building, squelching with every step.

"Sorley!" Lena's voice, from behind me. I turned. She was wearing her uniform, and she was holding papers. I frowned.

"Lena? Why are you in uniform? Where's Gwenna?"

"I'm working," she said, "and Gwenna is with her nursemaid." Said almost casually, but I heard a tightness, tension, in her voice.

I hesitated. "I'm drenched. I must change. Can we eat together at mid-day?" An hour, or a little more.

"Certainly. My time is mine to order, when I'm not needed in meetings. Our rooms?" I agreed, and with a quick smile she turned back the way she had come. A small fire burned in my room, driving out the damp, but it looked bare, somehow. I stripped off my wet clothes, found a light tunic and breeches, and went to the baths.

Just after mid-day I knocked on Lena and Cillian's door, and pushed it open. Lena looked up from where she sat feeding Gwenna. A young woman — I would have said girl, but she too held a nursing baby, its hair fox-red — sat beside her. Seeing me, she pulled a shawl over the baby and her bare breast, flushing.

"I'm sorry," I said. "I didn't realize —"

"Tyrvi, this is Sorley," Lena said. "You may have heard your father speak of him. Tyrvi has come from Berge to help with Gwenna. We needed a wet-nurse; I do not make enough milk to feed her properly. It's why she cried so much; not colic at all. Tyrvi is Turlo's daughter, Sorley."

"I know your father well," I said to Tyrvi. "Your child has his hair."

"Yes," she said shyly. "He does. He is called Darel, for my brother."

"How old is he?"

"Two months." She stood, holding out an arm. "I'll take Gwenna now, Lena, and finish both their feeds in the nursery." Lena detached Gwenna from her breast, gently, and gave her to the girl. Gwenna made a few noises of protest, but Tyrvi murmured to her as she carried the two babies to the adjoining room. Lena adjusted her shirt.

"How old is she?" I asked, very quietly.

"Fourteen. At least she was not taken into slavery. Kyreth brought her to me, not long after you left. Gwenna wasn't gaining weight, and she was lethargic, but always wanting to feed. Gnaius weighed her for two days running, and declared I needed a wet-nurse. Tyrvi wanted to be where her baby's grandfather mattered, not his father. How could I refuse?" She had walked over to me as she spoke. I held out my arms, and she came into them, sighing. "I'm glad you're home."

"Cillian?" I asked.

"He is — all right. Working too hard, and not sleeping well. He missed you."

"Is he coming to eat?"

"No, because he doesn't know you're here. He would if he did, but usually he eats with Casyn, or in his workroom. If he eats at all. Shall I fetch him? Or shall we talk, just the two of us?"

I could tell which she hoped for. I didn't mind; I was reluctant to face him, for many reasons. "Just us," I said.

Food — bread, olives and cheese — awaited us on the low table. "What is it you're doing?" I asked, as we sat. "What work, I mean?"

"Inventories, of weapons and harness and the like." She reached for a piece of bread. "Nothing interesting, but I needed something to do, and the Procurator insists this must be done. The man counts or measures everything."

"And what is Cillian doing?" I bit into an olive. I'd developed a taste for them in Casil.

"Thinking of counterarguments to the changes the Casilani want, mostly. Trying to predict what they will demand next, and reading through old records when he isn't in meetings. Talyn helps with that, now."

"Couldn't you help him too, rather than count swords?"

"He hasn't asked."

The tone of her voice made me put my food down. "Why not? What's wrong?"

"I think he's angry with me, because I…" Her voice trailed off.

"What? Because you couldn't feed Gwenna enough? That's not your fault."

"No. Not that. But, Sorley, I was — relieved, in a way. I cannot be just Gwenna's mother and nothing more. At Tirvan, I would have been working again a week or two after her birth, with Dessa or Siane, if I couldn't go out on the boats. There were always women around to help, and because of Festival and the babies all being born close together, someone else could feed her, too, if I'd gone out to fish. No one brought up their babies alone."

Nor had they at Gundarstorp, I reflected. "And you think Cillian is angry because of this?"

"Maybe. Yes. He adores her, Sorley; you saw that, before you left. When he is here, he's always holding her, playing with her. Singing to her, even, the cradle song you wrote. I don't think he understands how I can want to do something else."

"Because his own mother never had the chance?" I asked. She nodded without speaking. "Has he said this?"

"No. He is just — distant. Not cold; he's affectionate enough, but it feels as if he's reminding himself to kiss me, or put his arms around me."

"And…" I hesitated. "Nothing more?"

"No. And not because it is too soon after the birth now. He can't, still."

I winced. I had a tiny glimmer of understanding of what making love had meant to them. "Lena, couldn't that be why he is detached? Remember what he said when he was arguing to not marry: that under the circumstances, it was unfair to you. Why Dagney did not ask you to swear vows of bodily fidelity, even though he did."

"He didn't," she said. "Neither of us did."

"But — " I thought back. Hadn't he? "Oh, gods," I said. "Did he think it wasn't necessary, because he would never recover?"

She looked at me quizzically. "No. That wasn't why. Hasn't he said anything to you?"

"No. What?"

She shook her head. "I asked him not to promise it, although he would have. It would have been inappropriate. But this is all theoretical, Sorley, and likely to remain so for a while yet, Gnaius says."

"I'm sorry," I said gently. "But, Lena, shouldn't you talk to him?"

Her jaw tightened. "If I ever saw him for more than a few minutes, I might. But when he comes from his treatments in the late afternoon he goes immediately to Gwenna, and how can I interfere with that joy? Without you or Druise with us in the evening, he returns to his books soon after we eat. Maybe Irmgard was right, Sorley."

"I told her she was wrong then, and I'm telling you the same now," I said angrily. The Marai princess had dismissed Lena as not worthy of Cillian's intellect. "You were part of all the planning for the negotiations in Casil, and all the work we did together on the Boranoi treaty. He should be consulting you."

After the meal, Lena went back to her storerooms, and I went looking for someone in the Governor's retinue. I found one of his assistants and requested a meeting. I would be told when, he assured me. Then I kept myself busy until late in the afternoon.

The bath attendant frowned at me: I'd just been there, earlier in the day. "The Major Cillian?" I enquired.

"He is here, yes."

"Alone?" He confirmed it.

Cillian's greeting was genuine, his smile warm, but his face had grown thinner again, the lines on it more pronounced. "Gods," I said, after I had slipped into the water. I didn't offer the kiss of greeting. "You look terrible. Are you working too hard?"

"I must."

"Why?" I inquired, settling back on the bench.

"There is much to do, to counter what Casil demands of us, and what I in naivety agreed to."

"What does they want now?"

"To divide the country into administrative districts, each with a Sub-Procurator. The *mensores* are sending in more reports, which we are not allowed to see. Casyn — " he took a deep breath, "Casyn is not arguing, or not strongly. Token objections, I would say."

"And you?"

"I try to limit what is actually done, counter with carefully researched arguments about Ésparias's laws and traditions. But I fear in the end all arguments will fail. Did you bring the books I asked for, *mo charaidh*?"

'Yes." I'd nearly forgotten them. "They're in my room."

"Dagney had no objection?"

"None. They're yours, after all." I paused. "It's strange, at the *Ti'ach*, without Perras."

"It must be." He studied me for a moment. "As you will find it strange here this summer, without Druisius."

"I suppose I will," I said. I didn't really want to talk about Druise.

"You could have resigned your position and gone with him."

"Resign?" I almost said, 'I am going to', but Daoíre's last words stopped me.

"I did, if you recall."

"But you weren't in the middle of important negotiations," I protested.

"Were we not?" An enigmatic answer; they always were, whenever conversation touched on that time.

"Why did you resign?" I'd never had the nerve to ask before. He rubbed his chin, not looking at me.

"Too many secrets," he said. "Too many half-truths and evasions, and innocent people being caught by them. More than my conscience could allow, by then."

I hadn't expected such a raw answer. "Gods," I said, deflecting, "maybe I should resign, before I am corrupted."

"You? I doubt you could be, *mo duíne chiòntach*."

The description irked me. "Cillian, I am far from innocent." I saw the tiny flicker on his face. He'd seen, here in the baths, the marks Druise's teeth left on my skin; he'd given me an assessing look the first time, but that was all.

"In this you are," he said.

"Nevertheless," I said, "I cannot resign, not now. Ruar trusts me, and I will not disappoint my *Teannasach*."

"Another innocent."

"Why are you so cynical suddenly?" I spoke sharply. "Cillian, you sound like you did years ago. Before your exile. Before Lena."

"For some of the same reasons, I suppose," he said. Then he smiled, unexpectedly, reaching out a hand to touch mine under the water. "I am frustrated with the *Princip*, and a little angry at myself. It has been a difficult few weeks, with Gwenna not well, and the talks. Forgive me."

He would have worried about his beloved daughter; regardless, he would have tried to be calm and rational in the face of that worry and the demands of his work. I studied the lines on his face. Only fatigue? "How bad has it been?"

He glanced over at me, surprise evident. "Bad enough,"

"And no Druise, to help you."

"I must learn to deal with this on my own," he said.

"It's been — what? Eight weeks? Ten? Don't be a fool, Cillian. I'm here now." Without Druise, he'll need me, I thought, to my immediate horror. Did I want Cillian fighting the desire for poppy, just so I could be the one to help him through it? I wasn't an innocent, but I wasn't an adult, either, if I really thought that.

"It should not be you I turn to, when the cravings occur."

Irritation flared again. "Why not? Or don't you trust me to be capable of supporting you through them?"

"I have no doubts about your capabilities, my lord Sorley," he said. "My distrust lies elsewhere." He smiled, a little sadly. "Now we know what was wrong with Gwenna, I will be all right."

"I hope so," I said. He *was* distancing himself, from me, too. "I'll get your books after the baths. Do you want them in your workroom?"

He shook his head. "No. Our private rooms, if you will. Now, tell me how things are in Linrathe, and what happened at the council meeting."

"Very little, in truth," I said. "Most landholders see no issue with the treaty, and only one objected to Ruar as *Teannasach*, because of his age. He swore allegiance anyhow." I didn't think I'd tell Cillian what had been said about him, by Liam or Utar or anyone.

"And the tribute?"

"Likely timber." I heard Gnaius's voice in the antechamber. "It was fairly boring, if I am truthful."

"Often they are," he said. "And you must be circumspect: Linrathe's *toscaire*, not my friend. I understand."

I only nodded. What was there to say?

Chapter 19

ANGER AT MYSELF BUBBLED as I went to fetch the books and *xache* set. My thoughts had been those of a child, eager for the attention of an adult. Then again, I thought, Cillian is still treating me like one. That wasn't entirely true, I admitted immediately, but it wasn't wrong, either. *Mo duíne chiòntach.*

Lena was not in their rooms. I put the books and game down on the table. Tyrvi opened the door to the nursery. "Lord Sorley," she said. "I wondered who it was."

"Just Sorley," I told her. "Please."

She closed the door behind her. "The babies are sleeping," she said quietly. "You wrote the song the Major sings to Gwenna, didn't you?"

"Yes. Do you like music, Tyrvi?"

"I like to sing."

My interest sharpened. "Do you? Songs from your village?" She nodded. "Could I hear them, some time? I collect songs," I explained, "and Lena knows only one, I think, and it isn't even from Tirvan."

Her cheeks turned a pale pink. "But I have no training, and you are a musician."

"It doesn't matter. Just sing them to the babies sometimes when I'm here. Will you?"

"All right." She cocked her head at a sound from the nursery. "That was Darel. I had better see to him. Then I could sing a song for you."

I settled down on a chair, picking up one of the books I'd brought Cillian. I opened it, reading a few lines, then more. I was still reading when

Tyrvi returned with her son in her arms. She sat across from me, the baby on her lap. "This is a lullaby," she said, and began to sing a simple tune. I listened intently, recognizing similarities with cradle tunes I knew, but the words were very different.

I took the *ladhar* I left here from where it hung on the wall, and adjusted its tuning. "Sing it again?" I asked, and this time I played along. She smiled in delight. The baby gurgled on her lap.

After another repetition I had both the variations of the tune and the words. I'd write them down later, but as long as I knew the tune, the words would come. "You remind me of one of my students," I told her. "Niav, her name was. She loved to sing too."

Her eyes were older than they should be, suddenly. "Did the Marai take her?" I nodded, not sure what to say. She looked away.

"At least she can sing her songs to her baby," she said. "They belong to us, the babies, and they are needed, aren't they? Because so many people died."

"They are," I said softly. There was sense in the thought, a way to find something good after the violence and terror. I wondered who had suggested it to her.

Gwenna wailed from the nursery. Tyrvi got up. "She'll need changing and feeding again." She touched my *ladhar* with one finger. "I'll sing for you again, if you like, Lord Sorley."

I was engrossed in the book still when Lena came in. "I came to bring Cillian's books," I told her, "and then I started reading one." I closed it, not wanting to talk about its contents.

"Have you seen him?" she asked, unfastening her badge of rank and putting it on the sideboard.

"Yes. Briefly. He was distant with me, too, Lena, just as he was in Casil. It's not you."

"I suppose, then," she said, dropping into a chair, "I should be happy he remembers to be affectionate, even if it feels forced. Or was he not, with you?"

"Not really." Nor had I wanted him to be. "Lena, at the *Ti'ach* — I had never been to his room before this winter. Students do not go into the annex. But he wanted his books, so I did. It was stark. His only personal possession, the *xache* set — it's here, by the way — was under his clothes in the chest." Not quite true, but I didn't think it was my place to tell Lena about the diaries. "Twenty years, or more, probably, he has followed Catilius, and the other philosophers of his school, and I think they are solace and strength for him now."

"To deal with the pain, and the cravings," she said.

"And other things. Including the work."

She sat silently, her eyes unfocused. "Then I must find my own source of solace and strength, mustn't I?" she almost whispered. "Have I been foolish, Sorley? Thinking we would have again what we did for a few brief weeks away from diplomacy and politics?"

"Lena, he loves you. This is temporary."

"Is it? Do you remember saying that with me, he was truly happy for the first time? In the weeks before we met you, in the Kurzemë village and after, he was a different man. I saw him change, the moment he realized who was on the ship, and that our past lives had caught up with us."

"But, Lena," I protested, "not back into the man he was before. Nor is he that now."

"That may be true," she said. "It is true. But neither is he the man I came to love over that winter of exile. Nor am I that woman, I suppose."

What could I say? I hadn't known her, bar a few days at the *Ti'ach*, and I certainly hadn't known Cillian in the freedom of exile. I had seen only the change from the cynical and bitter man he had been in his last years in Linrathe. "He is," I said, "somewhere inside him." But so was the cold and angry man, too, by that argument.

"Perhaps," Lena said. "But the pain will never leave him, and his mind will always need occupation, both to distract him from that pain, and to challenge him. He would have stayed at the Kurzemë village out of a sense of obligation, a duty, but I argued, telling him the work was not sufficient for his intellect." She took a deep breath. "So I cannot complain now he has something that meets his needs. I can choose my reaction to this. That is what Casyn — and Catilius — would tell me. So I will. Soon. But right now, what I'm feeling is angry."

Not what I had expected her to say. "I suppose," I said, groping for words, "that's reasonable. You wanted to go to the *Ti'ach* as soon as possible, didn't you?"

"I did. And yes, I'm annoyed about that, but I almost understand. It is something else that angers me."

"Which is?"

"He has never taught me Linrathan. I can't talk to him in his own language, except a phrase here and there. It's another sort of distancing, isn't it? Dagney started to teach me, but he didn't make any attempt to continue it, after she left."

But he had found time to learn Heræcrian. My idea. I winced a little, inside.

"Do you want to, still?"

"Of course I do!" She frowned at me. "The *Ti'ach* is still our dream, even if it is postponed, and I'll need the language. But it's more than that. Long ago —" She stopped. "Not so long ago, really; a year, or less, Cillian and I talked of finding the voices of common people in history. He suggested perhaps the *danta* were the best place to look."

"Out in the wilds, trying to survive, and he's talking about books and history? Why doesn't that surprise me?"

"It shouldn't," she said drily. "But looking for those voices was my thought, not his, and one I would like to pursue. But to do so, I will need to read Linrathan, as well as speak it."

"I'll ask Dagney to send some from her collection," I said. "In the meantime, I'll write some out for you, and I will teach you Linrathan. If Cillian is going to insist on working all the hours of the day, it'll give us something to do."

A headache had begun its rhythmic pulse in my left temple as I returned to my workroom. I needed willow-bark, or the baths, and the first was simpler. Not only Lena's concerns fuelled the pain. *Be circumspect with the books*, Cillian had told me. I knew why now: the one I had so idly begun was a history of rebellion within Casil, of the overthrow of a dictatorial Emperor. A history of treason and betrayal, and of its planning.

Chapter 20

15 Years After the Battle of the Taiva

MARAI, RIDING OPENLY IN daylight in Linrathe? Druise shrugged. "I know what I saw." We waited. Two men rode out of the valley before us. They were indeed Marai. I pushed my cloak a little further back, my eyes never leaving them. Swords, but each rider had both hands on their horses' reins; cloth riding clothes, not leather.

"Good morning," I called in Marái'sta.

"Good morning," one called back. "Are we on the right track for the school? *Cillín's* school?" He pronounced Cillian's name as it would be in northern Sorham.

"And what might you want with him?" I asked. They stopped a few paces away. The speaker was young, mid-twenties, I judged, the other man closer to my age. Dressed the same, but I thought the one speaking was of higher rank, the way the second man remained just a little behind, his eyes alert and moving. Just at Druise's would be.

"I am Vidar," he said. "I am come at my father's behest, with questions."

"Who is your father?" I asked.

"Who is asking?" he replied, with cool confidence.

"Lord Sorley, *scáeli* to the *Ti'ach na Cillian,*" I said. I wasn't, actually, lord of anything, but Ruar had insisted I keep the title.

"Lord Sorley!" His face brightened. "I am a friend of Bjørn's. My father is the Earl Aaro."

That explained a lot, although I still didn't understand why they were riding in Linrathe alone. Perhaps Ruar had thought insisting on an escort would be interpreted as an insult to his wife's cousin? But surely, a guide, at least?

"I am surprised to see you without a guide, Vidar Aaroson," I said. "It is easy to lose the way among these hills."

"I refused," he answered. "I like wayfinding. It is a challenge, especially in a new land. We have not been lost," he added, proudly.

"Well," I said, "you are on the right track, to be sure. But I will ask you to wait while I speak to my companions." I turned my horse to ride back to where Druise and Gwenna waited. Gwenna spoke Marái'sta, but Druise did not. I switched to Casilan.

"If he is who he claims to be, he is cousin to the *Teannasach's* wife," I told them, "come to speak to Cillian."

"About what?" Druise asked.

"He didn't say," Gwenna said. "But he's very relaxed, isn't he? Sure of himself." Two years a cadet, I thought, and she's better at this than I was when I was made *toscaire*.

"He may be," Druise said, "but his guard is not. I don't like this." He chewed his lip. "I'll escort them to the *Ti'ach*. Gwenna, say nothing, and give no hint you can understand them. Sorley, tell them I'm your guard, and that you're sending me with them for their safety."

Which would not be a lie. The *torpari* guard at the *Ti'ach* would be on them as soon as they crossed into our lands.

"We'll wait for you at Dun Ceànnar," I said.

He nodded. "I'll send word if I can't come."

I reined the gelding around. "Vidar," I said, keeping my voice conversational, "I appreciate your liking for wayfinding, but I must send my guard with you to the *Ti'ach na Cillian*. You are lucky to have ridden so far into Linrathe without incident, and I would not want the *Ti'ach's* patrols to accost you in error. Ésparias ensures they are well-protected, and Linrathe cooperates."

He heard the veiled warning. His eyes narrowed fractionally, but he smiled and made a gesture of acquiescence. "I appreciate your concern for our safety, Lord Sorley," he said.

"Druisius speaks no Marái'sta," I added. "Do you speak Linrathan?"

"Some. Enough to get by, I am sure. Will we reach the *Ti'ach* today?"

"Easily. And so you know, the correct title within Linrathe for Cillian is *Comiádh*."

"*Comiádh*." He tried the word out. "I will remember. Thank you, Lord Sorley. Safe journey, wherever it is you ride."

We turned our horses off the track to allow them to pass. Druise rode up to us. "Do what Sorley tells you, Kitten," he said to Gwenna. He gave me a wry grin. "Maybe this will deflect Lena's wrath over the puppy," he said to me. "But if I take the brunt of it, *amané*, you will know."

I watched them ride away before I glanced over at Gwenna. For all the years of being guarded, she'd never been in a potentially dangerous situation before. Nor had she ever heard Druise give her a direct command, expecting to be obeyed. Her bodyguard, not her friend.

"Is *Athàir* in danger?" she asked me. "Or my mother?"

"You tell me, Gwenna," I said. "What did you see?"

"The second man was his guard," she said. "He was watching Druise, mostly. I guess he knew Druise was our guard?" I nodded. "But his hand didn't go to his sword. So he didn't feel very threatened."

"Good. What else?"

"The young man — Vidar? — seemed genuinely glad to know who you were. But you didn't give my name, so you didn't want him to know who I am. So you think there might be a threat."

"I'm being cautious," I agreed. "Again, Gwenna, why?" We had begun to ride again, at a walk.

"They are Marai," she said.

"And?"

"There are Marai who want to kill *Mathàir*. Or hurt me, or Colm. Because she killed Fritjof."

"Yes. I'm likely erring in caution, but I promised to take care of you. I think Vidar is who he says he is, but that he rides unescorted worries me a little. I wonder why Ruar would allow it. So I didn't volunteer your name."

"But if he had asked you, you would have had to tell him, wouldn't you?"

"I would, yes."

"So you can't lie to me about anything?"

"I cannot, no." Not to a direct question. I did not have to offer information, but my oath to the *scáeli'en* council required me to tell the truth if asked, unless what was requested was someone else's secret.

"Is that why you're asking all the questions, instead of letting me ask? And you didn't answer my first question. Are my parents in danger?"

"I doubt it. And I wanted to know what you saw, without being influenced by my opinion." She was Cillian's daughter. Why was I surprised she saw through my dissembling? "But I fully intended to tell you."

"Did you? And that's a question, Sorley."

I tried not to laugh at her indignant tone. "I know, Gwenna. Yes, I did, and here is what I think. Vidar is the Earl Aaro's son, and he's here to talk to your father about setting up a school of some sort in Varsland. He's old enough to have children of his own and he may be thinking of them, and their part in a larger world, now Varsland trades with Casil." None of this was untrue. I waited for her next question.

But none came. We rode a little faster on the broad track. Gwenna was a good rider, and the dun mare she rode a seasoned traveller. The horse had been one of Lena's army mounts, although not the one from whose back she had killed Fritjof at the Taiva. When it had been time from Gwenna to graduate from her hill pony to a horse she could take to the White Fort, Lena had given her the mare.

My own gelding had travelled from the *Ti'ach* to Dun Ceànnar so many times I thought I could have slept in the saddle and he would still deliver me safely. Ruar had granted me freedom from my *toscaire's* oath when he had appointed me to the *Ti'ach*: I could not be both an envoy and a *scáeli*. But I had remained an unofficial advisor to him, and a messenger, sometimes, and I made the journey several times each year.

We stopped by a stream to eat and let the horses drink. A ring of stones made a convenient place to sit, and we ate cheese and smoked fish and bread companionably. "Sorley?" Gwenna said when she had finished eating. "You're going to tell me why my father broke his oath, aren't you?"

"You should know. You are just old enough now, I believe. We believe, all four of us."

"You have known him longer than anyone, haven't you?"

"In a way, yes. Since I was sixteen, although I did not see him again for two years, until I came to the *Ti'ach*. And even then he was travelling quite a bit." Nor had we been close. Cillian had made sure of that.

"In our classes, the General has told us we need to learn as much as we can about both our enemies and our allies, to understand their motives," Gwenna said. "So I want to learn more about *Athàir*, before you tell me his reasons for betraying Linrathe."

I said a silent thank you to Casyn for implanting the idea in Gwenna's mind. He was an old man now, nearly seventy, but he still taught the officer cadets. "Something to do," he'd told us, the last time he visited the *Ti'ach*. "Faolyn needs advising, of course, but I cannot be seen to be too much of an influence on him."

"A sensible approach," I said to Gwenna, "and one worthy of a diplomat in training. The General would be pleased. Where would you like me to start?"

"Why are we at the *Ti'ach*? Shouldn't *Athàir* be in Ésparias, advising Faolyn?" She rushed on, forestalling anything I could have said. "I know what I've been told, that it is for his health, but when I said that at the White Fort there were looks and whispers. Tell me the truth, Sorley."

"It is a long story, Gwenna," I said. "His health is part of it. Your father," I grinned, "tends to work too hard, if you hadn't noticed, and there was so much to be done once the war was over. So many negotiations with Casil and at first he couldn't be part of it. He was too ill."

"Was he?" She thought about that. "I suppose he must have been. But no one tells me about that time, after he didn't die when he was expected to. All I know is that he recovered, and after a while we came here."

I glanced at the sun. I needed a few minutes to gather my thoughts, and to prepare myself for the memories. "We should mount up. The track is wide enough for us to be side by side; I'll tell you as we go."

Chapter 21

"I'M NOT SURE THAT even with all my *scáeli's* skills I can truly help you see what those months were like," I began, when we were riding again. "Your father was in immense pain: every movement was agony. He could not walk, and we did not know if he ever would again. Gnaius and Druise forced him through exercises twice a day; they exhausted him, and he needed strong drugs."

"Drugs? *Athàir*? But he hardly accepts even willow-bark, and he waters his wine more than mine," Gwenna protested.

"But then he had no choice," I told her. "Gnaius had been very clear about it. He told Cillian that if the pain was not controlled, it would place too much strain on his frail body, and the fever would return. So he accepted the drugs." Just as now, some nights, he accepted the mix of cannabium and willow-bark that helped him relax and freed him of the worst pain for a few hours.

"He must have hated that," Gwenna murmured.

"He did," I said. "They affected his mind, his clarity of thought. Can you imagine it, Gwenna? Your father unable to think clearly, unable to hold a book for very long, or write; he couldn't understand a *xache* game, or follow more than a simple conversation. These things bothered him more than his physical limitations, in truth."

"He wouldn't be himself," Gwenna said, aghast. "He couldn't be the *Comiádh*."

"Exactly," I said. "Your father's fear, and your mother's. And I was away a lot: I was *toscaire*, then, to Ésparias and to Casil. Your mother was frightened, and very alone. You know what happened at Tirvan, and at all the women's villages. Her mother was dead, and her sister was in Casilla, a very long way away, and with a newborn of her own by then. Not that she would have asked her to come."

"Why not?"

I did not know what Lena had told her daughter. "Her experiences were so different from your aunt Kira's," I said, "and from almost all the women's. Only a very few villages escaped the raids by the Marai. She was carrying you, who had been conceived in love — love and light and laughter, she told me once — and their children, born and unborn, came from rape. She did not feel comfortable being with Kira, I think."

"What about Talyn?"

"She was there, yes, but you have to understand how busy everyone was, in the aftermath of such a terrible war. Your father was far from the only severely wounded soldier, and there had been many deaths. Talyn simply could not spend much time with Lena."

"I can't imagine my mother afraid and…and weak."

"It's difficult, isn't it?" I agreed. "But she was. She had lost so much, and she was terrified she was going to lose your father too."

"But I thought…" She frowned.

"Oh, he was going to live. Your mother did not care that he was scarred, and not graceful any longer — because he had been, Gwenna. Cillian was the most beautiful man I have ever met, handsome and elegant, and he danced like a swallow in flight. But none of that mattered: what Lena feared was that his injuries, to body and mind, would make him bitter and withdrawn. That he would not love you, or her."

"*Athàir*? Not love us?"

"Love," I said, "is not simple, Gwenna. It comes with responsibility, terrible responsibility towards the ones you love, and what if you believe you cannot meet that obligation?" You run away, I thought. As I had, to my everlasting shame.

"He thought he would not love me?"

"Only before you were born," I told her. "I saw that doubt disappear when Gnaius put you in his arms when you were only a few minutes old. He was frightened of being a father, but he kept his promises."

"I thought he always kept his promises," she said. "He's told us they are binding, and should be made sparingly, and only if we can keep them. But he broke his oath to Linrathe, and that is a special kind of promise."

"He did," I said. "You asked me to help you understand. It's your father as a man, with fears and wishes, a man who made — makes — mistakes, that you need to learn to see, Gwenna. May I tell you something?"

"Yes," she said, a little doubtfully.

"When I first met him, I didn't see the man, either, only how…exciting he was, in my northern hall. And even through the journey to Casil, and back, and the war, and all that came after, I was a bit like you. I saw my hero, an ideal of unattainable perfection, I think, not the imperfect human he is. And learning he was indeed imperfect, very much so, was as big a shock to me as it's being to you, right now."

"But you were grown up."

"In years, perhaps. Not so much in wisdom." I had another truth I needed to begin to weave into the tale; one that she must acknowledge if she were to fully understand Cillian's actions. But gently. "For all his mistakes and his faults, he's the best man I know or have ever known, and he deserves your love, and your brother's, and your mother's and mine. Don't judge him too quickly." The sky was clouding over. I wanted to reach Gedwinstorp before it rained. "We need to ride faster, Gwenna."

We were drenched by the time we reached the *torp*. Our horses were led away to be fed and watered and groomed, and we went into the hall for much of the same. The *Konë* took Gwenna to change into dry clothes, and I was shown to the room they always gave me, the one every *Eirën* or *Harr* kept for *scáeli'en* and *toscairen* and travelling teachers seeking a night's accommodation.

Old Gedwin and his son Gedi were sitting by the fire drinking ale when I returned to the main hall, *ladhar* in hand. I would pay for our room and board with news and song. I accepted a mug of ale, settling down to talk of sheep and the price of wool: things that concerned me as the overseer of the *Ti'ach's* lands.

"Did you have visitors last night?" I asked, in a lull in the talk.

"Aye," Gedwin said. "Two northmen, with a letter from the *Teannasach* for safe passage. Kinsmen of yours, Sorley?"

Were they passing themselves off as men of Sorham? The news didn't help my vague unease about Vidar. "No," I said. "Kinsmen of the *Teannasach*. The letter didn't say?"

"It did not. Only that they were to be offered hospitality as we would any traveller from Linrathe. Bound for the *Ti'ach*, were they not?"

"They were. We met them on the road. I sent our guard with them. He may come through here tomorrow, or the next day; Druisius, his name is."

"There'll be food for him, and a fresh horse, if he needs it. But a guard, Sorley?" Gedwin frowned. "For a *scáeli*?"

"Not for me. For the *Comiádh's* daughter."

"Aye, of course. Because of what her mother did. You are going north?"

"To Dun Ceànnar, first, then north. The first *Ti'ach* in Sorham opens this summer, and I am going to arrange their music program."

He nodded. "And the lassie goes with you?"

"I do," Gwenna said from the door to the women's rooms. "Thank you for your hospitality, *Eirën* Gedwin. I am a cadet in Ésparias, training to be a diplomat, a *toscaire* of sorts. I should know the people and lands of Linrathe and Sorham better than I do, for that reason, and so Sorley agreed to bring me with him."

"You are welcome, my lady Gwenna," Gedwin said, rising with a glance to his son, who also stood. I wondered when she had prepared the excuse for travel; it was well thought out.

"Gwenna," she said. "I have no rank in Linrathe." She was correct; married *Comiádha* were rare, and there were no formal titles for their children.

"Perhaps not," Gedwin said. "But Ésparias is our ally now, and you have rank there. But we will not stand on ceremony, if you so wish. Will you indulge an old man, and let me tell you how much you look like your father?"

In the firelight, her dark hair brushed back off her forehead, and dressed in a simple tunic and breeches, soft indoor boots on her feet, she looked more like Cillian than I had ever seen her do before. For a moment, I simply stared. She met my eyes, and I saw confusion rise in hers.

"You do," I said quickly. "Or I think you do; Gedwin, you would have known Cillian at fourteen, wouldn't you?"

"I met him once or twice, with the old *Comiádh*," he said. "Aye, Gwenna, you could almost be his twin. But come and sit, lassie. There is ale, if you would like."

"A small cup," she said. She glanced at me, as if for permission. I nodded. She smiled naturally, and I thought the moment past.

After dinner, I moved again to sit near the fire, this time to tune my *ladhar*. The family gathered round; a *scáeli's* visit was always welcomed, for songs and sometimes dancing, and music was the one love of my life untouched by regret or compromise. Playing was never a hardship.

Gedi brought out his own *ladhar*: I knew from other visits he was a competent musician, with one winter at the *Ti'ach* under Dagney's instruction. He and I played for much of the evening, with breaks for ale to soothe our throats. I sang the dragon *danta* to his accompaniment, for the children, and after they had fallen asleep in laps or on the floor, we harmonized on familiar tunes.

We finished *The Two Sisters*. I raised the mug of ale to my lips. "Sorley," the *Konë* said. "You played a song once, one of yours, about war and partings. It was very beautiful. Would you play it again?"

Scáeli'en were bound not just to tell the truth, if it was theirs to tell, but also to play or sing the songs requested. I wished Gwenna had fallen asleep, but she sat cross-legged on the floor, enjoying the evening. "I will," I said. "But this must be the last song. My voice grows tired." Gedi, beside me, put his *ladhar* down. I checked my tuning, played the opening notes, and with a silent prayer that Gwenna was sleepy, and not truly listening, I began to sing.

My true love's eyes are darkly gleaming
In candlelight and music's lure;
One night alone, at spring's fair dawning,
To keep me longing through the years,
To leave my soul bereft and mourning.
You danced that night with grace unfettered,
A glance my way, a touch bestowed.
Your dark hair swept by supple fingers.
Too soon the day, the calling road,
The shaken head when asked to linger.

A long, long path, and distance boundless,
Years of sorrow and empty days
Till chance or fate together brought us,
So far from home, in summer's blaze,
With war behind and war before us.

I risked a glance at Gwenna. She was sitting more upright, and her eyes were wide.

The gods and time have blessed us both
With love's reward for all our years
Of wandering on lonely ways;
A respite offered for our cares,
A soul to hold ours, all our days.
But candlelight and music's memory,
Dark eyes gleaming over wine
Revive that youthful love and longing
For graceful fingers touching mine
For kisses left at day's first dawning.
My life's companion loves me truly
My heart is his and his is mine,
But older love is not forgotten
There is, by fate, or god's design,
A yearning still for paths untrodden
You danced that night with grace unfettered,
A glance my way, a touch bestowed.
Your dark hair swept by supple fingers.
Uncharted ways might be explored,
Still dreams this wistful, loving singer.

I repeated the last line, not looking at my audience. The final notes faded into the air. In my worry about what Gwenna was thinking, I had forgotten to change the words to the second-last verse: 'My heart is his and his is mine.' Usually I substituted 'hers', unless I was very sure of my listeners. But if I were lucky, no one would have noticed, or at least thought it odd. After all, I had sung *The Two Sisters* just a little earlier, and it had similar words.

"Ah," the *Konë* said. "As beautiful as I remember. Such a sad song." All Linrathan songs were sad, Druise maintained. "Bedtime," she announced, to the women. "Come, Gwenna, I will make sure your bed has been warmed and the fire banked."

Gwenna stood, as graceful as her father had been. "I have not heard that song before, Sorley," she said, challenging just a little. She is far too bright, I thought, not to understand I wrote it for Cillian, and to put that together with my reaction when Gedwin said she looked like her father. For the several-hundredth time in my life, I cursed my expressive face.

"I rarely play it early of an evening," I replied. "You have always gone to bed before, I believe."

"My parents know it, then?"

"They do."

Uncertainty crossed her face. But there would be difficult questions, tomorrow.

CHAPTER 22

I REMAINED RESTLESS, UNSETTLED, as the following days stretched into a week and more. My irritation with Cillian didn't go away. I'd argued myself back into rationality about the book: he could be reading it for any number of reasons. But I didn't ask him, about that or anything else, and I didn't know why, except I hadn't liked his dismissal of me as an innocent. I was annoyed, and worried too by what Lena had told me.

She and I worked together an hour or two most days learning the spoken *danta* and Linrathan, usually in the late afternoon when Cillian was with Gnaius. I often spent half a day in their rooms, just reading, or playing for Tyrvi and the babies. But I left them to themselves most evenings: Cillian had not asked me to play *xache*, or music.

"Why are you not eating with us?" Lena asked me one afternoon.

"He'll only discuss the treaty with me," I pointed out. "He should be relaxing with Gwenna and you, not thinking about work."

"He does anyway," she said bluntly. "And it should be our work. It is yours, for Linrathe, and his, but my name is on that treaty too. And he doesn't listen, when I do suggest something." I heard the irritation, the exasperation, and in the line of her jaw I saw anger again behind her controlled words.

What had happened now? "Lena," I began, but I had no chance to say anything further, stymied by Cillian's arrival. He did look tired, and more than that, vexed. He leant heavily on his cane, and his smile to me was perfunctory. Nor, I noticed, did he kiss Lena. He dropped into his chair with a sigh that was close to a groan.

"Should I even suggest cannabium?" Lena said.

"Just wine," he said.

"I'll get it." I barely watered his. After the first sip he shook his head.

"More water, Sorley, please. I need a clear head."

"What is it today?" Lena asked. I returned his wine to him, having added a few drops of water.

"The records I need are at the Eastern Fort, if they exist at all. I must know how land was granted to the women's villages, if I am to counter the arguments in any effective manner," he said.

"You really haven't listened to anything I've told you, have you?" Lena said, her voice tight. She stalked out of the room, returning with a book in her hand, putting it down in front of him with some force. "Colm's history, which you have never read, preferring to study obscure Casilani and Heræcrian texts over the history of your adopted land. There is a description, in the third chapter, of how lands were assigned to the villages, to be held in common rather than by individual ownership."

"Are you sure?" Cillian asked. Gods, I thought, that was foolish.

"Of course I'm sure," Lena said icily. "I may not be *Ti'ach* educated, Cillian, but I can read. Colm was impressed by my questions; they showed insight, he said. I remember a time when you said the same, but you seem to have forgotten that."

"No," he said wearily. "Lena, it is just — "

"Just what?" Her voice was high, and every muscle taut. "Cillian, the gods know you have suffered, and you are in pain and overburdened with this treaty you regret. But I have suffered too. For weeks I thought you were going to die, and leave me with a child I hadn't planned, and nowhere to go. My mother and aunts are dead; my sister and my friends brutalized by the Marai, and now this treaty that I signed — I, Cillian, for the women of my land — is taking away what little they have left, and I am not allowed to do anything to try to counter that. You dismiss my suggestions as if you know what the women here want, when you haven't bothered to ask any of us." Fury had not brought her to tears; instead, it was the flame of the furnace or the forge, shaping steel. This was the woman who had killed Fritjof. I held my breath, my eyes going from her to Cillian.

He had put his wine down. A small muscle jumped under his eye; otherwise, his face showed no emotion. He put a hand on the book. "May

I?" he asked quietly. She made a brief motion of assent. He began to leaf through it, and then to read.

As quietly as I could I rose to pour another glass of wine. I handed it to Lena. "Should I leave?" I murmured. She shook her head. I wondered where Tyrvi was, with the babies, and if she had heard Lena's words.

"May I take this to my workroom?" Cillian asked a few minutes later.

"No," Lena said. "I don't want it out of my sight. You can read it here, and take notes, and you can ask me questions if you think I might have useful insights. And if you want to show it to the Governor to support your arguments at some point, you will do it with me present. If he wishes to know how the lands were managed, a first-hand knowledge might just be useful."

"A valid point," he said. He moved, as if trying to find a more comfortable position. His jaw clenched.

"Gods," Lena growled, "would you stop being stubborn? Add some cannabium oil to that wine."

He shook his head. "Willow-bark, nothing more."

Without a word she went into the bedroom. He glanced up at me, his eyes unreadable. "Lena told me to stay," I said, "but I will leave if you prefer."

"Decanius thinks Lena no better than a *scrapta*," he said. "He would ridicule her, or worse."

"The common soldier not a fit wife for the Emperor's son?" I said. "Did he hear that from Eudekia, do you think?"

"More likely Quintus, his uncle, I would think. Palace gossip, but somehow Decanius also knows we were married only hours before Gwenna was born. He laughs about it. I would not subject Lena to that."

"Is that a wise choice? Lena is more than capable of proving her own worth, to Decanius or anyone. And if you keep her away, from the talks or from dinners, could not the Governor think you are ashamed of her, confirming what he thinks?"

Faint surprise showed on his face. "I had not considered that."

"Then maybe you should," I said, not masking my displeasure. He leaned his head back, closing his eyes, purpled with fatigue.

"There is so much to think about," he murmured.

"Then ask for more assistance. You won't let me, as I am Linrathe's *toscaire*, but Lena can help."

"What can I do?" she asked, returning with a cup in her hand. She set it down in front of Cillian. "I made it strong," she told him. "If it's too bitter, there is honey."

"Lena. May I explain?" he said, opening his eyes. I glanced up at her; she was watching him, concern battling with her still-obvious anger.

"No," she said, but her voice was calm. "Not now. I'm going for a walk, for a little while. When I return, you may tell me your justifications, if your pain has lessened. Sorley, would you stay to ensure Cillian sits quietly for half an hour, and does not attempt to work?"

"With pleasure." When she had gone, he slumped back in the chair. "Drink your tea," I said.

"I will. Music would not be unwelcome, *mo charaidh*."

I took the *ladhar* down from the wall where it hung and began to play. Cillian reached for his tea, drank it down, and sat motionless. I didn't sing, just let my fingers move from one familiar Linrathan tune to another. When I thought he looked a little better, I spoke over the quiet melody. "Could it be," I asked, "you have forgotten the difference between shield and shelter?"

"A subtle distinction," he said.

"But a distinction, nonetheless. Lena needs one from you, not the other."

"Such insight, my lord Sorley. How have you grown so wise?" A sardonic tone, raising my hackles again.

"Lena is my friend, Cillian. Friends talk, and often about the things — or people — that trouble them. *Mo duíne gràhadh*," I said, softening my voice, "can't you see that it is her friend and companion Lena is missing, as well as her lover? If you can't be the one just now, it is no reason not to be the other." I wasn't going to tell him what I feared: that Lena might yet leave him. I couldn't speak those words. They would destroy him.

He was quiet so long I wondered if he had fallen asleep. "I dislike what conclusions I have drawn from considering your comments," he said, "but I thank you for them. I would like to ask you a question. Do not feel you must answer, if it is uncomfortable."

So formal. "Ask."

"How have you learned to enjoy being only my friend, when it is less than what you truly want?"

"You know how," I prevaricated, taken aback by the question. "You did, after — after Ivor."

"Yes. But then Lena was hurt, and not being denied, in the same way. She had no interest."

"You were sheltering her."

"Those were her words, exactly. This is not the same."

"Then — " I paused, gathering my thoughts. "The truth, Cillian? Druise has made it easier, but only somewhat. I still want you, and sometimes that is more difficult than other times. I'm not sure that will ever change. But the alternative is to not be with you at all, and that is unthinkable now. So I accept the price I pay to be your friend."

"I doubt I am worth it." His eyes were closed again.

"That is my decision to make," I said. "As Lena made hers. We are honouring our choices, as much as you will let us. I don't blame Lena for feeling excluded, and for being angry about it."

He picked up the wine he hadn't finished, taking a mouthful. "Nor do I," he said. "Shield, not shelter, as you said. An effective turn of phrase, my soon-to-be-*scáeli* friend, as well as a mistake to be rectified. When Lena returns, will you leave us to ourselves?"

Ale, I thought as I left Lena and Cillian to talk, would suit me just now. I didn't feel like political conversation: someone at the soldiers' commons would allow me to be their guest. But at the door, the steward stopped me. "Best not today, Lord Sorley."

"Why not?" I asked.

He glanced behind him before he stepped out of the building. "Not here. Walk with me to the storerooms." When we were in the open, and it was clear no one could hear us, he began to speak. "The men are unhappy about the new cohort structures, and the way the Casilani *capori* treat them, or at least that is what it is today. One or two are being very vocal. They are mentioning Major Cillian, and not in a good light."

"I see. None of the Casilani are in the commons just now, I would think?"

"No. But there was a fight last night, and several have been banned for a week."

"They are blaming the Major for bringing the foreign troops here?"

"That, and for what the treaty says." We'd nearly reached the storerooms, and its guards. "Druisius would have told you," he said under his breath. "He is missed; he keeps the other Casilani in line. Although some accuse him of disloyalty."

I nodded to the guards. "Bribe them for better ale," I said with a grin, and kept walking, as if the steward and I had simply met by chance, heading in the same direction. I glanced at the sun. The *Princip* just might be at the baths; with Decanius gone. I circled around the fort to the bathhouse.

The attendant confirmed his presence. "Ask if I may join him," I instructed him. He came back quickly, ushering me in. I stripped and washed, and went through to the hot pool.

"What brings you here, Sorley?" Casyn asked, as I settled into the water.

"Something I was told today that I thought you should know," I said. I told him what the steward had said. "Do they need someone to blame who is not their *Princip*?"

"Plenty criticized my brother's policies." Casyn said. "I appreciate your information. Birel had told me of the fight last night, but not what was behind it. I will ensure proper consequences. They will serve to make the troops aware that we know what is being said."

Chapter 23

I LEFT CILLIAN AND Lena to themselves for a few days, arguing to myself they needed the time together — assuming they had managed to reach some reconciliation — but also sheepishly acknowledging that my stark words to Cillian: 'I still want you' embarrassed me. Although why it should, I wasn't sure. We all knew it. On the third day, though, hours spent transcribing music in preparation for the autumn examination, and more time spent on bending wood for the *ladhar* I was making left me with aching shoulders and a stiff neck. I went to the baths, hoping for a long soak and a massage.

I hadn't expected Cillian to be there. More of the afternoon had gone than I'd judged. But he seemed happy to see me, so I slipped into the hot pool and submerged all but my head, letting the heat of the water work.

"Lena," he said, conversationally, "has an excellent memory for what she has read. She knows Colm's history nearly by heart, which is proving useful."

"Now you're actually listening to her."

"Indeed. She had more words about my arrogance, which I fully deserved. Although I never thought Dagney's scholarship lesser than Perras's, only different. But we — I, but I doubt I am alone in this — carry presumptions, prejudices, of which we are not fully aware."

"I suppose we do." Or which we are fully aware of, but allow to sway us anyhow, I thought. I had proved myself for many years to be competent to succeed my father as *Harr* of Gundarstorp, yet one aspect of me would have led to my disinheritance in a moment, had he known. "Decanius doesn't bother to hide his."

"That he does not. We have spoken about how she will handle him, when she comes to the next talks."

"I assume it won't involve her secca," I said.

He looked at me, eyes narrowed a little. "What is wrong, Sorley?"

"Nothing," I said, and saw his frown. "I don't know. I'm just out of sorts. I miss Druise, I suppose."

His face softened. "I am sorry."

"You sent him away," I snapped.

"You *are* out of sorts," he observed. He reached out a hand, touching my shoulder.

"Don't," I said. "Cillian, just — don't."

He dropped his hand immediately. "I'm sorry," he said quietly. "That was insensitive."

"It was," I said. "I do miss Druise. But remember what I told you a few days ago. Will you be all right, if I leave?"

"Of course. Just tell the attendant." I climbed out. He said my name. I turned, looking down at him, conscious suddenly of his gaze, and my nakedness, and that we were alone. "*Mo duíne gràhadh,*" he said. "I wish — "

"Wishing," I said, cutting him off, "got me nowhere, did it? I'll send the attendant to you after I'm dressed."

I refused any assistance, drying and dressing as rapidly as my trembling muscles would allow. Anger and shock at my own behaviour combined to make me unsteady, disoriented. I walked outside, careless of my cloak, turning towards my room, then away: I didn't want to go inside. There were hours of daylight left.

The gate guard greeted me civilly, and I said something I hoped was a fair reply. My boots clattered on the steps down to the harbour. I headed south along the seawall and down onto the beach. Gulls cried and circled, or stood at the tideline, pecking at weed. Shells and starfish littered the sand. I walked along the hard strand, watching the tide recede.

"Lord Sorley?" A quiet voice, from beside the cliff. I stopped. The man stepped forward, just a little. I recognized him from the soldiers' commons.

"Evan, isn't it?"

"Yes. I haven't seen you out here before."

"I needed fresh air," I said, trying to be courteous. "I suffer from headaches, from time to time. And you? What brings you onto the beach?"

"The seals," he said, indicating the animals basking on rocks a little offshore with a tilt of his head. "And there's a pair of otters, too. I like to watch them." I turned to look. "When will Druisius be back?" he asked.

"I don't know."

He took a step or two nearer. "Are you in need of company, Lord Sorley?"

A tug, visceral and deep. He was my age, I guessed, slight, his lips slightly parted in a smile. He cocked an eyebrow. I hesitated for a moment, and then I moved towards him.

Arms around me, the touch of lips on skin. A growled laugh, the nip of teeth on my ear. The moment of utter oblivion. I lay still, avoiding thought, listening to my heart beating.

"Druisius is a lucky man," Evan said, sitting up.

"You won't — ?"

"Tell him?" He adjusted his clothes. "No. Neither will you, Lord Sorley. At least not my name."

"No." I sat up. Sand chafed. I looked at the ocean. Pulling off my tunic, kicking my breeches onto the beach, I ran into the waves. Evan called something, but I ignored him. When the water reached my thighs, I dived, swam a few strokes, turned around.

I stood dripping on the hard sand. The wind chilled me, but I would dry soon enough. I walked forward, bending to pick up my clothes. Evan sat still, watching me. I shook as much sand as I could from my shirt before using it to rub water from my hair. "I wouldn't have done that," he said. "Far too cold."

"Never gets any warmer, in Sorham." I crouched; I didn't want to stand over him. "I've been swimming in the sea since boyhood. Sometime there're chunks of ice in the water. "

"Look!" he said, pointing. A pair of otters crossed the beach to slide into the water. He grinned, the sight clearly bringing him enjoyment.

"We had otters at Gundarstorp, too," I said. We watched the animals in silence. One flowed up onto a rock, a fish in its mouth, and began to eat.

When its meal was done, it slipped back into the water with barely a ripple.

I was dry, and cold. I dressed. Evan didn't move. "I'll stay here," he said. "Watch the otters some more. A pleasure, Lord Sorley."

It had been. Demanding, brief, mindless pleasure. A hunger satisfied, as instinctual as the otter with its fish. I nodded, smiling, and he smiled back before his eyes returned to the animals. I turned to walk north, back to the fort.

Regret insinuated itself into my thoughts before I'd reached the stairs up the cliff. Regret, then disgust.

In my room I poured myself wine, not watering it. Behind my anger with myself was a memory, a familiarity to this feeling. I picked up my *ladhar*, letting my fingers find what they might. A few notes, bringing remembrance.

I had been seventeen. The visiting *scáeli* had been older by a handful of years, new to his title. My father thought nothing of me going to his room for lessons, encouraged it, in fact. Amlodd had taught me more than music, to my delight — but also to my guilt. I loved Cillian, did I not?

The young *scáeli* returned the next year, and then I did not see him for some time. Our last encounter had been chance: I'd ridden to the smithy at Hagenstorp, and he'd been visiting its *Eirën*. We'd talked a little of music: anything else, outdoors in daylight in Linrathe, was far too dangerous.

He'd taught me unintended lessons, too: that desire and love were not the same thing, and that a physical appetite temporarily slaked did not reduce my longing for Cillian. All you have done today, I told myself, is satisfy a need. There is no need for guilt.

Chapter 24

IN THE HEIGHT OF summer, Rufin returned from Casil, bringing Apulo, the body servant Gnaius had insisted Cillian needed. Newly freed from slavery, scared and looking younger than I had expected, he stood trembling when Gnaius brought him to Cillian.

"Sit," Cillian said to them both. Apulo remained on his feet. "Apulo," Cillian said, gently, "you are not enslaved now. Please take a seat." He did as he was asked, perching on the edge of the chair.

"I have had the pleasure of Apulo's massages, at the baths in Casil," Gnaius said. "His hands are skilled. Over the next weeks I will teach him all he must know about your needs, Cillian, and then perhaps by the autumn I can begin my travels in these lands, to teach and to learn."

"Of course," Cillian said. "You have curtailed your own interests too long, in caring for me."

"Not at all," Gnaius said. "I have learned much from your case. Your treatment and recovery will be the subject of a lecture I am preparing for when I speak again in Casil. Including," he bowed his head to me, "the role of music in that recovery, Lord Sorley. And speaking of music, Apulo, please sing."

The boy — he wasn't, but it was hard not to think of him that way, slight and frightened as he was — stood, obediently. What poured from his throat, words to a tune I recognized as one Druise played sometimes, was the voice of a trained singer, precise and controlled and beautiful. "Oh," I murmured involuntarily, listening with wonder and confusion. How had such a singer become enslaved?

"You sing beautifully," I told him, when the song was done.

"*Gratiás,*" he said shyly, but I saw a faint smile.

"I have told Apulo," Gnaius said, "that music is valued in this household. That the Lord Sorley is a musician, as is the absent Druisius. And," he looked at me again, his face showing me only the calm, impassive physician, "I have also told him nothing is expected of him in the treatment room or elsewhere, beyond Cillian's massage and exercises, and assistance with dressing and the baths."

I met Gnaius's eyes with equal impassivity. "A message for your Procurator, not me," I said. "In our lands, he is the only man who needs to hear that."

"Take no offense," Gnaius said. "A reassurance for Apulo, nothing more. But given that concern, would the *Princip* accept an oath of loyalty?"

"It would be wise," Cillian said. "I want no confusion over his status, as there was with Druisius. Are you willing to make an oath, Apulo, to the *Princip* of Esparias?"

"To you?" the boy asked.

"No. To Casyn, my father's brother. He is our leader."

"I am free? I have a choice?"

"You are," Cillian said. "You will be paid for the work you do for me; and you are free to leave my service if you wish, but if you do, it is better you are a citizen of Ésparias, and not Casilani. Do you see?"

"Yes," Apulo said. "I will swear. I wish not to go back to Casil, ever."

A knock sounded at the door. Lena got up, frowning, to answer it. It had sounded like Birel's double rap. "The *Princip* and the Governor require your presence," Casyn's soldier-servant said, a little apologetically. "Yours too, Lord Sorley."

"I will show Apulo where we work," Gnaius said. "Later, he can watch your treatments."

I handed Cillian his cane. "About the forts?" I murmured.

"Perhaps," he said, "but why include Lena? The timing suggests to me a message from the Empress, something about the treaty. We are all signatories."

"There is a decree from the Empress," Livius said. He'd greeted us with apparent pleasure, smiling, asking after Gwenna. Decanius had been barely civil, his usual aspect since Cillian had revealed his overstepping of his position as Procurator of a royal province.

"It affects the leadership of Ésparias; your local leadership, not my position or the Procurator's. Lord Sorley, I have asked you to attend as Linrathe's envoy, so that the exact message of the decree can be accurately conveyed to your leader. And," he added, "because of your close friendship with both the Major and the Lieutenant."

Cillian's eyes had narrowed. Gods, I thought, now he has recovered, has Eudekia countermanded his decision to renounce the leadership? With all the unrest there is around his position as advisor? But she would not know that. I glanced at Lena. Her set jaw showed me she had reached the same conclusion.

"The decree should be read by you first, *Princip*," Livius said. "Then give it to the Major, if you will."

Casyn could hide his feelings better than many men, but his lips parted as he read. He glanced at the Casilani men, and then at Cillian. Wordlessly, he handed Cillian the letter. Cillian's eyes scanned the page. He blinked once, and an expression I didn't understand — almost sorrow, I thought — crossed his face. Then he laughed. "This," he said, "borders on the ridiculous, Governor, and I shall tell the Empress so myself. How can the bastard son of a peasant girl and an army cadet be made a prince?"

A prince? I bit my lip to stop myself from gasping.

Livius laughed, genuinely, masking Decanius's grunt of anger. "You have just cost me a large amount of wine. The Empress wrote that you would say something close to this. I had wagered you would not. Clearly," he said, chuckling, "she knows you better than I thought."

"A prince?" Lena said. "What does this mean for our daughter, Governor?"

Her frown and her clenched hands told me — and Cillian — how displeased she was, as Livius explained, in detail, the Empress's decision. How their first child, boy or girl, was, after Faolyn, heir to Ésparias, returning the title to Callan's direct descendent. A rule second to the Empire's appointed governor, of course, but still the leader. Gwenna would be the *Principe*, someday.

"But you," Livius said, addressing Cillian, "as the last Emperor's son, are to be acknowledged as the senior prince, second only to the actual

Princip. The Empress was very clear on that."

"I imagine she was," Cillian said drily. *In another life, they would be well suited,* I had said to Lena once. It had been true. Regardless of the political games being played in those tense weeks in Casil, I thought they had genuinely enjoyed each other's company, intellect and wit equally matched. He put a hand on Lena's for a moment. "We will talk later," he murmured. "First, though — " He bowed his head to Casyn. "Prince Casyn of Ésparias. I repeat what I told my father: I have no wish to lead this country. You will forgive that I cannot kneel to offer my fealty, but it must be clearly witnessed that I did."

Casyn sat very still. Then, his lips tightening slightly, he nodded. "I understand the need. I accept your fealty, Cillian, prince of Ésparias."

Lena did kneel, offering Casyn her hands. "Prince Casyn. You have my trust and my fidelity." As Cillian's wife, this too was necessary, regardless of how she truly felt. She looked up at Cillian.

"No," he said sharply. "Never." He held out a hand. "Stand, *käresta.* There will be no oaths between us beyond the ones we have sworn. I will play this game, but not at that cost." His voice was firm. Livius sipped his wine, saying nothing. Watching and listening, detecting the undercurrents. Decanius hadn't moved, hadn't said a word, his face and head red with anger.

I stood to bow deeply to Casyn. "Prince Casyn. My deepest respect," I said. Then I turned to Cillian. Eudekia's Governor was a subtle, insightful man. I bowed again. "My heartfelt regard, Prince Cillian."

"A provincial title," Decanius had found his voice. "A sop to the barbarians."

"Procurator," the Governor said coldly. "Do not speak of a decision by our Empress regarding the leaders of her province in such a way." There had been the faintest emphasis on 'her'. "And as we are all here, I will take advantage of this meeting to tell you this: my captains inform me a lighthouse is imperative on the small islands just beyond the Eastern Fort. I myself was dismayed by its lack on my voyage here. Your oversight is needed, both for the work itself and to ensure the costs were kept low."

"I am still determining the division of lands, Governor," Decanius said. "Surely that is more important?"

"More important than alleviating danger to our ships?" Livius said mildly, arching his eyebrows. "You have a villa on the coast, I understand. Surely you wish to acquaint yourself with your lands, and ensure your steward is competent? I wish the construction of the lighthouse to begin immediately. A ship will be ready to take you to the Eastern Fort within a day."

He turned back to Casyn. "*Princip*, our business here is done. The Procurator and I will leave you. My lord Cillian, presents from the Empress have been taken to your rooms, as the *Princip's* have been taken to his."

"She was supposed to have a choice!" Lena said, as soon as we had returned to their rooms. Cillian had insisted I accompany them. "How could you accept this, Cillian?"

"How can I not?" he countered, gently. "Eudekia sees it as a gift of great value." I busied myself pouring wine. This gift, this elevation of status, was nothing Cillian could have expected. I handed him his cup. "No one can argue about the *li'itho* now," I murmured. He shot me a look, half-amused, half-irritated.

"It is utterly ridiculous," he said. "But there is an artful mind behind it, so let us consider what its purpose truly is."

"My lady Lena," I said, holding out her wine.

"Don't jest," she snapped.

"I'm not," I said. "You'll have to get used to it, as wife to a prince. Unless there was a more formal title for Lena, Cillian?"

"Not that Eudekia mentioned. An elevation too great in her eyes, I think."

"Good," Lena said. "I would have refused."

"You could not," Cillian said. "She is our Empress, Lena. Your signature is on the treaty, as you so recently reminded me."

She swore, walking across the room to stare out the window. "And Gwenna?" she asked.

"*Principe*." Princess.

"You said that it did not have to be the oldest child, or any."

"That is what I believed, *käresta*. Eudekia has changed the rules of inheritance."

"Does this increase your influence in the negotiations?" I asked. "Yours or Casyn's?"

"That may be one reason." He glanced at Lena and shook his head slightly. "I am only part of it. Faolyn is a prince now too, by this decree. There will be alliances he could be — offered for."

Lena spun around at that, her shoulders high and rigid. "I do want an oath between us beyond the ones we have sworn, Cillian," she almost spat. "Whatever game is being played here, Gwenna is not a piece in it. You will never allow our daughter to be used to further Eudekia's plans."

"I have already sworn that," he said evenly. "I promised to shelter you and our children, did I not?"

"Then I trust you will be more successful with her than you have been with me," Lena said.

Dear gods, I thought. She is trying to hurt him. "Go to Casyn," she added, her voice flat. He limped over to where she stood, putting a hand on her shoulder. She didn't move. He kissed her hair. The treaty between them had been so fragile. Had this ended it entirely?

I handed him his cane. He took it, and then to my surprise embraced me, kissing my temple. "Do not bow to me again," he said. "Never, Sorley. Promise me."

"Never? Not even in front of the Governor?"

"Not even in front of the Empress, were we ever to return to Casil."

"If that is what you want," I said.

"It is," he said, his voice as low and fierce as I had ever heard it.

"Then I promise."

"Lena?" I said, when he'd gone. "This is not his doing."

She took a deep breath. "I know. But you thought your intervention with Eudekia meant she gave him up, didn't you? But she hasn't. She is tying him — and now our daughter — to her. With subtle, silken threads, perhaps, but they are meant to hold tightly, Sorley, make no mistake."

"She is within her rights," I said. "She is your Empress."

"You think I need reminding? Did you also know Casilani law gives me no rights over my own daughter? She is Cillian's, to use as he chooses."

"What?"

"It's one of the things being argued over. Talyn tells me Livius is being reasonable, given our traditions, and is likely to accept our ways. Unless the child is born within a recognized marriage, and then Casil's laws will take precedence."

"Oh, gods." I sat down. "Oh, Lena."

"Neither of us knew," she said. "Or I suppose Cillian might have, in an abstract way. But if he did, he didn't mention it when he was arguing against us marrying, so I suppose I cannot blame him."

"Then why are you so angry with him?"

"Because…" She too sat, twisting her wine cup in her hands. "Because even though he negotiates with Livius about the details of the treaty, I think all those years of following Catilius, of reading the books about Casil and Heræcria, the philosophy and stories and poems — I think he believes my little country should take its place again in the great Eastern Empire, so superior in thought and education. That we need its oversight and guidance, and we will be better off as its province than we were before."

I licked dry lips. "How can you possibly think that?"

"Who does he talk to, other than you and Casyn? Gnaius. Rufin. What do I see him reading?"

Reading. "You can't read Casilan, can you?" I asked.

"You know I can't."

"Then — " I looked around. "Where are Tyrvi and the babies?"

"Out. She's been taking Gwenna over to Berge. She says they see just another baby if she takes her, and they are coming to accept her."

"Good," I said. "Lena, listen. I will wager anything you like Cillian talks to Gnauis and Rufin for reasons other than what you think. I brought those books from the *Ti'ach*. I know what they are about."

"Then what is he doing?"

"I can't be sure," I said. Even knowing the rooms were empty, I dropped my voice. "But the books have a common theme. They are about resistance to an unfair government."

She stared at me. "Resistance?"

"Yes. One is a biography of a Heræcrian philosopher who lost his life for speaking out against corruption; one is a history of rebellion against an early Emperor of Casil. I don't know about the third. When he asked me for them, Lena, he told me to be careful, that they could be considered subversive. He has said nothing to you?"

Silence, for several heartbeats. "Of course not," she said. "He wouldn't, because he is sheltering me, isn't he? And I accused him of the opposite." A wave of pain washed over her face. "I am surprised he told you."

"He didn't," I said. "He asked for the books, nothing more. And I read part of one when I was waiting in your rooms one day."

"Where he'd left them, knowing I can't read Casilan," she said. "Safer there then in his workroom, where Gnaius or Rufin might see them. Oh, Sorley, I have been so wrong."

"But not about one thing," I said slowly. "Eudekia is an intelligent woman, and shrewd. She hasn't held onto the throne without being an astute judge of character and motive. In the weeks of negotiation, and the late-night talks, perhaps she understood Cillian better than we knew. By making Gwenna the heir, she becomes a hostage, doesn't she?"

Lena understood immediately. "If Cillian is guilty of treason — and, gods, Sorley, he would be, wouldn't he? — then his rights over Gwenna are forfeit. Eudekia would take her, bring her up in Casil as some prince's bride." Fear laced her voice.

"I think that is the implicit threat, yes," I said, trying to sound calm. "Cillian must give in and accept Casilani rule, so that someday in her old age Gwenna may be a figurehead *Principe*. Resist, and he loses both his daughter and his life."

CHAPTER 25

I WALKED OUT TO meet Tyrvi, returning from Berge. I did this occasionally: sometimes alone, sometimes, as today, with Lena. Both of us needed sky and sea, space away from the confinement of the fort. We didn't talk much. But when we returned, with Gwenna asleep in my arms, Cillian was sitting in the living area. He looked almost haggard, exhausted.

Tyrvi took both babies into the nursery. Without a word, Lena went to Cillian, kneeling in front on him, burying her face in his chest. His arms went around her. I moved towards the door.

"Sorley," Cillian said. I looked back. He held out one hand. Reluctantly I went to him. He took my hand, raising it to his lips. "Thank you," he murmured.

"Don't thank me," I said, annoyed. "What did I say to you, not more than a few weeks ago, about excluding us? I didn't realize just how guilty of that you were. And yes, I understand I'm Linrathe's *toscaire*, and that changes things between us. So talk to Lena, since you can't to me."

I turned on my heel and left, stalking down the hall out to the commons. I chose the junior officers' building tonight, finding an officer from my classes to sign me in as a guest. I listened to the usual talk, about the soldiers under their command and speculation about deployment to the Sterre or the coastal patrols, but it irritated more than it interested me. I went back to my workroom and my *ladhar*.

My head hurt a little, from the wine at the junior commons, but I wasn't ready to sleep. One of the *danta* I might be asked to play for my *scáeli's* exam had a difficult fingering: I would practice that. Lost in the music, I nearly didn't hear a gentle tap at the door. My lamp guttered as I looked up; hours had passed. Was I disturbing someone?

Cillian stood there, leaning on his cane, Lena beside him. "May we talk?" he asked.

"Of course. Come in. I don't have wine, but there is some next door."

"Do you have *fuisce*?"

Fuisce? He must be in some pain, I thought. "Yes. Sit down. I'll fetch it."

I handed him the small cup of the distilled spirit, placing the water jug on the table. He added a few drops, swirled it. "*Meas,*" he said, taking a tiny sip. I poured a little for Lena, as well, and then for myself.

"Are you all right?" I asked.

"Yes, if you are asking about my back and leg. The usual discomfort, nothing more." He took another sip. "I have come to ask a favour."

"Which is?"

"Have you noticed that Lena and I remove our insignias of rank, before we allow ourselves to be — ourselves, you might say, not major and lieutenant?" I nodded. I had noticed, but I hadn't understood the significance. "We have done that since the Eastern Fort. Could we do the same tonight, Sorley? Forget for an hour or two that we are diplomats, the bearers of our countries' secrets, and just be friends?"

I hadn't heard such fatigue in his voice for some time. What could I say? "We can. We are."

Lena sat silently with her *fuisce*. He glanced at her. "Then do you remember me saying that in asking Casil for help, we might be exchanging a known horror for an unknown?" he asked, very quietly.

On the ship, before we reached the city; the moment I had realized I must speak for Linrathe, decide for Linrathe, in any negotiations for support. "Yes."

"I am afraid we have."

I recoiled. "Casil is not that bad, surely? Worse that the Marai? How can you say that?"

"I did not say they are worse than the Marai. Only that they are a horror. We had hoped their idea of a civilized life was much like ours. Sorley, I was not wrong, except in my understanding of what this land — Lena's land — considers civilized. How could I have thought I could speak for a people I did not understand?"

I too sipped the fiery *fuisce*, considering. "You're saying that their idea of how a society works is closer to Linrathe's?"

"Is it not? A more stratified society, with clearer roles for men and women, structured land ownership, a traditional view of marriage and inheritance. Not identical, by any means, but closer. Easier to find commonalities. The only commonality here is with the army; that has been reasonably easy to adjust. But beyond that, almost everything is in conflict. Is that not right, Lena?"

"It is," she said. "We might have been a province of the Eastern Empire once before, but we kept almost none of its laws and traditions, except in the army."

We drank, not speaking. Cillian shook his head when I offered more *fuisce*. "What are you thinking?" I asked finally.

"Nothing now. Nothing…overt. Eudekia, as you surmised, has seen to that. But tell me this, Sorley. If I had died, would you have stayed with Lena?"

"Yes, of course. You asked me to." I hesitated. "Just as I promised her I wouldn't leave you, were she to die."

"Did you?" He turned to Lena. "You asked that?"

"Of course I did," she said. "I do know what he is to you, Cillian."

"You are the sun, Cillian, around which we orbit, Lena and I," I added bluntly.

He half-smiled. "If we keep to that analogy, then just now Casil is also a sun, is it not, shining its lights of history and order on us?"

"Go on."

"Had I died, then you and Lena, and Druisius, perhaps, would have found a way to make a life together, adjusting your differences of upbringing and expectations to live together reasonably harmoniously, would you not? Just as you and Druisius make your two musical traditions work together, with some adaptation?"

"I would hope so."

"Then what if Casil 'dies'?" he said softly. "What if they go away again, as a study of history tells us they — as every empire before them — will? *Look back over the past, with its changing empires that rose and fell, and you can foresee the future, too,* Catilius wrote. Heræcria failed, and I have learned from Gnaius that before that another great leader ruled an empire that reached far into eastern lands. What happens to our countries then?"

"I don't know," I said. "How can we know?"

"We cannot. But we can plan for that day, whether it is fifty years or a hundred or more. My fear is that our countries would fall again into discord and war. But just as the three of us made plans for my death, or Lena's — and yours, *mo charaidh,* for I would have asked Druisius if he wished to stay — perhaps our countries should make private plans for the day the East leaves us to our own defences, too."

"Private plans?" I said. "Secret? Cillian, isn't this as seditious as whatever else you might have been thinking?"

He regarded me gravely. "Is it? Or is it simply good sense?"

"It's not good sense if it results in you being tried for treason again." I looked at Lena, who simply shook her head.

"There is no chance of that," Cillian said. "My thoughts are only for those whom I love, and who love me, and I can trust. You and Lena."

"Cillian," I said, bewildered. He half-smiled.

"Say nothing," he said. He pushed himself up. I rose automatically to steady him, holding out a protective hand. He took it, pulling me to him, his hands tight on my back. His lips brushed my hair. "Keep my words close."

He let me go. I didn't know what to say. "Good night, my lord Sorley," he murmured.

"I will be a moment," Lena said. "I have something to say to Sorley." She let him leave before speaking. "Can you do this?" she asked. "Hold this secret?"

"Can you?"

"Yes. I see the sense. But he did say 'countries', Sorley, and that means Linrathe, and perhaps even Sorham and Varsland some day. And you have an oath to keep."

"Shouldn't Cillian have asked me this, not you?"

"It was not Linrathe's *toscaire* that he told." She hesitated. "You don't understand what you are to him, do you? What you have always been, I think."

"His friend," I said.

She shook her head. "More than that, Sorley. I want a promise. You will not leave him."

"Have I not already said that?"

"That was before this…revelation. But I will say this. If you ever abandon him, Sorley, you will hurt him more than you can understand. And I would never forgive you, regardless of how much I love you." Tears shone in her eyes.

"Lena! I won't. What's wrong?"

She blinked the tears away. "So few years ago, Maya told me — the night Casyn came to Tirvan — that she was scared of what the future held. I told her we had to face it, and do what was needed, or it would overwhelm us. I didn't understand how she felt. I do now." She smiled. "Just late-night fears, I suppose. Come to us tomorrow, and we'll open the packages from Eudekia."

Chapter 26

THE PACKAGES CONTAINED NOT just presents for Cillian from the Empress, but letters. Delighted, apparently, to hear of his recovery, Eudekia had sent him a walking stick of a wood so dark it was effectively black, decorated with an eagle of silver. For Gwenna, she had sent a silver rattle, and a small half-moon pendant of gold. An amulet, Cillian explained, to ward off disease and misfortune.

I had a letter from Druise. He wrote exactly as he spoke, which amused me a little. It didn't tell me much, but its last line: *I will be back in the autumn, amané*, both cheered me and incited a new wave of guilt over Evan, although I doubted Druise was sleeping alone in Casil. I was reading it for the second time when Cillian called my name. I looked up.

"Come and see," he said. Lena had been untying the string around a squarish parcel when I had begun to read. The wrappings, I saw now, had protected a hinged silver box. Cillian had just opened it. Inside, jewels in various settings lay on a bed of cloth. Among them were a pair of earrings, gold wire set with matched green stones, about the size of my smallest fingernail. "These were meant for you, *käresta*, I am sure," Cillian said, showing them to Lena. "They will enhance the green flecks in your eyes." She took them from him, holding them in the palm of her hand.

"Why is she sending jewels?" she asked. "I will have to have my ears pierced. I never bothered, although Maya did, and other girls at Tirvan. But only for formal occasions. I am not teaching cadets wearing these."

"That would seem inappropriate," Cillian said, with a quick grin. It had been clear from the moment I had come in that they were reconciled. From the box he took two rings, set with deep red stones. "Sorley," he said, "look at these." The stones were each carved with a figure. "Carnelian," Cillian told me. "The Empress's seal was made of this stone, if you recall."

I didn't, but I had no reason to doubt that he was right. "What incredible detail," I murmured, taking one of the rings. The figure carved into the stone held a stringed instrument.

"The motif on the other is similar," Cillian said. "Would they not grace the *ladhar* you are making, the jewels mounted one on each side?"

I looked up. "You can't give me these," I said.

"Why not?"

"They were meant for Lena, and Gwenna."

"I doubt it," he said. "Not with those motifs. Lena?" She looked up from the earrings. "Should not these be Sorley's?"

"Of course," she said. "What would I do with them? I have no need of jewellery beyond these earrings and Irmgard's pendant. And Gwenna's a baby, with no need of jewels at all."

"And there are smaller stones here, for what she might want in future years," Cillian pointed out. "The Empress's note says I may give them to whom I wish. They are yours, *mo charaidh*."

I would have an instrument like no other. But still I hesitated.

"Please take them," Cillian said. "Not in exchange, but for the same reasons you gave us the *li'itho*."

"Then I must accept," I said, around the constriction in my throat. *Those whom I love*, he had said last night. "Thank you. I will bring the *ladhar* to show you when it's done."

I had hoped that with Lena and Cillian reconciled, my own simmering anger at him would subside. And it did, a bit, but not entirely. I found myself unexpectedly worried by his idea of an alliance among our western countries, and not entirely because of the danger inherent in it. Did it not also speak to a willingness to forget a treaty signed, an oath spoken? My mind went back to the first night he had been free of the poppy juice, clear minded and as precise in his thoughts and speech as ever. *Asking Callan to acknowledge me was not the betrayal*, he had said, and then he had repeated the words of the *toscaire's* oath. There was an implication here I couldn't believe. Not Cillian, for whom promises were sacrosanct. But I couldn't find the courage to ask.

Nor did words spoken in the night over *fuisce* or the gift of the jewels for my *ladhar* return us to the closeness we had once had. He was always happy to see me, but there was something — a distance, almost a formality — dividing us, as if he could not forget now that I was Linrathe's *toscaire*.

"Come and eat with us," Lena insisted one day. I'd seen little of Cillian recently: he played *xache* with Rufin when the Casilani captain was in port now. Livius, too, gave him the occasional game, and the Governor had also brought an extensive library with him, and was free in the loan of books. Between Cillian's dinners with the senior officers, and his other occupations, I spent little time alone with him. "We've barely seen you, and I am returning to active duty next week."

"Are you?" Gwenna was five months old now.

"Training cadets. I wanted to ride patrol, but Casyn said no. But I am looking forward to working again. Although," she said, "I am horribly soft. I haven't shot a bow or thrown a secca in almost a year."

"You'll need the baths for a while," I said, "but your muscles won't have forgotten." I agreed to come to them that evening, and, accordingly, arrived at their rooms in the early evening. Over roast lamb — the kitchen had improved with the addition of a Casilani cook, I thought — we talked of Gwenna's latest achievements, and Lena's studies of the *danta* and Linrathan. Casual talk among friends. But Cillian's eyes bore the stain of fatigue, and he was quiet, letting Lena and me carry the conversation.

After the meal Lena went to the nursery to change Gwenna. Cillian sat silently, but his hands were slightly clenched, and he rubbed his fingers together without ceasing.

"You're not really here, are you?" I said.

"No. I am failing, Sorley." He shook his head, lips thinned. "Not negotiations now," he said. "Just planning. We managed to curb Decanius's excesses, but Livius is no less adamant about the changes that must be made in our laws and the administration of Ésparias. More gracious with it, and he has compromised on some issues, but the result remains the same."

"Was there ever much chance?" I asked.

"Probably not." He sighed. "It is the women's villages that will bear the brunt of it."

"But he has agreed that the villages own their land, at least," Lena said, coming back into the room.

"That is true, and he has no argument with their council structure. The governance of local matters should remain in local hands, he said. And, thank the gods," Cillian added, "Decanius remains in the south."

"You have done your best," I said.

"I suppose I have." Gwenna gurgled from Lena's arms, and he smiled up at his daughter and held out his arms. She smiled back, and he took her, to her obvious delight, and we spoke no more of politics. But later, when Gwenna had gone back to the nursery, and Lena had gone to bed, our talk turned back to his worries.

"That we — Casyn and I — are not given the *mensores'* reports to read troubles me," he said. "All we are given are summaries; with maps showing the proposed new roads, and divisions of lands. It will be his friends now who control the new land divisions, not Decanius's, but is that truly an improvement?"

Apulo had started to help Tyrvi with the baby, and with meals and other little chores. I went to visit Lena one day, late in the afternoon when I thought she'd be back from the training grounds. Apulo was picking up Gwenna's toys from the floor, and singing as he did. Lena put a finger to her lips. I stood still, listening. He hadn't warmed to me, despite my overtures: I thought he'd been told — or intuited — my nature, and was understandably wary.

Seeing me, he stopped. "Don't stop," I said in Casilan. "Your voice is remarkable. Do you play too?"

He shook his head. "Not properly," he said. "Excuse me, Lord Sorley. I will take these to the nursery."

"I wish he'd talk to me," I said to Lena, going to sit beside her. She had a pot of tea in front of her. "Is there enough for me?" I asked.

"You don't want that," she said. "It's anash. I'll make some mint."

"Don't bother." A tiny smile played on her lips, I noted. "Anash? Is this just for a few days, or...?"

"Both," she said, the smile blossoming. "Gnaius was right; time was what was needed, that and Apulo's skill with massage lessening Cillian's pain. Gwenna will not, perhaps, be an only child now, but I don't want to be pregnant again, not yet. So I will drink anash every day. At least there is honey to be had here."

I hugged her. "I am so glad," I said.

"So am I," she said. "It has been a long year."

"Ah well," I said with a grin, "we weren't playing *xache* late at night very often, anyhow." Or at all.

"I wish you were." I still had an arm around her shoulders. She nestled a little closer. "I know there are distances between you just now, but…" She bit her lip. "I wish I could tell you what is on his mind, but I can't. It is a decision he cannot make lightly, and perhaps one he is slightly afraid of, or at least afraid of the consequences that might ensue. As am I, a little. But you should know that if he decides the way I think he will, it is with my blessing."

Oh, gods, I thought, is he contemplating offering to be regent for Faolyn after all, to let Casyn retire? Now? "When did Cillian ever make any decision lightly?" I said, adding, "I don't expect you to tell me. I will let it be. There are things I can't say to him, either. But we will not be diplomats forever, or at least I won't. I have had a letter from Dagney. The date of my *scáeli's* exam is set. I can't be both *toscaire* and *scáeli*, so assuming I pass, Dagney will formally request I be relieved of the *toscaire's* role. Not immediately, but soon."

"Assuming you pass?" Lena said. "Of course you will. That's wonderful, Sorley. Will your *ladhar* be ready? What will you play?"

We were still talking about music when Cillian came in, looking tired. "Sorley!" he said with evident pleasure. He limped to the sideboard, unpinning his insignia of rank before bending to kiss Lena. "If I sit," he said to her, "I will not want to get up again."

"You're in pain," she said. "Baths and massage, *kärestan*."

He nodded. "Is Gwenna sleeping?"

"Yes. Don't disturb her, please. I'll get Apulo." She started to get up.

"No. Not if — Sorley, will you come to the baths with me? Apulo can massage me afterwards. Will you send him to me later, *käresta*?"

"Yes, I'll come," I said. "I have news." We hadn't shared the baths privately since I had told him not to touch me, months before. The afternoon I had found Evan on the beach. The distances were not all his doing, I reminded myself, and perhaps I hadn't done enough to bridge them, either.

He was as delighted as Lena had been, asking questions about the process and what songs were required, and which I could choose. "I would like to sing *War in Winter*," I told him. "If I may?"

"In translation? Certainly. But are you not judged on your ability to write poetry too? Shouldn't you be singing your own words?"

"I will be. The *danta*, and," I hesitated, "one other, at least."

"Come and sing them for us tonight. It has been too long since we have made time for music, *mo charaidh gràhadh.* Work should not keep us apart."

"It hasn't been just work," I said. "I will."

"A long time since I have sung for you without Druise," I commented, tightening a string after finishing the *danta*. Apulo, who had been sitting quietly, invited to listen by Lena, got up to bring me wine; after such a long song, he knew my throat would need it. "He has some interesting harmonies to add, and some counterpoint, in Casilani tuning, at the appropriate points."

"You've lost me," Lena said. "I understand harmony, and grace notes — Cillian explained those to me, once — but counterpoint?"

"Easier to show you," I said. "Apulo, will you sing with me?"

He hesitated, glancing at Cillian, who nodded. I explained what I wanted, in Casilani. He asked a question or two, a slight smile beginning. I played a few notes and sang part of the *danta* again. Apulo joined in with a different but complementary tune.

"Oh," Lena said. "How lovely. It deepens the music, doesn't it?" She smiled at Apulo. "*Gratiás.* Thank you, Apulo."

"You said that song, and another?" Cillian asked.

"Yes." I'd had a growing certainty that I should do this, although not one I could explain. I was glad of Apulo's presence: he would not understand the words, but this would be easier with someone else listening. "I wrote this in the winter. I shouldn't sing it publicly before you hear it. I wouldn't sing it for the exam, except that it may be the best song I've ever written. But I'll need your permission, as you will understand once I play it." I played the first run of notes, and began to sing.

My true love's eyes are darkly gleaming
In candlelight and music's lure….

I looked up, once. Lena was watching Cillian, a shadow of a smile on her face. His eyes were on me, and the look in them almost made me stop singing. Regret, and something I couldn't fathom. I held his gaze for a line or two of the next verse.

But candlelight and music's memory,
Dark eyes gleaming over wine
Revive that youthful love and longing
For graceful fingers touching mine,
For kisses left at day's first dawning.

He glanced down at Lena. She met his eyes with nothing but love. I looked away.

You danced that night with grace unfettered,
A glance my way, a touch bestowed,
Your dark hair swept by supple fingers.
Uncharted ways might be explored,
Still dreams this wistful loving singer…
Still dreams this wistful, loving singer.

Silence. I put the *ladhar* down. "You see why I have to ask. Dagney will understand. The others won't." Cillian said nothing.

"It is beautiful," Lena said. "If I have a say here, then my vote is that you sing it."

"And mine," Cillian said. "It is beautiful. More than beautiful. You have outdone me as a poet, *mo duíne gràhadh*. Use it to gain your entrance to the *scáeli'en* with my blessing."

"Thank you." It felt inadequate, but I could find no other words. Lena sat up.

"I'm going to bed," she said. "Are you playing *xache*?"

"Sorley?" Cillian asked.

"No. I'm tired. Soon, but not tonight." For some inchoate reason I did not want to be alone with Cillian just now. I had never, even earlier this summer, been so honest about my feelings. I couldn't quite identify what I felt: embarrassment again? Regret that I had sung the song? As I walked the dark corridors back to my room, the un-nameable feeling coalesced into frustration; frustration and jealousy, and, when I recognized it for what it was, anger at myself.

CHAPTER 27

WE LEFT SHORTLY AFTER breakfast, the day cloudy and cool, but not yet raining. We could reach Dun Ceànnar today, if we didn't dally; if not, there was a *torp* a couple of hours south that would provide us with bed and board, although then I would need to sing again. The land was rising now in a series of long, low hills, carpeted with heather, resounding with birdsong on this spring morning.

Other than commenting on the day and the surroundings, I didn't talk. Nor did Gwenna. The track was wide enough for us to ride side by side, but Gwenna lagged just a little behind, her mare's head at my gelding's flank.

Mid-morning, we stopped to water the horses and relieve ourselves. Gwenna returned from around a small rise. I held both horses' reins, waiting. "You taught us," she began, "that new songs use words and images from older ones, to make them part of a tradition."

"They can."

"And you do that?"

"Sometimes." How many Linrathan songs began 'My true love's eyes'? Countless, probably, if I included every minor variation in my tally.

"How did you meet my father?" she asked abruptly.

"In his role as *toscaire*. He was visiting Gundarstorp. I was sixteen."

"Oh." She took her mare's reins from me.

"He gave me and my brother a *xache* lesson," I told her, as I mounted, "and the next day we went hawking, he and my father and the two of us. Most of the rest of the time he spent with my father, talking."

"About what?"

"Varsland and the tribute we paid them, and possible ways to reduce it," I said.

She made a face. "It doesn't sound very interesting."

I laughed. "It is what *toscairen* do, Gwenna. It is very likely what you will do, or something very similar."

"I hope not," she said. We rode on. I let myself remember, no pain in the memory now after so long. Cillian's fingers, so light on my hand and knee, the look on his face. I had loved him from that evening, loved the grace of him, the intelligence, the unattainable beauty, and that love had survived his rejection at the *Ti'ach*, and years of barely seeing him; it had survived his love for Lena, and the darkness that was the other side of his brilliance. I had believed, briefly, it had changed into a brotherly love, that of close and dear friends, but I had been wrong. Or perhaps that might have happened, had not fear of his death forced me to face what I truly felt.

The clouds parted occasionally, the day warming. We shed cloaks, and swatted at midges near the streams and bogs. At midday, I halted on a hilltop where a breeze would ensure no biting insects, and I had a clear view of the track behind us.

I handed Gwenna the waterskin, and a chunk of cheese, along with bread the *Konë* had insisted we take this morning. I remained standing, arching my back against the hours in the saddle. My side ached where the ribs had been cracked, years ago. "You're getting old," Gwenna teased.

"I am," I agreed. "Thirty-nine, now. My back hurts, and my knees, and there will be no baths to soak in to relieve the aches."

"Or Apulo to massage you?"

"He only does that for your father," I said. "Even if he offered, I wouldn't make him uncomfortable by accepting."

"Why would it make him uncomfortable?" She sat on a rock, taking a bite of the bread.

"You know his story, Gwenna. You can deduce why."

She chewed the tough barley crust, thinking. "Is he afraid you might hurt him, the way he was in Casil, because you love men?"

"That is it exactly."

"But you *wouldn't*."

"Of course not. And he knows that now, so I probably could accept a massage. But Druise gives an adequate one, so why would I bother Apulo?"

"Would Apulo have worked for my father, if he loved men?"

"Your father doesn't love men," I said, "so it is not a question with an answer." I glanced down the track. "Look!" I said. "That's Druise."

Gwenna stood up, and we watched as Druise galloped along the track and up to where we waited. He slid out of the saddle. "Kitten," he said, "will you walk my horse, and find it water?"

"*Amané*," he said, when she had led the horse away. "I was as quick as I could be."

"When did you leave the *Ti'ach*?"

"Dawn. But this new horse is strong and fast." Lena had bought the gelding on her last trip to Han, a journey she made alone once or twice a year. The guard needed better horses than the *torp's* ponies, and it gave her some time under the wide skies and space of the grasslands.

"You could have ridden a little slower," I said, shaking my head at his foolishness. "Met us at Dun Ceànnar."

"My job is to guard Gwenna," he said, seriously.

"In Sorham, *amané*, not Linrathe," I said. He shrugged, as I knew he would, and I laughed. I wanted to hug him, but somewhere there could be a shepherd watching us. I settled for a hand on his shoulder, briefly.

"Vidar?" I asked, giving him the waterskin.

"Cillian appeared unconcerned by his arrival," Druise said, wiping his mouth. "Less than unconcerned. As if Vidar was expected, yes?"

"Perhaps," I said. We exchanged glances. "Perhaps that is why he agreed so easily to Gwenna accompanying us, so that both you and me would be gone for the summer?"

After Druise had eaten, telling us as he did of Lena's exasperation and Colm's delight when the puppy had arrived, we moved on. I'd travelled only rarely with Druise, and except for his desperate ride to find me after the Taiva, he'd never been this far north. What little time we had spent on the road together had been south into Ésparias.

I can finally show him my country, I thought. I can take him to Gundarstorp. The thought made me smile. I glanced over at Druise, sitting easily on his horse, looking around. Our eyes met.

"You look happy," Gwenna said.

"I am," I said. "I've always wanted Druise to see where I grew up, and now he can."

"Like *Mathàir* making sure I went to Tirvan," she said, "to see her village."

"Yes," I agreed.

"Why doesn't your son inherit Gundarstorp?" she asked.

"Because he is acknowledged, but not legitimate," I said. "You know the rules."

"You could have married his mother."

"I could not have," I said. Entirely true. I picked my words carefully. "Some men find pleasure freely with both men and women. But I am not one of them." I could, I knew now, find some pleasure with a woman, if I must. But learning that had made me only more certain of where my desires truly lay. "His mother is happy with her husband."

"And you are happy too? The two of you?"

"Do you think, Kitten, I would have stayed in this cold and wet country for all these years, were I not?" Druise said. "But you are asking if Sorley and I together are happy, yes? We are."

"What about my parents? I want Sorley to answer that." she said, as Druise began to speak.

"Gwenna, do you need to ask? You have seen them together in private," I said.

"An hour a day. Anyone can pretend, for an hour," she replied.

"The pretense is when they are in public, when your father is the *Comiádh* and your mother the Lady of the *Ti'ach*. That is the act, just as it is for Druise and me. We are very good at it, all of us."

"You have not answered," she said.

"In all my years and travels, Gwenna, I have met no one whose commitment to each other, or whose love, runs as deep."

"Nor I, Kitten," Druise added. "Do you not see how your father looks at your mother, or hear what is in his voice when he calls her *käresta*?"

"Yes," she said in a small voice. "I know he loves her. But she doesn't do the same."

"Not in front of you," I said, "and perhaps that has been a mistake on your mother's part." One I understood but had never quite agreed with.

"But she does, when it is just the four of us together, and I am sure even more so, when they are alone." I would raise this with Lena, I thought, when we were home. Above us a bird gyred in the warming air, hunting. *Fuádain*, I thought, looking up at it. I pointed it out to Gwenna.

"What is it after?" she asked.

"Grouse," I said, "over these moors." She seemed content with what I had said about her parents. Were Cillian and Lena happy? Together, yes. Of that I was convinced. But their separate happiness was another question. Lena was satisfied with her life, and I believed she was happy. Cillian would never be completely at peace.

"Listen!" Gwenna raised a hand. We reined the horses to a stop, to quiet the creak of leather and the jingle of metal. A dog barked, high and sharp and insistent, an edge of panic in the sound.

"Over there." Druise pointed. We turned the horses off the track and over the moor. The barking grew louder. A sheepdog ran to us, whining, circling us. I gave it the 'find' command and it started back the way it had come.

At the base of a crag perhaps three times a man's height, the dog led us straight to a body, unconscious or worse on the ground. A dead lamb lay nearby, blood clotted at its mouth. The story was clear: the shepherd had tried to rescue the lamb from somewhere on the crag and fallen.

Druise was off his horse and at the man's side. He felt for a pulse. "He's alive," he said. The shepherd's leg was bent underneath him at a horrible, unnatural angle.

"I'll go for help," I said. "Gwenna, stay with Druise." I reined my horse around and rode for Sullistorp.

Several hours later, we had the shepherd on a table in Sullistorp's hall, and Druise and the *Konë* were splinting and binding the leg. A bad break, Druise said, but the bone had not torn through the flesh. Birgit, the *Konë*, had dosed the shepherd with poppy before the cart journey to the *torp*, and again before beginning to work on his leg. Gwenna had made herself useful holding horses' heads and opening gates, but otherwise had stayed out of the way.

They finished their work, and two men who had been waiting at the edge of the hall carried the shepherd to a bed somewhere down a corridor. Birgit watched them go. She had run the *torp* since Sullis, her husband, had died fighting the Marai. Her *torpari* respected her competence and authority.

"I hope he recovers," she said. "A dry day, too. I wonder what made him slip?" She shook her head. "A drink now?" She looked at Druise. "I didn't catch your name."

"Druisius. Captain of Ésparias," Druise replied.

"You are Casilani," the *Konë* said. Not a question; no man of Ésparias or Linrathe had skin as dark as Druise's.

"I was," Druise said, in his accented Linrathan. "Ésparian now. I guard the *Comiádh's* daughter."

Birgit turned to look at Gwenna, sitting quietly against the wall. "I did not realize who you were," she said to her. "My apologies."

"There is no need to apologize, *Konë* Birgit. Why should you know who I am?" she said, standing. She repeated her explanation of why she was travelling with us.

"My daughter will show you to a room," she said, calling a name. A girl about Gwenna's age appeared, wiping her hands on her apron. Birgit introduced her to Gwenna, and they went off together. "They are both heirs," Birgit said. "My daughter to these lands, and the *Comiádh's* to Ésparias."

"In theory," I answered. "But with the *Princip* less than ten years older than Gwenna, it's unlikely she'll ever take on the role, or not until she's an old woman herself."

"Unless they marry," the *Konë* suggested. "That would ensure the inheritance in both lines."

"I suppose," I said. "I wouldn't say that in Gwenna's hearing, though."

"She cannot choose whom she marries," Birgit said. "My daughter is pledged to Gedwinstorp's heir, already."

"Ésparias thinks differently," I said. Although it didn't now in a few places; one of the changes nearly fifteen years of Casilani rule had brought. And when it came to the *Princip,* it certainly didn't; that was part of why I needed to be at Dun Ceànnar tomorrow. "*Konë,* I forgot to ask when we arrived. My horse should have grain tonight and tomorrow morning if possible. I must ride at speed to Dun Ceànnar at first light. Will you arrange it?"

"I'll do it now. We need more ale, too. I won't be a minute." She strode off. I took the mug of ale she'd poured for me off the table.

"You must ride at speed?" Druise asked.

"Yes. You and Gwenna can follow at a slower pace. I've half a mind to go tonight, except my horse needs the rest. Ruar expects me."

The evening followed the usual pattern: the meal, then music, this time with Druise accompanying me. He played a few Casilani songs, to polite interest, until I used my early start as an excuse to end the singing. In the hall, sharing a last round of ale with some of the men of the *torp* and Birgit, Druise took me aside.

"Gwenna asked me tonight about what the shepherd was given to ease his pain. Why we did not have this drug for her father," he told me in Casilan.

"What did you say?"

"That I would ask what it was and tell her tomorrow."

"Will you?"

"Should I?"

"Yes. I think you should. He told us we could tell her what we chose."

"About why he broke his oath to Linrathe. Not this," Druise pointed out.

"Finish your ale, and walk me to my room," I said. We said our goodnights to the men. "I have a few things to discuss with Druisius before I leave," I told them.

"Fill your cups again, and take them with you," Birgit said. "Singing is thirsty work, and talking, too. Good night, Sorley. Your horse will be waiting for you in the morning."

At my room, I closed the door. The only light was from the banked fire, and the candle Druise had carried to light our way. He put it down on a table. I put my arms around him, holding him close for a moment, his strong, familiar body reassuring. We kissed, briefly, before I opened the door again.

"There is more to what Gwenna's classmates have been saying to her than just doubts about Cillian's loyalty," I told him, reverting to Casilan. "She's heard a lot of things, and if the poppy isn't part of it, I'll be surprised. More than just the three of us and Gnaius knew, and people talk."

"Likely you are right," Druise said. "The questions about her parents' happiness — rumours from the same source, you think?"

"Yes."

"I will not talk to her about that," he warned.

"I will. If she asks again, and I think she will." I said with a wry grin. "Sooner or later she'll realize I didn't answer her question,"

CHAPTER 28

RAIN AGAIN THE NEXT morning; I was drenched by the time I reached Dun Ceànnar. The steward took me to the room I requested. "Not your usual, Lord Sorley?" he asked, but I explained my need to be close to Gwenna's guardsman.

"Not that there can be a problem, here," I told the man, "but I promised her father." He simply nodded and gave me the room. I changed quickly, rubbing my hair until it didn't drip. Then I went to find Ruar.

The *Teannasach* was in the big room he used as a workroom, Daoíre with him. I accepted the brief kisses of welcome, from Ruar first, and gladly assented to the offer of tea. We sat at the big table, talking at first of the *Ti'ach*, and my reasons for going north. I told them Druise and Gwenna would be arriving later, but I guessed that with this rain, they might delay until tomorrow.

"I would have liked to see Gwenna again," Ruar said. "She was at the White Fort when I was last at the *Ti'ach*, so I have not seen her for some years. She is — how old?"

"Fourteen." He had been *Teannasach* at fourteen.

"You'll be taking her to Casil soon." I had taken him the year he was seventeen. We'd spent three months there, and Ruar had hated it.

"Cillian wants to wait another few years, until Druise and I can take both children together."

"He won't go?"

"I doubt he can," I said. "That much travel? Lena might, though." Although I guessed she would not leave Cillian for so long, if I was gone too.

"To business," he said briskly. "Are all the plans for the wedding in place?"

"They are," I told him. "A joint ceremony; Casyn will preside for Ésparias. He is a follower of the soldier's god, and I believe he holds high office in that practice, although that's only a guess."

"And you, as head of the *scáeli'en*?"

"I can. But would not Siusàn prefer Amlodd, as Dun Ceànnar's *scáeli*?" I had always thought Amlodd should have been head of the council before me, but the members had had a different view.

"Likely. If she wants him, he will officiate," Ruar decided. We spoke a while longer about the marriage of his sister Siusàn to Faolyn, *Princip* of Ésparias. The second in the web of relationships binding our western lands together, Cillian's vision slowly becoming real.

"Ruar," Daoíre said, after a while. "You must prepare to leave."

"I need to do nothing but mount my horse," Ruar replied. "And I had best say my farewells to Helvi; Sorley, would you accompany me?"

We walked down one of the maze of hallways to the women's rooms. Helvi was at her desk, writing. She looked up as we came in. "Leave us," she said to her companion.

"Lord Sorley," Helvi greeted me in Marái'sta. "How good to see you."

"My lady," I said, kissing her extended hand. "I met your cousin, on the road to the *Ti'ach*. Was it your idea that he pretended to be from Sorham?"

"Mine," Ruar said. "I couched his letter of safe passage in uncertain terms. Did it serve?"

"It did. He would have been apprehended by the guard on the *Ti'ach's* lands, of course, except that Druise escorted him back to Cillian. Who was not the least surprised to see him, Druise tells me."

"Of course not," Helvi said. "Cillian invited him."

"In one of the letters I brought last time?" I asked.

"Yes," she said. "Bjørn wants a school in Varsland, and he had written to Cillian to tell him that. The children of the king, when he has them, and those of the earls need to know of the wider world and its philosophies, if they are to be part of it, and not barbarians on the edge of civilization. He does not want to wait another ten years, nor will he countenance sending children of Varsland to Sorham to be educated."

"This is faster than Cillian had planned," I said.

"So perhaps the next *Ti'ach* is not in Sorham, but across the sea," she answered. "There are those in Varsland who do not like the forts Casil has built along the coast. They see them as a threat, because, after all, who else could the enemy be but the Marai?"

Who indeed? "At least Casil does not completely control the trading harbour," I said. As they so easily could have.

"At least," she agreed. She glanced at her husband. "Should I speak of the other matter, Ruar, or you?"

"Better me, I think," he said. "I wish in some ways you hadn't needed to come north to me, because I do not think Cillian will like what else they had to say. But there is some truth in it. I have done my part, in marrying Helvi, although," he smiled down at her, "it has been no hardship at all. My sister goes to wed Faolyn in a few weeks. Varsland and Linrathe, Linrathe and Ésparias. What of Ésparias and Varsland? Where will Gwenna wed, Sorley?"

"She is fourteen," I protested, my throat suddenly dry.

"Not too young to be promised," he said. "My sister was nine, and Helvi thirteen, if you recall."

I shook my head. "Cillian not liking this will be an understatement. Who are they suggesting?"

"The king, of course," Ruar said. "She is appropriate, given her relationship to the *Princip*. He is twenty-three. Not an unsuitable difference in age."

Nine years. Cillian could make no objection on that basis, with thirteen years between him and Lena. If Cillian would recoil at the suggestion, Lena might kill someone, I reflected. Or at least threaten.

"Cillian will say no," I said. "Ruar, surely you see it is impossible. What Fritjof and his men did…Gwenna's own cousin, Lena's sister's son, is Marai-fathered. For her to marry a man of Varsland, as much as he also hates what Fritjof did, would be repudiating the murder and rape of Ésparias's women, not to mention everyone who died in the war." I heard my voice rising. "I'm sorry," I said. "I am letting my feelings override courtesy."

"I do see," Ruar said. "But it is what will be suggested. What counter-suggestions are there, Sorley? We need Varsland with us, and without that marriage, the connection with Ésparias is tenuous. The long history that Linrathe has with Varsland is lacking between those two lands."

"Faolyn has a sister, "I said, thinking "Lynthe. She is seventeen, maybe. And Casyn's other daughter has children — but she renounced any claim on the inheritance, for herself or her children. But it is Ésparias, Ruar. Their women have different expectations. With all respect, Helvi, you knew you would be required to make a marriage for political purposes, and women in Linrathe expect to marry for reasons of land and property. Ésparias has acknowledged marriage, yes, but rarely for such reasons."

"Sorley?" Ruar's voice was uncharacteristically hesitant. "Is there not a daughter of Cillian's somewhere in Linrathe that he could claim? From before he met Lena? He did travel, extensively, and for many years."

"No," I said. "No children, male or female."

"How can he be sure?"

"He is," I said bluntly. "He swore to leave no child fatherless, because he had been, and so he ensured it could not happen. But a late-acknowledged bastard would not be acceptable to Bryngyl, anyhow."

"Perhaps not," Ruar said. "Although it would have been to the Empress Eudekia, so how could he gainsay?"

I had no answer to that. Had Eudekia known Cillian had been thirty-three when his father had acknowledged him? Perhaps he had told her, in one of their late-night talks. "How did you know that?" I asked Ruar.

"Cillian told me," he said. "We were discussing the treaties, and how he had negotiated them."

"I see. I have no solution for you, *Teannasach,* but I can't believe Cillian hasn't foreseen this, and planned for it. But that plan will not include Gwenna."

There was a sharp rap at the door, before it was opened by Daoíre. "Ruar," he said, "we must leave."

"All right," Ruar said. He ran a finger down Helvi's cheek, bending to kiss her. "I will be home in a week, no more, and maybe less," he told her. He looked up. "Daoíre, wait for me with the horses. I will be there in a moment."

He pushed his dark hair out of his eyes. "Walk with me." I bowed again to Helvi, and side by side Ruar and I went through the corridors to the great hall.

"Where are you going?" I asked.

"West, to the coast. To settle a land dispute. One *Eirën* wants to break a marriage contract for his son, and he is alleging the girl is not the other *Eirën's*, but Marai-fathered. Her age makes it possible. But the first has his eye on a better alliance, in terms of property, so he may well be manufacturing the claim."

"What will you do?"

"If the *Eirën* acknowledges the girl as his daughter, and will swear she is his heir, then the contract must stand." A servant handed him his cloak. "Otherwise there will a rash of these disputes, I fear." We walked out into the morning. The rain had stopped. He gave me the kiss of farewell and swung up onto his horse; Daoíre and the bodyguards were already mounted.

"Stop," Ruar said, looking down the track down the long valley. I followed his eyes: two horses and riders approached. Druise and Gwenna. "We will wait," he said. Daoíre made a sound of protest.

"I am the *Teannasach*, cousin," Ruar said mildly. "The *Eirënnen* in question can wait another day for their hearing, if I so choose. But I do not; we will ride in only a few minutes more. Be patient."

Gwenna halted her mare, Druise behind her as befitted his role as her guard. She did not dismount: Ruar had stayed in the saddle. "My lady Gwenna," Ruar said. "Be welcome. I am sorry I will have no chance to speak with you, but my duty lies elsewhere."

"*Teannasach*," she said. "I thank you for your hospitality. I regret too that we will not have time to speak together." Mud-spattered or not, she was flawlessly correct; she had been well-taught, at home and at the White Fort. I watched them: Ruar in his prime, the resemblance to Donnalch evident in hair and the shape of his face, but he had his mother's blue eyes, and her slightness of build. I remembered him at thirteen, grim-faced, wielding a sword beside me against the Marai. He had earned the men of Linrathe's loyalty that day, nearly fifteen years ago. Gwenna, not yet fully grown, carried herself with confidence.

"Your parents?" Ruar asked. "They are well?"

"Quite well," she answered. "And the Lady Helvi and your children?"

"Looking forward to meeting you," Ruar said. "And now I must go. Druisius, welcome. You are a guest here, not a guard; my men will ensure no harm comes to Gwenna." With a raised hand, he urged his horse forward along the track. I turned to Druise and Gwenna.

"Leave your horses and your bags," I said. "They will be taken care of."

"Not my *cithar*," Druise said. He removed it from his saddlebag before allowing the servants to take them. I led them into the great hall, where the steward met us.

"I will take the lady Gwenna to the women's rooms," he said.

"Go," I said to her. "You will want to wash and change. I'll show Druise to his room."

"She was in tears earlier," he said, with no preamble, as soon as the door to his room was shut. "I had her wash her face at a stream."

"A hard thing to learn," I said. "How much did you tell her?"

"All of it. The tears were for her father."

"He has induced tears from all of us, over the years," I said. "Except you, I suppose, and Colm."

"Only Colm."

"What? When did he make you cry?"

"You think I could do everything I did that winter, day after day, and not feel the pain I caused him?"

"Why am I suddenly learning these things about you?" I asked crossly. "First you reveal you wanted to be a doctor, and next that you cried for Cillian's pain? Why didn't you let me know that at the time? And don't shrug!"

He gave me a wry grin instead. "Could I risk such weakness?"

"I cried in front of you."

"You cry in front of everyone."

I put my arms around him. "Druise, I couldn't have survived that winter without you. None of us could have. Especially Cillian. We asked a very great deal of you. I should have realized the strain you were under."

"My job," he said, as I knew he would. I kissed him, once, and again.

"I asked for these rooms because there is a door between them," I told him.

"Was that wise?" He pulled back to look at me, his eyes troubled.

"I told the steward I needed to be close to Gwenna's bodyguard. And there will be no chance, after we leave here."

"I thought no chance at all," he said, smiling slightly. "I am going to have a nap. Wake me when you need to, *amané*."

He was asleep in minutes, a knack I had never developed, and often wished I had. I wondered how often he had been up in the night to check on the shepherd; I hadn't thought to ask. I'll let him sleep for as long as I can, I decided. I used to get angry at Cillian when he said he didn't deserve Lena, or me, but I understood now. Why did I deserve Druise?

Chapter 29

14 YEARS EARLIER

IT WOULD HAVE BEEN very easy that night to seek out company: Evan, or another. Some of my frustration was simple physical hunger too long unsatisfied, but I wanted more than that. I wanted to be held, to hear soft breathing — or even snoring — beside me, and the ease and excitement of a partner whose rhythms and desires I had begun to know. My jealousy, I gradually understood, came not from knowing that Cillian and Lena were lovers again, but from the security inherent in the intimacy they shared. The shelter. I was alone, and lonely.

I did not go in search of comfort. I slept, with the help of more wine, and the next day and the next I met with Livius and wrote letters and did all the things asked of me as Linrathe's *toscaire,* and one day I did play *xache* with Cillian in the late afternoon, joining him after his massage in his workroom. Before Apulo arrived, the adjoining room had been connected internally, and a treatment bed and shelves for Apulo's creams and unguents and the mild drugs Cillian allowed himself. The requirements of the massage used to treat Cillian's injuries was unsuitable for the public tables adjoining the baths, Gnaius had decreed.

But just as after Gwenna's birth, I felt inconvenient, superfluous to Cillian and Lena's life. Some nights I drank in the junior commons, some officer from my classes always willing to name me guest, and once or twice I diced with the soldiers. I did not accept the propositions that came my way, although later, in my empty bed, I wondered why.

I spent a day in the carpentry shop: the pieces of the *ladhar* had been cut; now I was shaping them to produce the curved frame, alternating darker and lighter strips. The *ladhar* would look like the Casilani bows, I thought. I wondered if that was where the idea for the instrument had come from: you could pluck a strung bow to produce a note, and differently-sized bows — or bowstrings of different thicknesses — made different sounds. Something to think about.

Satisfied with my hours of work, and needing to wet my dusty throat, I went to the senior officers' commons. I was avoiding the soldiers' commons, not wanting to meet Evan. Talyn, my frequent sponsor, sat at a table across the room. To my surprise, Lena was with her.

The steward nodded at me. I walked over to their table. "Am I interrupting?"

"Sit down," Talyn said. "I needed a drink, and Lena too. We spent the day with Livius's staff, going over land ownership again."

"Are you done?" I asked, accepting wine from the steward.

"No. We have maps to look at, tomorrow. Village land boundaries," Lena said. "I can remember Tirvan's, I think, and Talyn is sure she knows Han's. If we can show the maps are accurate for those two, and perhaps Berge's — Kyreth might know theirs — then Cillian believes we can argue for all the boundaries being right on the maps."

"Are the boundaries clear?" Gundarstorp's land was delineated by physical markers: standing stones, mostly, but sometimes the run of a wall, or an ancient tree. I'd walked and ridden them since earliest childhood, learning the extent of the land I was to inherit.

"Mostly. Decanius, apparently, has been critical of the stones being just stones, though; in a proper Casilani province, they would be engraved with the details, apparently. He is doubtful of their precise positions, we are told, because it would be easy to substitute another stone or tree, to claim more land."

"Gods," I said, taking a drink. "What does the Governor say?"

"That if he is satisfied, the boundaries will remain as they are, but not all villages will remain in the hands of women, or only women."

"That will not be popular."

"No," Lena said slowly, "and yet I think he is right. There are not enough women now, and so many are young. Settlers are coming from

Casil, and eventually from Linrathe, aren't they?"

"Someday," I said, "probably."

"Be careful where you say that, Lena," Talyn said, "and to whom. Don't add to the problem you already have."

"What problem?" I asked.

"Not here," Talyn said. "Shall we go to see Gwenna?"

No one but Tyrvi was in their rooms, Tyrvi and the two babies. Lena picked up Gwenna, handing her to Talyn, who held her with experienced hands and half her attention. Gwenna gurgled and smiled: now she wasn't hungry all the time, she was a happy baby.

"Tyrvi, I have work to discuss with Lieutenant Talyn," Lena said. "Would you take Darel out for half an hour? Gwenna can stay with us."

"More wine?" she asked, when the girl had gone. I accepted a cup, but she made tea for Talyn and herself.

"What problem?" I asked again, when we were settled. The two women glanced at each other.

"Cillian," Lena said.

"My cousin," Talyn said, "is not well thought of by either soldiers or officers. What is said ranges from his bad advice being the cause of the Emperor's death, to siding with the Casilani in the talks." She held up a hand at my splutter of denial. "He is also accused of purposely giving away much of our land's autonomy to save Linrathe's."

"He hates this treaty!"

"You know that, and I, and Lena. But think, Sorley," Talyn said, with force. "Who are Cillian's friends? He plays *xache* with a Casilani ship's captain and discusses philosophy with his Casilani physician. He does not go to the baths publicly. He prefers the company of his Casilani soldier-servant and you, a Linrathan musician and envoy, to the officers of his rank. On top of which he holds a commission as a Major seen as undeserved by many. Why Turlo and Callan insisted on that, I do not know. Colm was Advisor, with no military rank; why could Cillian not have just been given that title?" Gwenna began to fuss, probably at Talyn's tone, I thought. Lena took her, jiggling her into silence.

"Turlo said he had to have rank," I said, "to be his adjutant at the negotiations with Casil. I can't speak for the Emperor." Druise had mentioned the unrest among the soldiers. So had the steward, not very long ago. But if it had spread to the officers… "When did this start?"

Talyn shrugged. "There's always been a bit of it, complaints about this unknown Linrathan exile influencing the Emperor and my father. But it's grown worse as the changes are implemented."

"Does the *Princip* know?"

"I imagine he's heard rumours," Talyn said. "But — Sorley, this is only for your ears, please — my father sees his dead brothers in Cillian, especially Colm, and because of that will tend to ignore what is said. There were complaints about Colm, too, officers and men who thought a castrate should not advise an Emperor."

"Casyn is tired," Lena said. "He's had no time to grieve, and he never wanted to be *Princip*." She had got up to walk with the baby, who was turning her head to look around.

"I almost wish I could have taken the title," Talyn said, "but I have neither the rank nor the experience. Cillian nearly has the rank, but it would be impossible now. I would worry even if he were co-regent, were my father to die. By the time Faolyn is eighteen, I hope the position will be that of a figurehead, but just now it requires an active strategist."

"Which Cillian is," I said. "The question in many minds seems to be for whom? He has to be told, Lena."

"Yes," she said thoughtfully. "He must. I'll do it, Talyn."

"Better you than me." Casyn's daughter grinned. "Although I would have, you know."

"I cannot blame people for thinking much as I did, and for the same reasons, at least about his feelings toward the Eastern Empire," Lena said to me a few minutes later. She dropped her voice to a murmur. "But now we know his real thoughts — the irony, Sorley."

"That they see him as favouring Linrathe worries me," I told her. "It all worries me, Lena. Do you want me there when you talk to him?"

"Not this time," she said. "I think, Sorley, there are things he may not want you to hear. Don't be offended; it would just be from a fear of hurting you, nothing more."

I didn't like it, but I couldn't argue. "About Linrathe?" I guessed.

"In a way."

Cillian himself told me what Lena had said to him, in summary, at least. "She is completely right," he said with a wry smile, over wine and *xache* two nights later. He'd sent a messenger to ask me to join him. "I have consulted with Casyn, and I must spend even less time with Lena and Gwenna, and with you, and be seen around the fort. I will dine with the senior officers at least three times a week now and attend the baths on occasion. Casyn tells me the scars I carry will remind others of my service to Ésparias."

"What does Lena think of Casyn's directives?" I moved a piece, capturing one of his. He raised an eyebrow.

"An interesting move," he said. "Lena? She is resigned to the need, and perhaps a little pleased."

"Pleased?"

"She believes I need to listen more to other officers. She also has valid concerns about her own authority as lieutenant, which should not be compromised by what factions within the army think of me." He moved a piece, effectively blocking what I planned to do next. I shook my head at my failure to see the obvious.

"She has told me often enough that I have become too authoritative," he went on. "And again, she is not wrong. I must appear very sure of my arguments in discussions with the Casilani, and that spills over, into my private life. I am attempting to amend that." He watched me slide a piece along the board, a stalling move on my part. "I am surprised you have not complained."

I looked up from the board. "Sometimes I feel like I am still your student, so I suppose it's much the same thing."

"Do you?" he asked. "I do not intend that, *mo charaidh*. I am well aware you are not. Why have you not told me?"

"I haven't seen that much of you," I said. Another stalling move. I took a breath. "Cillian, Talyn told us you were being accused of giving up too much here, to keep Linrathe free. I have never claimed that, but I did say to Liam once that the treaty you negotiated for us was proof you loved the land of your birth. Could that have got back to the men here, perhaps through Randall?"

He leaned back. "Perhaps. Or perhaps it is a conclusion anyone can make who sees the differences between the two agreements. Do not worry over it, *mo charaidh*."

Anger flared. I had voiced a reasonable concern. "By Rögnir, Cillian, stop condescending to me!" I stood, pushing back the chair noisily. "We can finish this later."

"Sorley." I stopped, my hand on the door. His voice was very quiet. "The student I have made you recall? Is it the one I last saw at the *Ti'ach*, almost ready to leave us, or the one you were at eighteen?"

"Is there a difference?" I didn't wait for an answer.

I stalked around my room, swearing. Why did Cillian still treat me as — what had he called me? An innocent. Someone who had to be treated with care. Even Lena had said as much. And Druise: *Be careful with Sorley.* I swore at him. Hadn't he concurred with Cillian that I needed gentle handling?

I went back over the overheard conversation in my head. Slowly, grudgingly, my anger at Druise dissipated. Whatever he had been saying to Cillian, it had not been to diminish me. Then had Druise known of Cillian's treasonous thoughts? *Certain indications.* It fit.

Had Druise been concerned how I would react, what position I might take? Pain stabbed at my temples, my jaw and neck too tight. My churning mind needed more space than this room. The night was warm enough to be out. I closed my door and walked softly down the corridor.

I should have turned left from my room, to reach the first exit from the building. But I didn't. I let my feet take me right, and right again to the corridor where Cillian's study was. Light flickered under the door. I stopped. My head pounded in time with my heart. No, I told myself. You are too angry. Keep walking. I continued down the corridor, toward the door that would take me out into the night.

Then I turned. At Cillian's door I knocked, my quick triple tap.

"Come," he called, just loud enough. I went in. He was contemplating the *xache* board, studying the game we had left unfinished. "Sorley," he said. "Have you come back to finish the game? It was your move."

I picked up a piece almost at random, moving it the requisite spaces.

"Are you sure?"

"Does it matter?"

He frowned a little. "You are still upset."

"Yes," I said.

He sat back. "Will you pour us both wine?" I did as he asked, but I didn't sit. "How do I make amends?" he asked. "I was dismissive, I admit."

I drank a little wine, for courage, although it would not help my head. "Before Druise left," I said, "he came to talk to you. About me. I overheard much of that conversation."

"I see," he said. "I believe I remember the conversation to which you refer. What do you think you heard?"

"That in your eyes I am still a boy," I let anger blossom again. "That I don't know you, and that I need to be treated carefully. Still, Cillian? After Casil, after your illness, after trusting me with your plans? How dare you treat me as if I am a child?" I had never spoken to him like this. I could feel myself trembling.

The lamplight flickered. He picked up a *xache* piece, turning it in his fingers, his eyes hooded. I waited. His fingers tightened around the gamepiece. Deliberately, carefully, he put it down, spreading his fingers wide as he did. "You misunderstand," he said.

Chapter 30

15 Years After the Battle of the Taiva

A LOUD SNORE BROUGHT me back to the present. I forced the memory away: it was not for here, not in this room where I watched Druise sleep. He and I had our rules: our lives might be interwoven with Cillian's and Lena's by work and vision, responsibility and love, but some aspects were our own, kept distinct and discrete. The dilemma Ruar had handed me was not one of those, though, and I wanted Druise's thoughts. But he needed sleep. Later would do.

I did not see Gwenna until the mid-day meal, served in a small chamber off the great hall to just the three of us, along with Helvi and Amlodd, the *scáeli* to Dun Ceànnar. I thought her subdued, although she handled the light conversation adroitly.

"Will you play tonight, Sorley?" Amlodd asked. I could not, unless he gave me permission, not here where he was *scáeli*.

"I will. May Druisius play too? You will not have heard the *cithar*, I expect?"

"I have not," he said. "But would you show me the instrument before tonight, Druisius? I am curious to see its construction and hear its tunings."

"Gladly," Druise said. He would always talk about music; it was what had brought us together, in Casil. "I must speak with Sorley after the meal, yes? After that?"

"I will be in the hall," Amlodd said. "By the fire."

"May I speak with you too, Sorley?" Gwenna asked. I heard the plea.

"After Druise and I are done, yes," I said gently.

"You might like to stay by the fire too, Gwenna," Helvi suggested. "You would play for the Lady Gwenna, Amlodd?' Her suggestion was a command, couched politely.

After a suitable time, Helvi rose to indicate the meal was done, and I took Druise back to my room. I told him, in Casilan, what Ruar had proposed, that morning.

"No!" he said.

"No. It will not happen. Cillian promised." He had never mentioned anything about this third alliance, the completion of the triangle linking our lands together.

"Will the Governor expect it? He was happy with Faolyn marrying Ruar's sister."

"He was," I said, "because he saw it as bringing Linrathe even closer to Ésparias, especially once he understood that Faolyn could then influence the choice of *Teannasach*, should something happen to Ruar." Livius had been subtly and masterfully convinced of the benefit, sealed by the offer of a percentage of the tariffs imposed at the trading port. He in turn had convinced the Empress. "But," I said reluctantly, "Gwenna is Faolyn's heir, and her children after her. I doubt marriage into Varsland is what Casil would consider appropriate. But Cillian must have a plan to join the Marai to our...confederation."

"He must," Druise agreed. "He will not have told you, *amané*; he tells none of us all the parts of his designs, so we cannot be complicit if the charge of treason comes."

"Even though we are," I said. I sighed. My thoughts were no clearer. "I will write to him, letting him know Ruar has raised the issue."

"I will go to explain the *cithar* to Amlodd," he said, "and send Gwenna to you."

She came in hugging herself. I stirred the fire and added a brick of peat, and made her sit by it, even though I did not think she was cold from the air of the room. "Shall I call for a hot drink?" I asked. She shook her head.

"I feel like I don't know my father at all," she said.

"In a way, you don't," I said. "This all happened a long time ago, *leannan*."

"But...was he like old Póli, who stumbles around and shakes and sees things?" Póli was a wanderer, lost to ale and cider, and *fuisce* when he could get it. I thought he might have been an aspiring *scáeli* once, but his stories made no sense.

"No. Póli cannot, or hasn't chosen to, break himself of his need for drink. Your father became dependent on poppy, yes, but he broke that dependency, and he has never once given in to the craving."

"Does he still want it?"

"I don't know, Gwenna," I said. "There is none at the *Ti'ach*. He asked for that. And you know how rarely he accepts any drug, willow-bark or valerian." He had an exception to his strict self-restraint, but not one Gwenna needed to know.

She nodded. "*Mathàir* gets irritated with him, when he is clearly in pain and won't even drink willow-bark tea."

"Did Druise tell you to whom your father made the vow that he would free himself of the drug?"

"To my mother, I suppose."

"No, Gwenna. To you. Or to the child unborn, who turned out to be you."

"Oh," she whispered. "Truly?"

"Truly. He would not go through with the ceremony that would make you legitimate in the eyes of Linrathe unless his mind was clear, undrugged. He made the vow to do so in my presence, so there was a witness."

"They say at the White Fort that my parents only married because of me. Is that what they mean?"

"Did you think it meant otherwise?"

"I thought...that they wanted not to, but because of me, they had to."

I chose my words carefully. "Your mother had promised your father to swear any vow he wished, if they lived past the war, long before you were conceived. You complicated things a bit, I suppose; they might have waited until your father was stronger. But that is all." A version of the truth. I had not answered her direct question once again, but as I could not know what her classmates had intended in what they said to her, I had not violated my oath.

"Sorley? What did my parents vow, at their ceremony?"

"It was fourteen years ago," I said. "Let me think." But my *scáeli's* memory for words didn't fail me. "There was no land to consider, so the ceremony was nothing more than an affirmation of the vows your parents had made to each other before Turlo and Irmgard and I found them in those empty lands. Then they each answered 'yes' to a question from Dagney." I could still hear her firm voice asking, 'Will you affirm to these witnesses your belief that your friendship, the love you share, and your trust in each other, will endure all things?' I told Gwenna the words. "When they exchanged the bracelets, the words said were 'In love and trust, I give to you the *li'ítho.*' That is all."

She looked at the fire. "Didn't it bother you, watching them marry?"

"In what way, Gwenna?" She didn't answer. These past few days must have been difficult for her, I thought. I stood up, going to a sideboard where a wine jug stood. I poured two small cups, watered them. Gwenna took hers, but she didn't raise it to her lips. I took a sip of mine, putting in down on the low table. I wasn't going to play *scáeli's* word games now. "Yes, it did bother me, a little, then." Her face was still, her eyes wide and dark. "I think you have realized I love your father, Gwenna, and not just as a friend or a brother. I lost my heart to him watching him dance, the second night he was at Gundarstorp when I was sixteen. I was playing, but my eyes were on him. He looked over at me and smiled." I smiled myself, the memory no longer painful. "Twenty-three years ago."

"I thought so," she said. "But...Druise?"

"I love him too," I said. "It's possible, you know." Although the closest we ever came to acknowledging that was in the newer verses to my song. I smiled a little, remembering the first time I'd sung them to Druise. He had simply grinned, but he hadn't denied their truth.

"And everybody knows?"

"Of course. Your mother has known since a few days after we met on the river, and Druise since our first night together. They've both been extraordinarily understanding."

"And... *Athàir?*"

Careful, now, I told myself. "He knew that night. He didn't encourage me, Gwenna, in the slightest. For me to show...longing...for another man would have meant disinheritance in Sorham, and immense shame for my family. So he kept his distance from me, hoping I would outgrow the love. That is was an infatuation, nothing more."

"But it wasn't." She was smiling now, as if she were listening to a *scáeli's* tale.

"No. We couldn't escape each other, on that small ship or in Casil, and over those weeks Cillian and I allowed ourselves to become friends. I accepted that he was vowed to your mother, and then I met Druise, and that helped. It was your father's wish that we would all be together at the *Ti'ach*."

"The marriage bracelets were yours, weren't they?"

"They were. Brothers often give them, if their father is dead."

She didn't answer, staring into the fire. I didn't speak either, lost in memories of that night. I'd shown Cillian the *li'itho*, asked him to accept them as a brother. He'd picked up the larger of the bracelets to examine its intricate woven strands. "Beautiful work. From Varsland?" he'd asked.

"No. From a silversmith in Sorham."

"Lena might have baulked, were they Marai," he'd said. "If she does not see them as jesses, if she will wear them, I will accept your *li'itho*, and not just as a brother's due." He had looked up at me, his eyes dark in the lamplight. "It is not a brother who braves the underworld with only his instrument and his voice to bring another home."

"The Marai say it was," I'd replied.

"Not successfully."

"Nor was Oraiáphon."

"His music convinced the god. It was his own impatience that lost him his love. When you thought I was not following, when death seemed certain, you just kept singing, Lena tells me."

"To ease you, if you could hear me. To make you feel loved, and safe, so —" I hadn't been able to go on, hot tears rising.

"So I could sleep," Cillian had said. "But I followed your voice past the sleep you were gentling me towards, and into the sleep of healing. I heard you that night, and the love with which you sang. I owe you my life, Sorley."

"I did it for Lena," I'd answered. "Lena and your child."

"But not only." He'd let the silver bracelet slide from his hand to the table again, gently. "It is not an hour for half-truths, is it?"

I had swallowed, or tried to, my mouth dry. "No," I'd said. "Perhaps not." I'd reached my hand out to him, almost involuntarily. He'd taken it, entwining his long fingers with mine, raising it to his lips.

"Lena is the greatest blessing of my life, and the greatest love. I will wear this bracelet as a symbol of my bond with her, but I will wear it for you, too. Never doubt that you too are loved, my lord Sorley."

I'd said his name, and then I'd leaned forward to kiss him. He'd allowed it, his fingers tightening on mine for a heartbeat. It had felt like a goodbye, and for me it had been, to the vestiges of a dream.

"Sorley?" Gwenna's voice broke my reverie. "You are very brave, aren't you?"

"Brave?" I said. "No. I have followed my heart, Gwenna, and that is a privilege allowed to few. If it is bravery you want, look to your parents."

Chapter 31

WE JOINED DRUISE AND Amlodd in the great hall, where they were having a detailed discussion about the construction of their respective instruments. But how long can three musicians together simply talk? Amlodd found a *ladhar* for Gwenna, and we began to play. The steward came through once or twice, stopping to listen. We were just explaining a tuning to Gwenna — she was competent with the *ladhar*, but not inspired — when the doors to the hall swung open, the guard calling for the steward.

Beside him stood a woman, cloaked and hooded — it must be raining again, I thought — and with her a girl, similarly attired. "May we go to the fire?" she asked the guard. A shiver ran through me. I knew that voice, or at least a younger version of it. I put down my instrument.

"Jordis?"

She pushed the hood back. "Sorley?" she breathed. Then she said my name again, and ran to me, throwing herself into my arms. I held her, ignoring her soaked cloak, feeling her body racked with sobs. How was she here? The Marai had taken her from the *Ti'ach*, fifteen years earlier, she and little Niav, Isa's niece.

I looked up, seeing the girl standing uncertainly beside a man I recognized. I'd taught him, the winter I had spent at Dugarstorp. The oldest son, known as Dugi. He'd be seventeen or eighteen, now.

"You know this woman, Lord Sorley?" the steward asked me. I hadn't heard him come in.

"I do," I said. "This is the lady Jordis, daughter to *Eirën* Egan. She was a student at the *Ti'ach na Perras* with me. The Marai took her in the war."

Jordis stepped away from my arms. "And this is my daughter, Elsë," she said, beckoning to the girl. She slipped an arm around the girl's shoulder. "My...her father had brought us to the boy's family for her marriage. There was a gathering, in celebration, and Dugi — the lord Dugi — was there, and he saw I was not Marai, although I do not know how, and approached me. I asked him to bring me home, and he did."

Dear gods, I thought. The diplomatic implications of what Dugi had done could be serious.

"Gwenna," I said in Casilan. "Go to Helvi. Explain who is here, and what has happened. You understand there may be repercussions from this?"

"I will tell her a Marai's captive wife, an *Eirën's* daughter, has fled her husband, and a lord from Sorham has aided her," she said, in the same language.

"Correct."

"What language was that?" Jordis said, clearly bewildered. "And who is the girl? There is something familiar about her."

"Much has happened, Jordis," I said, helping her take off her wet cloak. I gave her wine, and at her nod a cup for Elsë too. "I was speaking Casilan, as it should be spoken, not as Perras taught us. The girl is Gwenna. She is Cillian's daughter."

"Cillian's daughter? But who is her mother?" I laughed, gently, at the genuine surprise in her voice.

"Lena. Do you remember her?"

"Yes," she said slowly. "They were exiled together. Are they home again?"

"A long story," I told her. "Not one for now."

"Yes," she said. "Tell me, Sorley. I want to hear about home. Elsë, come and listen."

"There is a *danta*," I told her. "I'll sing it for you, later, if you like, but there isn't time now to tell you everything. Suffice it to say the Emperor pardoned both Cillian and Lena. Cillian is *Comiádh* now. Perras died fifteen years ago, and Dagney eight. Lena is Lady of the *Ti'ach*. They have two children, Gwenna and Colm. And I am the music teacher there, and a *scáeli*. Isa and Anndra are still with us, and will be overjoyed to hear you are alive." I gestured to Druise. "And this is Druise — Druisius, I should say — from Casil in the Eastern Empire, Jordis. He teaches at the *Ti'ach* too."

She smiled at his greeting, but I could tell her thoughts were elsewhere. "Isa and Anndra," she said. "Niav is dead, Sorley. She died giving birth, and the child with her. She was too small, too young."

I closed my eyes against the news. Little Niav, full of questions, turning everything into a song. Hatred for the Marai welled from wherever I had hidden it, deep inside. "Oh, Jordis," I said. "But perhaps it will give some peace to Isa, to at least know her fate."

The guard by the door straightened. Helvi came into the hall, Gwenna behind her. Jordis scrambled to her feet, pulling her daughter up. Bearing and dress had told Jordis who this was, I guessed.

"My lady Helvi," I said. "May I introduce the lady Jordis of Eganstorp, and her daughter Elsë? She asks for sanctuary from her daughter's father. Lord Dugi has brought her from Varsland."

"My dear," Helvi said. "You are wet, and no doubt cold. Will you come with me to the women's rooms? We will find dry clothes for you both. Gwenna, will you come too? I guess that Elsë speaks no Linrathan?"

"No, my lady," Jordis said.

"Then we had best speak Marái'sta, hadn't we?" she said, switching to that language. Jordis glanced at me.

"Go," I said. "You are safe." She must have known Ruar had married a Marai bride, I thought. Whatever remote farm or village her Marai captor had taken her to, that news would have spread through the kingdom.

"Dugi," I said when they had gone. "You do know how serious this may be?"

"And how are you, Sorley?" he replied.

"Sorry," I said. "But there is little time for pleasantries. The *Teannasach* left for the coast this morning. He must be apprised. Tell me who the man who took Jordis was, and who the girl was to marry. And how did you recognize Jordis as Linrathan?"

"Wine would be welcome," he said, coming over to the fire. I gave him a cup. "As for how I recognized her," he said after a mouthful, "she was humming to herself when I happened to be close. The tune was yours, the one you wrote for Halmar's poem."

War in winter sends sorrow soaring... I had written the tune for Cillian, for his translation of the poem, when I was eighteen. I had taught it to Dugi and Gefen, his brother, when I was their tutor.

"The man?"

"Eluf. A farmer, from all I've heard. The boy Elsë was to marry is the son of a man who deals in fish. He's wealthy: the business does well, and he has a fleet of boats. I was there to make an agreement over some of our catch, in fact."

"Is either family close to any of the earls?"

"They'll owe duty to someone. The merchant...Earl Gosta, I think. Don't know about Eluf." He drained his cup. "Gosta's lands are mostly coastal, and his people fishermen. He's cautious in declaring allegiance. Canny. Markets matter more to him than who sits on the throne, I'd say."

"So unlikely to send men after the girl?" I asked.

"I doubt it. There's no shortage of girls to marry a rich man's heir," he said. So unless Eluf had connections, Jordis and her daughter were likely safe.

"Where will she go?" Dugi asked.

"I don't know," I admitted. "Her father and brother died in the war. The lands are in the hands of her uncle now; the *Teannasach* may need to decide." I turned to Amlodd, who had been sitting quietly, listening. Remembering what was being said and done, as his role required. "Amlodd? How is Eganstorp held? In trust, or were the lands ceded?"

"Ceded, after seven years," he replied.

I should have known that. "Can she stay here?"

"For a while, yes. Helvi will offer, I have no doubt."

"Or," I said, thinking out loud, "she could go to the *Ti'ach*. It's familiar to her, and isolated, and guarded, if that were ever important."

"Sorley!" Druise said in Casilan. "You cannot send a woman perhaps chased by Marai men to the *Ti'ach*. It puts Lena in danger."

"She is unlikely to be pursued," I said.

Druise compressed his lips. "No," he said. "I will not allow it."

I stared at my lover, and he stared back, his jaw set. I looked away.

"Their protection is my job," he said quietly.

"Yes," I said. "I know. But Jordis was my friend, and both Lena and Cillian know her. If I write to them, and they say yes, what do you say?"

"Lena is the senior captain," he said. "If she says yes, then I must. Although," he added, "I would argue with her, were I there. Is there space in your letter for my thoughts?"

"Yes. Of course. Or write you own, and I will include in with mine under the *Teannasach's* seal. We will let Lena decide." He nodded, his lips still tight. We rarely argued, but the safety of our family and the *Ti'ach* was his responsibility, and I should have spoken to him before making the suggestion. I would apologize privately.

Chapter 32

LATER I SPOKE ALONE with Dugi, for more information on the men involved with Jordis and Elsë. I should tell Cillian and Lena as much as possible, so Lena could make an appropriate decision. He had little to add about the man who had taken Jordis, but much more about the bridegroom and his family. "There's a daughter," he said. "My father is considering offering for her; he thinks a connection to Varsland's fish trade could be valuable."

"For you or Gefen?" I asked.

"Gefen. I inherit the *torp*; he'll need something."

Always the way, for second sons; sometimes there was a *torp* with only daughters to make an alliance with, or the army, or for some the path of a scholar or a *scáeli*. And some crossed the narrow sea to take the coin of the Marai.

I wrote my letter. Then I went to find Jordis. "She has eaten and bathed," Helvi told me, "and she's sitting quietly now, resting." She opened the door to a small sitting room. "In here."

Jordis was watching Gwenna combing Elsë's hair in front of the fire, her movements gentle. I supposed she had done this with the other girls at the *Ti'ach*, or at the White Fort. "Sorley," Jordis said as I came in. "Of all the people to find. Why are you here?" She looked tired, but much of the tension had gone from her. "I am so glad you are."

I sat beside her. "Do you remember me saying I am a *scáeli* now? The *Ti'acha* are expanding, Jordis, into Sorham and into Ésparias." She frowned at that.

"Ésparias?"

"The land south of the Wall. Casil renamed it, when they reclaimed it as a part of the Eastern Empire. One of many changes there."

"You are going to explain all this?"

"In time. But to answer your question, as *scáeli* to the *Ti'ach na Cillian*, I am travelling north to the newest *Ti'ach*, to ensure the music program is properly organized. I had business with the *Teannasach*, so we stopped here for a day or two."

"The *Ti'ach na Cillian*," she said. "It sounds so strange. Do not mistake me, Gwenna," she added, seeing her look up. "I can think of no one better than your father to succeed Perras. But I have thought of it with its previous name for all these years."

"I must ask, Jordis. Will Elsë's father come after you, or her?" I asked. "Or the bridegroom?"

"Eluf? No. Not after me. But perhaps after her. It was a good marriage." We were speaking Linrathan, so the girl could not understand. "There are two boys, too: younger, and Eluf thought perhaps one would be taken into the business."

"Where are the boys?"

"At the farm. They're not mine. Something went wrong after Elsë. I was ill with a fever and a flux that caused great pain here — "she touched herself, low on her belly — "and after that I did not conceive. He has another woman."

"Are you his wife?" I asked.

"There was some ceremony, so in his eyes, yes. The other woman is another captive, from the Southern Empire. Ésparias," she corrected.

"Her name?" Her answer meant nothing to me, but it might to Lena.

"I'm sending letters to the *Ti'ach*, to ask if you may go there for a while," I told her. Gwenna straightened, looked my way. I told Jordis, as gently as I could, why she could not just go home.

"All dead?" Tears welled. She brushed them away. "My uncle will not want me. The *Ti'ach* would be a refuge, for a while. But what will I do, Sorley? No man will want me; I am barren, and I have no lands to offer. And no skills beyond that of house and farm, now."

"My mother," Gwenna said, "could use help this summer. She is Lady of the *Ti'ach*, and if you were there you will know what that entails. But she also teaches, the bow and secca, and some aspects of the *danta*, and she will insist on riding patrol, with Druise gone. If you were there, you could help with the students, and lessen her work. Why cannot Jordis and Elsë just go, Sorley?"

"Druise forbade it," I told her.

"Why? — oh," she said. "I see."

"Who is Druisius?" Jordis asked. "And patrols? And the *Ti'acha* do not teach the use of weapons."

"They do, since the war," I said. "Druisius is a captain in Ésparias's army. His responsibilities include the protection of the *Ti'ach*. Lena killed Fritjof, Jordis. Did you not know that?"

"Oh. No. I didn't know."

"With a bow, from horseback," Gwenna said. "A long shot, halfway across a river, and the arrow hit him in the neck. She was pregnant with me, at the time."

"Then I can't go to the *Ti'ach*," Jordis said. "I might be a danger to her."

"It will be her decision," I said. "Druise forbids you to go now, but Lena outranks him. If a letter comes saying you may, then you shall, if you wish."

"Outranks him? She is still in the army, then?"

"Yes. Her rank is captain too, but she is the senior, seconded to the *Ti'ach* to teach weaponry, officially."

"A high rank to teach weaponry," Jordis said. Fifteen years of captivity had not completely dulled her mind.

"She has other duties," I said. Personal bodyguard was one of them, but Jordis did not need to know that. Or did she? I doubted Lena and Cillian would turn Jordis away, but I would not be here to find out. And wherever she went, she would soon hear the tale.

"Gwenna," I said. "An opportunity to practice some of your diplomatic skills. Would you introduce yourself to the lady Jordis, as you would if you met her at Wall's End?"

"At Wall's End?" Her eyes flicked from me to Jordis. "At a formal occasion?"

"Yes, if you will."

She shot me a look of displeasure, but she rose in one fluid move to stand in front of Jordis. "I am so very pleased you could join us, Lady

Jordis," she said. "I am Gwenna. My father is Cillian, prince of Ésparias."

"Prince of Ésparias?" Jordis said. "But.... How? *Cillian*?"

"His father was the Emperor," I said. "You did hear that?"

"Yes. But still..." Her face reflected her bewilderment, trying to adjust to the idea that the sardonic, distant teacher she had known was now a prince. An Ésparian prince, but also *Comiádh* of a Linrathan *Ti'ach*. It was a lot to take in, all at once.

"It was the Empress Eudekia," Gwenna said. "She made him a prince, because he should have been Callan's heir. It makes me a princess, but I do not like to be called that at all. And in Linrathe, I am only Gwenna, so please do not call me anything else. Please?"

"How old are you, Gwenna?" Jordis asked.

"Fourteen."

"Much the same as my daughter. The Marai believe that is old enough to wed. Your people do not, if I remember rightly...but there is no marriage, in the southern Empire, is there? Then how are your parents married? Have things changed?"

"They have," I said, glad the questions had been directed to Gwenna. "Or at least they are changing. When Casil agreed to support us against Fritjof, Ésparias agreed to live by their laws, ending the Partition agreement. Some men and women marry now, but it is far from all. Some women's villages were rebuilt, and still keep to the old tradition of Festival. But children, boys or girls, now stay with their parents until twelve, and choose an apprenticeship then."

"Even you, Gwenna?" Jordis asked.

"Yes. I am an officer cadet at the White Fort. I am not quite decided on my future; either the army, like my mother, or diplomacy, like my father. I think it will be the latter, but I have two more years in which to consider. Officers and diplomats learn together until we are sixteen."

"I always thought of Cillian as a teacher," Jordis said. "I knew he was also a *toscaire,* but was that not mostly the gathering of opinions for the *Teannasach*?"

"That is what he would have had us believe," I said. "You remember he would never talk about what he did as a *toscaire*?"

"He would rarely talk about anything," Jordis said, "unless it was our course of study. What was he doing, then?"

A direct question. "Negotiating, mostly about the tribute agreement between Varsland and Linrathe regarding Sorham, and other things related to that. He spent more time in Varsland than any of us knew, even Perras, I think."

"But he went to Casil, with my mother, and Sorley, and a general who is dead now," Gwenna said, "and he made the treaty with them that saved Ésparias and Linrathe. Then after the war, when the Eastern Empire wanted Ésparias to follow all their laws and their rules on how we should live, he made them change their minds. On some of it, anyhow." She was trying to speak neutrally, I could see, but her pride in her father shone through. "Even though he wasn't well enough, or so my mother says."

Jordis looked at me quizzically. "He was badly wounded, at the battle of the Taiva," I told her. If she were to go to the *Ti'ach*, she had better know. "Very badly. In his leg and back. His ability to walk is limited, and he is often in pain."

"I see," she said.

I laughed a little at her confusion. "Tonight," I promised, "I'll play the *danta* that tells all our adventures, and you will be a little less bewildered."

After the evening meal, we again gathered in the hall. "This is a long song," I told everyone, my fingers plucking notes softly. "I'll sing a few verses, then just the tune for a minute or two, to allow Gwenna to tell the story to Elsë. Now, listen." I spoke the formal, opening words. "This is a story of great deeds and great valour, and it began..."

The song took some time. I chose the simplest of several endings for the *danta*, the one which told only of victory and peace, Gwenna's birth representing hope and renewal. The last notes fell into silence before I spoke again. "My tale is told."

"Our thanks, Lord Sorley," Helvi said, formally.

"You were all so brave," Jordis said, her voice barely above a whisper.

"Bravery comes in many forms." Gwenna said, unexpectedly. "My mother told me that once. She said Casyn said it to her, when she was only a few years older than I am now. You have been brave, too, lady Jordis."

"You are kind," Jordis murmured.

"It is time to retire," Helvi said. "Sorley, are you leaving in the morning?"

"Unless there is heavy rain," I said. "But there's little urgency, except to leave in time to reach a *torp* for the night. Mid-morning will be soon enough."

"Then I'll see you at breakfast." We said our goodnights, Gwenna leaving with the women. Druise took my *ladhar* along with his own instrument, leaving me with Amlodd.

"My thanks for allowing us to play," I said, as I must. He nodded.

"Will I see you at Faolyn and Siusàn's wedding? I understand I am to preside."

"Not if Cillian attends," I said. "We can't all leave the *Ti'ach*. But if he doesn't, then likely Lena and I will." If he did, I thought, he would be in immense pain upon reaching Wall's End. Apulo would have to go too, Apulo and Druise. But that could be decided at the end of the summer. "Good night, Amlodd."

He smiled. "I am glad to have finally met your Casilani. A fine musician. Good night, Sorley."

Torches flickered along the corridor to my room. I closed the door quietly, sliding the bolt home. A flask of wine sat on the table. I picked it up, and the two cups, before opening the door that led into Druise's room. He was sitting on the edge of the bed, playing very quietly.

"Wine?" I asked.

"I hoped you had been given some," he replied. "I had not. Ale only." He laid the *cithar* aside.

"I should have asked for wine for you," I said, pouring a cup.

"No. Wine is not appropriate for a bodyguard, even if I am an officer." I knew it didn't bother him. He took an appreciative sip.

"I'm sorry I argued with you this morning," I said, sitting beside him.

"The woman and her daughter are a risk. But there is another concern, yes? The Marai that are at the *Ti'ach* — would they take her husband's side?"

I hadn't even thought of them, in my wish to send Jordis somewhere she would feel safe. But a wife fleeing a husband could not become an incident involving two — or three — countries, disrupting a dozen years and more of patient, secret negotiation.

"No," I admitted, "I'm not. Better they stay here, then."

Druise drank. "It is for Lena to decide. The letters were sent?"

"Yes. I saw the steward seal them, and the messenger he gave them to rode out in the early afternoon."

"Good," he said. He leant over to kiss me, the stubble of his beard rough against my own. He tasted of wine. I broke off the kiss to drain my own cup. My lips moved to his neck, knowing after fifteen years together exactly what excited him. He pushed me down onto the bed, laughing deep in his throat. "Would your friend be shocked?" he asked.

"I don't know," I said. "I don't care. Stop talking, Druise."

Chapter 33

14 YEARS EARLIER

"IF YOU'RE LEAVING TOMORROW, will you ride with me today?" Lena asked, on a sunny, still morning. The first purple of the heather had begun to colour the hills, and the air was crisp. A year ago, we had been preparing for war.

"I should attempt to ride again soon," Cillian said, from where he sat holding Gwenna. We'd breakfasted together, as we did now often: still a wonder to me, after the night I had gone to Cillian, angrier than I had ever let myself be. I had expected that anger to finish our friendship. Instead, we were closer, the three of us, than we had been since Casil.

"Ride?" Lena asked. "Is that wise?"

"Gnaius approves, with certain restrictions," Cillian said, holding Gwenna upright on his lap. "A placid horse, a mounting block, and no more than a few minutes at a slow walk to begin. And, yes, *käresta*, I will accept a little cannabium, at least at first. But I may need to ride in the future, and better my leg and back are prepared."

"I suppose," she said doubtfully.

"Talyn has offered to supervise," he said. "Will you trust me to her? No, *mo nihéan gràhadh*, do not pull my hair." He untangled Gwenna's tiny fingers gently, eliciting a wail of frustration.

"I'll take her," Tyrvi said, coming out from the nursery. "May I go to Berge today with the babies, Lena?"

"Of course. But I am off duty all day, so perhaps you could bring Gwenna back late in the morning?"

"Or we could ride over and bring her back, so Tyrvi and Darel can stay there," I suggested.

"We'll do that," Lena decided. She bent to kiss Cillian. "What are you discussing today?"

"Altars."

"Altars? To what? Or should I say to whom?"

"Casil's gods. They must be honoured, Livius says. At the forts, and in Casilla, and eventually throughout Ésparias. But the forts first."

"Shall I devote myself to their huntress goddess again?" Lena said with a grin. "I should, I suppose. I did pray to her, before I loosed the arrow that killed Fritjof."

"I will ask for a shrine to her, then," Cillian said, his voice light. He would not ask for the darkest god to be acknowledged, I knew. He had found other ways to make his offering of thanks or supplication. Not thoughts for daylight and sunshine, I told myself, and turned to Lena.

"I'll meet you at the stables. Your mare?"

"Yes."

"Sorley," Cillian said softly. I glanced at the nursery door: closed. I crossed the room to drop a kiss on his forehead. He smiled up at me. "Enjoy the day. You will have little relaxation at Dun Ceànnar, I imagine."

We rode quite a way along the Wall, and then, because there was nothing now to stop us, crossed over into Linrathe at a guardpost and spent an hour or two among its hills and moorland, for no other reason than we could. I taught Lena some of the names of plants and birds in my language, and we didn't talk of treaties or negotiations or politics, or even Cillian. Only when we reluctantly turned for home did Lena bring the conversation back to the immediate.

"Druise," she said. "He'll be home soon."

"I know."

"And?"

"He will not have slept alone," I said bluntly. "He was clear about that, before he left."

"So? Neither did I, before I left Tirvan and on the road south, and yet I was seeking Maya. Nor have you. But grace notes do not make a melody, do they? And you and he do make good music together."

I laughed. "We do," I admitted. "I don't know, Lena. I suppose I won't know, until he is here and we have talked."

We saluted the guard who opened the gate for us and rode back into Ésparias. The sun was tipping toward afternoon when we reached Berge, and my stomach was growling. Outside Kyreth's house we dismounted. I held the horses while Lena went in to fetch Gwenna.

She was out again in a moment, Kyreth with her. "Tyrvi's not here," she said. "Nor has she been."

"But we saw her walking with the babies as we left the fort," I said. "Where was she going, then?"

"Maybe just along the beach?" Lena said. "Perhaps Gwenna was fussing; she is teething. So Tyrvi may have changed her mind."

But she wasn't in their rooms, either, and Apulo hadn't seen her. Apprehension tightened my gut. "Lena, a few weeks ago, I met Tyrvi coming back from Berge. I carried Gwenna home, do you remember?"

"Yes." She was pacing, tension in every fibre of her being.

"I called Gwenna 'princess', teasingly, and Tyrvi grew angry. She said it wasn't right; that in the women's villages, girl children belonged to their mothers."

"And?"

"And once before she told me the babies were needed, because so many people had died. Would she — could she have taken her? Away from Berge, I mean?"

Lena swore, and then she began to run. I followed, sprinting to the stables with her. "A horse," she shouted as she grew close. I repeated her call. "No," she said. "I know where she's gone. Stay here. Don't let Apulo tell Cillian." She was up on the horse almost before the cadet had the girth tightened, kicking it into a gallop.

"Saddle a horse for me," I told the girl. "I'll be back for it, soon."

I jogged back to the fort. I found Apulo, told him what Lena had said. "Say nothing," I repeated. "But find Gnaius, and tell him that the baby is missing, and we think Tyrvi has taken her. Tell him he might be needed." I didn't know what Apulo had been told about the weeks when Cillian could not function without poppy, and the cravings that still challenged him, sometimes.

"I understand," Apulo said. I had to trust he did. I collected the horse the stable cadet had waiting for me, and rode for Berge.

A group of women stood on the jetty. I joined them. "Lena?" I asked.

Kyreth pointed at a boat already well out from the shore. "One of the little boats is missing. We think Tyrvi took it."

"But where is she going?"

"Tirvan, Lena thinks."

"Gods." Lena had no experience with the currents and shoals of the coast this far north. "Who went with her?"

"She wouldn't let anyone. Said the boat would be faster if she went alone," someone said.

I waited with the women as the sun moved inexorably toward the western horizon. In mid-afternoon I noticed eyes looking repeatedly to the sky north of us, and I turned to see clouds, heavy and grey, building over Linrathe. The wind had picked up, northerly and off the land; a boat returning from the south would have to tack against it in a rough sea.

After another half an hour, I took Kyreth aside. "I must go back," I said. "I cannot leave Cillian to find empty rooms."

CHAPTER 34

HE WASN'T ALONE. GNAIUS was with him, and Apulo. The relief I felt at that came with a twinge of self-disgust. Cillian stood at the window of their sitting room, the shutters opened to the sky and wind. He turned when I came in. He'd have heard my triple rap, known it was me.

He didn't speak. "They think Tyrvi took a boat to sail south. Maybe trying to get to Tirvan. Lena went after them." I said, forcing the words through a dry mouth.

Cillian turned back to the window. "I have sailed with Lena," he said, "in weather not so different. She is more than competent."

But they had been sailing with the wind, the storm behind them. I had navigated the waters off Gundarstorp since I was twelve, and I had known experienced fishermen lose their lives fighting to bring a boat home in the teeth of a storm. "No doubt you are right," I said. I couldn't think about Tyrvi, inexpert and with two babies in the boat with her. I could only hope Lena had reached them before the weather worsened.

"Why has Tyrvi done this?' Cillian asked. He was too calm. Detached, almost, as he had been in Casil. I told him what I thought, what I had told Lena. He nodded.

"So she is taking her to Lena's sister, you believe? To Tirvan and her people?"

"That is what Lena concluded, yes," I said.

"Did I not say almost everything Casil asks conflicts with this land's traditions?" he said. Apprehension prickled along my spine. If he said more in front of Gnaius…

"Forget that," I said, sharply. "We can concern ourselves with it later."

He looked at me then. "Do not worry, *mo duíne gràhadh*," he said. "This is not a price the god will ask of me." He sounded completely certain. What drug had Gnaius given him? I turned to the physician, frowning the question. He beckoned me over.

"Cannabium," he murmured in my ear, "and certain other herbs, in wine. I will give him more, in another hour, if there is no news. Or if it is not good."

I couldn't settle, unable to think of anything but the rough seas and a little fishing boat battling against them. I paced for a while, and then I sat, wrapping my arms around myself. Cillian remained at the window. Rain drummed on the roof and flagstones, the wind blowing it away from the open shutters.

Apulo lit lamps around the room, and then made his noiseless way over to me to place his hands on my shoulders. I looked up, surprise dimly registering. He began to gently massage me. Behind him, I heard Gnaius at the sideboard, busy with wine and drugs. I wondered if he would give me a little, if I asked, to stop me thinking of drenching waves and the tiny body they could so easily sweep away. Bodies: Darel was out there too.

"Thank you," I murmured to Apulo, before I rose abruptly to stand beside Cillian. This time I could hear the unsteadiness in his breathing. The effects of the drugs were fading. I put an arm around him, feeling tautness and a faint trembling.

"By my side, as Lena asked," he said.

"She isn't dead," I said. "They aren't." I had to believe it. *She is as necessary to me as breathing*, he had told me once, in a place and time I couldn't think about just now. I slipped both arms around him, resting my cheek against his back, feeling his heartbeat, light and rapid, under my hands.

The wail of a baby made us both turn. Apulo ran to the door, pulling it open. Lena stumbled in, dripping rain, Gwenna in her arms and another woman behind her. An incoherent sound from Cillian, and he moved towards her, steadying himself on the furniture. He wrapped his arms around them, murmuring words I couldn't hear.

Tension drained from my shoulders and neck. I grinned at Gnaius and Apulo like a fool, and Gnaius smiled back and emptied the wine cup he held into a bowl. Refilling it, he handed it to me. I drank half of it in one swallow. I exhaled, deeply, and at that sigh Cillian looked my way. He held out one arm. "Come here, Sorley," he said softly.

"No," I said. Lena turned her head.

"Yes," she said, and so I did.

Gnaius allowed us our reunion and reassurance for a few minutes before asserting himself as the physician. He made Lena sit while he examined the baby in the nursery, ordering Apulo to make tea for the sodden women. When Lena raised a hand to take the mug Apulo offered, both he and I gasped.

"Your hands," I said.

"What?" She looked at them, bleached and torn, flayed, I realized immediately, by the wet, salt rigging she'd handled for so many hours on the sea. Once her hands would have been callused, inured to the work, but that had been years ago. "Oh," she said.

The other woman clucked her tongue. "I did not see, in the dark."

Apulo had disappeared into the nursery. He came back with a cloth, wrapping it around the mug. "Not hurt so much," he said. Lena took the mug, holding it gingerly before taking a sip.

"Thank you." She seemed to remember the other woman was there, suddenly. "Marcail, you are soaked. Sorley, ask Apulo to find her a towel, and show her where my clothes are, in the bedroom?"

"You should change too," I said. Cillian and I were wet too, but we hadn't spent hours out in the storm.

"I will. In a minute. Why is Gnaius taking so long with Gwenna?" Cillian had gone with his daughter. I heard the note of panic in her voice.

"I'll see," I said, but I didn't need to. The two men returned, Gwenna in Cillian's arms, grizzling a little. Gnaius walked beside him, a hand on Cillian's elbow.

"She is fine," he announced. "But hungry, I believe."

"It's why Marcail came," Lena said. "She left her own baby with the women in Berge. But let me hold her first?" She reached out for Gwenna.

"Your hands?" I said. "Gnaius, look at them."

An hour later all was calm, Lena in dry clothes, her hands salved and bound, and Gwenna fed and sleeping on her mother's lap. I'd tried to leave, to sharp objections from both Lena and Cillian. Apulo had brought us food and built up the fire. Marcail had gone to the nursery and the bed there.

"You miss the baths, and massage," Apulo said to Cillian, quietly.

"Then twice tomorrow, if I must," Cillian replied.

"You can go," Lena said. "I'm all right."

"No," he said. "Not tonight." He sat close to her, stroking her hair every so often. "I should have seen this could happen."

"You cannot see all outcomes," Lena said. "I've told you that before. Not even you."

"I should have said something," I admitted. "When Tyrvi made those comments to me."

"Why would you?" Lena asked. "The thoughts of a young girl? I don't think I'd have taken them seriously either, even if she'd said the same to me. No, the fault lies with me. Talyn and I were speaking last week of the new law, that within a marriage both boy and girl children belong to the father. Tyrvi was in the nursery, and I thought the door closed, but it must not have been."

"An extreme reaction, but Tyrvi will not be the only woman to object," Cillian said.

"How is Tyrvi? And Darel?" I hadn't thought to ask until now.

"I left them with Kyreth," Lena said. "Darel was well wrapped; Tyrvi took great care of both babies, but I'm worried for her. She was near exhaustion when I reached them, soaked through and terrified."

"She's lucky to be alive," I said, without thinking.

"So is Gwenna," Lena said sharply. She leaned forward. "I want you both to hear me. I know there will be complications with your work, Cillian, and with Druise, but nonetheless: I want us in Linrathe. I want Gwenna in Linrathe, away from people who would risk her life to claim her for one faction or another. I'll resign from the army: it doesn't matter that much to me. There will be work I can do at the *Ti'ach*, of some sort."

"Not a conversation for tonight, *käresta*," Cillian said. "You too are exhausted."

"Perhaps," she said. "Yes. But do not brush this off, Cillian. I mean it."

"I am not," he said. "We will talk tomorrow."

She gave him a level, unsmiling look. "Yes," she said, "we will. And tell Livius I want that statue of the huntress. Three times I have prayed to her, once to guide the bowshot that killed Fritjof, and twice now for Gwenna's life. She needs to be honoured."

Chapter 35

RELUCTANTLY, I LEFT THE next day for Dun Ceànnar, for more talks with Liam. The Governor had accepted timber as tribute, and a delivery schedule needed developing.

The planning took time: Liam had little stamina, and his weakness frustrated him, but he insisted no decisions could be made without him. All of us —

even the *Teannasach* — endured his withering remarks.

"Liam does not look well at all," I commented to Daoíre the first afternoon, while the old man rested.

"He isn't," Daoíre said. "But he won't admit it, and for all we guide his thoughts now, he'll know if we decide something he didn't approve." He drank some of his ale. "It's teaching Ruar patience and subtlety, though, so there's value to his obstinacy, in a way."

Our short meetings left me with time on my hands, and I took advantage of it. Bhradaín had no objection at all to working with me to improve aspects of both my playing and singing. "Gladly," he'd said, when I'd asked. "We'll concentrate on your voice; it's where you're least skilled."

We were practicing in the great hall a few days later, discussing how different inflections changed how a listener interpreted the words of a *danta*, when Liam appeared unexpectedly. "You are *toscaire*, not *scáeli*," he growled at me. "Leave this and come with me."

I didn't hide my displeasure; Liam's eyesight wasn't good enough for him to see the look on my face in the dimly-lit hall. Bhradaín touched my arm in commiseration. "Lessons in influencing an audience's responses are appropriate for both *scáeli* and *toscaire*," he said, his voice level.

"Aye, maybe," Liam said. "But my *toscaire's* time is mine now."

My toscaire? I saw Bhradaín's eyes narrow slightly, but he said nothing. I followed Liam, not into our usual meeting room with its large table, but into a smaller one, where even on this summer's day a small fire burned.

"What have you to tell me about the trading port?" he snapped, as soon as the door was closed.

"Nothing," I said. "The Governor wishes to discuss that directly with the *Teannasach* and his advisors. I assume it will be Daoíre who accompanies Ruar to Wall's End later this summer?"

"I do not want Ruar in the south," he said, his face purpling with anger. "He should never have been sent as hostage. I do not know what Donnalch was thinking."

"He cannot always have a go-between," I said. "Casil will expect his direct involvement. Or," I added, "will they not wonder why? You do not want the Governor thinking Linrathe's leader incapable, do you?"

His face grew even darker. "You will keep him away from Cillian na Perras, do you hear me? I want none of his influence on the boy."

"Cillian, Prince of Ésparias," I said coldly, "is a senior diplomat for his country. I have no say in who meets with the *Teannasach* on a political visit. I am only Linrathe's *toscaire*. Give those instructions to Daoíre, if you must."

He'd heard my emphasis on 'Linrathe'. "Get out my sight, *toscaire*," he spat. I'd never been so happy to obey him.

Twelve days later, I rode into Wall's End just after midday. I went in search of Cillian or Lena. Neither was available, but Apulo, tidying their rooms, greeted me with genuine pleasure, I thought. They were in talks with the Governor, he told me, but yes, Gwenna was well, and there was a new nursemaid. Relieved, I left a message that I was back, and went to the carpenter's shop to oil my *ladhar* one more time.

Late in the afternoon I tried their rooms, finding Lena feeding Gwenna something that looked like mashed peas. Cillian was having his treatments, she told me. "Both of you with the Governor?" I said. "I thought the question of land ownership had been settled."

"It has," Lena said. "We are discussing the age of marriage now. Did you know girls marry in Casil at fourteen?"

"Fourteen?" I said. "Actually marry, not a betrothal?"

"Marry," she confirmed. "And Casil's laws are ours now. Or are supposed to be: it is what Talyn and I are arguing against."

I poured tea from the pot on the table. "Are you getting anywhere?"

"Perhaps. We are arguing that Ésparias needs its women to be skilled at their trades, so the apprenticeship structure makes seventeen the more reasonable choice. He is listening, at least, but I am not sure he is convinced." She held the spoon to Gwenna's lips. "No? Well, you've eaten enough." She wiped the baby's face and put her down on the floor.

"You're weaning her?" I asked.

"Yes. I know it's early, but it will be easier for everyone." The door opened. I stood to greet Cillian.

He smiled down at me after our kiss of greeting. "I must spend the evening in the senior commons," he said. "I wish now I did not have to, but I have made the arrangements. How is Ruar?"

Lena picked up Gwenna. "She'll need changing. You can have her in a minute." She went through to the nursery. I poured tea for Cillian.

"Ruar is well," I said, handing him the cup. "Maturing rapidly. Liam tires easily now, and can work for no more than an hour at a time. So I spent as much time, or more, with Ruar talking of our travels as I did in the actual tribute discussions. But it got done in the end."

We talked about Dun Ceànnar until Lena returned to put Gwenna down in Cillian's lap. She babbled happily, and he kissed her hair.

"Dinner here tomorrow night?" Lena asked. "Cillian's missed you. Eat, and then go and play *xache*."

"With pleasure," I said.

We'd left the game unfinished, moving eventually to the chairs by the hearth where Cillian could rest his aching leg on a footstool. I'd been adding fuel to the fire when he'd said my name, softly. I'd looked up, smiling, but his face had not held the expression I'd expected.

"What is Liam doing, behind Ruar's back?" he asked.

"There are…certain negotiations," I stammered. "You know I can't tell you."

"Then I will tell you. You do not need to comment. Liam is offering Casil timber, the tribute once paid to Varsland now given to Casil, as we discussed. And he is also suggesting a trading fort with a deep harbour, where perhaps ships may be built, and the Marai ships can come to trade."

I tried to keep my face impassive, but I doubt I succeeded. I picked up my wine glass to take a sip, hoping it would disguise my thoughts. Cillian barely glanced at me, though. "It all seems reasonable," he said, "especially since Liam hopes for support from Casil to retake Sorham. But beware of those you ask into your house, for they may make it their own. A deep harbour on Linrathe's coast may be protection, and a trading base. It may also be a foothold from which to bring Linrathe, and perhaps even Varsland, under Casil's complete rule. Is the mouth of the Tabha the suggested location for the harbour?"

"Cillian," I said helplessly, sinking back down into my chair. His interpretation made chilling sense.

"Do not forget your *danta*," he went on, "and how far up the Tabha Halvar brought his ships."

"How did you know?"

"Now it is I who cannot say. To protect the man who told me, you understand."

"What do I do?"

"Talk to Ruar, privately. Just the concern, this alternate explanation of Casil's interest. Plant the seed of suspicion. That is all you can do."

I put my wine down on the low table. "Is this what you would do, were you *toscaire* for Linrathe, and not me?"

"It is where I would start. Be careful, though, Sorley; judge first the relationship between Ruar and Liam. If he has influenced the boy too greatly, say nothing."

"And let Casil take Linrathe?"

"No. If Ruar is too much under Liam's control, look to see who in the family is unhappy, excluded, and who his followers are." He paused. "Then I would prefer it if you did not act, before consulting me. But you must do what your conscience tells you."

"Should you be saying this to me?"

"It is advice only, from an experienced diplomat to one new in his role, nothing more."

"I doubt Eudekia would see it that way," I said. "She'd say you were speaking treason. Again."

"If I am, it will not be the first time I have forsworn an oath," he said, "and this is for love of my country, my true country, whether I can ever go home again or not."

My true country. The scream of gulls over the harbour; the sheep on the hills, the curlew crying. Waves, always beating, like a heart. I had signed it away, on Cillian's advice. Cillian's, and Turlo's. Liam had suggested Casil might help regain it.

Ésparias had asked for the same help, and the price was to be reshaped in Casil's image. I took things at face value too easily, not considering other motives.

Words forced themselves to the forefront of my mind. *My true country. Not the first time I have forsworn an oath.*

"Cillian," I said, "did you…is Linrathe's treaty favourable, because Ésparias's is not?"

He didn't answer immediately. When he did, his voice was low. "I believe not. I hope not, Sorley. But I cannot be sure."

But you were sure of the need to surrender Sorham. I ignored the thought, intrusive and unwelcome. "Why shouldn't you go home to Linrathe?" I asked instead. "Lena is insistent that you must, and it would remove Gwenna further from Casil's influences."

"Can the heir be taken to a foreign land?"

"Will Gwenna ever be *Principe*? Faolyn isn't that much older than she is."

"Perhaps not," he agreed. "But nor will she have a life of free choice, I am afraid. No more than I do now, if ever I had. We are bound, she and I, by what fate has brought to us. Or what an Empress will allow," he added wryly. "So while Lena wants Gwenna to be brought up at the *Ti'ach*, and I too wish for the peace of a scholar's life, I wonder if it can be."

"You've said this to Lena?"

"I have. She is unhappy about it. Casyn insisted on a guard, so now there is always someone with Gwenna, as well as the new nursemaid, which lessens Lena's fear, and mine, but does not solve the problem fully."

Another intrusion into their life. "Perhaps," I said, "when Druise returns, he could be the primary guard?"

"I think he might insist," Cillian said. "Would he trust anyone else to protect his Kitten, do you think?"

"Not easily," I said, grinning.

"He is a good man, Sorley."

"I know." I didn't want to talk about Druisius. "If we are staying," I said, "I'll need to think what a *scáeli* can do in Ésparias, then. Perhaps as the *Princip's* senior advisor, you can convince him that music is a necessary part of the education of officers. I am sure Livius would agree."

"*Scáeli'en* are supposed to wander, gathering songs and teaching our history."

"Wander where? I doubt there's a song left to gather in Linrathe. Here I can learn songs from both Ésparias and the Eastern Empire. Music can create bonds between people: think of how both Linrathe and Varsland agree about the battle between Orri and Neilan, on the Tabha so long ago: *a shining river dulled by blood*. It's the only line the songs have in common."

A smile flickered and faded. "I ask too much of you."

"Never. Do you want to finish the game?"

"No. Just sit, *mo duíne gràhadh*, and watch the fire with me for a while. And then I will rouse Apulo, and go to the baths."

CHAPTER 36

"HOW ABSOLUTELY BEAUTIFUL," LENA said, running a finger along the curve of the *ladhar*. I'd finished it that morning, the carnelians set with the help of one of the fort's metalworkers.

"I'm pleased," I admitted. "And the sound is so rich; listen." I played a few notes, letting them hear its timbre and resonance.

"Dagney will be proud of you," Cillian said. A rap at the door stopped anything else he had to say. Lena went to open it. A cadet stood there.

"A letter for the Lord Sorley," she said. "I think it's important. The messenger is exhausted, and his horse worse, so I ran with it here."

The seal on the letter was Ruar's. I read, quickly. Significant news, and by rights the *Princip* and the Governor should know first. But Cillian would be next to be told in any case. My face, I knew, reflected the gravity of the contents.

"It is from Ruar," I said, looking up. "Liam is dead. Ruar has declared himself fully *Teannasach*, free of a regent, with the agreement of his advisors. His advisors support — " I stopped. Cillian was not listening. He stared beyond me, at something not in this room at all, I thought.

"Cillian?" Lena said.

He blinked, returning to us. His fingers flexed. "May there be no peace for him," he said, his voice cold, laced with hatred. He turned, going to the window, leaning heavily on his cane.

Lena moved first. She put a hand on his back. "Tell us."

"I cannot."

"You can. Do not keep this to yourself, *kärestan*."

"I must."

"No," she said. "Never again, remember? Both of us told you that."

He laughed, a dry, bitter sound. "I told you in our first days of exile that you did not know me. What I had been, or done. But in exile, I thought, what did it matter?"

"Did what matter?" Lena asked.

She was not Linrathan; she had not sworn the oath that both Cillian and I had. *Be careful,* he had told me, months before. *The oath demands that no man has sway over you. Some — including Liam — may try.* So many things began to make a terrible sense.

"Your *toscaire's* oath?" I said, my voice tight. "You broke your oath, and Liam used that against you?"

"I broke my oath to become Liam's man, for several years," Cillian said, with no emotion at all.

"No," I said. "You couldn't have."

"I did." He turned to face me. Lena stood completely still, watching. "*Why?*"

"Do not ask me that," he said.

"Oh, *kärestan,*" Lena said. Her arms went around him, but his eyes never left mine. "Liam was at Gundarstorp that night? What did he threaten?"

"Liam was not there. One of Liam's traders was, there to make deals for fish and fleece."

"What has he to do with this?" How could Gundarstorp and a night of music and dance so many years ago matter?

"He was looking for a way to entrap me, on Liam's instruction. He would have watched, seen which *Härra* approached me, waited outside her door that night." He shook his head slightly. "But it would not have worked, would it? That game is not played unless the rules are understood. Instead, I did something even better, in his eyes. I went to speak to you."

One hand had touched mine, on the *ladhar*; the other had rested, lightly, briefly, on my knee. If that had been seen… "He threatened to tell the world you were *channàdarra*?" I said. "No. I don't believe it. Too many women would have said otherwise. No one ever said that of you. You had nothing to fear."

"Sorley," Lena said. "You are right. Cillian did not. But you did."

"I did?" There was a hollow in my stomach, echoing and cold. "No. You barely knew me."

"What would your lot have been?" Cillian asked. "Disinheritance and shame. You were newly a man; I was ten years adult. The fault was mine."

"You could have just denied it."

"The tale would have been told, and the damage still done."

"No," I said again. "You were so beautiful. So full of laughter, delighted with hawking and riding and dancing. Delighted by life. And then you weren't; you were cynical and — and cold, and detached. And it is my fault? I am responsible?"

"You are not, *Somhairle*. Not at all." An unevenness now, in his voice.

"Breathe," Lena murmured. "Breathe, Cillian."

I swallowed, wiped my eyes, blinked. Saw the pallor of his skin, the damp hair. The ice had spread to my limbs. He had betrayed Linrathe. I didn't move. Lena growled my name.

I stared at them, at the trembling man and the fierce, strong woman who held him. "I'm not — I can't — " I stammered. I turned toward the door, took two steps, three.

My *ladhar* leaned against the wall where I had put it down to open the letter. I picked it up, turned to face them again. He had betrayed Linrathe. For me. "I must ride north tomorrow," I said. "For my examination."

"You must," Cillian said.

"But you will come back as soon as you can," Lena said.

"I — I should go to Dun Ceànnar."

"Would you abandon him now?" No compassion now, only sharp anger. "Remember what I told you: I will never forgive you, if you do."

"Lena." Cillian's voice was so tired. "Let Sorley go." His eyes met mine. "Did I not say there would be a reckoning? If it is truth you seek, remember the *xache* game. Go safely, *mo duíne gràhadh*. Come home to us if you can."

Chapter 37

15 Years After the Battle of the Taiva

"YOU RAN AWAY?" DISBELIEF coloured Gwenna's voice. I hadn't seen her at breakfast — with no one to insist she eat, I guessed she had chosen to forego the meal — but she had found me not long after.

"Why will my father not talk about what he did as a *toscaire*?" she had demanded. "When Jordis said that, yesterday, I realized it's true. He never answers my questions about it, either, except with the briefest explanations."

Perhaps, I had thought, it was best for this to be told here, where she had some chance of solitude. We didn't need to leave today. She could avoid me if she wanted to, for a day or two.

I found a small room where we could talk privately. "Sit down," I said gently. "Gwenna, I can't tell you why your father won't speak of his time as a *toscaire* without finally telling you why he broke his oath. Are you ready to hear it?"

"Yes."

"Do you want me to find Druise, first, and ask him to join us?"

"No."

The story had taken some time to tell, and I had watched the emotions on her face as I spoke. Anger, just now. Tears glinted in her eyes. "How could you? You said you loved him."

"I was angry and frightened, Gwenna. You do understand the enormity of what he had done?"

"No," she said, but I thought the answer at least partly defiance. "I don't."

Nor had I, that night, not fully. But I had known, viscerally, that if Cillian had been Liam's man, Liam's voice, persuading the nobility of Linrathe and Sorham to the point of view of a man not the *Teannasach* — although that would have been a betrayal too — then he had violated not just my trust, but a covenant promised to every man and woman north of the Wall, noble or *torpari*. Isa's trust and that of Perras, equally.

Could I explain? Did Gwenna really not understand? She was only fourteen, and not truly Linrathan, regardless of where she had been raised. But I was being unfair. There was another interpretation. Ruar had been fourteen too, when he had learned the truth, and his response had been measured, practical, not my instinctual revulsion. Like Gwenna, he had been brought up to be rational, to think rather than react.

I took a deep breath. "The *Teannasach* is leader of his people, but not their overlord, although all but *toscairen* swear fealty to him. He is advised by the council. You know all this. But a *toscaire* to the people of Linrathe, or rather, *for* the people of Linrathe, is separate even from that council. His role is to listen to everyone, whether they live in a hall or a cottage. To ensure their voices, their concerns, are heard by the *Teannasach*. He is sworn to them, to the people and the land. Not to one man and that man's priorities."

Distance crept into her face. Good. She was thinking, analyzing. "Then he chose you," she said. "Over all the people. You were more important than his oath."

"Not me, not really," I said. I still, after all these years, hadn't fully accepted that. "Someone he had harmed, not young Sorley of Gundarstorp." In my mind I heard Druise's snort of derision.

"You would have been disowned?"

"Almost certainly. Gwenna, try not to judge him too quickly. That is what I did, to my shame. A shame I still feel."

"So he did it to prevent harm. Not for the Marai, or for money, but to keep you safe." I tried not to flinch at that, the exact words of her father's unspoken vow to me.

"Yes."

She stared down at her hands. "Will you tell me one more thing?"

"If it is mine to tell."

"Did he — did Liam's trader see what he thought he saw?" She wouldn't look at me.

"On my part, certainly. You know how hard it is for me to disguise what I am feeling." Would she accept that?

"And on *Athàir's*?" She did look up then, meeting my eyes in challenge.

"Yes," I said.

The look that crossed her face was not one I understood — satisfaction? triumph? — followed quickly by doubt. "But you said he did not encourage you."

"Nor did he," I said. "Gwenna, music and dancing and night — they can be a potent mix, and sometimes lead us to do things we would not in the light of day. Your father paid a terrible price for one such moment."

"But you did too," she said, "didn't you? Didn't it make you feel responsible?"

"In a way, yes," I said. She got up from her chair to give me a hug.

"Thank you," she said. "For telling me. Could I go out? Maybe for a ride?"

"Find Druise. He won't be far away."

She hesitated. "Do I have to?"

"You can't go out unaccompanied. Ask the door guard for an escort," I told her, understanding. She nodded.

When she'd gone, I dropped into the chair. I needed some time alone too. *Didn't it make you feel responsible*? The acknowledgement so hard won, the third thing that bound me to Cillian, and him to me. What I could not forget, but only forgive, for love.

Chapter 38

I REACHED THE *Ti'ach* in late morning. I was expected, of course, Anndra himself waiting in the courtyard to take my horse. "The others are all here," he confided in me as he led my gelding away. I inhaled, deeply. My mind still roiled, but I had to calm myself. Whatever lay ahead of me, I had worked towards this day all my life.

The hall was empty. Isa hurried out from the kitchen to greet me. "They are all in the Lady Dagney's rooms," she said in a low voice. "I am to give you a bitty food, and time to tune your *ladhar*, and then you are to go to them."

I thanked her, and pulled open the door to the annex. Shouldering my bags, I walked down the hall, my eyes going to Cillian's room as I passed. Later. In my bedchamber, I washed my face and hands. Isa brought me tea and oatcakes. I ate a little, and drank the tea, then I picked up my instruments and went to knock on Dagney's door.

My throat was too dry. I put both my instruments down, carefully, and faced the three people in front of me. Dagney and Bhradaín, and the unforeseen third. Amlodd. His dark hair held a few traces of silver now. He smiled, a neutral welcome.

"Sorley," Dagney said. "Welcome."

"I must ask," Bhradaín said, "before we begin the examination. Did the *Teannasach's* messenger find you? He came here first, knowing I was here, and of course the lady Dagney had to be told of Liam's death, but he thought you might already be here too."

"He did," I said. "Sad news."

"But not unexpected," Bhradaín replied. "Now, to your testing. You will play the set songs, of course, then three of your own composing: one *danta*, and two others. Then a brief pause, for tea to soothe your throat, then a dozen short songs you have collected. You will tell us a little about each, and at least half must have words to be sung. Do you have any questions?"

I would play and sing for over two hours. All confusion fell away, replaced by still composure. "One question, but it can wait," I said. I settled onto the stool to check the tuning on the *ladhar*. Dagney nodded, and I began.

The three *scáeli'en* were listening for precision, not improvisation. But even with the careful attention I gave to expression and phrasing, the traditional *danta* they had chosen for me to play were easy; I had known them for so long. At the end of the third, the dragon *danta*, selected, I knew, because it was deceptively simple, I stopped for a cup of water.

"One short song I would like to play is my music, but not my words," I said. "Is that acceptable?"

"The other two are yours?" Dagney said. They would be listening now not just for skill on the instrument, not just my ability to use my voice to stir feeling, but also to how good a poet I was. I had agonized over including this song, for that reason. I vacillated over another, now, but it was too late to substitute something different.

"They are."

"Then, yes." I nodded my thanks, tightened a couple of strings, and began to sing.

War in winter sends sorrow soaring…

Perhaps I could not equal Cillian's skill as a poet, but the tune had been my first offering to him, and even now I could not hide the love with which I had written it. When I finished, the last notes played, Amlodd spoke. "That is by Halmar," he said. "Who translated it?"

"Cillian na Perras," Dagney answered, before I could.

"He has done the original justice," Amlodd said. "Does the tune fit the Linrathan words too, Sorley?'

I sang the first few lines in our language, to show him, before I began the second song, the *danta* about our journeys to Casil and home again to war. It was my *danta*, so I could deviate from the traditional presentation, and I did. In the last verses, the ones speaking of cost and reckoning, I let the anguish inside me reveal itself. When I was done, blinking at my own hot tears, I began my last composition into the respectful silence of the room.

My true love's eyes are darkly gleaming
In candlelight and music's lure...

Only in the second verse did I begin to play the melody. I left the line 'My heart is his and his is mine' alone; I had no need to change it in this company. On Dagney's face, as I glanced up, I saw understanding, and a profound sadness, and my own bewilderment rose again, infusing the last verse.

You danced that night with grace unfettered,
A glance my way, a touch bestowed.
Your dark hair swept by supple fingers.
Uncharted ways might be explored,
Still dreams this wistful, loving singer.

I repeated the last line, my voice nearly breaking. I put the *ladhar* down. Tea was brought, a few words exchanged, but protocol said no comment could be made on my performance.

My throat eased with herbs and honey, and my composure regained, I switched to the *cithar*, explaining first its tuning and construction. I played a few Casilani songs, before going back to the *ladhar* for some Ésparian songs. I had planned the final song, but I did not now trust myself to sing *An Dithës Braithréan*. I chose instead a song in a language I did not truly know, although I understood what the words I sang meant.

I played the last notes. I had done well, and I knew it. But well enough? The council needed to confer. "My thanks," I said, the expected words, "for your indulgence, *scáeli'en*. You have heard my *ladhar*; now it is yours to examine." I handed the instrument to Dagney.

"Yew," she said, running a hand along its curves. "And the jewels, Sorley? I have never seen their like." She passed the instrument to Amlodd.

"Look at them," she said. "Tiny, exquisite musicians, carved into the stone."

"Carnelian, I am told," I said. "From Casil."

"They grace a fine instrument," Bhradaín said, when he took the *ladhar* from Amlodd. He plucked a string, listening to its resonance. "Very fine."

I murmured words of thanks. "Now, Sorley," Dagney began. She would dismiss me, while they conferred. Perhaps I would go to the kitchen and let Isa fuss over me. My neck and shoulders ached. I turned to go.

"Wait," Dagney said. She looked from Bhradaín to Amlodd. Both were smiling. I saw each nod.

"Was there ever any doubt?" Bhradaín asked, sounding amused. Dagney laughed.

"None at all," she said. "Come back, Sorley. We will officially welcome you to the *scáeli'en* once you are free of your *toscaire's* oath. You cannot do both, as you must know."

"I am honoured," I said, "that you have found me worthy."

"You should have been one of us several years ago," Dagney said. "May I say that while we have had, over the years, several tunes from south of the Wall sung as part of the recital, this is the first time we have heard Casilani songs. But what was that last?"

"A song of the Kurzemë people, who live in the foothills of the Durrains, on the eastern side," I told her. "A mid-winter's petition to the sun." She raised an eyebrow, but she said nothing further. My *danta* had told them of Lena and Cillian's winter there. Bhradaín asked a few questions about Casilani music. Then Amlodd, reaching for his instrument, asked me to teach him the tune that went with Halmar's poem.

"And I," Bhradaín said, and we were just four musicians together, sharing one of the passions of our lives.

Later, after food, Amlodd came to sit beside me, his wine cup in his hand. "The *Teannasach* must release you from your *toscaire's* duties as soon as he can," he said. "Dagney will write the letter, and Bhradaín will deliver it. He is expecting it, of course."

"Daoíre will take over," I said. "How are you, Amlodd?" I asked, in a different tone.

"Very well. What will you do now?"

"I have a message to take to the Sterre, and then I'll go to Dun Ceànnar, to resign as *toscaire* effective whenever Ruar allows," I told him. When might that be? I had promised my help in regaining Sorham.

"Back to Wall's End, then?" he said. "Dagney said you still had much to learn from a Casilani musician stationed there."

"Druisius is a fine musician," I said, not confirming or denying his supposition. "He taught me the *cithar*, and the Casilani songs I played today."

"An instrument I would like a better look at. Would you show me privately, later?"

"No," I said gently.

"I thought not," he said, without bitterness. "Your Casilani, or your dancer?"

A direct question. I wasn't truly a *scáeli* yet, but still... I hesitated. "There is no dancer," I said. Not a lie. Cillian would never dance again.

"A *toscaire's* answer," he said, "but a *scáeli's*, too. I won't press you."

"And you? " I asked.

"In Linrathe? Welcomes here and there. You may hear soon that I have accepted an extended stay at a certain *torp*. The *Harr* appreciates my skills, and wandering is growing tiresome."

Chapter 39

I SAT ALONE WITH Dagney in her room, drinking tea. It was very late, and she looked weary, slumping just a little in her chair. How old was she? Well into her sixties, I guessed.

"My dear, I must say this," she said, a smile on her lips. "Your playing has matured considerably. Druisius is very skilled with his cithar. Is this his influence?"

"I suppose it must be," I answered. Not a lie. *Play,* Druise had said, handing me my instrument, that terrible night Gnaius had said Cillian would die. *Better than shouting. Use your anger, amané. He may hear it, yet.* I had played, in love and anguish and to petition whatever gods there were, and when I could play no longer, I had sung. Something from that night had stayed with me, Cillian's life not the only gift granted, perhaps.

"Did Lena teach you the Kurzemë song?" Dagney asked. "I had not thought her particularly musical."

"She isn't. Cillian taught me."

"*Cillian*? But he would never sing, beyond what I insisted upon."

"He sings to Gwenna," I told her. "Music has become more important to him."

She straightened. "Three — no, four, if I include the Kurzemë song — involved him in some way. Sorley, I would not say this in front of the others, but I heard the pain as you sang. What is wrong, my dear? Has living with him become too difficult for you?"

I started to shake my head. Then I stopped. "Yes," I said. "But not for the reasons you might think. Dagney, when did Cillian become bitter? He wasn't always that way, was he?"

"No," she said thoughtfully. "I thought he had found a certain contentment in his work, in the years after he left the *Ti'ach*. Then one year he returned — he had been away a long time — and something had changed. He was detached, and more ascetic, I would say. Denying himself pleasures of almost any sort, except scholarship."

"How old was he?"

She thought back. "It was the year Ingold's daughter left us. I remember that, because I had thought, once," she smiled, "as mothers do, that she might be a match for him. But he never showed a flicker of interest. So he would have been twenty-six, almost twenty-seven."

"Was that when he began to hate the Empire?"

"Yes," she said. "He had not seemed to, before, but he began to speak more of his unknown father, and his irresponsibility. I thought perhaps his bastardry had been raised again, by Donnalch, or some *Harr*, but he would tell me nothing more. What has this to do with you and Cillian, Sorley?"

"It is not mine to tell," I said, the formal words. She gave me a measured look.

"Do I need to worry?"

"Not for him." The fire glowed in the silent room. My mind whirled. "You are tired," I said. "I will leave you."

"Sleep well, *scáeli* Sorley," she said. Standing, I bent to kiss her cheek. "My lady," I replied, the title doubly appropriate now from me: she was Lady of this *Ti'ach*, and head of the *scáeli'en* council. Her eyes were on the fire, distant, lost in thought, when I closed the door quietly behind me.

Just inside the annex I paused. Amlodd's room was down the hall. I felt a tug of temptation, in gratitude and celebration, and perhaps, too, to briefly silence the confusion that warred inside me. But no. I walked as silently as I could to the door to Cillian's room, opening it slowly. I put the candle on the desk and knelt in front of the chest. I removed the few items that remained to pull open the false floor. The diaries were dated. I sorted through them, found the right year, opened it. Glancing at headings, I forced myself not to read the entries, until I found the one entitled Gundarstorp. I skimmed over the first paragraphs, a summary of his discussions with my father. Below those, and separate, was what I searched for.

Catilius writes often of what he learned from his father, Cillian had written in Casilan, in his precise hand. *I had thought I could not emulate him in this, but it appears I can. One thing my unknown father taught me, indirectly: not to give in to desire when doing so has consequences for the one desired. Had he had a stronger character, I would not be here to write this.*

I must acknowledge two things: he was much younger than I am now, and, if I am fair, I must also acknowledge that had the encounter tonight with the young musician gone further than a brief touch and a few words, I doubt my own strength of character. I hope I have averted the damage threatened.

I am forsworn, my word broken. I saw no choice. What has more value, a vow, or the life of the young man? I will balance the broken oath with another: to protect him, as best I can.

He will not understand why I turned away. Time will lessen his confusion and disappointment, I hope.

I closed the book. Disgust at what I done was all I felt, disgust and a hollow, gaping loss. I put the diary back, dropped the false floor back in place, piled the blankets on top. Lowering the lid, I stood. Then I looked again at the chest. The journal from the year I came to the *Ti'ach* would be there, too.

No, I told myself firmly. Do not add to your trespass. You have the confirmation you sought.

I stared at the random pinpricks of light behind my closed lids until a fitful sleep claimed me in the early hours. I woke to the same numb blankness, an unwillingness to think. You are a *scáeli,* I reminded myself, but the thought brought no joy.

Over breakfast I managed a credible semblance of happiness, keeping the talk to music and poetry. "Are you riding north today?" I asked Bhradaín. He would need to go home to Dun Ceànnar, to officiate in the rites of burial for Liam. By tradition, the burial would be for the men of the family only, so I wasn't expected to attend, but it would be impolite if I didn't ask to ride north with him. *Toscairen* and *scáeli'en* often kept each other company on the road.

"Not today," he said. "Bones as old as mine need a drier day to be out, or there will be another burial. The weather will change tomorrow; I'll ride then."

"I am staying too," Amlodd said. "I'll take the opportunity to share music with Bhradaín and Dagney while I can. Won't you wait, Sorley?"

"I can't," I said, hoping I sounded regretful. "The message to the Sterre should not be delayed."

"Come to my rooms," Dagney said, "before you go."

I expected questions, but she asked nothing, only offering a long, tight embrace. "You are always welcome here, Sorley, for a night or for as long as you wish."

Under my hands her shoulder blades jutted. Too thin, I thought. A lonely life here, now. "Thank you," I murmured.

"Whatever troubles you," she said abruptly, "he is worthy of your love, Sorley. Or I am wrong, and Lena, and Perras was, and I think it unlikely we could all be mistaken."

A laugh strangled itself in my throat. If they knew… "But am I worthy of his? Ask him, the next time you are together, what I cost him." I freed my arms. "I must go. May I leave my new *ladhar* here, Dagney? I don't want to risk it on the road if I don't need to."

"Of course. I will keep it safe until you return." She reached up to kiss my cheek. "Go safely."

CHAPTER 40

BEFORE WE LEFT DUN Ceànnar the next morning, Helvi took me aside. "The lady Jordis can stay here, if she cannot go to the *Ti'ach*," she told me.

"And if Lena writes to say 'yes', someone will escort her?"

"Two guards, at least," she promised.

Parting meant a long embrace for Jordis, and a smile for Elsë. "Do not worry," I told the girl in Marái'sta. "You are safe here." They watched us mount. Our fickle weather had turned, and the day was as sunny as anyone could have hoped. It could well be raining again by mid-day, but I rolled up my cloak and stuffed it in a saddlebag, enjoying the sun's warmth. Gwenna hadn't worn hers, but Druise left his on; he and I had different opinions on what 'warm' meant.

We rode south again until the long track that followed the valley met the wider road running northward to the Sterre. There was no other way to leave Dun Ceànnar, not on horseback: the house sat on the southward facing slope where the valley suddenly ended, and above it, along the crest of the hills, a wall and guardposts protected it. The greater threat had always been from the north.

"Elsë told me that among the farms and villages where she grew up, there are many men who wish that Fritjof still led them," Gwenna said suddenly. "That they liked raiding and fighting."

"Was her father one of them?" I asked.

"Yes. At least when he had been drinking, she said. Are they a threat, Sorley?"

"Possibly. That there are men who think this way is not unknown to either the *Teannasach* or the *Princip*, and we're keeping an eye on them," I told her. Did this increase the chances that Eluf would come after Elsë? I glanced at Druise. His eyes were narrowed: he was wondering the same thing, I thought.

"We?"

"Ésparias and Linrathe. Faolyn and Ruar."

"And you and *Athàir*."

"We advise our respective leaders, yes. You know that."

"But do you go to Varsland? Like *Athàir* did?"

"No. Nor has your father, for at least twenty years," I said. "Others provide the information, Gwenna. All I and Cillian do is help interpret what's learned."

"What did he do in Varsland? You said he was *toscaire* to the people of Linrathe. Why would he go there?"

I'd been expecting this: I knew she'd heard the exchange between Jordis and me. I was just glad she hadn't asked yesterday.

"Are his travels there widely known?" she went on. "Is that why some of my classmates say the Marai invasion was his fault?"

"What?" I said.

"Who says that?" Druise demanded.

"Cadets. Not in front of others. Just to me."

I sighed. "No, it is not widely known he went to Varsland. There is a way your father's actions could be interpreted as precipitating the Marai invasion, yes. But neither Callan, nor Casyn, nor Ruar ever accepted that. Nor I," I added. "It was Ruar's uncle, Lorcann, who invited the Marai. Fritjof had promised him something: the lands south of the Wall, we think, and so he welcomed him. He used Callan's decision to sentence your father to exile, rather than death, for violating the terms of the truce between Linrathe and Ésparias as the excuse to side with Fritjof. But if it hadn't been that, it would have been something else."

She nodded. Nothing more was said. We rode steadily north, the day remaining sunny, the breeze warm. After another hour, we halted to let the horses drink and to attend to our own needs. When Gwenna returned from around a small hill, Druise went to speak to her. I saw him put his arm around her shoulders. I wondered what he was saying to her.

What would she think when she learned why Cillian had crossed the narrow sea at Liam's behest? Considering everything that had happened, it had been almost providential, an action that in the end had borne unlooked-for benefit. But Cillian — and I — had not seen it that way.

Druise and Gwenna returned to where I was holding the horses. Gwenna had been crying, from her red-rimmed eyes. "Are you all right?" I asked her.

"Why do they say such terrible things about *Athàir*?"

"Did anyone actually suggest that he was actively involved in bringing the Marai into Linrathe and Ésparias?"

She shook her head. "Just that it was his fault. I…put pieces together. I thought…" Tears glinted again. "I thought that my mother married him so I would be legitimate here, but she didn't want to, and that was why. And that it was why *Mathàir* never is affectionate to him."

Druise snorted in derision. "You do not see affection, Gwenna, because your mother thought that when you were little, you would tell the other students how they behaved in private, and it would undermine the *Comiádh* in their eyes, or something equally foolish. But it is not what Sorley and I see," he continued. "I will tell you this: why you only have one brother is not for any reason but the will of the gods."

"Druise!" I said, half embarrassed, half laughing.

"She is fourteen," he said. "Old enough to be married herself, in Casil."

Gwenna had turned pink. "Don't tell me things like that," she muttered.

"You should hear them," Druise said. "Kitten, you know the facts. But we are not like animals, or not always. Sometimes people make love just to satisfy desire, for pleasure or for comfort. Sometimes it is more. Your mother should have told you this, but as she has not, I will. For your parents, always, it has been much more."

"Still?" she asked. "Even —?" She stopped.

"Yes. Still."

"How do you know?" she asked, without looking at him.

"Friends talk," he said briefly. Lena, letting him know that all was well, I thought, a habit of reassurance.

I thought about Druise's words as we rode. Pleasure and comfort. That was enough for Gwenna to know at fourteen. But there were times in my life when making love transcended the slaking of desire, became an act to which I, for all my *scáeli's* skills, could put no name; an offering made in humility and thanksgiving to whatever gods there might be. Or perhaps to only one. I had no words for the experience, but I heard its music: the clear triple notes of remembrance: one for loss, one for love, one for forgiveness.

"I can't imagine being married at my age," Gwenna said a little later. "But Elsë seemed to think it was normal. In Casil, too, you said, Druise?"

"Yes. And not just in the *subura*. High-born girls, too."

"Why not in Ésparias, then?"

"Because the women of Ésparias would not have accepted it, and your father and Casyn agreed with them." I said. "Before the war, women could choose to bear a child once their apprenticeships were done, at seventeen, and men had to be beyond cadet age to attend Festival. Casil wanted to impose their marriage rules, but your mother — and other women — made it very clear that could not happen."

"And the Empress agreed?"

"Her governor did, after some long argument, and she didn't veto his decision. So yes, I suppose she did."

She considered this. "And Linrathe's marriage age is sixteen, is it not?"

"Correct. Although Siusàn wished to complete her years at the *Ti'ach na Asgaill* before marrying. She'll finish this summer, and the wedding is planned for a few days after the autumn equinox."

"Are they in love?" she asked.

"Faolyn and Siusàn? Yes, so the *Teannasach* says."

"And Ruar and Helvi?"

"I would say so, seeing them together now."

"Now? Were they not, before?"

"Not when they married, no," I answered. "Surely, Gwenna, you understand the reasons for their marriage."

"To create a lasting peace between Varsland and Linrathe," she said. "And to regain Sorham."

"Exactly," I said. "Ruar swore he would do anything possible to regain Sorham, and he did. That he and Helvi are happy together, too, is the best outcome that could be hoped for."

"So even though they didn't know each other, when they make love it is more than…making the heirs?"

Druise, I thought, I will have words for you later. "Gwenna, how would I know?" I asked, hoping my tone reflected disinterest.

"Is not Ruar your friend?" she asked.

"Yes, but this isn't something we have discussed," I said. "Friends do not always talk about this, regardless of what Druise just said."

"This is true, Kitten," Druise said. "I was your father's nurse, when he was ill, yes? So we know more about each other, maybe, than four other friends would."

She thought about that as we jogged along. Why was she asking these questions? It wasn't like Gwenna to be prurient. Still, she was fourteen, the same age I had been when my father had started to welcome me when he gathered with his men of an evening. The talk I'd heard had satisfied any curiosity I might have had. Which hadn't been much, because they spoke of women.

"So if a couple isn't in love at first, but they learn to love, like Helvi and Ruar, does making love change?" she asked, suddenly. "Or like you and Druise?"

"Why are you asking, Gwenna?" I said.

"I am trying to understand about political marriages."

I glanced over at my lover, raising my eyebrows. Could I talk about this? He shrugged, spreading his hands. "We came together over music, a shared passion. I suppose we both thought it was something brief, while I was in Casil. But, yes, things between us have changed, over the years, and for the better."

"So if I married Bryngyl I might grow to at least enjoy being with him?"

"What?" Druise growled. "You are not marrying Bryngyl, Gwenna."

"Did Helvi suggest this to you?" I demanded.

"No, she didn't," Gwenna said. "All she said was that he was still unmarried, but that he would need to change that soon. If the peace is to be maintained, then doesn't Ésparias need a better alliance with Varsland? And if Ruar can marry Helvi to ensure peace between Linrathe and Varsland, why shouldn't I marry Bryngyl for the same reasons?"

I swore to myself. Both her parents made connections rapidly, and usually accurately. Why should I have thought Gwenna would be any different? For once in my life, the right words came to me quickly. "Because Bryngyl is twenty-three, and he can't wait another three years for you to be of age, Gwenna. He needs heirs to establish his line. He's already old to be unmarried in Varsland's eyes. So while you're not wrong that an Ésparian bride would be advantageous in maintaining peace, it will not be you."

But who would it be? I waited for Gwenna to ask the question, one I didn't have an answer for. When I glanced at her, her eyes were distant.

"I have cousins in Han, don't I?" she asked.

"Yes. Talyn's sister's children. I don't even know their names," I said. One was a girl, though.

"*Mathàir* goes to Han twice a year. To buy horses, I know. But she would never take me."

I remembered those arguments, when Gwenna had been ten or eleven. Lena had cited safety, and the difficulty of bringing horses back even without a child to supervise. Privately, I had thought she wanted the time alone, free under the grassland sky. Then Gwenna had turned twelve and left for the cadet school, and the opportunity was past.

But I did not know what Lena's part in Cillian's vision was, just as she didn't know mine. Gwenna's question had raised a possibility I had never considered. Its implications kept my thoughts occupied through most of the next hours.

We reached the Sterre in mid-afternoon. Sheep grazed on the dyke, and the ditches on both sides were filling in, slowly, heather encroaching. Druise snorted. "This was meant to stop the Marai?"

"There were guardposts, like the Wall," I said, "and it was well-manned." I understood his derision, though: Casil's walls made the Sterre look like a series of molehills.

"Once we cross it, we are in Sorham, aren't we?" Gwenna asked.

"Once we have crossed the ditch beyond," I told her.

"And the Marai just gave it back when Helvi married Ruar?"

"As part of the agreement to the alliance, yes. There are trade arrangements beneficial to them as well, and a series of payments over ten years. But when those are paid, and they nearly are, Sorham belongs completely to Linrathe."

We rode across a wooden bridge and up to the top of the dyke and along it, scattering sheep, until we reached a place where the sides of the northern ditch had crumbled under the hooves of the flock. The horses picked their way across it and up onto the moorland. My heart felt absurdly, immediately, lighter. I grinned.

"It is not different," Druise said.

"Not in appearance," I said. "Nor is the land on either side of the Wall. But it's a different land, Druise. Wilder. Harder, and the more so as we go north."

He grunted a reply. I glanced at Gwenna, but she was looking ahead at the track. We rode on. Grouse scattered, calling, and deer trotted off as we approached. There was a stream to ford not too far ahead, I remembered. We'd water the horses there.

Gwenna stayed silent. Druise began to hum a tune, and I joined in with the words. He rarely sang, for no good reason: his voice was untrained, but true. "Sing," I called to him. "The sheep won't mind." He grinned, shaking his head. Pure happiness washed through me, and I laughed out loud.

We dismounted at the stream. The horses dropped their noses to drink. I put an arm around Druise's shoulder for a quick hug; there was no one for miles. "Sorley?" Gwenna said. "If *Athàir* wasn't helping the Marai, why was he in Varsland? You told the lady Jordis he mostly was negotiating tribute. What else he was doing?"

Chapter 41

14 YEARS EARLIER

I RODE NORTH. THE weather stayed fair, and I claimed a *toscaire's* bed and food at several *torps* before I reached the Sterre. One day, I told myself, I'll return as a *scáeli*. The thought brought little joy.

I turned east just a little, on a track that bypassed Dun Ceànnar and would bring me directly to the fort on the Sterre where I should find Turlo. I reached it in the early afternoon. The General Turlo, I was told when I inquired, was not at the fort. The Linrathan commander was at the Sterre itself.

"Sorley!" the commander said, grinning hugely, when I found him.

"Gregor?" I returned the grin. "How did I not know you were commanding here?"

"You've been down at Wall's End, and busy, from what Turlo has told me," he replied. We'd known each other from before the war, when he, a landholder's son like me, but one with an older brother, had been part of Donnalch's guard.

"It's good to see you, but I can only give you a minute."

"What's wrong?" I asked. "Can I help?"

"Nothing wrong, exactly," he said. "A Marai inspection party approaches. They do this, every few weeks, assuring themselves we are not encroaching on lands north of the Sterre. Or so they say. I believe, as does Turlo, that they are assessing our numbers, and the repair of the earthworks."

"I speak fluent Marái'sta," I said, "it that is of any help."

"It might be," he conceded. "Come."

"Turlo should be here," Gregor said, as we waited.

"Where is he?"

"He and his scout rode east some days past, to investigate the fortifications where the Sterre meets the mountains, he said. He thought it a point of weakness. But I expected him back by now."

"Are you his second-in-command?" Turlo had been assigned overall command because of the Casilani troops on the Sterre; it had been thought they might not obey the Linrathan officers. If this was a formal Marai delegation, they would not be pleased to be met by a subsidiary commander.

"I am." We watched the riders approach. Three Marai men, two more from Sorham, by their cloaks. A dozen guards. They crested a small rise and halted, unfurling a white standard.

"What is this?" Gregor muttered, but it barely registered. My eyes were on the grey-and-green cloak of the man to the right of the Varslanders: the colours of Gundarstorp. Too slight to be my father, though. My brother?

"Come." Gregor snapped commands to a junior officer. Aides brought his horse, and mine. We rode along the Sterre. At the gate built into the high earth-and-stone dyke, where a wooden bridge had been dropped into place to span the ditch that ran along the Linrathan side of the border, we halted. Guards massed behind us; archers took their places on the Sterre.

A bowshot's distance from the dyke the Marai stopped. Deliberately, they removed swords and knives, dropping them to the ground. My brother — I was sure it was him now — and the other Sorham noble, who wore the colours of Dugarstorp, did the same. I watched carefully, but even the boot knives were tossed aside.

At the edge of the ditch on the Sorham side, where no bridge crossed the gap, the men halted. I tried not to look at Roghan, hoping my tell-tale face was schooled to impassivity, and that any flush would be attributed to the cold wind. "What do you want?" Gregor demanded, in Linrathan.

"This is the Earl Olavi, and his brother Tavö," the man from Dugarstorp replied, pitching his voice to be heard, "and the Earl Aaro. They come with a proposal for the *Teannasach* of Linrathe, one to bring peace to both our lands. I am Dugar, *Harr* of Dugarstorp, and with me is the lord Roghan, who holds Gundarstorp."

My brother held Gundarstorp? Then my father was dead. I tried not to react, focusing on Dugar. He was a good ten years older than I, and his body had broadened and his hair thinned since I had seen him last. Nor had he been *Harr*, then. He waited. I saw his eyes fall on me, and the recognition, quickly mastered. He did not turn to Roghan.

"You will submit to being searched, and your guard will remain where they are," the commander said. "I am Gregor, commander of the Linrathan troops here. With me is the lord Sorley, *toscaire* of Linrathe. He will act as translator, so that I am convinced that no words are misconstrued. That is acceptable, my lords?"

I rode forward to repeat the instructions. As the Marai made gestures of assent, I allowed myself a glance at my brother. He met my gaze with no expression at all.

We reined our horses off the bridge, allowing soldiers to put the second bridge in place over the northern ditch. Gregor watched as the five men were escorted into Linrathe and searched, carefully.

Satisfied, Gregor nodded. "Your horses will be fed and watered," he said. "You too could use food and drink, I expect?"

"We would prefer to ride to the *Teannasach* as soon as possible," Dugar said, not bothering to translate for the Marai.

"Nonetheless, it will be an hour before I can allow that," Gregor said civilly. "Your horses too must be searched, and your harness, and a messenger sent ahead to the *Teannasach*, as you must realize. Five northerners riding into Dun Ceànnar without advance warning to their guards, even with our escort, would be met with force."

Dugar nodded. "As you say. Food and ale, if you have such, would be welcome. My thanks, Commander."

Gregor swung down from his horse, so I did the same. As I did, Roghan moved so he was close to me, although he continued to look away. I turned to the Marai, repeating what Gregor had said, as Dugar hadn't. Questions jumbled my thoughts. Why was Roghan here? How had my father died? The commander had begun to move towards the fort. Beside me, I heard Roghan murmur 'kelika'.

Kelika. Our local word for a sled. We had been eight and eleven, that March day. The weather had been mild for a week before it had turned, a wind from the northeast bringing temperatures below freezing overnight, and an icy crust on the snow the next morning that meant fast sledding.

But while the snow had frozen, the lake ice, weak from the thaw, had not, or not beyond a surface skim. We had swept down the hillside, laughing together on the sled, and onto the lake. And through the ice, almost immediately. It was the immediacy that had saved us, the lake just shallow enough for me to stand, to pull Roghan up into my arms and struggle across the short distance, through the energy-sapping freezing water and the soft ice to the shore. I remembered his terrified tears, and my shaking fingers as I tried with flint and steel to light a fire, praying incoherently, huddling close to it when it caught and began to burn. When its heat had warmed and dried us enough, we made a pact of silence before we plodded over the hill to home, to explain how we had jumped off the sled just before it went into the lake.

Kelika had become our private code for any secret to be kept from our father and the other adults. I had forgotten it until now. I met his eyes, smiled a bland, *toscaire's* smile. "Yes," I said, in Linrathan, pausing for a moment before I continued. "You have travelled far. I am sure you will glad of a short rest."

"Your understanding does you credit," Roghan replied. His hair, once nearly as pale as mine, had darkened. When I had left Gundarstorp, he had been shorter than I, and slight; now he stood half a head taller, and his shoulders told of hard work with sword and axe. But his voice, uncannily like my father's, held the soft accents of Sorham I had worked hard to lose, a requirement for a *scáeli*. I swallowed, hard.

In the headquarters, we gathered round a table; ale and bread and sheep's cheese were brought. The northerners were hungry. After some minutes, Dugar pushed his empty plate away. "So," he said. "You will want to know why we are here."

"I will," Gregor said evenly. "What is this offer that will bring peace?"

"Nothing I can speak of, except to the *Teannasach*," Dugar said, with a shake of his head. "But it is a real one, not a ruse to bring the Marai into Linrathe. I risk my life, and so does young Roghan, and the earls, were any of our countrymen to have seen us crossing the Sterre." He looked my way. "You, Lord Sorley, I trust."

"You know these men?" Gregor said.

"I do," I replied. "From childhood."

"You will go to Dun Ceànnar with them? Act as a translator for the earls?"

"Certainly. It was where I meant to go next, in any case."

CHAPTER 42

IT WAS LONG PAST dark when our tired horses plodded along the long track leading to Dun Ceànnar. Men with torches had joined us, our faces examined in the flaring light, mine and the officer riding with us given a long examination. But I had recognized the man who held his torch up to see my face, and called him by name, and even remembered to ask after the health of a child who had been ailing the last time I had been here. Satisfied, he moved on.

In the confusion of torches and men and barked questions, Roghan brought his horse close to mine. "Sorley," he said, his voice barely audible. "An unexpected meeting. You are well?"

"Well enough, Roghan," I murmured back. "I am *toscaire*, as you heard, and *scáeli*, too."

"It was all you ever wanted," he answered. "I am glad. I have a son. He is two now."

"An heir then, for Gundarstorp," I replied, genuinely pleased. "He is Gundar, I suppose?"

"No. Hairle, we call him. For the rightful heir, you understand, for whom I hold the lands as a steward."

Roghan had named his son for me? "What did Gundar say to that?"

He looked away. "Nothing good. He would not call the boy by that name. But he is dead."

"I know," I said. "Dugar said you held Gundarstorp."

He nodded, a bare shadow of movement in the dark. "He drowned, trying to save a fishing boat from the rocks."

"When?"

"In the spring."

There was time for nothing more. The Dun Ceànnar guards shouted, and we rode up to the house. In the arched great hall, Ruar waited for us, noticeably more a man than he had been in the spring, taller, his face more defined. Daoíre sat beside him.

In adequate Marái'sta, Ruar greeted his unexpected guests, telling them firmly there would be no discussion this night. "Food, and drink, and a little music," he said, "and then to bed. The morning is appropriate for diplomacy, not a late night after a long ride."

Music. Ruar's words had given me an idea. I could not talk with my brother as I wished, but I could sing. With Bhradaín absent, it would be I whom Ruar expected to entertain his guests.

When the food was eaten, and only cups of ale remained in front of our visitors, I stepped up to the low dais with my *ladhar*. "Our *Teannasach* has called for music," I said, "and as Dun Ceànnar's *scáeli* is absent, I will be your singer tonight."

I sang the *danta*, the last verses completely unaccompanied, as the last verses of a lament sometimes were. I sang the more complex ending, speaking of the debt owed, the reckoning of the price paid that must be made in every heart after war. I had written these verses over this last summer, after Cillian's warning to me of Casil's possible intentions towards Linrathe. I wanted Ruar to hear them, before the Marai made their proposal.

And, I admitted, I had wanted Roghan to hear what I had done since the invasion, and where my loyalties lay. Had lain. He had named his son for me. There was a message there, just as there was in the fact that he was here with these Marai earls, proposing a marriage alliance between Linrathe and Varsland.

I finished, bowed, and left the dais, returning to my chair and a cup of ale. Down the table, Roghan caught my eye. He nodded, in acknowledgment and approval. I wondered, suddenly, what Ruar thought, and Daoíre: they both knew the two brothers of Gundarstorp sat at their table tonight.

"Your usual room is damp, my lord Sorley," the steward said, "so I have put you here." He opened the door to a smaller room, but one with a fire burning brightly and wine warming on the hearth. Wine? I saw the door that would open onto the adjoining room. There were two cups on the hearth.

"It will do nicely," I told the man, closing and locking the hall door. I heard noises in the hall, voices, doors opening and closing. I waited. When there was only silence outside, I opened the interior door.

My brother spun at the sound. He had removed his heavy tunic and boots, and stood in his breeches and light shirt, his feet bare. "Will you share a cup of wine with me, Roghan?" I asked. "In memory of our father?"

"Sorley," he said, and then, "brother," before we moved into a long, hard embrace. I kissed his temple, and then his lips. "He even looks like you," he said, when he could find words.

"Your son?"

"Who else?"

"Who is his mother?" I poured the wine, handed Roghan a cup. He told me. I flushed. "That match was proposed for me," I said.

"I know. But you were still at the *Ti'ach*, and her father wanted her wed. I liked her, and I didn't think you'd mind."

"I don't," I said. "Your son is heir, Roghan, as I said. I will father no children."

"I — " He hesitated. "I have long thought that." He took a drink. "You are still my brother." Brave words, from a man of Sorham. "Are you happy?" he asked.

"I have what I want," I said carefully. "I was made *scáeli* only a week ago. I have good friends, and work to do that matters."

"Don't you miss Gundarstorp?"

"Yes. But I chose, Roghan. I cannot come home."

"You could, one day, if we are successful in our proposal to the *Teannasach*."

I gestured him to silence. "Follow me," I whispered, and went back to my own room. I took paper and pen from my pack and wrote quickly. 'We may be being listened to. Say nothing of your proposal." He looked surprised, but nodded. I threw the paper in the fire.

"The *danta*," he said. "You wrote it? Was it all true?"

"Yes, to both questions. Do you remember Cillian?"

"Yes. We went hawking. I liked his horse." I smiled. He had been only thirteen. I hadn't had eyes for the horse that day. But I thought Roghan looked worried.

"What's wrong?" I murmured.

"Not now," he whispered. "You will understand tomorrow."

We talked then of Gundarstorp, of who had died among the *torpari*, and of marriages and births, of boats lost to summer storms and new barns built, and my longing for my land grew with every word. It was very late, and the wine finished, when Roghan stood. "I must sleep," he said. "As should you. *Mo bhráithar,* this has been an unlooked-for joy. I thought never to see you again."

"Nor I you, Roghan. I might have played *An Dithës Braithréan* tonight, except I would have wept in the playing," I told him, "as I have every time since war separated us." Not untrue, and some of my tears had been for my brother.

"I envy you the music, to express what you feel," he said unexpectedly. "I will see you in the morning."

CHAPTER 43

VERY EARLY THE NEXT morning I went in search of Ruar. The hall guard challenged me, but I gave him a look and reminded him I was Ruar's *toscaire*, and I had information that could not wait. Reluctantly he escorted me to the boy's bedroom.

Ruar was awake, and dressed. "Sorley," he said in surprise. "I was just going out for a ride before breakfast; it will be the only chance I have today, I think. Will you come with me?"

I could have asked for nothing better. Once on the horses, and riding up the long valley, he told his guard to fall back. The man protested. "I am well-guarded along this valley," Ruar said calmly, "and if the lord Sorley could keep me safe in battle, then he can here, too."

"What is it?" he asked, as soon as the guard had dropped behind. "You're not in the habit of dawn visits."

"Two things," I said, "and perhaps not unrelated. The first concerns our talks with Casil. You do know Liam asked me to negotiate with them not just to build a trading port at the mouth of the Taiva, but also a ship-building harbour?"

"Ship-building?" he said. "I heard nothing of that. Tell me." I did, summarizing the discussions of the summer. His eyes narrowed, concentrating.

"That is more than I agreed to," he said. "These talks must stop."

"There is more, Ruar. I have come to wonder what their motives are. Is it only a deep harbour in which to build ships, close to a supply of timber? Or do they want a base for a fleet from which to make Linrathe more than an allied land?"

He pulled up his horse, turning to face me. "A valid concern," he said. "A very valid concern. Tell me. Is Ésparias aware of this offer my great-uncle made?"

"No." I'd agonized over this, on the ride north. It was partly why I had made the detour to the Sterre, to give myself more time. Ruar was my *Teannasach*, and deserved truth from me. As a *scáeli* I must give it, but I had not yet sworn that oath. Cillian's words to me would be treason in the eyes of the Eastern Empire, and as hurt and angry as I was, I could not — would not — do that to him.

"Your concerns are noted, Lord Sorley," Ruar said, "as is your diligence in bringing the matter to my attention. Casil must be told ship-building will not be allowed. A port for the transport of timber, yes; and perhaps for Marai trade, but under our control."

"The governor will be displeased," I said. I would not be diplomatic, out here where no one could overhear.

"He may be," Ruar agreed. "But I have made it clear that I am *Teannasach*, and Liam was only one voice that advised me. What my other advisors will think of this will be informative."

Fourteen, he was. Donnalch had taught him well.

"We must return," he said, reining his horse around. "What do these northerners offer me, Sorley? Did your brother tell you?"

"I wouldn't let him," I admitted. "Were the connected rooms your doing, Ruar?"

"They were."

"Thank you," I said. "I haven't seen him for seven years, and our father died this spring. He holds our lands as steward for me, by our laws of inheritance, and his son is my heir. We had much to talk about."

"I thought you might," he said briefly, urging his horse into a gallop. At the doors to the house we left the animals to other hands and went to breakfast. Dugar and Roghan were there, and the Marai earls, looking impatient.

"I will hear your thoughts shortly," Ruar told them, "but I am newly-come from riding, and both thirsty and hungry." As only boy of his age could be, I thought, watching him eat twice what I did.

"Now," he said, with a nod to the servers to remove the plates and food, "I am ready. You will address only myself, and my *toscaire* the lord Sorley." Ruar's two older cousins had joined us.

"Ruar," Daoíre said, warning in his voice.

"Please leave me, Daoíre," Ruar replied. The man crossed to crouch by Ruar's side, murmuring something. The *Teannasach* considered his words.

"A fair thought," he conceded. "You stay. Oisín, you will be advised of my thoughts later."

"Well?" Ruar asked, turning to the northerners once the door had been closed. "What is this proposal that can bring us peace?"

Dugar cleared his throat. "With respect, *Teannasach*, we had hoped for another at this meeting. But from the *danta* Lord Sorley sang last night, it is clear that hope is in vain. Perhaps we could ask for your great-uncle Liam, instead?"

"He is dead," Ruar said. "Explain."

"You may not be aware of certain negotiations begun between Linrathe and Varsland nearly a decade past, regarding a marriage between your sister and a prince of the Marai?"

It has been many years since we traded thoughts. Irmgard, Ádla of Varsland, greeting Cillian on a distant river a year and more ago. Cillian, whom they had hoped would be here. My stomach constricted.

"I am not," Ruar said. "My sister would have been newly born. Under whose authority?"

"Liam's," Dugar said.

"A decade past? He had no right. Who conducted these negotiations, behind my father's back?"

"The man we hoped could be present," Dugar answered. "Cillian na Perras."

"Cillian na Perras?" Ruar derided. "I don't believe that."

"I was there, when he came to talk to my father, to see if there was support in Sorham for the idea," Dugar said.

Bile rose, burning my throat. I reached for my cup, and the dregs of tea it held.

"Lord Sorley?" Ruar turned to where I sat in silent shock. *I was Liam's man.* Liam's man, brokering a marriage between Varsland and Linrathe that would allow the Marai to influence the choice of *Teannasach*, that would make a Marai man an advisor to our country's leader. A betrayal of not just Linrathe, but of its ancient line of chieftains and its generations of independence. For me.

"I wasn't aware," I managed to say. "Not of the specifics. But that Liam had asked something of Cillian, yes."

"We will speak of this later," Ruar said shortly. "*Harr* Dugar, there are no princes of Varsland now. What marriage are you proposing?"

"But there are," Dugar said. "I will have Earl Aaro speak; Lord Sorley can translate as needed. Although you speak my language, *Teannasach*?"

"Some," he said. "I will have my *toscaire* confirm what I believe I hear."

Aaro spoke succinctly. I listened with half an ear, enough to catch the gist of what he told us. With only one legitimate son himself, Fritjof had not killed his brother's boys, but separated them and sent them to foster, to be brought up to honour their uncle. Aaro had one prince, Earl Olavi the other. Fritjof had thought the earls loyal, and for some time they had been, he admitted. But Fritjof's cruelty had disturbed him, that and his usurping of the authority and voice of the Varsland earls, disbanding the council that spoke for the people and advised the king. Slowly he — and Olavi and others, he added — had come to think there must be another choice.

"We fought for Fritjof. I admit that freely. I saw no other path at the time. But we have no leader now, and already there is strife among the earls. It is time for me to reveal I protect the legitimate prince of Varsland, Ásmund's oldest boy Bryngyl, and declare myself and Olavi regents for the boy. A betrothal to the sister of the *Teannasach* of Linrathe will strengthen our position, I believe."

"How?" Ruar asked sharply. "It implies Linrathe would come to your aid in a war, Earl Aaro, and that I will not promise. We have fought the men of Sorham, our own people, once. I have no stomach to do so again."

"There are many in Sorham who tire of Marai rule already," my brother said.

"Many, perhaps, but not all," Daoíre said.

"And if we promised to return Sorham to you?" Aaro asked.

"Can you make that promise?"

"As regents to the true prince? I believe so."

Ruar pushed his chair back, standing to pace the room. "That is enough," he decided. "I must speak to my advisors. There is much to be considered here."

"*Teannasach*," Dugar said. "We must return to Sorham, or questions may be raised about where we were."

Ruar nodded. "You will be escorted," he said. "For the risks you have taken to bring me this offer, and for the possibility of peace, I thank you."

CHAPTER 44

DAOÍRE REMAINED QUIET UNTIL the northerners had left. Roghan held my eyes for a long moment, the faintest hint of a smile on his lips, before he turned away. As soon as the door closed, Daoíre spoke.

"No, Ruar. We cannot consider this."

"No, cousin?" the young *Teannasach* said. "What do you think, Lord Sorley? What do you know of Cillian na Perras's role in this treachery? I understand finally why my father never trusted him."

I had regained a little control. "That is unfair, Ruar," I said

"Is it? Then tell me why he would do such a thing." A flush stained Ruar's face, and I could hear the anger in his voice.

"I will tell you," I said. "But only you."

"Daoíre." With a sweep of his head Ruar indicated the door. His cousin frowned. "I have trusted the lord Sorley with my life," Ruar snapped. "Go. Wait outside." Daoíre did as he was ordered, shaking his head in disapproval as he left. "Well?" Ruar demanded. He is still a boy, I reminded myself, and he likes Cillian. He defended him to Liam, before, and he is afraid he was wrong.

"Ruar," I said, softening my voice. "Will you listen?"

"Why should I?" he said. Then he relented. "I will, of course. But you will tell me all of it. You must, of course; your *scáeli's* oath demands it."

I would do as he asked. "One of Liam's informants witnessed something compromising. He gave Cillian a choice: do Liam's bidding, or have what he saw revealed."

"Cillian na Perras forswore his oath to save his reputation?" Ruar scoffed. "That seems unlikely, from what I know of the man."

"Not his reputation," I said. "That of a young man only a little older than you, who stood to be disinherited and cast out, shamed through all Sorham and Linrathe."

Ruar said nothing for a long minute. "I see. Or rather, I do not. What you are implying — I have never heard such things said about Cillian."

"But you have about me, from my own lips," I said.

"Yes. They are of no matter. I may have only been in Ésparias for a short time, but while I was, I learned to think in different ways about certain things." He turned. "How do you know Cillian speaks the truth in this, Sorley? It could be a tale to cast him in a favourable light."

"It is not," I said. "I have reason to know. I was the young man, *Teannasach*."

"You?" Ruar repeated. His brow wrinkled. "Have you been part of this, then?"

"No. I learned that Cillian had been suborned by Liam very recently. But these talks I knew nothing of, nothing at all."

"I see." He paced the room. I waited, watching him, seeing the confusion on his face. Abruptly he stopped. "But perhaps he did us no wrong," he said. "What if the ideas he planted seven years ago are our map to peace, and to regain Sorham?"

"You cannot accept!"

"No," he said calmly, "I cannot. I do understand that I must not allow the Marai to have a say in who might be *Teannasach* after me. Nor do I wish to force my sister to marry. But who I marry is my choice, and I will ask if either of the earls has a daughter of the appropriate age. Do you not think that would bind them closer to us than sending my sister to Varsland?"

"I'm not your advisor, *Teannasach*," I said, temporizing.

"No. But you are my *toscaire*. I am going to ask something very hard of you. I need eyes and ears I can trust in Sorham." He held up a hand, stopping my instinctive protest. "I won't ask you to violate your *toscaire's* oath, and do what Liam asked of Cillian. Your task is not to influence, but only to listen, to gather opinion. I am sending you north, Lord Sorley."

To go home! A surge of longing swept through me. But the leap in my gut that said 'yes' was not just about walking my lands again. I couldn't explain; that would come, later, when I had my *ladhar* in my hands. But it felt like deliverance from a weight I hadn't known I was carrying.

"This is a commission from me, and not to be mentioned to my cousins," Ruar added.

"Then where will I be?"

"You have volunteered to search for General Turlo, and his scout," Ruar said. "He may have gone north himself, along the Durrains, as he did once before. A route you know, and therefore you are the best person to attempt to find him."

"And I'll insist on going alone, to risk no one else's safety?"

"Just as you say, Lord Sorley. How could I refuse such bravery?" Ruar grinned.

"I must write some letters," I said. "Ruar, one other thing — could a letter be sent to Casil, to inform Irmgard that her sons are alive?"

"Please write it," Ruar said. "Now, I must meet with my advisors. You don't need to be present. Take today for preparation; write your letters. I'll have my steward gather the food and supplies you will need. Tomorrow is soon enough for you to begin your journey to the Durrains."

"One last thing," I said. " Who will replace me, as *toscaire* to Ésparias and Casil?"

"Daoíre. He told me he was prepared to, when you were made *scáeli*. So perhaps you and he had best talk, later today." He stood. "Thank you, Sorley. I'll see you before you leave. Give your letters to my steward; he will ensure they carry my seal too, and are sent."

I had been dismissed. Ruar, I thought in something bordering on awe, was going to be a formidable *Teannasach*. Perhaps already was. He had, I admitted, manipulated the emotions raised by my unexpected meeting with Roghan to get me to agree so readily to his plan. I could not yet look at my other reasons for accepting.

In my room, I sat at the small desk to write the letters. I began with the one to Irmgard; that was easy, good news to be shared. A few brief lines, and then I folded the paper and sealed it. The second was to Druisius. He might be back, by now. I wrote his name, continuing in Casilani. *I have work to do for my leader. I may be gone some time.* I stopped writing, thinking how to express my feelings. *You are my well-loved friend. Take care of them.* It would have to do.

Then the third. My last minutes with Cillian haunted me. I could not forget how I had left him, or his last words to me. I stared at the paper. I wrote his name, and stopped again. Not only my own doubts made me hesitate: I could not guarantee these letters would not be opened. *I have a task to do for the Teannasach,* I wrote again, this time in Linrathan. I put the pen down, picked it up again. That *Teannasach* saw potential in what Liam and Cillian had done. I wished I could think of a way to tell Cillian that.

I wracked my mind for a line from a *danta,* something to tell him that good might yet come of his actions in Sorham and Varsland. Nothing quite fit, but if I changed a few words... I picked up my pen.

Did you ever hear this variant of the danta *of Hrothgar in your travels?*

His earl unknowing, Hrothgar travelled,
Seeking a bride without consent
Or license, leaving his lands
And people unprotected.
No union found he then. Ten years passed;
His earl, not wed, made query,
Heard word of Hrothgar's seeking,
Found his wooing welcome where Hrothgar
Went before, west and north,
A herald honoured.

I might not be Cillian's equal as a *toscaire* in most things, but the language of song and story I could manipulate. Then, on impulse, I signed the letter *Somhairle of Gundarstorp.* No one could argue that I was not entitled to do so, and it would tell Cillian where I was going.

Then before I was tempted to add more, I sealed the letters and went in search of the steward. I gave him the letters, instructing him they were for Ruar's seal as well, and that they were to be sent south to Wall's End fort as quickly as possible.

"You need clothes and provisions for winter travel?" he enquired, although he must have known the answer.

"I do," I said. "I'll be on foot."

He assessed me. "Clothes I can choose," he said, "but you must try on boots. Come." I followed him to a storeroom, where he glanced down at my feet, and then handed me two pairs of deerskin boots, lined with a thick fur. Neither pair fit.

"I'll keep my own," I said. "Send the rest to my room, will you?"

By mid-afternoon I had clothes and provisions, with just enough space in the pack for my travelling *ladhar*, and a tent and blankets that, rolled tightly, could be tied beneath. I had spent time writing notes for Daoíre, on every aspect of the negotiations with Casil I could think of. Now I joined him in in a small room, sparsely furnished with a table and chairs. It was an interior space, without windows, lit by lamps and the fire, but outside the sun had set long before we finished talking.

"Your letters?" Daoíre asked, as we shared ale to ease our throats.

I gave them to him. He glanced at the names. "Whom should I entrust with the Lady Irmgard's?"

"Rufin. He is a ship's captain of the Casilani, and a good man."

"Do I trust the *Princip*, and his advisors?" he asked bluntly.

"Casyn, yes. Cillian, yes. Be cautious around the others, I would say." I hesitated. How to say this, without endangering Cillian? "Prince of Ésparias he may be now, but Cillian remains attached to the land of his birth."

"Clearly," Daoíre said. "The treaty was favourable, in my eyes." He made a sound of disgust. "My wife's father was an old man, and his ideas were old too. But he had his supporters, so we must balance our approach." He eyed me. "Neither I nor Oisín were among those, as you may have gathered."

"I am glad to see our *Teannasach* advised by men who look forward," I replied. Was he speaking the truth? I thought so, from his voice.

"Cautiously forward," Daoíre said. He finished his ale and stood up. "Time to eat," he said. "We both ride tomorrow, in different directions."

"Ruar is sending you so soon?"

"He wants it known now this harbour will be under our control, not Casil's. I will be at Wall's End until midwinter, at least, to be Linrathe's voice to this Governor."

"More so than I was," I murmured.

"Aye," he said, gently. "You are not hard enough, Lord Sorley. You have done well, but this needs a stronger voice than yours now. I need not tell you to be careful in your search for General Turlo: you will know the dangers of travel at this time of year."

CHAPTER 45

15 YEARS AFTER THE BATTLE OF THE TAIVA

GWENNA HAD BEEN QUIET these last few days. Not sulky, but thoughtful. She behaved impeccably at the halls of the *Härren*, to the credit of her upbringing and training, and, I reflected, her own strength of character. But away from other people, she said little. Today she had been even quieter, and when we stopped she had buried her head against Druise's chest and sobbed.

Later, when we had eaten and were readying to ride again, I put a hand on her shoulder. Her eyes were still red. "I cried for weeks," I said.

There was little more I could say: she knew now what her father had done, and its implications, and she would have to find her own peace with it. She'd been horrified, disbelieving and angry, shouting at me, and since then she'd barely spoken to me except in public. Much like her mother, once.

She didn't flinch from my hand. "You went back to him," she said. "You still loved him, after he betrayed your land."

"Kitten," Druise said, buckling a saddlebag. "Think about this: I broke an oath too. I deserted Casil for Ésparias. Your father saved my life, when I would have been executed for that."

"But," she said, "you were only a soldier."

Druise chuckled. "What was your father, when he broke his? Only a man, Kitten. Younger than I was." He swung up onto his horse. "Listen to me, Gwenna. Your father is the best officer I have ever served. I guard both him and you, and I would give my life for either of you. But he is not a hero. Sorley had to learn that. So do you."

Blunt words to his beloved Kitten, I thought, mounting my own horse. But needed.

"Druise?" Gwenna's voice broke my reverie. I'd been riding beside Druise, but I had been lost in thought, letting my horse keep pace with his. *Sorley had to learn your father is not a hero,* Druise had said. I'd known this journey would be difficult; I hadn't expected the memories would return with the force they had today.

Gwenna had been riding a length or two ahead of us. She'd reined her horse to a stop and was staring ahead of her.

"Sorley!" Druise said, his tone sharp. "Stay there," he ordered Gwenna. "Secca out." I swore, silently. What had they seen?

Then I saw them too, emerging from a group of boulders that had shielded them from my sight. Three men. Three Marai, on horseback, riding purposely. Two older men, and a young one, swords and axes hanging from their saddles. Chasing a fleeing wife and bride, I guessed. Jordis had been wrong. I'd been wrong. I scanned the countryside. Whose land was this?

Open moorland lay on either side of us, low hills rising in the distance. I listened, searching for one sound: the bell around a sheep's neck. Out here, where fog and storm might mean a lost flock, every *torp's* bells made a different sound. Above the high piping of a plover, and the distant, steady baa-ing, I heard the tone, once, and again. Karlstorp's bell. My jaw tightened.

"There'll be no help here," I told Druise, "even if Gwenna could reach the house." He nodded, his eyes, like mine, on the men. We'd been seen: their swords were out.

"Gwenna?" he asked, without turning.

"One secca in each boot, and one in my hand," she said calmly. "The mare's reins are knotted on her neck. I wish I had my bow, though."

"Do not think about that. Remember your training."

We didn't move, letting the Marai spend more of their horses' strength in riding to us, slightly uphill. They'd been travelling at some speed already, and probably since daybreak. Nor were their animals likely trained to battle. But it had been fifteen years since I — since either of us — had fought, and Druise's gelding was completely untried.

I glanced at my partner. His eyes flickered to mine for the briefest of moments, followed by a tiny nod. I rode forward a few paces.

"Men of Varsland!" I called, in Marai'ista. "What business have you riding in Sorham with weapons drawn, against our laws for foreigners?"

They pulled their horses up some distance away. "Who asks?" one of them called back.

"Sorley of Gundarstorp is my name, brother to *Harr* Roghan."

Their apparent leader circled his horse, talking to the others. I guessed he knew my name, but as what? It mattered. The Marai revered *scáeli'en*: they had prohibitions against wounding or killing a bard. But if I were just a *Harr's* brother, they'd have no compunctions about attack.

"Your father would not have named us foreigners," the man called, facing us again.

"My father is long dead. Gundarstorp's loyalty is to the *Teannasach*."

"We want no bloodshed," he replied. "We seek only two women, and the man who took them. Let us pass."

"You seek Jordis of Eganstorp, a woman you took in war, and the daughter she bore you through force," I said. I didn't need my *scáeli's* training to make my voice cold and menacing. "You will not have her. She is at Dun Ceànnar, under the protection of the lady Helvi. Go home, Eluf."

I'd hoped to disconcert him by using Jordis's name, and his. Druise rode up beside me. Eluf had neither spoken nor moved. We began to ride towards the three men, a tactic practiced over and over. Druise and I would move apart, flanking the Marai, pulling their attention — and attack — to us. I said a silent prayer to Lena's goddess that Gwenna's nerve would hold. "Sorley," Druise hissed, as the distance between us widened. He tossed me his long sword. *Scáeli'en* did not carry weapons save their belt knives, but we could defend ourselves if attacked by any means available. There was more than my life at stake here.

The young man kicked his horse forward at a gallop, past the older men, then wrenched it to a stop, axe in hand. He was not facing me. I screamed Druise's name, saw his shield go up. The axe turned in the air. The Marai had twisted in his saddle to make the throw, his arm raised. Metal flashed in the sunlight. Gwenna's secca sliced into his stomach, embedding itself deeply in his flesh.

He fell. I ignored him. Druise's shield took the axe-blow, spinning the weapon. It hit his thigh, hard, and he rocked in the saddle. I heard hooves near me, raised my sword, swept it at the attacker. Our swords hit, rebounded. I swung again, feeling the blade slice flesh. He gasped, pulling his horse back, and as he did he transferred his sword to his left hand, reaching for his axe with his right. I lunged forward, too late. With utter horror I watched the axe fly at Gwenna, heard Druise's desperate shout. I drove my sword into Eluf. He writhed, fighting for balance.

I didn't wait to see if he fell. I turned, praying. I'd heard a wet thud as the axe hit, a scream of pain. Gwenna was off her horse — but she was tumbling free of the gutted animal. She came up on her feet, secca in hand, to throw with unerring accuracy at the Marai man whose sword was raised against Druisius. The knife took him in the side. Druise's short sword finished him.

Relief coursed through me. I looked down at the man on the ground. Eluf spread his arms, his sword held loosely. "Will I be ransomed?" he rasped.

"No," I said, dismounting. "The girl is the heir to Ésparias."

The briefest flicker in his eyes, before he nodded. "I should have known," he said bitterly. "*Scáeli'en* do not ride guarded. You will let me have my sword?"

Druise slid off his horse beside me with a grunt of pain. "Go to Gwenna," he said. "This is for me to do."

"Let him have his weapon," I said. "It matters." I turned away, starting towards Gwenna. A moan stopped me. I looked down at the young man, and the blood draining from his belly. No help for him but one. I put Druise's sword in his hand before I cut his throat.

He died in seconds. I retrieved the sword and went to Gwenna. She sat on the ground trying to calm the dying horse, the smell of blood and excrement strong. "You are unhurt?" I asked.

"Yes. How do I stop her suffering?" She wasn't crying. There was blood on her hands and clothes, but it wasn't hers.

"Go to Druise. I'll do it."

"No. She is mine. My responsibility. Show me how." Her voice was firm. I crouched to show her where to position the knife.

"Don't hesitate," I said. "Push hard. You must cut through hair and skin and muscle."

She took a breath before she ended the animal's pain. Stroking the mare's head, she waited until the final shudders had run through its body, and the eyes had clouded. "You did the right thing," I told her.

She stood up, as graceful as a dancer. "Why did Druise kill the man who had surrendered?" she asked.

"He tried to kill you. There can be no mercy after an attempt on the life of royalty."

"He didn't know who I was."

"It makes no difference. By our laws and his, too, his life was doubly forfeit: he knew I was a *scáeli*."

"And our lives are worth more than Druise's?"

"For who you are, and the knowledge I bear, yes. Gwenna, do not argue, please. This isn't the time. Druise is hurt, and we have a long way to go."

Her eyes widened. "Druise is hurt?"

"A bruise only, Kitten," he said, approaching us. "The head of the axe hit my leg, that is all. What do we do with the bodies?"

I considered. We could take them with us, draped over two of the horses, but the smell of blood and the unfamiliar dead weights would make the animals hard to handle. And I was not sure where we would spend the night now.

"Leave them. Put a weapon in the hands of the boy, though."

"Why?" Druise argued. "I know it is so he can go to his gods. Does he deserve that?"

"Why doesn't he?" Gwenna asked.

"Because he was a fool. He should have waited for the older men to choose what to do."

"My mother did not wait for older men to choose at the Taiva."

"Not the same," Druise said. "She knew her orders, and she could see the Emperor was distracted. She acted on experience. This boy acted on impulse. Reckless."

"And paid the price," I said. "Put the axe in his hand, Druise." His lips tightened, but he did as I asked.

The three horses stood together by a boulder. I approached them, leading my own and speaking softly. They sidled and tossed their heads, but I caught them all easily enough. Solid Varsland horses, much as mine as a boy at Gundarstorp had been. That didn't tell me if the Marai had brought them across the sea, or if Karl had lent or sold them to the men. I led them back to where Druise and Gwenna waited. They'd taken her saddle from the dead mare. She studied the three horses. "I'll take the dark one," she decided.

I helped switch saddles, placing the extra one on top of the one the largest of the three wore. "Do you need help mounting?" I asked Druise. He was favouring his left leg. But he shook his head, and I knew better than to insist. "Before we ride," he said, "water, and some food."

Always practical, always sensible. I unfastened the waterskin from my saddle, handing it to him. Surprisingly — and telling me how much pain he was in — he took a long drink before passing it to Gwenna. I frowned at him as I handed him bread and cheese, receiving only a shrug in reply. We would stop at the first chance, I promised myself, once we were off Karlstorp's lands.

He was right about the food, I thought, as we began to ride north at a walk. Faster was out of the question. The rush of concentration and energy the attack had brought was already fading, and even with food and water we would feel the aftereffects soon. Gwenna, I noted, appeared absorbed in her new horse, but that too could be a shield against her emotions. I dropped back. "Ride between Druise and me," I said to her. "He should set the pace."

I studied the land around us, a faint memory beginning to rise. The shape of the hills to our right tugged at me. "Druise!" I called. "Go right, along that valley." He raised a hand to show he'd heard, and we turned away from the track that would have taken us to Karlstorp's buildings.

About an hour later a shepherd hailed us. We halted, waiting for the man — old, and walking slowly — to come down off the hillside with his dog. He looked at the three of us, and then at me again, assessing.

"My lord? What are you doing with these horses?" His northern accent was thick.

"I am Sorley of Gundarstorp, *scáeli* to the *Ti'ach na Cillian*," I told him. "I ride to the *Ti'ach na Barì*, for certain discussions. Have you a boy you can send to Karl with a message?"

"Aye, I do. What is the message?"

I swung down off my horse. "I will write it down. We were beset by three Marai, an hour or two ago. They are dead, and should be buried. The bodies lie near the track. The aggression was theirs, and unprovoked: I say this on my oath as a *scáeli*."

He chewed the inside of his cheek as I found what I needed in my saddlebag. "The *Harr* will not be pleased."

"Nor will the *Teannasach* will be pleased that Karl gave assistance to three Marai men bound on their own version of justice. There are diplomatic routes that should have been pursued." A fruitless choice, that would have been, but the shepherd did not need to know that. "These are Karlstorp's horses, then?"

"Aye." The dog whined, feeling the tension. I finished writing the note, signing it with my full name and titles. I handed it to the shepherd.

"I am claiming them as payment for damage done. If Karl disputes that, I will be at the *Ti'ach* for some days, and after that he can find me at Gundarstorp. The note also tells your *Harr* that the wife and daughter these men pursued are at Dun Ceànnar, under the protection of the *Teannasach* and the lady Helvi."

"As you ask." He would do as I had requested, although reluctantly. His eyes went to Gwenna. "You must be someone very important," he said to her, in the direct way of Sorham's *torpari*, "to be guarded by more than a *scáeli*."

She glanced at me. I didn't know Karl's true loyalties, but the news that I had travelled north with the heir to Ésparias was likely already being spread. I nodded.

"I am Gwenna, daughter to the *Comiádh* and the Lady of our *Ti'ach*," she said.

He studied her. "Then I know what else you are, outside of our land. I understand the need for a guard." I remounted. The shepherd was already turning away, his dog at heel. Abruptly he turned back.

"The wife they were after. Was she Marai?"

"No. A Linrathan woman, a girl they took in the war."

He buried his hand in the dog's ruff. "They took my daughter. I'll go to Karl myself, Lord Sorley."

Chapter 46

HOURS OF LIGHT REMAINED when we rode into the courtyard of the *Ti'ach*, the northern summer nights not ever truly dark. We were hungry, and our horses tired. Druise's leg had tightened into cramp more than once on the ride, and I could tell from his face it pained him. A girl came to take the horses, telling us to go inside.

But the door to the hall opened before we reached it, and the young *Comiádh*, Barì, stepped out. "Sorley," he said. "We've been expecting you, but I thought you'd be alone. Druisius, you are of course welcome. And this is — Gwenna? I haven't seen you since you were seven." Barì had been one of our *Ti'ach's* first students, a fourth son with no land to inherit, even though two of his older brothers had died in the war. He'd come to the *Ti'ach* at eighteen for five years of learning with Cillian. His time had overlapped with Ruar's, and they had remained friends.

"Barì na Cillian," I said, stepping forward to kiss him lightly. He'd spent some weeks with us in the autumn, discussing curriculum with Cillian. "How prospers the *Ti'ach*?"

"It flourishes. We already have eight students. Druisius, are you well?"

"He is injured," Gwenna said.

The usual shrug. "It is nothing."

"I doubt it. Come in, and we will see what can be done. Food and ale would be welcome, I expect."

We'd missed the evening meal, and I wasn't sorry: after the day's events, I'd no wish to eat with eight students. But the *daltai* were in the hall for their evening's instruction and entertainment, of course, and they stood as we entered.

"*Daltai,*" the woman with them said, "welcome Lord Sorley, please, and his companions. When you have done so, the rest of the evening is free. After you put your instruments away, of course."

They chorused a greeting, and as they scattered, I smiled at Eithnë. I hadn't taught her, but I had been one of the three *scáeli'en* who had judged her fit to join our ranks. "Thank you," I said. "We are tired. Eithnë, you will not have met Gwenna, or Druisius. Gwenna's name you will know; Druisius is captain of the guard at our *Ti'ach.*"

Gwenna greeted her appropriately, *dalta* to teacher. As one of the students crossed the hall, Eithnë called to him. "Tell the kitchen we have guests who are hungry."

"And one who is injured," Barì added. "Come with me, Druisius. I have some skill with wounds. How did it happen?"

"It is just a bruise," Druise protested.

"Which will benefit from *arnek.*"

"Druise," I said, "go. And tell Barì everything."

When they had gone, I sank down into a chair at the big table. Without asking, Eithnë poured me ale; wine at this *Ti'ach* would be only for very special occasions. She gave Gwenna a cup as well, then sat across from me. "What has happened?"

I told her, as succinctly as I could. She turned to Gwenna. "Well done. I can throw a secca, of course; we all learned to. But I am not sure how I would manage in real danger."

"You didn't have my mother to teach you, my lady," Gwenna said. "I was sorry to lose my mare, though. She was my mother's, once. Do you think she will be angry with me, Sorley?"

"*Dalta,*" I said gently. She realized, immediately.

"Lord Sorley," she amended. "Forgive me."

"You're tired," I said, "and you need food." She looked pale. The lapse in protocol told me just how upset or tired, or both, she was. In this setting, just as at our *Ti'ach,* she should have called me by my title. She and Colm had been adept at this by their seventh years, switching easily between public and private spaces.

"There's a table in my teaching room where you can eat," Eithnë said, "if privacy would be preferred."

"Yes," I said, "thank you." We followed her to the rooms, almost identical to mine. Eithnë knelt at the fireplace.

"It's summer," I protested, as she lit dried moss and shreds of peat.

"Fires are comforting," she said, adding more peat. She stood, brushing her hands on her breeches. "I doubt you will say no to *fuisce*, either. And a little for Gwenna, well-watered?

"I don't like it," Gwenna said, "but thank you, my lady."

"Wine, then?" Once Eithnë had left, I put my arms around her. She leaned against me, but she wasn't crying.

"Did I kill either of them?" she asked.

"Not directly. I did, and Druise did."

"*Mathàir* says killing made her sick. I…I don't feel that. Only sad about my mare. Am I unnatural?"

"Sit down," I said. She took one of the stools; I pulled another up close to her, so I could keep an arm around her. "You are not," I said. "Each of us reacts differently. Your father believes he could never have killed; the act makes you mother vomit. But Talyn has killed without revulsion, and so has Druise. I dislike it, but it doesn't make me physically ill." I let her absorb that. "How do you feel, about the dead Marai?"

"I wish they hadn't had to die. They shouldn't have attacked. It was…a waste."

"That's what I feel too: regret at the necessity, and a little angry at the squandering of life, especially the young man's."

"But if I wasn't me…you would have let the older man live." Here was the crux of her disquiet, I thought. It hadn't been a question, but I would tell her the truth anyhow.

"No," I said, "I wouldn't have. It would have been merciful, and perhaps he would have gone back to Varsland to talk of the leniency he received at the hands of a *scáeli*. Or perhaps he would have bragged how he had ignored the prohibition against harming one of us, and the talk would grow and spread, putting us all at risk."

The door opened. Eithnë came in carrying a tray. On it was a jug of water, and one of wine, and a small flask I knew held the *fuisce*. She put it down. "Food in a few minutes," she murmured, and slipped out again.

"Sometimes," I said, "I am not just myself, Gwenna, but a representative of all *scáeli'en*. I must act for us all, regardless of what I feel personally."

"As I will have to," she said.

"Yes." I poured her a cup of wine, adding a little less water than usual. My own *fuisce* got barely a couple of drops. There was a third cup, but I would let Druise decide if he wanted wine or something stronger.

"If killing does not bother me — does not make me sick," she said, "I could be a soldier, and not a diplomat."

"You could," I sipped the *fuisce*. "Officers and diplomats use many of the same skills. Both exercise leadership, and discretion, and both must learn to read a situation and the people in it. And both," I said with a smile, "are going to do boring work around supplies or trade when they are junior, as we are not at war."

She wrinkled her nose, but she smiled as well. "Is Druise all right?"

"Yes. Just a bad bruise."

"He could have died today," she said. "And you."

"Protecting you is his job," I said. "And I promised your father I would guard you with my life. Instead, *leannan*, you helped save ours."

"I suppose I did," she said. She drank a little wine. "Sorley, why did you forgive my father so easily for his betrayals?"

"Easily?" But why would she think otherwise? "Oh, Gwenna," I said. "It was far from easy."

"But you did."

"In the end. But it was a difficult journey, in more than one way."

"Will you tell me?"

I would have to, I thought, although the memories would rob me of sleep; they could, still.

"When you've had some rest," I said.

The food and Druise arrived together. "Are you all right, Kitten?" he asked.

"Yes. Did the *Comiádh* give you a salve for the bruise?"

"He did. It hurts less. Can we eat?" He accepted wine, and we settled down to the meal. A little later Eithnë came for Gwenna, to take her to a bedroom on the girls' floor.

"You have the first two rooms in the annex, on the left side," she said to us.

Druise put down his wine. "I want to look around, outside."

"Then lock the door when you come in," Eithnë said. "Sleep well, both of you."

Stars fogged the sky. We walked silently around the house and its ancillary buildings, Druise's eyes studying every door and window, every wall and byre. I didn't interrupt. I listened to the night sounds, the rustle of some small animal in the grass, a distant owl. Nothing untoward, and no unnatural silence.

"All is well." Druise stopped at a wall, looking out into the fields beyond. In Casilan, he added, "Before the attack, *amané*, where had your thoughts gone?"

"Why?" I asked, prevaricating.

"You do not always remember to school your face," he said. "Some of it I understood. But anger? Still, after all these years?"

"At myself," I said. "For doubting his motives." I had no need to say whose. "For thinking he would use me for political gain." I leaned on the wall beside my lover. "Should I have forgiven myself for that?"

"Yes. It is in the past. Just as my actions in Casil are."

"What do you mean?"

"I was not just a guard. I was meant to report back to the palace."

"You were?" I turned to look at him. "Lena and Cillian believed you might be, I think. Lena warned me not to speak of anything political to you."

"I did not follow my orders." He shrugged. "I liked Cillian from the start, this man from so far away who knew about Casil. I liked Lena. And you. So talented a musician." He grinned, his teeth white in the moonlight. "So I lied to the man who sent me. I did not like him."

"Quintus?"

"Who else?"

"Does Cillian know?"

"I told him, yes. On the ship. He said he had guessed, and it was part of the reason he had decided I should join you."

"He never told me. Nor Lena, I think."

"No. And I would not have, either, except you are still disturbed by your thoughts from so long ago."

I looked up at the stars. "I'm not, really. The memories were strong, though, this afternoon."

"Do you mind what I was?"

Did I? "No. What matters is that you are here, protecting Gwenna. And still playing duets with me."

"Even if your songs are sad," he said with another grin. He put his hand on my shoulder. "You too are just a man, Sorley. Forgive yourself."

Regardless of time and forgiveness and what I had told Druise, regret and a quiet disgust at what I had thought — and done — had never wholly left me. *How we respond to circumstances is what defines us*. Casyn's words.

Druise, I thought, did not agree. Although perhaps that was unfair: his response to circumstance was simply different, his own survival, and perhaps advancement, always predominant. Or they had been, until Gwenna's birth. He would die for her; he well could have, today. As I could have too, but for all I loved her, in the moment I realized what was happening, what I had heard in my mind had been Cillian's voice: *Take care of my daughter.* Different responses. Different loyalties.

Loyalties. I grinned, thinking of Druise deciding, on instinct, to ignore his orders, because he liked us; because he was bored as a palace guard; because he didn't like the man who had issued them. And perhaps because he and I had made music together. His confession hadn't surprised me; I'd probably realized it on some unspoken level long ago. He'd been too unperturbed the times he'd been asked to extract information from his fellow soldiers, in Ésparias and in Casil, through whatever means he though best. Whatever his motives in bedding me that first night, neither of us could have expected our long partnership would result.

Pragmatic Druisius, his behaviour not so different from Cillian's in his days as a *toscaire*, using physical intimacy to encourage indiscretion. I'd known what Druise was doing in Casil, that summer. I'd told myself it didn't matter. But had that been true? Or had it, pushed to the back of my mind, insinuated its way into my doubts about Cillian's motives?

Maybe. It was too long ago, and there were too many twisted threads to separate now. But if I took the sword of truth to that that knot, the answer was simple: the fault had been mine. I had not, in the depths of my heart, believed I was worthy of Cillian's trust, or his love.

What a fool I'd been. I turned over and pulled the blanket closer. Go to sleep, I told myself. Tomorrow your concerns are music and the *danta*. I'd probably have to teach a lesson or two in my time here, especially if Eithnë had a student she thought exceptional. Druise could rest his leg, and demonstrate the *cithar*, and Gwenna could just be a girl among the *daltai*, for a few days.

CHAPTER 47

14 YEARS EARLIER

THE STERRE BLENDED INTO a slope of earth and rock climbing up into the Durrains; impossible now, after centuries, for me to see where the hand of man ended and the natural landscape began. I stood with Gregor on the ridge, looking north.

"The last anyone saw of the general and his scout, they were heading north on that trail," he told me.

"And that was three weeks ago?"

"Close enough."

"What were they looking for? Did they tell you?" I asked. I knew this trail; I'd travelled it myself, two years and more past. I couldn't help glancing east, although the path that Lena and Cillian had taken to begin their climb into exile lay further south, at the end of the Wall. Galen had brought them to that spot, I remembered. How difficult would it be to go north a short way, and then circle back to that eastern trail?

Turlo had become increasingly subdued since the war with the Marai, Lena had told me once, worried. His once-irrepressible cheerfulness had settled into reflexive politeness. Too much loss, she'd said: Darel, Arey, Callan. Son, lover, Emperor; all the soldiers he had seen fall, and on top of that Turlo knew it was his treaty — his and Cillian's — that had stripped his land of its autonomy. Too much loss. Enough to send a man into voluntary exile?

But I was not really looking for Turlo and Galen. I would pay attention for signs, but it was not my purpose. I adjusted the pack on my back.

"Thank you," I said. He hadn't reacted when I had given him the note from Ruar, with its instructions keep my direction of travel secret. I wondered if he would. I doubted everyone now, I thought wryly.

"Best of luck," he said, turning to go back to his horse. I waited in the dawn light until he was out of sight, so that he could honestly say he did not know where I had gone. Then I scrambled down the northern side of the Sterre, and back into darkness.

The huge evergreens that grew on these western foothills allowed little light to reach the forest floor at midday, and almost none at dawn. As my eyes adjusted, I could just see the trail, snaking among the thick trunks. A trail used by trappers and hunters, mostly, and in these weeks of autumn that was who would be out here, gathering pelts made thick and glossy by the riches of summer. I would almost certainly meet one or more of them. In my pack was my smallest *ladhar*, to support my claim that I was a *torpari* man aspiring to be a *scáeli*, risking my life to collect songs to meet the requirements of the council.

I touched my chin. I hadn't shaved now for three days; if I were lucky, I wouldn't run into anyone until my beard had grown in enough to help disguise me. But I hadn't lived in Sorham since I was eighteen, and in these eastern foothills the chances of being recognized, even without a beard, were slight. As long as I remembered to speak in the accents and dialect of my youth, and didn't play or sing too well.

A squirrel chattered at me as I passed, its body flattened along the trunk of the tree. It might well be its alarm call, or that of a jay, that would alert others to my presence. But if I paid attention, I would be alerted of an approaching hunter by the same sounds. I could not let myself be distracted or let my mind wander into writing songs.

More light filtered through the dense evergreens now. I began to study the path in front of me, looking for scuff-marks in the layer of needles that covered the soil. Where exposed roots stretched across the trail, I paid more attention; a walker was more likely to catch a foot here, leaving a mark. But I found nothing. No one had been on this path for some time.

Days later, I eased the pack, lighter now, off my shoulders and onto a moss-covered boulder at the side of the trail. A small stream ran down off the hills, adequate to fill my waterskin and my kettle. I thought I recognized this place, the trail hugging the edge of a drop to the west. Hadn't I camped here before? If so, I was more than half-way to the coast. Galen had captured me just a day's journey north.

There should be a small fire-ring across the stream, I thought, if I'm right as to where I am. I crossed the stream, and there it was, hidden behind another boulder, a good, sheltered place for a fire. I began to gather twigs and cones. I'd been lucky with the autumn weather; rain had been light and seldom, and the kindling I piled up would burn easily.

The fire had caught and was burning steadily, and the squirrel I had killed earlier in the day spitted and waiting for coals, when I heard the warning call of a crow, and then another. I crouched down behind the boulders. The fire smoked, and any experienced hunter would smell it. You are a travelling musician, I reminded myself.

I heard voices. Two men, I thought, coming from the north. I reached for my pack, and took out my *ladhar*, running my fingers over the strings. It was out of tune, but that didn't matter.

"Music?" I heard one man say.

"I smell smoke," the other replied. "Someone's at the campsite. Musician!" he called.

I stood up. "Aye?" I called back. They came out of the shadows. Two men: trappers, it appeared, from the bundle of marten pelts one had strapped to his back.

"Who are you?" the lead man asked. "And what are you doing here on my lord's land?"

"No harm," I said, making my voice fearful. "No harm at all. I am only passing through."

"Going where?"

"To the coast, and to the Raske Hoys if I can find a fisherman to take me," I said. "I am gathering songs."

"A *scáeli,* then?" the man carrying the pelts asked. He shrugged the bundle off his shoulders. "A bit of music would help pass the evening."

"Not a *scáeli,*" I said. "Not yet. I have not enough songs. That is why I hope to reach the Hoys; I am told there are different songs there." I watched them, hoping I only looked nervous. They had relaxed as I spoke. The first man was unbuckling his pack.

"I don't care about new songs," he said. "Old ones suit me. You sing for us, and we'll share some food. A bargain?"

"A bargain," I agreed. I laid the squirrel on its spit over the fire, the branch resting on a pair of taller rocks, and began to tune the *ladhar*. The two men settled on the ground, leaning against rocks.

"I am Saaren," I said. A common-enough name in the north, and close enough to mine.

"Engus," the taller of the two offered.

"Janni," the other said. "We are *Harr* Snetti's men. You?"

"I was *Harr* Pietar's," I said, naming the owner of the lands that ran to the south of Gundarstorp. I was gambling on these two not knowing the north. "I fought for him in the war. When I was wounded, he left me behind." I shrugged. "So now I am no one's man, and I can sing, so I thought, be a *scáeli*. It is not a bad life."

"I suppose," Janni said. "You don't speak like one, though."

"I can learn," I muttered, as I thought a man who doubted his dream might do. I turned the squirrel over. Engus pulled some bannock from his pack.

"We'll share this. Janni, fill our waterskins."

"Wait," Janni said. He reached over to touch the fur that lined my cloak. "Where did you get this? No wandering would-be *scáeli* has a cloak like this."

I swore, silently. "It was given to me," I said, the first thing that came to mind.

"For singing? I don't think so. I know what my lord used to give wandering singers, and it wasn't a cloak like this." Engus said. He stood over me. "Did you steal it?"

"No," I protested, my mind desperately sorting through explanations. "No, honestly. It was given to me in Linrathe."

"Then what did you do to earn it?" Engus asked. "Or can I guess? Good with your hands and mouth, are you, all that playing and singing? Is that it, *piteog*?" He kicked my leg, none too gently.

"No!" I said. "I — I know a bit of medicine. For animals, not people. I made a poultice that cured a horse's leg, that's all. It was the lord's favourite horse," I added. Cold sweat beaded on my neck and under my arms.

"I don't believe it," Janni growled. "Look at his kit, Engus. It's all too good for what he claims to be." I cursed my luck. Ruar's steward had given me soldiers' gear, but what was issued to the men of the *Teannasach* was far better than my clothes and pack should be.

"Except the instrument," Engus said. He picked it up. I reached towards it, involuntarily. "Ha!" he cried. "So you really are a musician. You've been some southern lord's *channàdarra* pet, haven't you? Did he grow tired of you? Or did his wife find out?" He kicked me again. I scrambled backwards, trying to stand. My hand went to my knife, in its sheath on my belt. Janni knocked it out my hand in a move too swift for me to counter. He kicked it away before punching me hard in the gut. Grabbing my arm, he wrenched it behind me. I screamed.

I remember Engus smashing my *ladhar*, laughing as he did, and the first few blows. I remember trying to protect my hands, terrified they would break my fingers. They were strong and wiry and fast, fuelled by anger, and once Janni pulled me upright, my arms behind me and a hand tight across my throat, I could do nothing. I was going to die here. Jumbled images flashed behind my eyes: Druise. Gundarstorp. Cillian. Forgive me, I thought, through the pain, as darkness descended.

Chapter 48

COLD WOKE ME, COLD and pain. I was alive. For now. Shivering, I moved each limb. Nothing broken, as far as I could tell. I tried to sit up. That hurt, terribly, my gut and lower back and sides exploding. I lay down again and examined my torso with my hands. No blood. I hadn't been stabbed. I held my breath, and sat up again. It seemed more manageable this time.

I propped myself up until the throbbing in my abdomen eased, looking around. Daylight filtered through the mesh of evergreen branches above me. Above me, the ground sloped upward. They'd thrown or pushed me down the scarp to the west of the trail, leaving me to die.

A violent shiver ran through me. I must move, I thought. I need a fire. My pack might still be up there, or a few coals in the fire ring. My legs felt colder than the rest of me, my breeches clammy. I felt them: wet, and when I brought my hand near my face I could smell urine, the tang sharp in my nostrils. I'd pissed myself.

But, no. My crotch was dry. I gagged when I realized what they'd done. I fought down the impulse to retch: it hurt too much. I collapsed back onto the earth, tears seeping from my eyes. Sobbing took energy I didn't have. I can't get up there, I thought. Just go back to sleep. Dying of exposure is supposed to be kind. My mind drifted.

Sorley, get up, Druise's voice said. *You made Cillian live, but you don't have to*? I jerked awake. "Druise?" I whispered, but I knew the voice hadn't been real. My fists clenched. Swearing, I pushed myself up again, moaning, and began to crawl.

I passed out at least once more, but much later I dragged myself over the lip of the scarp and onto the trail. I used the boulders to help me to my knees. Scattered around the campsite, my belongings had been smashed and fouled, and my cloak and what food I had had was gone. Fire, I told myself. Make a fire.

I searched the campsite on my hands and knees, finding first my flint, and then, at the base of a tree, my steel. Deep in the fire ring a few coals held some warmth, and those and the sparks from my flint were enough to make dried needles catch, and then twigs. Finally I laid the pieces of my broken *ladhar* on top to make a decent blaze.

I shook with exhaustion and hunger and pain. The bones of the squirrel lay in the dirt. I rinsed them in the stream, filled my kettle to just below the split in its side, and threw them in. I set the kettle on the fire. A few mushrooms grew along a fallen log. I added those, hoping I recognized them correctly as edible.

The thin broth revived me a little, enough to give me strength to gather what of my things were worth keeping. My tent had been slashed, long rents making it useless except as a ground cloth. I spread it out as best I could. I had had one change of clothes: Janni or Engus had taken a knife to those, too, so I simply put the rags on over what I wore. Then I pulled the tatters of blanket over me, cushioned my head on the folded pack, and fell into a fitful sleep.

I woke to add wood to the fire, and to relieve myself, a burning stream of urine that made me gasp in pain, then slept again until morning. When I woke again, I felt better. Not well, but better. I could think. I sat up, the strips of blanket around my shoulders. My stomach spasmed with hunger. I needed to eat, but first I added twigs to the fire, blowing on it as best my ribs — cracked at the least, I thought — would allow.

Food. I couldn't hunt; the pain in my ribs prohibited it. I looked at the stream, a memory stirring. Had I seen the silver flash of a fish last night? I followed the burn eastward, and found a pool worn into the rock of the hillside, and in that pool, fish.

I had the strings from the *ladhar,* and perhaps I could fashion a hook from thorns or a sharp piece of twig. But these were little fish. From a tangle of bushes, I picked a red berry, dropping it in the pool. Fish swarmed to it. I grabbed one, wincing at the pain even that quick motion caused. But I had a fish.

I realized I needed to scoop the fish out when they came to the berries, not try to catch individuals. A remarkably short time later, my left side throbbing, I had a meal. I gutted them, laying the bodies on the coals of the fire, flipping them over with a twig. The first two I swallowed half-cooked.

For the next two days I ate fish and berries and mushrooms, and even mice that came nosing around for what tiny bits I dropped. I slept a lot, my body demanding it, but on the third morning I woke with a strong sense that I needed to leave. If there had been one trapping party out here, there could be others.

I still hurt, but when I relieved myself my urine looked yellow, the red tinge of the last two days gone. Standing made the world swirl and spin. I sat down, hard, my ribs screaming: it was that or fall. I waited for the dizziness to pass, my head bent. After some minutes, I turned my neck gingerly, assessing the effect. Under ferns to my left, I saw the glint of metal.

I edged over, reaching out. My knife! They hadn't bothered to search for it, I realized, thinking they were leaving me for dead. With a knife, I had a chance. I pulled myself to my feet. With difficulty, I cut a walking stick, whittling one end into a dull point to dig into the ground. Resting every few minutes, fighting light-headedness, it took me most of the morning to pack up.

I'd forced myself to smoke some of the fish I'd caught, not eat it, so I had a little food, and the low-growing blue berries that clambered over stumps and fallen trees were plentiful. I ate some, and a few fish, and then I lifted my pack onto my shoulders, gasping at the pain, and began, very slowly, to walk north.

I doubt I made it more than a mile or two that afternoon, before fatigue and pain made me stop. My sleep was broken, and my dreams fragmentary and frightening, engendering strange and powerful thoughts. *Some southern lord's channàdarra pet,* I heard again. Wasn't that what I had been? Cillian's plaything? Part of my mind knew this was wrong, but the thought wouldn't go away. He'd known I loved him, and he'd used that to convince me to sign away Sorham. Betrayed his country, again. Betrayed me.

For perhaps a week I made my painful way north along the trail, travelling only a few miles each day. I suppose my body healed, but I was constantly hungry and light-headed, and the insistent fear of discovery meant I slept badly, adding to my disorientation. I thought there were voices once, and hid, shaking and dry-mouthed, behind a fallen trunk, only to realize after some time that what I had heard was the cawing of crows. At night by my fire, I recited *danta* to myself, under my breath, just for the comfort of it, and in the darkest hours I railed angrily at Cillian, for all the wrongs he had done, both to me and to my land.

Early one morning, just as I rounded a bend in the trail, I saw a marten on the trunk of a tree ahead of me, a squirrel in its mouth. Without thinking, I threw my walking stick at it. The stick bounced harmlessly off the tree, but to my surprise the marten dropped the squirrel, flowing up the trunk to challenge me from a branch. I picked up the walking stick, and keeping an eye on the marten, reached for the squirrel, still warm.

Well away from the marten, I gutted the squirrel, and at the next appropriate spot I built a fire and cooked it. The smell of it roasting! But I waited, although my hunger overruled prudence, and I ate it all. After enough to eat—at least for my shrunken stomach—for the first time since I had been attacked, I sat, considering my situation.

I would starve to death before I reach the coast, I concluded. Already I was gaunt, my clothes loose. But what options did I have? I couldn't hunt; I'd tried throwing the knife, and the pain in my ribs made an accurate throw impossible. Berries and water weren't going to keep me alive.

Water. The streams ran down off the mountains. To where? I closed my eyes, trying to remember maps. Wasn't there a river? I became convinced there was. I got up and went to the edge of the trail, looking down the scarp, my walking stick well planted. I could see nothing: no glint of water, and certainly no path down.

Food had sharpened my mind. In my condition — possibly in any condition — trying to climb down the scarp without a path was folly. But if trappers and hunters came up from the lowland *torps,* then there should be trails. Had I passed one? I couldn't remember, but for days I had walked with my eyes only seeing the path immediately in front of me.

In the lowlands I could not likely hide from other people. But it was my only chance of survival.

CHAPTER 49

I FOUND THE DESCENDING trail the next day. It was steep and precarious, and I edged my way down with the help of the walking stick. It took me hours, sometimes clinging on to trees for several minutes before attempting a step. At one almost-vertical drop I stopped, convinced I would fall if I continued, and after many minutes I sat down and scrambled and slid down the rocks. Tears of pain and fatigue wet my cheeks by the time I reached the bottom, where the river I had correctly remembered ran between the scarp and the rolling plain beyond.

Reedmace grew along its bank. Reedmace roots were edible, even raw. I dug my hands into the mud, pulling them up, rinsing each one in the flowing water before I ate it, although I tasted mud regardless. My stomach full, I found a sheltered place along the bank, covered myself in my tatters of tent and blanket, and slept.

I woke to rain. I wrapped myself in both layers of my rags, pulling the blanket up over my head for added warmth. An hour's walk north, I met two trappers taking beavers along the river. I stopped, uncertain. They stared at me, but no hand went to a knife. Instead, one made a sign I remembered the *torpari* using in my boyhood.

"A *gubbë*!" he said to his companion. "I thought they were all gone, after the war." I had forgotten the northern belief that the god wandered the land as an old man with cloak and staff. It meant any apparent beggar, if the description fit, was treated with courtesy, in case he was more than he seemed. But even if I had remembered, did I look that bad?

I must, I realized. Mud caked my clothes and skin, and at a distance my pale beard and hair, half-obscured by dirt and the blanket over my head, could be white. And I stank, so no one would come close to me by choice. A useful disguise, I thought. Perhaps I would forgo the swim in the river I had planned.

Gubbë!" the trapper called. "Are you hungry?"

I tried to make my voice low, and hoarse. "Yes," I said. He bent to a pack, and straightening, tossed me half a loaf of bread. I managed to catch it. "*Takkë*," I said. "*Meas*. I wish you good harvest."

"*Takkë*," he replied. He hesitated. "You'll find a carcass or two, up the path. They're fresh. I would have taken them back for our pigs, but you're welcome to one, if you want."

"Óski's blessings on you," I said, silently thanking the deity I had invoked. Maybe, I thought, I should just become a *gubbë*, wandering the land, sleeping in barns and byres and haystacks, begging my food. I would be free. Free of my allegiance to Ruar, free of Gundarstorp. Free of Cillian. I tore a bite off the bread and chewed.

Fool. Druise's voice again. *You cannot be free of Cillian. You are too angry, and, amané, you promised Lena.*

"Lena already hates me," I muttered. "And why should I not be angry? So many betrayals, Druise."

"*Gubbë*?" one of the trappers called. "Were you speaking to us?"

"No," I said, startled. "No. Only a blessing, over the bread. I will go my way." Ten minutes down the path I found the beaver carcasses. I took one, hefting it over my shoulder; the blood would add to the smell of my garments, but what did that matter?

Later, I found a cave where the escarpment and river met. At its mouth I fashioned a smoking rack from branches, lashing it together with the strings from my *ladhar*. I cut most of the meat into strips for curing: I'd have to stay here a few days, but the cave provided shelter, and the local trappers would leave me alone, so why not?

I was wrong on only one thing: the trappers did not leave me alone. In the late afternoon the two men reappeared, this time with their wives and children. "Will you give blessings to our families?" the one who had given me the bread asked. They had brought the other beaver carcass and some cheese as an offering. I nodded. "Óski's benediction on you all," I said. Then, remembering, I sang a verse of a song dedicated to the god.

"*Takkë*," the women breathed, and urged their children to thank me too.

"You will remember this," I said to the oldest child, a boy, not knowing why I did. "All your life." He looked at me, a long stare, and nodded silently. "I will be here three days," I said. "Tell no one else."

For three days I added bracken to the fire, and twigs, and ate cheese and meat and bread, the oldest boy sent daily with a new loaf. He never spoke to me, just put the bread down and backed away a few steps before turning to run home. In preparation for packing the cured meat, I washed a section of my blanket in the river, and dried it over the fire, so I had a clean wrapping. When the sun was high on the third day, I wrapped the dry meat, put the remnants of the loaf on top of it in my pack, and moved on.

I had slept well the last two nights, dry and warm in the small cave, and with a full belly. The frantic flickering of thoughts and images through my mind had ceased, and for the first time I took a deep breath without serious pain. I would, I decided, maintain the disguise. No one looked closely at a *gubbë*, and I would be fed at any cottage or *torp* in exchange for a blessing.

I made better progress on the flat trail along the river, and when I reached the coast some days later I had gained both strength and sanity, thanks to sufficient food and sleep and a lessening of fear. I was drenched, though: it had rained for the last three days. The river had broadened and slowed. I had crossed to the west bank at a ford a few days past, carrying my boots and gritting my teeth against the icy water. My feet were the only clean part of me, save my hands.

As I had expected, a fishing village occupied part of the headland above the river's mouth, cottages nestled half-way down the cliff, tucked into folds of the land in partial protection from the unceasing wind. The tide was out, and with it the fishing boats, so only women and children, and a few old men repairing nets and traps in the shelter of the cots were to be seen. I approached cautiously, not speaking: *gubbë* never did. I might be welcomed, or ignored, but I wouldn't — shouldn't — be in any danger, if the old ways were kept to here. And if they weren't, on this north coast that had always looked far more to Varsland than Linrathe, well, then I was in trouble.

A woman emerged from the closest bothy, carrying a bucket. Seeing me, she stopped, and putting the bucket down ran back into the dwelling, calling to someone. Another woman, older, came out.

"*Gubbë*," this one said. "We've not seen your like here for a long time."

"I have been in the hills," I answered. She would not press me for more, I knew.

"Are you hungry?"

"You are kind," I replied, "but no. But is there space in the byre for me to rest?"

"Yes," she said. "You will bless us, *gubbë*?" The price expected.

"I will." She led me to the half of the bothy the animals occupied, the milk cow and the pigs, if they had them. Although this should be slaughter month, so the pigs might already be ham and bacon, hanging in flitches above the hearth. The byre was empty, as I had expected; what animals they had would be out foraging, but it was dry, and the reed bedding tolerably clean.

I settled into a corner, spreading my tattered blanket, which served as my cloak, out flat. I wished the cow had been indoors; her warmth would have been welcome. But I piled reeds over me, and the wife of the cot brought me hot tea, tasting of berries, and slowly I warmed and dried.

In the adjoining room of the bothy, I could hear the women talking: first about me, and how long it had been since the *torp* had had any chance of a blessing.

"I thought perhaps the gods had deserted us," a voice said. "That when our lord rebelled against the south, it angered them?"

"Why should it?" The older woman, I thought. "The gods should be happy we supported those whose ancestors we share. The Marai are our cousins,"

"Cousins?" a wavering voice answered. "Cousins who take our girls away, and increase our tax? They are worse overlords than Linrathe ever was, daughter."

"Mother! Do not say such things."

"Why? You are worried about the *gubbë*? He is probably asleep."

"But if he is Óski?"

"He is not. But if he were, should he not know how we are mistreated by men who call themselves his sons?"

Here was some of the discontent Roghan mentioned. Taxes and taken women; Linrathe had always taxed, but it had treated Sorham's women with respect. Did the men object to the same things? I wondered what might have happened to my sister: Roghan had not mentioned her, and I had not asked. I had simply assumed she had married.

I must have slept then, because I woke to men's voices, and the byre door opening. "Let's have a look at this *gubbë*," I heard a deep voice say.

"Yes, my lord." A lantern was held up. I shielded my eyes, hoping the movement would obscure my face.

"*Ja*, well, he certainly looks like a *gubbë*," the *Harr* said, looking down at me. "Have you a name, wanderer?"

"Sören," I said in a hoarse whisper, "my lord." I hoped my shock would be taken for fear. The *Harr* in front of me was Dugar. The river must have bent further west than I had realized, and in the days and nights of heavy cloud, I hadn't noticed.

"Hmmph," he muttered. "Well, spend the night, give the animals and boats a blessing, and be on your way in the morning."

"I will, my lord," I replied. He couldn't have recognized me, could he? The light was poor, and he had not come close. I settled back into the straw and waited for my heart to stop pounding.

The milk cow — my only companion, so the pigs had been slaughtered, I concluded — did warm the byre when she was brought in for the night, and a woman brought more tea and a warm cake, before the house slept. All the conversation I could hear, little enough over the cud-chewing cow, had to do with fishing and the farm, nothing more.

In the morning, I blessed the cow, and then went to the harbour to say words over the boats. "D'ye want to come on board, *gubbë*?" a fisherman asked. "We can leave you in the next cove, save you the walk."

In the proximity of a small boat, someone was bound to notice I wasn't old. "No," I said, "you are kind, but I do not like water. I will walk."

"Suit yourself," he said, already turning to his day's work. I set off along the shingle of the beach to where a rough path climbed up onto the headland. The day had dawned sunny, for once, and when I was well beyond the village, I began to sing quietly to myself. It helped pass the hours, and I needed music.

The wind was off the water, and strong. I didn't hear the horse until it was nearly upon me. "Sorley of Gundarstorp!" Dugar called. He reined his horse to a stop in front of me.

I couldn't run or hide. I pushed my makeshift hood off my face. "Dugar," I said. "I was out of my reckoning. I didn't realize whose lands I had reached."

"Gods, you stink," he said cheerfully. "How do you bear your own company? The *Teannasach* sent you, I warrant, to gather information?"

"Ruar, yes," I replied. "And my task is not known to anyone else."

"Where are you headed? Home?"

"I was."

"Bad idea," he said. "Someone will recognize you. You speak Marái'sta well, I expect?"

"I do."

"Then come spend the winter with me. I have two boys you can teach, and no one here will know you." I stared up at him. "Think, man," he said. "You go home, and even if Roghan can keep you hidden away, and the *torpari* don't talk, you're risking his life if it becomes known he's harbouring a traitor. I can always claim I didn't recognize you; he can't."

He's right, I thought. I would be a danger to Roghan, and to his family. To the boy named for me, who was my heir. I nodded, slowly. "All right," I said. "Thank you, Dugar."

"I'm not having you up behind me, smelling like you do," he told me with a grin. "The house is that way." He pointed. "The bathhouse is the outbuilding closest. I'll have water heated." He turned his horse and cantered away.

That bath was worth what I had suffered to get it, almost. "Feeling better?" Dugar asked, coming in with two tankards of ale and a servant carrying a pile of clothes. "Burn the others," he told the woman. He handed me ale, settling down on a bench. "You're beyond thin," he observed. "And you had no bow, and only rags to wear. What happened?"

"I was robbed, for my fur cloak," I improvised. "And beaten. Two trappers. I don't know whose land," I added, forestalling the question.

"They took your *ladhar* too?" he asked, after a draught of ale.

"Smashed it, and my bow."

"Fucking scum," he said. "There'll be one you can use here somewhere, although probably not up to your standard." He got up. "The mid-day meal's almost ready. Join us. Don't shave. The beard will help disguise you."

Clean, my still-wet hair combed back, I found my way to the central hall of the house. Men were taking places at the table; women brought food in from the kitchen. Two small boys, perhaps five and six, looked at me curiously.

"Sören, welcome," Dugar said. "He's a teacher," he told the others. "Time the boys had some proper lessons this winter." He made introductions. I wouldn't remember all the names, but his wife was Eilis. The older boy was Dugar, of course, known as Dugi, and his brother Gefen. I'd learn the rest in time.

No one but the boys showed any interest in me. Travelling teachers had been a part of Sorham for generations; I supposed they still were, scholars who had chosen the Marai cause. I'd better be careful, if asked my allegiances.

After the meal Eilis showed me to the room that would be mine, small but adequate, and told me she would find me a few more clothes. After I'd thanked her, she took me to another room, with a small central table and a few books. I could teach the boys here, she suggested.

⸺◆◇◆⸺

THE DAYS SETTLED INTO a routine. I taught the boys in the morning: neither knew their letters, although both could count, and add and take away to some extent, so we began with that. The *ladhar* I had been given wasn't one a professional musician would have used, but I didn't mind. Sounding like a *scáeli* would be unwise. When I sang, either when I was teaching the boys history through the simplest of the *danta*, or occasionally for Dugar and his household in the evenings, I purposely kept my voice rough.

I'd thought I might be expected to oversee the boys all day, but that wasn't the case. Dugar took them out with him many afternoons, much as my own father had, teaching them about the responsibilities of the *Harr*, and the work the men and women of the *torp* did. They had riding lessons, too, or one of his men instructed them in the use of their tiny bows and wooden swords. All what I had learned at Gundarstorp.

One small problem did arise. After an evening of music and ale, Dugar had stopped me on my way to my room. "It's a cold night," he'd said. "Shall I send a girl to warm your bed?"

I'd thought this would happen. "Thank you, but no," I replied. "I — I have someone, in the south."

"So?" he said. "She's not here."

"I promised," I said.

He shrugged. "Suit yourself. You change your mind, the red-headed one from the kitchen is good."

"I won't," I told him, "but thank you."

He eyed me. "Is this something they teach at that southern *Ti'ach*? I remember when the *toscaire* Cillian came to talk to my father, he wouldn't either. He and I are much of an age, and I'd've not turned down a girl then. Or now, come to that. And you must be, what, twenty-five?"

"Yes."

"Not natural," he said, and I tensed, waiting for him to make the connection, to slur the words together into the derogatory *channàdarra*. But he just grinned. "I hope she's worth it. And I'll lay a bet you won't keep your promise. It's a long winter."

Chapter 50

I HAD DONE A fair job of not thinking about Cillian, pushing my anger and confusion to the back of my mind. The obsessive recounting of our last conversation which had circled in my mind after I had left Wall's End had receded, but the idea that he had used my love for him to convince me to sign away Sorham had not.

It nagged at me when I was alone, and so I tried not to be. Someone was usually happy to have music of an evening, and I could play until fatigue forced me to bed. This night, Eilis had asked for *An Dithës Braithréan.*

"I—I don't know it well, my lady," I said. Dugar made a sound, disguising it by a cough. I didn't know if Eilis knew who I really was: probably not. But Dugar knew full well that I would have sung this song all my life.

I sang it, but badly. I heard the tightness in my voice, and afterwards I pleaded a sore throat and went to my room. I did not want company, suddenly: I needed to think. Weeks earlier, speaking to Casyn of the Procurator, I had told him why I thought the Casilani official was hiding something. *I can hear when a voice is being constrained by fear or tension,* I had said.

Think back, I told myself. For most of the years I had known him, Cillian had treated me with detachment. He'd never been anything but polite, gentle in his refusal of my tentative advances at eighteen, never letting there be real friendship between us. Much the same, I thought, as he treated everyone, except Perras and Dagney and Isa. His voice had reflected that: restrained, and often sardonic.

But from the first days on the river, he'd been different. Still a distance between us, but it hadn't seemed so cold. Then he'd taken me aside one day, for a private conversation, and after that there had been genuine and growing warmth in his tone. I had felt welcomed, wanted. I'd sensed detachment only when we talked seriously about what Casil might demand, and the difficulties of defending Sorham.

I picked up my *ladhar*, considering those conversations. Cillian's analytic, reasoned tone had not just been for me; he had spoken to Turlo in the same way, and Lena, when the talk had turned to her land. The more demanding the work had become, the more he needed my concurrence, and Lena's, with his terms for the treaty, the more distant he had become, cold and logical. All his warmth had been reserved for Eudekia. But I had seen him with her, and I could not equate that expertly flattering attention, his smooth tone when he spoke to her, with what I heard when he called Lena *käresta*.

Or sometimes when he said my name. Notes rose from my *ladhar*: the tune I had been playing that night at Gundarstorp, so long ago. I closed my eyes, seeing the scene again, Cillian kneeling before me. *Sorley,* he had said, before his fingers had rested lightly on my knee. *Somhairle.*

Somhairle. All the proof I needed, spoken in the dialect of Sorham. Subtlety with words, the precision of utterance, the fine division of meaning: these were Cillian's skills, as honed as my own ability with the *ladhar*. On his lips, my cradle name was an endearment; a promise, perhaps. A pledge, and one given more than once in the past year. *He has loved you since you were sixteen,* Lena had told me once.

I put the *ladhar* down on the bed, burying my face in my hands, the tears beginning. I flung myself onto the bed, muffling the sobs in my pillow. Only ever my own doubts. My own unworthiness. My own betrayal.

Chapter 51

HARD WINTER HAD NOT arrived yet, not down here by the sea, and late one morning Dugar came to the schoolroom. "Go outside," he told the boys, shouting after them, "and close that door behind you!"

He sat down on the bench the boys had just vacated. "There's a few *Härren* arriving today, and tomorrow," he said. "You'll be interested in our talk. Your brother's one of them. Thought I better tell you, so you don't react, although you handled that fine at Dun Ceànnar. Easier to forget here, though, among your own people. I'll tell him the same."

I thanked him. "Is there anyone else who might recognize me?" I asked.

"Don't think so. Pietar — he's your closest neighbour, am I right?" I nodded. "He's all for Marai rule. He won't be here." He reeled off other names. Some I'd never met; a few I might have when my father had taken me to Dun Ceànnar when I was seventeen. Or I might have met their fathers: Sorham's convention of maintaining the *torp's* identity through the name of the heir could be confusing. One, though, concerned me.

"Kitrig," I said. "He'll know me." We'd ridden to Dun Ceànnar that year with him, and his son of the same name. Kitri, the son, had been interested in swordplay and weaponry, and we'd had next to nothing to do with each other once we'd reached the council meeting, but still…

"The young one?" Dugar inquired. "Old Kitrig was killed in the fighting, same as my father."

"Yes." I explained. He rubbed his chin, thinking.

"He doesn't like the Marai rule, but that might not stop him thinking of you as a traitor," he said. "They're all like me; they fought for Fritjof and saw the error of that later. You didn't. How do you deal with that, by the bye? Not that you didn't fight for Fritjof," he clarified, "but that I did."

By not thinking about it, but I couldn't say that. "It's past," I said. "Linrathe has blood to atone for, too." Cillian's injuries and Callan's death were not Sorham's doing, or even Varsland's. "But why did you allow the Marai to take the girls, Dugar?"

"Couldn't stop them," he said. "It was one of the things that turned me against them. Was there someone special? Maybe I can find out where there are."

Would it ease Dagney and Isa, to know? "Two students from the *Ti'ach na Perras*," I said. "Jordis, who is an *Eirën's* daughter, and Niav, a *torpari* girl with a fine voice. They would have been sixteen and twelve, or thereabouts," I added, bitterness sharpening my tone.

Dugar chewed his lip. "I'll enquire," he said. "Was the *Eirën's* daughter a possible bride for you? Because you know she'll be a mother by now."

"No," I said. "Just a friend. I was meant to marry a girl named Betis, but her father wed her to Roghan, instead. I don't mind," I added at his look. "It wasn't a love match."

"Better that way," he said, getting up. "Wives die. My first did: two dead babies come too soon, and then she died with the third. Eilis has done her duty with the two boys, and I leave her alone. She's a good mother, so why risk her life?"

It explained the age of the boys. I had wondered. With Dugar in his mid-thirties, I would have expected them to be ten or twelve.

"I have an idea about keeping Kitrig from recognizing you," he said. "But I need to find something, and I shouldn't send a servant to look for it. We'll talk again."

I went out into the yard to find his sons. They weren't in sight, but I had a fair idea of where they'd be, and I wasn't wrong. They'd bridled one of the shaggy dun ponies and were riding it in the field behind the barn, Dugi handling the reins and Gefen behind him. Dugi was fearless with the ponies, and even at six a good rider. I saddled one for myself and joined them. We'd ride a while, and practice Marái'sta words while we did.

Late in the afternoon Dugar found me again. He handed me a leather band, wider in one section. "It covers one eye," he explained. "It was my grandfather's; he lost an eye. Don't know how. It'll need some softening, but there's beeswax in the kitchen. Ask anyone. You sure you don't want Bearga, by the way? She's good with her mouth, if you're leery of leaving a bastard behind."

I flushed. Dugar was getting insistent about this. Could I? Just to keep him from wondering? The girl would talk, so I couldn't just have her stay in my room for an hour before her on her way. I'd done some youthful exploration with the *torpari* girls, hoping it would change my inclination. It hadn't been entirely unsuccessful, although I'd kept my eyes closed, imagining different hands and mouths on me. I wasn't sure what had worked at fifteen would now, but I might have to try.

"Maybe," I said, to let him think I was weakening. He chuckled.

"Said you wouldn't last," he said. "Anyhow, wear the eye-patch, hunch your shoulders, speak badly. I thought to pass you off as a servant. A *torpari* hit in the head in the war. You lost some of your wits along with the eye, but you can still bring drinks and food."

We talked for a while longer. Eilis had taken the boys to visit her sister at the neighbouring *torp*; they had left just after mid-day and would not return until after the visiting *Härren* had gone. I was not to be present at supper, but to come to the hall later. The kitchen servants had been told to clear the food, fill ale jugs, and leave a full barrel in the hall. "I told them I don't want my visitor's minds on the girls, not until we finish talking. They'll do as they're told," he said. He stood to leave.

"You're sure you can do this? Act as half-witted servant?" he asked.

"I think so," I said. "But clothes? My cloak gave me away the last time I tried to pretend I was *torpari*. These," I indicated my tunic and breeches, "are too good."

"Leave that with me. You go find Bearga and get acquainted. I expect the first of the *Härren* to arrive any moment, so don't linger."

Chapter 52

IN THE KITCHEN THE women were busy preparing food, so even if I had wanted to dally with Bearga she'd have had no time for me. She gave me a pot of beeswax and shooed me out, but with a smile. I wondered if Dugar had told her I might want her company at some point. Tonight she'd likely prefer a visiting *Harr*, who would probably give her a coin or two.

In my room I found a pile of worn clothes, and a plate of cheese and barley bread. I rubbed beeswax into the leather eyepatch until it was supple before I tried it on. It was uncomfortable, and I found it disorienting to be half-blind, but perhaps that would add to my awkwardness. I ran my hands through my hair, so that it stuck up, and smeared ash from the fire on my breeches and tunic, and under my fingernails. Running my now-ashy hands through my hair and beard, I thought I would pass. No one looked at servants, anyhow.

I tried out a few appropriate phrases, hoarsening my voice and using the local dialect. I thought I sounded convincing. There was nothing else I could do. I ate my bread and cheese and waited.

Hours passed; I played my *ladhar* almost silently, planning for how I would remember everything I heard tonight. I couldn't risk writing anything down. I would have to remember the facts as a song. I could keep hundreds of poems and songs in my head, and if I used an old tune, then I could play it, reciting the words silently to fix them in memory, and no one would be the wiser.

A rap at the door told me it was time. I opened it, expecting to step out into an empty passage. But Dugar and my brother stood there, and with them a boy of about eight or nine. I frowned. This wasn't my nephew. Dugar pushed his way past me, indicating for the others to follow. "Shut the door," he said. My brother kept his hand on the boy's shoulder.

"Sören," Dugar said. "You can guess who this is. You'll teach him with my boys. He'll need to learn our tongue, but you'll know best how to do that."

Irmgard's younger son, the heir after Bryngyl. He had been sent here, I realized, to keep him safe. Aaro must be close to declaring himself regent, in Bryngyl's name.

"Bjørn," my brother said to the boy in Marái'sta. "You stay here. You can sleep; it is safe. Do not leave the room. Do you understand?"

"*Ja*," the boy said, very quietly. He walked over to the bed, sitting on the edge.

"He is exhausted," Roghan said. "A rough crossing, and we have been riding for two days. I think he will sleep, now."

The boy lay down on the bed. I went over to him, removing his boots and tucking a blanket and the fur over him. I'd worry about where I slept later. The floor would do. "Well done, Sören," my brother murmured.

"We'd best go," Dugar said. "Follow us in five minutes, Sören. Or should I say Saar?" By the end of this, I thought wryly, I'd be like a dog, answering to anything that sounded like the first part of my name.

The boy was asleep. I set a candle in the hearth, a safe place for it to burn; it would provide a little light if Bjørn woke disoriented. Poor child, I thought. He'd been torn from his parents at six, and uprooted again at nine, to a place where he knew no one. He didn't even speak the language.

I closed the door quietly. Slowly, shambling a little, I made my way to the hall. The *Härren* would have gone out to relieve themselves, and perhaps to stretch a little, after the meal. I leaned against a shadowed section of wall, waiting. Dugar returned, and shortly after, my brother. Neither man glanced my way. The other three men wandered back in over the next few minutes.

"Saar! Ale!" Dugar called. I picked up a jug, tilting my head to ensure I had the handle firmly in my hands, and shuffled over.

"Who's this?" one of the men asked, sharply.

"Saar? Just a servant. He's half-witted," Dugar said easily. "Took a sword-stroke on the head. Luckily for him the blade was turned, or he'd be dead. He won't understand most of what we say, and wouldn't remember it if he did. "

"What month is it, Saar?" a *Harr* said. I'd had my head bent, but I thought it was Kitrig.

I paused in pouring the ale. I blinked, as if I were thinking. "Winter, lord?" I ventured. Laughter, from Kitrig and others.

"Enough," Dugar said, but mildly. "We've work to do, and if you addle him any more he'll spill the ale. Finish filling the cups, Saar."

For the next three hours I filled cups when ordered to, from the jugs and then the barrel, ensuring I fumbled with its bung. Mostly I crouched or stood against the wall, listening, sifting out the important things said and converting them to lines of song. At a break when the *Härren* went to divest themselves of the ale they had drunk, I reflected, wryly, on what Cillian had said when he had first had to both speak and understand Casilan, and translate it too. Exhausting, he had told us, and now I understood why.

As good a *toscaire* as he had been, he could not do what I was doing tonight. The thought appeared in my head, unprompted. His bearing, and the trained grace in him; he could never pretend now to be *torpari*, although that is what he had been born. His years spent at the *Ti'ach* and in the subtle dances of diplomacy had left their mark. And I, who was born noble, was passing as *torpari* with a simple disguise and a small change in my speech.

I felt an odd pride, and something more. But the men were returning; I could not examine the feeling now. I began to refill tankards.

"This man of yours looks familiar," Kitrig said. "Saar, let me see your face." He put a hand on my chin, turning my head to his. "I'm sure I know him."

His fingers on my chin prevented me from speaking, but I whimpered, and tried to back away. Kitrig's eyes narrowed. "Who does he remind me of?" he said to the room.

I could smell the tang of sweat in my armpits, the sharp smell of fear. I clutched the jug. Roghan came to stand beside Kitrig. "Let me look," he said. Kitrig let go of my chin. I ducked my head. "Look at me," he ordered.

I met his eyes. Roghan gave a bark of laughter. "He looks like my father," he said. "He visited here often enough. I think that explains it." He turned away. "Gods, that makes this idiot my half-brother," he said, disgust in his voice.

"Well, we all have those," one of the other *Härren* said. "Be careful which girl you bed tonight, Roghan; if Gundar left one bastard behind, he could have left others." He began to tell a complicated story about a *torpari* half-sister, to ribald comments and laughter. I finished pouring the ale and retreated to my dark corner.

"So," Dugar said to the assembled men. "We're agreed? We do nothing until Earl Aaro's made his announcement, and even then not until the word has spread and we see if Pietar and two or three others support him."

"I still say we should be among the first to give allegiance," one of the men said.

"Among the first. Not first," Dugar said patiently.

"And if Pietar and his followers don't support Aaro?" someone asked.

"Roghan?" Dugar turned to him. "Pietar's your neighbour. What's he been saying, recently?"

"He's been making excuses for the infighting," my brother said. "But my feeling is he's tired of it, of not knowing where his tribute should be paid. You know it was demanded twice, on our shore? I paid both earls, but only a portion. I think he'll support Aaro just because he declares from a position of strength."

"I'd agree, knowing Pietar," Dugar said. "And where Pietar goes, most of the others will follow."

"The real question remains," Roghan said quietly, "if the *Teannasach* will play his part." He was so much like our father in his manner, I thought, even if I bore a stronger resemblance.

"The marriage alliance?" Dugar said. "I've no reason to doubt it. We'll send the boy to Dun Ceànnar in the spring, for his safety."

"Sorley." I turned to see my brother in the doorway. It was only an hour or two before the household would stir; in the kitchen, the ovens might even now be being prepared for the bread that had risen over night. He stepped in, closing the door behind him.

Bjørn slept deeply. He wouldn't understand us, even if he stirred. I motioned Roghan to the one chair, and settled myself on the end of the bed.

"You will take the boy south in the spring," Roghan said.

"Me? No." My gut tightened at the idea.

"Yes. Who else will be trusted by the *Teannasach*?"

"Any of you who met with him," I argued.

"Not like you will be." He chewed his lip, assessing me. My father's habit, too. "Aren't you expected back, anyhow? You're not here to offer allegiance to Varsland."

"I was going to send a letter," I said. "Not go back myself."

"Why not?" The boy made a small sound, moving a little in the bed. Roghan had spoken with force. He grimaced, and his next words were quieter. "You can't stay here, Sorley."

"I can," I said. "The boys need a tutor."

"What happens the next time Kitrig comes by and notices the tutor looks like Gundar? He's not stupid. He'll remember the fuss he made about the servant, and make the connection. Anyhow, what about your music? You're a *scáeli* now. Doesn't your council have something to say about what you do?"

"Not as long as I'm gathering songs and teaching," I said.

He grunted. "In disguise? What are you running away from this time?"

"I'm — " I began.

"Yes you are," my brother said, without heat. "It's what you do. You either go inside yourself, into your music, the way you did after our mother died, or you leave. You went to the *Ti'ach* so you didn't have to marry, didn't you?"

No disgust in his voice, but the twitch in his jaw told me more than his tone.

"And you don't want your *channàdarra* brother near your family," I said. "Isn't that the real reason you want me gone? I'm surprised you're entrusting me with Bjørn."

"By Rögnir, no," he growled. "Yes, you're a danger, but not for that reason. I've never heard a whisper of your…tastes from anyone, so you've kept it well hidden."

"I did," I said. "But south of the Wall is a different country, Roghan, and there I am known to share my bed with men, with no shame attached. And I'm not the only man from Linrathe at Wall's End."

A shadow of repugnance had crossed his face at my blunt words. But his reply was not what I expected. "Then why don't you want to return?" His mouth crooked, a little, at my silence. "I'll ask again, brother: what are you running away from?"

"A betrayal," I said.

"A lover's quarrel?" he said, and this time I could hear the disgust.

"No," I said. "Something bigger. I can't tell you." *If you hurt him, I will never forgive you.* Lena's words. The betrayal was not all Cillian's.

Roghan leaned back. "When you didn't come home when the war started, Gundar, well, he was angry. Betrayal was a word he used, too. I won't repeat most of what he said; it doesn't matter now. And for a while I thought the same. But then I started to wonder. You knew more of the world than I did, or Gundar did. Maybe you had your reasons. Maybe, even, you were right." He eyed me. "You sang a *danta* at Dun Ceànnar. Heroic deeds, I'll admit, if not all with sword and axe. You've chosen your path, Sorley. But men are just men in the end, not heroes, and men make mistakes."

He pushed his chair back and stood. "Take care of the boy. Maybe I'll see you again some day."

I felt the inevitable sting of tears. "At Gundarstorp, one day, the gods willing," I said.

<h1 style="text-align:center">Chapter 53</h1>

I ACCEPTED THE COINS the *Harr* offered, slipping them into my belt pouch with a nod of thanks. We'd been here nearly a week, helping with the lambing. "There's work here any time you want it, Saaren," he said. "You're sure you won't stay?'

"*Na*," I said, in the accents of the far north. "I can't settle, lord. Not yet."

"Come back when you've walked your grief to rest," he said. "You'll not be short of work this spring, wherever you go."

Bjørn waited, holding the pony. The sheepdog crouched at his feet, tongue lolling, her eyes on me. We were half a day from the Sterre; weeks from Dugarstorp. I would send the dog home later today.

Our progress south had been slow, and not just because I was travelling with a nine-year-old boy. Weather and work had restrained us. In my guise as a shepherd and shearer wandering with his son, trying to forget the death of his wife, I needed to accept employment in exchange for food and a bed in barn or byre. We'd been storm-stayed twice, too, waiting out the snow in a hut on a hillside the first time, and a barn the second.

No one, hearing my story, questioned Bjørn's silence, and as we were both pale-haired and blue-eyed, no one doubted he was my son, either. He'd proven adept with the pony, and quick enough to see how to help when needed, and when he did speak a few whispered words, his accent was close enough to mine not to incite comment. Nor did the privations of our travelling life cause him to complain. A resilient boy. I hoped his brother had the same strength.

We halted at mid-day for a little food. The pony, which carried my shearer's tools and our other supplies, browsed for grass. We sat on stones that marked the meeting place of the track from the *torp* we had left this morning and a broad valley running roughly north to south. We'd come up this valley, a week or so earlier.

I unwrapped the offal I'd boiled the night before and tipped it onto the ground, giving the dog permission to eat. She swallowed the meal before looking up at me for its next command. "Down," I told her. "It's time," I said to Bjørn.

He nodded, and crouched to hug the dog, his arms circling its throat. He would miss her, I knew, but we couldn't take her with us.

When he had let the dog go, I spoke. "Nell. Go home." She stood, the breeze ruffling her black and white coat. "Home," I said again. She turned and began to trot north, along the valley floor and the ancient droveway, the wide paths along which sheep and cattle had been moved for generations beyond count.

Bjørn watched her for a minute, his eyes dry. "Will she really find her way home?" he asked. "It's a long way."

"She's done it several times," I told him. "That's why Harr Dugar chose her to accompany us. The *torps* will feed her, don't worry." I pulled up the pony's head. "Do you want to ride?"

We reached the guardpost on the Sterre closest to Dun Ceànnar at dusk. In mid-afternoon we'd stopped in a sheltered spot, and with Bjørn's help I'd cut off most of my beard and trimmed my hair. Gregor would know me. Just before we came into sight of the dyke and ditches, I removed my cloak, adding it to the pony's burdens. Better it be clear I carried no weapon, even if it meant I shivered.

A shouted command stopped me a distance away. I could see the silhouettes of two archers on the dyke, bows drawn. "Who are you?"

"A traveller, with news for Lord Gregor, your commander," I called back. "Tell him this: *war in winter sends sorrow soaring.*" The code we had decided on: Gregor's idea, remembering Jordis speaking the words of Halmar's poem at the *Ti'ach* so long ago.

"You will wait there," the soldier said. Bjørn had been walking beside me. I pulled the cloak back off the pony, wrapping it around the two of us. I positioned the pony between us and the steady breeze. Bjørn leaned against me, and together we remained a bowshot's distance from the border with Linrathe, as the moon rose in night sky.

I'd had time to think, both over the winter and then walking the long miles south from Dugarstorp. I knew what I had to do, and what I might do afterwards. But before any of that, there was Bjørn. I had to take him to Ruar first.

We'd waited about two hours, I estimated, when a voice called out of the dark. "Come." We crossed the bridge dropped for us over the ditch and through the guardpost gate, Bjørn stumbling with cold and drowsiness.

"Wait, please," I said to the soldiers escorting us. I picked up the boy and put him on the pony's back. "He's tired." They didn't argue. He looked younger than his nine years, short and slight. Something to be used to our advantage.

Gregor met us at the headquarters. "Leave us," he said to the guards, and nothing to me until we were inside and the door closed. "I'd given you up for dead, Sorley."

"I wintered north," I said, moving closer to the fire. "Bjørn, come here." The boy did as I told him, crouching down and holding his hands towards the flames.

"Who's this?"

"My son."

"Didn't know you had one."

"Neither did I," I said, grinning in what I hoped was the right way. "I hadn't been home since I was eighteen."

"*Torpari* born, then?" Gregor asked, pouring ale.

"But a bright lad," I said. "I'll find a place for him somewhere." I'd decided the lie was necessary; even the most loyal officer could let something slip. Only Ruar had to know, for now.

"Did you find any trace of the General?" Gregor asked, as I slowly sipped another cup of ale, and Bjørn slept in a chair. Food had been brought, and the boy had eaten a little before his eyelids had drooped.

"He'll make a soldier, if he can sleep that easily anywhere," Gregor commented. Druise could do that, I thought, and pushed the thought away.

"None," I said, responding to Gregor's earlier question. "I went all the way to the narrow sea, but no sign, and no one on the coast had seen him either."

He pursed his lips. "A loss," he said. "You're going to Dun Ceànnar in the morning?"

"Is all well there?"

"Aye. The *Teannasach's* well, and his cousins too. He refused to allow forts to be built on the coast, to the displeasure of the Governor of Ésparias, I heard. But the treaty gave him the right."

We talked a while longer, until I began to yawn. I picked up Bjørn, who barely stirred, and carried him to the bedroom prepared for us, and we slept in comfort under woven blankets and furs until well after the usual breakfast time the next morning. Then I found the bath house, and by the time the sun was high, we were cleaner than we had been in weeks. Or perhaps months.

Even the pony had been groomed, and its rough harness cleaned. A horse waited for me as well. I wondered what Gregor had told the soldiers who had brought us over the Sterre last night, but when he came to bid us farewell, I didn't ask. I wasn't a *toscaire* now, privy to such things. I wasn't Lord Sorley, either: Dugar had witnessed the instructions I had written, ceding Gundarstorp to Roghan, and by Sorham's traditions I had relinquished any title too. I was a landless *scáeli*, and nothing more.

"Bjørn," I began, when we were away from the Sterre and not yet being followed by Dun Ceannar's guards. "We are in Linrathe now, you understand?" He nodded. "I am taking you to this country's leader, the *Teannasach*. Only he, and perhaps his advisors, will know who you really are. To everyone else, you remain my son. Your mother was a girl from Gundarstorp."

"Can I say she was Irmgard?" he asked.

"It would be safer to call her Irmë."

"I'll try to remember," he said. He looked up from the pony. "Am I going to live with the…the *Teannasach*?"

"Perhaps. Or perhaps you will go to a school. That might be better. You should be well educated."

"I can't stay with you?" I heard just a hint of plaintiveness in the question.

"No," I said gently.

"Why not?"

"Because," I said, "I don't know where I'm going."

We were in luck; the Dun Ceànnar guards recognized me, and so there was no tiresome questioning, or searches, and we were in Ruar's presence by early afternoon. He'd grinned hugely on seeing me, and the embrace that accompanied the kiss of welcome had been enthusiastic. His cousin Oisín's was more subdued, but he too was genuinely happy to see me.

"Daoíre is at Wall's End. I have met the Governor, too; in the autumn." Ruar told me. He turned to the boy. "But who is this?"

"My son," I said, with Oisín in the room. "Bjørn."

I would not be the first *channàdarra* man with a child, or several. Ruar gave me a level look "Oisín, please leave us."

When his cousin had gone, he looked at the boy closely. "Who are you?"

Bjørn glanced up at me. I nodded. "You can tell the *Teannasach*." I wanted the boy to speak the words, to keep his true identity clear in his mind. "Bjørn, prince of Varsland," the boy said, pride evident. "My father was Ásmund; my mother is Irmgard."

"You are the younger prince?" Ruar asked. He'd shot me a look, but he addressed Bjørn.

"Yes. My brother Bryngyl is the heir. I have been sent here for safety."

"And to test my support against Fritjof?" the *Teannasach* asked. "Who knows he is here, Sorley?"

"My brother, and the *Harr* of Dugarstorp, and perhaps their wives." I explained how we'd spent the winter, and how we'd travelled.

"You have no objection to the deception continuing? That he is your son?"

"None," I said. "I'd be proud if he was."

"Then," Ruar said, coming to a rapid decision, "he shouldn't stay at Dun Ceànnar. Where would you send him, were he truly yours, Sorley?"

"To the *Ti'ach na Asgaill*," I said. I'd noted Bjørn's quickness with numbers, his ability to estimate the number of sheep in a flock almost at a glance; how easily he divided up food for a given number of days.

"Then Asgaill will have him. But I would like him to stay with me a few days."

"Of course." Why not? It would delay me only a little, and it would be a valid postponement of what I had to do next. I hadn't quite told Bjørn the truth when I'd said I didn't know where I was going: I did, but it would be briefly. I couldn't stay; Lena had made that clear. After that I truly had no idea.

Ruar called for food then, and while we ate I explained to Bjørn what his life would be like at the *Ti'ach*. He nodded solemnly. "Like the schoolroom at Dugarstorp, but bigger."

"Exactly."

"Can I have the pony?"

"Yes." The shaggy animal was the right mount for a *torpari*-born boy acknowledged by his noble father. He'd need something better in a year or two. I'd have to arrange for that before I left.

Later, when the steward had taken Bjørn away to find him clothes and the other trappings he would need at the *Ti'ach*, Ruar questioned me in detail about the *Härren* of Sorham; who he could trust, who would follow a strong leader, and who would consider profit before anything else. He'd matured, physically, over the winter, dark hair shadowing his chin and cheeks now, his chest and shoulders and neck broader.

"I can marry next year," he said. "Or at least betroth a girl. Who is there? Did you learn that?"

"Bjørn says Earl Olavi has a daughter, and so does Aaro. Olavi's is older, thirteen, he thinks. Helvi, her name is."

"Won't she be destined for Bryngyl?"

"They want a marriage alliance. Offer soon, and I think they'll accept. Take the fish that's in the net, we'd say in Sorham."

He nodded. "She could come to be schooled here too, maybe at the *Ti'ach na Iorlath*? Skills in healing are good for a woman to have. If she's thirteen, it will be some years before we can actually marry, and I too could further my learning."

A sound plan, I thought, although it would need to be carefully executed. But Ruar was still speaking. "If I am to offer marriage to the girl, a message will need to be sent."

Why not? It would be something to do. I could be Saaren again. "I must go to Wall's End first," I said. "I have a duty to discharge there."

Ruar smiled. "Not you, Sorley. I have another task for you. I am not risking Linrathe's newest *scáeli* again. Bhradaín was horrified when he learned where you had gone."

"What is it you want me to do, then?"

"On your way to Wall's End, there is a letter that must go to the Lady Dagney. It concerns appointments to the *Ti'ach*, and as you are riding south, I would prefer you deliver it."

Chapter 54

15 YEARS AFTER THE BATTLE OF THE TAIVA

WE'D BEEN AT THE *Ti'ach* for five days when Karl arrived. He came alone. Barì offered us his teaching room. At my request, he stayed to hear our discussion.

Karl sat across from me, his arms folded. Shorter than me, and stockier, but about my age. "I sold them those horses," he said. "That's all."

"You aided Marai men bearing arms." I kept my body relaxed, my voice reasoned.

"His wife had been stolen, and the young one's bride."

"Is that what they told you?" I didn't believe him, although the tightness in his voice could, just possibly, be fear. I had Ruar's ear, and he knew it.

"*Ja.* They said Dugi wanted the girl for himself, and he took them both to ensure her compliance." If he knew they were with Dugi, then why had the Marai been riding south?

"You didn't just sell them horses," I said. "You told them to avoid the coastal *torps,* and how to come at Dugarstorp from the south. They knew you would assist them, which is why they brought their boat to your lands."

"I trade with them," he said. "Just as your brother does, and Dugar, and all the *Härren* on this coast."

"Trade," I said, "is one thing. Abetting an armed raid in Sorham is quite another."

"And what are you going to do about it?" he snarled.

"Very little, just now," I said. "I'll keep the horses, unless you want to pay the price of a trained war animal."

"Ridden by a girl?"

"Ridden by the daughter of the woman who killed Fritjof," I said, allowing my voice to become cold. "A girl who put knives into two of those Marai."

His eyes widened fractionally. So the shepherd hadn't told him who Gwenna was. No love lost between him and his *Harr*?

"Fuck," Karl said. "I didn't know. I mean that, Sorley. I thought she was just a girl being escorted to this school. *Scáeli'en* do that, don't they?"

"You didn't wonder why there was a guard with us? *Scáeli'en* travel alone, as we are meant to be free from attack."

"Didn't know he was a guard. I suppose I thought he was just someone you met on the road."

I was inclined to believe this part. I waited, wanting to hear what else he would say.

"Keep the horses," he offered.

"I will," I said mildly. "*Comiádh*, is *Harr* Karl supporting the *Ti'ach*?"

"I have been considering how," Karl said, before Barì could speak.

"Shall I tell you how, or would you prefer to wait for the *Teannasach's* judgement?" I asked. "Ruar may still impose his own penalties, of course, but it will go easier for you, I should think, if you have cooperated with my suggestions."

Karl rubbed the back of his neck. Ruar could strip him of his lands for what he'd done. "What do you want?"

I knew what the *Ti'ach* needed, from a conversation in the baths at my own school, weeks ago. Karl's hands clenched when I told him, but he didn't argue. A hundred sheep, and the grazing lands to support them, where his land ran along the valley almost to the *Ti'ach*. "And if the shepherd who brought you our message wants to come with them, him and his dog, all the better," I added as an afterthought. I didn't want the man punished.

We wrote two copies of the agreement, and signed them both. One would stay here; one I would take to Dun Ceànnar. I was — just — within my rights and power as the senior *scáeli* of Linrathe to do this. Perhaps.

I walked with Barì and Karl out into the summer sunshine, and after a word to the *Comiádh*, walked a little further with Karl.

"No one," I said, "has to know why you ceded the land, except the three of us here, and the *Teannasach*."

"Now what do you want?" he growled.

"A promise. That whatever talk happens in your hall about the superiority of Marai rule stops. You'll think of a reason you've changed your mind. And — how old are your children?"

"Grown men and women," he said. "The youngest boy is sixteen."

"Send him here for a year or two," I said. "He'll be company for Roghan's son."

"He'll hate it."

"So will Hairle," I said. I bade him a civil farewell. Barì and I watched him ride away. "I know little of sheep," the *Comiádh* said. "I hope the shepherd comes with them."

"I rather think he might. But you may need more than a shepherd. I'm going to tell Pietar and Roghan that Karl gave the *Ti'ach* land and sheep, but not why. They'll almost certainly do the same, or be shamed in the eyes of other *Härren*. You'll need *torpari*, but if Karl sends his shepherd, the others will find someone willing to move."

Barì threw his head back in a deep laugh. "And here I thought Cillian was the negotiator. But who will manage all this?"

I grinned. "You'll shortly have two sixteen-year olds who don't want to be here. Hairle will certainly be competent to manage a small *torp*: I was, at his age. Likely Karl's son will be too. Teach them some history and thought when you can, and leave the lands to them."

CHAPTER 55

I CALLED A HALT beside a small burn, at the spot where its descent to the sea began. Before us lay Gundarstorp, the hall nestled against the side of a low hill, its cottages and outbuilding scattered along the same rise of land. White crests of waves ran to the shingle of the crescent cove, and the breeze carried the scent of drying fish. The tears I blinked away had nothing to do with the wind.

I'd been back several times in the eight years since Ruar had married Helvi, her bride-gift of Sorham making it possible. I knew my nephews and my nieces, and my half-brother, and my father's second wife, and I was welcomed as both family and *scáeli*. My brother had tried to give me the lands back, but I had refused. "You should be *Harr*," I had told him, "not steward, and Hairle is the heir in either case. My life is elsewhere, Roghan." It was, and I had no regrets, but not everything or everyone I loved was at the *Ti'ach*.

"The sea is beautiful," Gwenna said from beside me.

"It is," I agreed. "But not always as calm as it looks today. In storms, it can be vicious."

"What's that?" she asked, pointing to the ruins of a circular tower on the headland.

"The *tårn*? I don't know. It's ancient."

"A lighthouse, maybe?" Druise suggested.

"Maybe. Maybe a watchtower. The sheep shelter in it, sometimes." Roghan and I had climbed among its stones and in the hollow between its inner and outer wall, pretending to be Marai raiders. I wondered if his children had done the same, if he had allowed them to play at what had really happened such a short time before. Probably.

Gwenna still stared at it. *"Look back over the past, at the empires that rose and fell,"* she said, almost under her breath. "It wasn't the Eastern Empire that built that, was it?"

"No one knows who built it, or when," I told her. "Shall we keep going? It's nearly time for the midday meal."

I hadn't seen my brother for two years. He hugged me, his grin wide. I hadn't told him I was coming; I didn't need to. *You are going home*, Cillian had said. I'd demurred, but he wasn't wrong, not entirely. "Roghan," I said after kissing him, "you are well?"

"As can be. Who is this with you, brother?"

Gwenna and Druise had dismounted and waited by their horses. Roghan's hand was on my shoulder. He was looking at Druise.

"Druisius. Gwenna's bodyguard." Druise stepped forward to clasp his hand. "And a fine musician in his own right," I added, "as you will hear tonight, perhaps." Roghan's expression changed, but it was my first words that had caused his reaction. He'd heard me speak of her, often enough.

"My lady Gwenna," He inclined his head. "Welcome to Gundarstorp."

"Harr Roghan, thank you," she said. "Are your lands the northern reach of Sorham?"

"As far north as it is possible to be, except for the Raske Hoys," Roghan said with a smile. From the doorway to the house, a young man stepped out into the sunlight. Pale haired, of medium height, solidly muscled from the work of the *torp*. His eyes flicked among us, but they rested on Gwenna.

He was sixteen. She was graceful and assured, and as beautiful as her father had been, twenty-three years earlier. "Hairle," I said, to break the spell. I held out my arms. "Come here." He came, with a last glance at Gwenna, for the kiss of greeting. My namesake.

Then the other children spilled out of the house, followed by calm Betis, who had been meant to be my wife, and Maj, my stepmother, who was barely older than I. Kisses and hugs and introductions done, I looked around, not seeing my half-brother. "Where's Nyle?"

"Gone trading," Roghan said. "He's nineteen now, and there's little for him here. So he took a place on a ship heading east to trade furs and amber."

"East?" I said. "Down the Ubë?"

"Your fault," he said, grinning. "After he heard your *danta,* he could talk of little else. Come, brother, let's eat."

After a meal that went on much longer than it should have at midday on a busy *torp,* Betis stopped by my chair. "You have posed us a problem," she said. Gwenna had gone off with the oldest girl, for reasons I guessed after seeing them speaking together in low tones. Better here than during our travels, I thought, and we'd be home again in less than a month. But it reminded me I had a package of anash to give Betis: the plant did not survive this far north.

"And that is?" I asked.

"The princess should have the best room. Unless I ask Hairle to move back with his brothers, we only have Nyle's room unoccupied, so you and Druisius will have to share. And that is disrespectful to a *scáeli.*"

"I am not here as a *scáeli,*" I said. "Sharing is not a hardship. But do not call Gwenna 'the princess' in her hearing. She is not fond of the title."

"She did not baulk when your brother called her 'my lady'," Druise said. He'd been quiet throughout the meal. "She is beginning to accept who she is, I think."

I had noticed. "Just use her name, Betis. Let her be just a girl a little longer."

Roghan came back in from outdoors. "Are you coming, Sorley? The barley is doing very well this year, and we have new racks for drying the fish."

"All right," I said, getting up. "Come, Druise. I've seen your *subura*; it's time you saw my childhood home."

Farming had been as foreign to Druise as his marketplace upbringing had been to me, but over the years at our *Ti'ach,* with me managing the *torp,* he'd learned some things. Enough to ask intelligent questions about how this thin land was kept fertile, and he made admiring comments about the horses.

After I'd inspected the fish racks and the horses, and greeted and spoken to a fair number of the *torpari,* we walked up the hill to look at the sheep. The breeze blew our voices away from the shepherd further up the slope:

I'd had to shout to acknowledge him. He'd only raised a hand, making no effort to join us.

"Roghan," I said, "I must tell you something. Druise and I killed three Marai men on Karlstorp's land, six days ago." I told him what had happened, but not Karl's part in it. "What do you know of them, and of Earl Gosta?"

He chewed his lip. "Gosta's hard-headed, but not stupid with it. Do you know who the third man was?"

"No. Just that he was perhaps a little younger than Eluf, wouldn't you say, Druise?"

"I think so." Druise had squatted, listening.

"So he could have been either Eluf's brother, or Lotar's father. What colour was his hair?"

"Dark," Druise said. "I thought odd, for a Marai."

"Then it was Eluf's brother, almost certainly. A little better for you."

"Better for me? I had given them my name, Roghan. Eluf knew I was a *scáeli*."

He was looking out to sea, reflexively watching the waves and the fishing boats. "Neither Eluf nor his brother have children old enough to farm the land by themselves. Gosta will send a steward for this harvest, but he'll want payment for taking that man from other work. I'd say pay it. It's not worth all — " He stopped, his eyes dropping.

"Speak freely," I said. "Druise is part of it."

"I see," my brother said. "Then — "

"Wait," Druise said, straightening. "I know some things, but not all. Cillian's choice, yes? I will go look at the ocean." Roghan and I stood silently until he was out of earshot.

"A good man, I think," Roghan said. "Loyal to Cillian."

"And even more so to Gwenna, who will be heir not just to Ésparias, but to her father's plans, some day. What were you going to say, Roghan?"

"Pay the price Gosta asks: it will not be unfair, and better you — we — are seen as magnanimous. You can say he did not know you were a *scáeli*, and the presence of a guard argued against it."

"We can't. Karl knows the truth, and I don't trust him to keep quiet."

"Ah. Can we not just be generous?"

"No. It weakens the traditional protection of the *scáeli'en*. They were riding armed, which is already against the terms that returned Sorham to us, and they attacked both a known *scáeli* and Ésparian royalty, although they did not know who she was. Ruar will never agree, nor — " I paused, thinking.

"What?" Roghan probed.

"They didn't know who she was," I said. "What if Ésparias paid the fee asked?"

He shrugged. "I doubt Gosta will care where the money comes from. But he is the smaller problem. Lotar's father has a hot head, not a hard one, and you robbed him of his heir. He'll want blood as well as coin. Who actually killed Lotar?"

"I did." A fine distinction, but the truth. He'd been dying: Gwenna's secca had pierced his liver. A minute or two more was all he'd had, but I had cut that short.

"Who knows that?"

"No one except the three of us, and you now."

He grimaced. "Druisius is an Ésparian officer. Gwenna is Ésparias's heir. Lotar's father may be hot-headed, but he'll not go after them. It'll be you."

"Or you," I said slowly. "You and your family."

"Possibly." No inflection, just agreement.

I swore. "I didn't mean to put Gundarstorp at risk."

"It's not the first time. There was more risk when I helped bring the young prince to safety." We turned by some mutual understanding, heading back down the hill to the path that ran along the cliff. Druise was looking out at the waves, and the seabirds wheeling and crying over the water.

"Come," Roghan said when we reached him. "Old Iosaf rarely stirs from his chair these days, but he'll want to see Sorley, and there will be *fuisce* to be had, I'm sure."

Druise adjusted the tuning of his *cithar*, sitting on the edge of his bed in the room we were sharing. "Iosaf barely cared I was here," I said, running a comb through my hair, "with you giving him something to wonder over and talk of until he dies. A man from Casil!"

He looked up. "So isolated here," he said. "A man from Ésparias would be excitement, I think."

"Possibly, for the *torpari*, at least. But even my own nieces and nephews are more interested in you than me." Druise adored children, the smaller the better, and they him. Roghan and Betis's youngest, five-year-old Lairís, hadn't wanted to leave his side.

"I am different." He was, of course, his dark skin making him stand out in Linrathe and Sorham. In Ésparias, where men from the southern coast and Leste served on the Wall, his appearance wasn't remarkable, a matter of degree rather than sharp contrast. He put down his instrument. I bent to kiss him.

"Careful," he said.

"I bolted the door. I didn't want Lairís following you in here."

"Lairís should be at a *Ti'ach*." He grinned at me. "Are you sure she's not yours? You were here six years back."

"Of course she's not," I said. It was another old tease between us, ever since I had told him about Bjørn, and then Bearga.

"Could she not come back with us?"

"She's five," I said. "No. Why are you suggesting it?"

"She sang for me earlier," he said. "Her voice is pure. Apulo could teach her so much."

"Really?" I shook my head. "Even so, there is a *Ti'ach* half a day's ride away now, and its specialties are the same as ours."

"I suppose. I miss little ones. Lena and Cillian should have had more children."

"Not from lack of trying, as you so embarrassingly told Gwenna," I said with a chuckle.

"I had reasons," he said.

"I know," I replied. I put a hand on his shoulder. "She needs to be sure of them."

After dinner we played and sang, all the family joining in. Music had always mattered at Gundarstorp; it was why my father had agreed to my years at the *Ti'ach*, and why, I had realized some years ago, he had chosen Betis for me: she played the *ladhar* with skill, and sang well. Maj, like his first wife, my mother, had musical talent too, clear indication of its value to my father.

But while they all could sing with some proficiency, Lairís's voice was exceptional, I had to admit. "Can she play?" I asked Betis, taking her aside while Druise tuned his *cithar* to play a Casilani song or two.

"I am teaching her, yes," she said. "She knows when the *ladhar* needs tuning, and she has started to pick out melodies I haven't shown her."

I clicked my tongue, thinking. "She should have proper instruction, later," I said. "Not that yours is not," I added hurriedly. "But with that voice, she could be a *scáeli*, Betis. Would you like me to ask Eithnë if she could ride over from the *Ti'ach* to give her lessons occasionally?"

"Oh," she breathed. "How I would have loved that. Yes, if Roghan does not object."

"Why would he? Shall I ask him, or you?"

"I will," she said. She glanced at her family, but they were immersed in Druise's music. "Sorley, I — I was upset, a little, when my father told me I was to marry Roghan instead of you. Because of the music. But not for long."

I could have married her, I reflected. Could have fathered heirs, probably, if nothing more. But it would have been a false life, and unfair to both of us.

She smiled, looking younger than I knew she was. "He will want the best for Lairís, and if you say she might be a *scáeli*, well, it is an honour for the family."

"A different life, for her."

"That is not a bad thing. We are not all meant for the same fate." Her eyes went to Gwenna, sitting between their oldest girl and Hairle. "Although I would not want hers," she said softly.

<h1 style="text-align:center">Chapter 56</h1>

THE NEXT DAY I went down to the harbour with Roghan before the fishing boats went out, to talk to the men who crewed them. The fishing was good this season, they told me, not halting their work but letting their hands do the familiar tasks while they talked. We watched them set off on the tide, and when the last boat was out in deep water we turned to go back to the fields. Hauled up on the shingle and roped securely was another boat, not so different than ours, and yet not the same. I frowned. "Whose is that?" I asked, indicating it with a jut of my chin.

"The lord Vidar's. Earl Aaro's son. He came — "

"I know," I said. "We met them on the road. He was in Linrathe to see Cillian, with a proposal or two. I'd thought he'd have gone home by now."

"He's also the Lady Helvi's cousin," Roghan reminded me. "Perhaps he's spent some time with her."

"Perhaps," I said, not really listening. "Is this just the shortest distance between Varsland and Sorham, or did he land here because he counts you as a friend?"

"A friend," Roghan answered.

"I wonder," I said, thinking aloud, "if he would assist us in convincing Lotar's father to forgo demanding blood."

We continued walking, Roghan hissing a little through his teeth, a habit he'd had since boyhood when he was thinking. "Did you really kill Lotar?" he asked abruptly.

"Yes," I said, "in that I cut his throat. But he was dying when I did."

"Who, then?"

"Gwenna. She put a secca into his gut."

He made a face. "That can't be known. Those in Varsland who think Fritjof was a hero already hate her mother. Eluf and his brother were firmly in Fritjof's camp; Lotar's clan weren't so open with their thoughts, being merchants, but the sympathies were there."

"I have no intention of allowing it to be."

"What would you tell Vidar?"

"That we were attacked unprovoked. Lotar threw an axe at Druise. In the melee he was wounded to the death. I put my sword in his hand before I cut his throat."

"Mercy and an honourable death. The same for the others?"

"Yes. Druise didn't like it, but I insisted."

We'd reached the barley fields. Roghan bent to pull ears from a few plants, giving me half before biting down on his. "Four or five more days," he said.

I chewed. "I agree. The next field looks greener."

"It was planted later. It rained for a week just after we sowed this one." I nodded. Vagaries of weather always challenged farmers, here or further south. "They were buried properly?"

It took me a second to realize what he meant. "I left the burial to Karl. But I'd think so."

"More than they deserved, then," Roghan said, spitting out remnants of the barley. "I can tell Vidar all this?"

"Everything except Gwenna's part."

"Then when he comes back, I'll tell him what happened, and I'll go to Varsland with him. Put the case to the king." He crouched, feeling the soil under the barley stems. "Can you convince Ésparias to pay compensation?"

"One way or the other." The money might flow from Ruar, or some of it, but any payment to Varsland would come officially from south of the Wall. We had worked too long to weave our web of alliances for one group of rogue Marai to sweep it away. "Can you go to Varsland at harvest? Won't you be needed?"

"Hairle's here. Might delay him going to the *Ti'ach*, though, not that he'll mind." He stood up, wiping his fingers on his breeches.

"About that." I told him what I'd said to Barì: history and politics, and managing the *torp*.

"Where's the land come from?"

"Karl and Pietar." I'd stopped to see Pietar on the way here, his lands lying between the *Ti'ach* and Gundarstorp.

"By Rögnir, Sorley, what made them do that? Now I have to do the same."

"You won't miss it," I said cheerfully. "I was thinking the west side of Beinn Agheàr, and the sheep hefted to it."

"You were, were you?" He stared up at the hills. "It's closest, it's true."

"You can send a *torpari* lad, too, and his bride if he has one. Fair compensation for the lessons Lairís will be having." Eithnë would come, I knew. As head of the council I could require it of her, but I wouldn't need to: she'd leap at the chance to shape a voice with the potential Lairís's had.

Roghan swore, but there was no heat behind it. I grinned. "I'll write a song," I said, "about the generosity of three *Härren* in the bleak north." He growled something, and punched me lightly on the arm.

"Gods," he said. "I miss you, brother. Come home more often, won't you?"

Late in the day the wind began to blow from the northwest, heavy clouds rolling in over the sea. I stood in the courtyard of the hall with Roghan, looking at the sky. "Every year," he said in disgust. "A ten-day more, and we'd have that barley harvested."

The rain began no more than an hour later. It continued all the night, and in the morning it still rained, steadily, the wind hard enough to make candles gutter in the house and the fireplaces smoke. Other than the most necessary work — milking the cows, feeding the stabled horses — we stayed in. Not idly, of course, or not all of us. I sat with Roghan and Hairle, tallying the expected worth of the fleeces this year, and discussing markets. For all the ten years since Ruar's marriage to Helvi, I'd come back to Gundarstorp every couple of years, and my brother had always treated me as if the estate was half mine. Perhaps had I not been effectively the factor for the *Ti'ach*, he might not have, but the price of wool and the grain harvest were my concern there too, even if I left the day to day management to others now.

Betis and Maj and the oldest girl had the endless work of women, cooking and mending, and if that was temporarily done there was always wool to spin. Druise and Gwenna played, Gwenna using my *ladhar*, and the women sang as they worked. The rain drummed on the roof.

After the midday meal, we lingered at the table. "How do you know all the northern tunes?" Betis asked Druise.

"Sorley taught me, over the years," he said. I had just turned to Roghan to pour him more ale from the jug on the table, in time to see the flicker of sudden comprehension on his face. He glanced from me to Druise, and back again, tension visible — to me, at least — in his jaw and throat.

"Tell us about Casil?" Hairle asked. "It is your home, isn't it?"

"Was," Druise said. "I came to Ésparias fifteen years ago. It is a city, Hairle, thousands of people, and huge buildings, and always many ships at the harbour." He continued his stories, speaking of the aqueducts that brought water from the hills, and the sewers that kept the city clean, and the massive bread ovens that helped to feed the people. Lairís slipped off her chair to crawl up on Druise's lap. He shifted to make room for her, cuddling her close with one arm the way he had used to hold Gwenna. "*Philomela,*" he said to her. Nightingale.

"Lairís!" she said in protest, and we all laughed, even Roghan. But in the late afternoon, he indicated the door with a movement of his head. "Hairle, you feed the penned cows. Sorley and I will see to the horses."

In the stable, smelling of horse and hay, he pulled the door closed behind us. Dim light filtered in through tiny gaps. "Druisius," he said.

"Is my companion, Roghan. What difference does it make? You know the truth about me."

"There is knowing, and seeing."

"Seeing what?" I kept my voice down. "What have we revealed? Or are you worried about Hairle? His desires are set, Roghan. You've seen how he looks at Gwenna."

"Gods, Sorley." He had picked up a leather bucket in preparation for filling the water trough. Now he put it down again. "I — you are my brother, so I made myself not think about — that side of you. But Druisius — " He swore. "I like him, Sorley."

I couldn't help laughing. "And why shouldn't you? I assure you that some of the other men you know and like have the same appetites, kept well-hidden."

He grimaced at that. "I suppose," he said. "Other *scáeli* — well," he shrugged. "But Druisius is a soldier."

"Roghan," I said, "what in Rögnir's name does a man's choice of bedmates have to do with how well he wields his sword?"

He stared at me for a moment, and then he began to laugh, hard enough that he leaned against the stable wall for support. "And how well does he wield his sword?" he asked.

"Extremely well," I said, grinning.

In the long summer twilight, the clouds and rain now blown eastward, we walked up to the barley fields. Much of the grain lay flat. Roghan clicked his tongue. "Harder work for the men," he said. At the greener field, he shook his head. "It will mould before it ripens. We'll try to rake it, but likely I'll turn the cattle out on it in the end."

"Will you go short this winter?"

"No. Just less to trade. There's good yield on the ripe fields." He looked westward. "Decent weather for a few days now, I think. If this wind stays strong, it'll help dry the barley." The baa-ing of sheep drifted down from the hills, and from below the cliff I could hear seals barking. Everything I had missed. But suddenly I saw Cillian in my mind, chuckling as he took a piece in *xache*; saw him presiding gravely over the meal table, questioning the *daltai*; the softness in his eyes when he looked at Lena. My silver bracelet on his wrist; the tone of his voice, sometimes, when he spoke my name. His fingers brushing mine. Longing surged.

I felt Roghan's eyes on me. "We need to begin our journey back soon," I said. "Gwenna has to be back at the White Fort in a few weeks."

"Tomorrow," he said, "Hairle and I are going, separately, to talk with the neighbouring *Härren*, to agree on a price for the fleeces the Marai will soon come to trade for. I'll go east; he'll go to Pietarstorp. We could ride together that far, if you like."

"I would. But, Roghan, should I stay, to go to Varsland with you? Druise can take Gwenna home without me." I hadn't planned to say that.

He smiled, a little sadly. "No. Not that I wouldn't like you to. I don't have your *scáeli's* ability to convince, but if it goes wrong — well, you're needed more than me. If the worst happened, Hairle's old enough to be *Harr*."

"No," I protested.

"Be sensible," he said. "Like it or not, your death would be a greater loss. Head of the *scáeli'en* council, advisor to the *Teannasach* — and you're needed at your *Ti'ach*, too. For teaching, and more. You're an important man, Sorley."

What he was saying was not different than what I had told Gwenna when she had asked why Eluf had to die. "I'll write a letter for you to take," I said. "At least I can acknowledge my part in it, and my responsibility."

He nodded. "I won't leave too early. Go for a walk, one last look at the sea, and we'll leave mid-morning. Hairle's got further to ride, so I'll send him off before you leave."

"Better that way," I said.

"There's no chance, is there?"

"None. She's only fourteen, Roghan, and regardless, she's — "

"Ésparias's heir. A princess. She'll have to marry someone important."

"Likely, yes." Were there plans for her? A conversation to be had.

He shrugged. "He'll get over her."

"Perhaps. I hope he does."

"Because you didn't?" my brother asked, his eyes still on the western sky. He put a hand on my shoulder. "You can come home, you know," he said. "Bring Druisius. We'll find a place for you, both of you."

Tears pricked, hot behind my eyes. I put my hand on his. "I can't," I said. "My appointment as *scáeli* to the *Ti'ach* is for life, and Druise is an officer in the Ésparian army. And — "

"And you will never leave him."

"Not again, no."

His hand tightened on mine, then let it go. "Gundarstorp is here, if you ever change your mind. Hairle will know my wishes."

CHAPTER 57

13 YEARS EARLIER

DUSK HAD FALLEN WHEN I rode into the stableyard, drenched by the day's rain, and cold. I was looking forward to a bed tonight: for the past days, I'd slept rough, or in barns. I hadn't wanted the hospitality of the *Eirënnen*, hadn't wanted to be *toscaire* or *scáeli*. I had too much to think about.

I dismounted, and a man I didn't know came out from the stalls, peering up at me in the dim light. I'd hoped it might be Anndra. "Lord Sorley," I told him, "with a letter for the Lady Dagney."

"My lord." He led my horse away. I had just picked up my saddlebags when a figure stepped out from the shadow.

"Sorley," Druisius said. I dropped the bags.

"*Druise*? What are you doing here?" I stepped forward to embrace him, but he offered his arm, the soldier's greeting. I felt a twinge of disappointment, but no surprise. "Tell me, Druise."

"The *Princip* sent me. I will explain later. Come," he said, with a shake of his head when I tried to ask again. Confused, I followed him along the familiar path, the rain and growing wind making talk difficult. At the steps into the hall he turned. "Give me your bags." He opened the door, and I went in, rain dripping off my hair, blinking in the light.

I pushed my hair back. From beside the table where she stood speaking to Dagney, Lena turned. And froze, staring at me. I couldn't move, either. She said my name, barely a whisper. Her face showed me nothing.

I stood still, suddenly colder, waiting for her to turn away. With a tiny part of my mind I heard Druise's receding footsteps on the flagstones of the hall. I straightened, preparing to accept judgement. "Lena?"

"How dare you come here?" she said. Dagney made a sound of protest.

"The *Teannasach* sent me," I said, "with a letter for Dagney. I didn't know — "

"Sorley," Cillian said from the annex door, as calmly as if I had only been gone for a week or two. "*Mo duíne gràhadh*. I have been waiting for you." He held out his free hand.

"Cillian," I said, not moving. "I — I'm wet. I can't — I will give Dagney her letter, and there are things I must say. I was going to Wall's End, to find you," I managed. "And then I will go away again."

"Why?" he asked, very quietly.

"I cannot stay. You will not want me to."

"That is for me to judge, is it not?" His dark eyes studied me. He was still so thin, and I thought his hair greyer. "Not just now, though. Shall we sit, and share wine?"

"A very good idea," Dagney said. "Sorley, my dear, welcome."

"I will not drink wine with him," Lena said. "I am going to our rooms, Cillian. I suppose he'll have to stay the night, but I want him gone in the morning."

"But I do not," Cillian said evenly. She stared at him, her shoulders high. "Stay, *käresta*, please?"

"If I stay," she said, "I will not be quiet. Is that what you want?"

"Say what you need to, Lena," I said. "I deserve it."

She took a deep breath, and let it out, a long exhale of frustration. "Not now," she said. "I will not spoil everyone's relief at knowing you are safe."

"Thank you," Dagney said. "Druisius, will you pour wine for us all?"

"No," Cillian said. "I will. I always do." He limped to the table where a jug stood, along with cups. Propping his cane against a chair, he poured the wine, handing the first cup to Dagney. The next he gave to me.

"It's yours," Lena said, as I offered it to her.

"No," I said. "Always you, first, Lena." She grimaced, but she took the cup. Druise was given his. Cillian held mine out; this time, our fingertips brushed as I took it, his familiar gesture of affection. My heart caught.

"My lord Sorley," he said. "We have missed you. Welcome back."

We drank, still standing. "Dagney," I said, my confused mind remembering. "Your letter." I found my bags and handed it to her. Inside it was another note, which she gave to Cillian. She glanced at the content of hers: whatever was in Ruar's letter pleased her. But she folded it again, and made no mention of what it said.

"Tell me," I said, the first shock subsiding a little. "How are you here? Why?"

"Sit down," Cillian said. We took chairs around the long table, Cillian sitting at the head. "We are here for my safety, among other reasons," he began. "I am a target, it appears."

"Someone tried to kill him," Lena said bluntly.

"What?"

"I was riding with Druisius, the usual route east along the Wall," Cillian said, calmly. "The man — presumably — was on the Linrathan side of the Wall. Druise saw movement just in time, and slapped my horse."

"Druise," I said, turning to him. "Thank the gods."

"My job," he said, shrugging.

"Who?"

"It is unclear," Cillian said. "Druise stayed with me to ensure I wasn't unseated, rather than pursue the archer."

"A good thing he did," Lena said flatly. "Trying to stay on a galloping horse wrenched Cillian's back. Badly."

"I am better now," Cillian said. "More importantly, Randall was found stabbed to death the next morning. Stabbed and robbed, but that may not have been the motive."

"He was Linrathan too," I said.

"One possibility," Cillian said, "and a likely one, as this happened only a few days after Daoíre and Ruar had met with the Governor."

"Resentment about the perception the treaties favoured Linrathe," I said. "And you the negotiator." The simmering anger finally acted upon?

"Yes. Although I was careful not to be involved with their meetings with Livius, I did, of course, meet with them privately. There are few secrets at Wall's End."

"Someone knows who killed Randall, and tried to kill you, yes?" Druise said. "But maybe not about the treaty."

"What then?" I asked.

"Maybe Randall knew too many of someone's secrets. Whose translator was he for many weeks? And who hates Cillian?"

I stared. *"Decanius*?"

"Another possibility," Cillian said. "There is no proof."

"But for Cillian's safety," Lena said, "we have been sent away. Once he could stand to travel, heavily drugged. We came here in a cart, a few hours a day."

"Drugged?" I asked.

"Cannabium and willow-bark, nothing more," Druise said.

"There is no poppy here, nor will there be," Cillian added. "Do not worry."

"Do not worry?" Lena snapped. "You were ill half the winter, and worrying about Sorley did not speed your recovery. Have you forgotten the anguish, and because of that the cravings, and the sleepless nights? The melancholy? I have cursed your name more than once this winter, Sorley, and you deserved it."

"I know," I said. "I did. I do. I am not staying, Lena."

She put her wine down abruptly, turning away. Her shoulders heaved. Cillian put a hand on her back. "Yes you are," she said through the tears. "You must." She scrubbed at her eyes before she looked up. "Remember what I said." She gave me a hard stare. "Not about not forgiving you. About bindings."

You brought him back from death. I believe you are bound to him by that, and he to you. She'd spoken the words on a morning at the end of summer. I hadn't forgotten. What she'd said had been unexpected, but with a deep ring of truth, of inevitability, like so much that had happened in the previous hours. I couldn't find anything to say.

"He thinks," Cillian said, "he has done something I will not forgive. Or is it still I who have made it impossible for you to stay?"

"No," I said. "Not you. I — I see things differently now, Cillian."

"Take Sorley to your library," Dagney said. "This is between you and him, Cillian, not for all of us to hear."

"Everything is for the four of us," Cillian said.

"Not everything," Druise said. "Not this. Lena agrees, I think."

"Yes," she said, sniffing a little. "Druise is right. This is private."

Cillian pushed himself to his feet. "Come, Sorley," he said. I followed him to the annex door. His library? But of course, his small bedroom would not be big enough for him and Lena. There would be larger rooms somewhere, maybe even several together, as a nursery was needed, too. Dagney must have prevailed with the new *Comiádh*, whoever that was, to allow him to keep his old room for his books.

But the door he opened was one down from his bedroom. Shelves lined the walls, and a table piled with papers stood near the middle of the room. A *xache* game, partially completed, sat on a sideboard beside a flagon of wine and two cups. In the interior wall was a door, the mortar around the stones indicating it was new. Cillian followed my eyes.

"What was once my bedroom is now my treatment room," he said, without inflection. "Apulo sleeps on its far side, just as at Wall's End. Now, my lord Sorley, sit, and tell me why you feel you cannot stay." He hadn't touched me, hadn't offered an embrace again.

"I do not deserve your trust," I said. I didn't sit.

"I doubt that."

I ploughed ahead. "There are two things I must tell you, and they are not trivial. But I don't know how to begin, because I don't know which transgression is worse. One involves my trust in you, and one your trust in me. Where should I start?"

"I know how I lost your trust," he said immediately. "The other is likely erroneous."

I shook my head. "It's not. But there is more to the first than — than the obvious." I took a breath. "Even before Liam died, I thought — not voluntarily, Cillian, but once the idea appeared, I couldn't ignore it — that you had manipulated me, used my feelings for you to convince me to sign away Sorham." I forced myself to meet his eyes, expecting anger. It wasn't there.

"Can I fault you for that?" he said. "You know what I did as a *toscaire* for many years, and you know what I would have done in Casil to secure the treaty. You made a logical conclusion, and one I should have seen you might reach. But did you, in the light of day, believe your thoughts?"

"I would like to say I didn't. But I was not myself, for some time." I told him of the beating, seeing him wince in pain at my description, and the days of near-delirium and the angry, circling thoughts that followed. "Then I did believe it could be true. Perhaps because I deserved it to be," I added, seeing for the first time the connection between my duplicities.

"Because you believe you broke my trust? Should I not be the judge of that?" He reached out, touching my arm to stop my pacing. "But finish this first confession. What do you think now? Did I coerce you to give up Sorham?"

"What do you think I think?" I said crossly. "No."

"No. I will swear to that, if you like."

I shook my head. "It isn't needed. I know you didn't. But when I found out what you had done, the negotiations with Varsland — I was horrified. Appalled. You betrayed Linrathe."

"I cannot deny that," he said. "Nor will I make excuses. I hated what I had done, and hated myself for doing it. I knew what the outcome might be, the Marai influencing Linrathe's choice of leader. But I could not allow you to be cast out of your family as a result of my actions. The first I thought I might mitigate, somehow. What could I have done, if the second had occurred?"

"So you chose to protect me," I said. "A vow to replace the one you had broken."

He leaned back, regarding me. "You read my diaries," he said quietly.

"Yes. I am ashamed that I did. You see why you cannot trust me." I managed, just, to keep my voice steady.

"But you were free to read them."

I didn't understand. "How can you say that?"

His lips twitched. "Because I told you to."

"What?"

He smiled, quirking an eyebrow. His amusement irritated me, suddenly. Too much had happened, too quickly. "If it is truth you seek, remember the *xache* game," he murmured.

Almost the last thing he'd said to me before I had ridden north. In a flash of understanding, I realized he'd been referring to his childhood game, stored in the chest above his diaries. Irritation flared into anger, deep and hot. *The anguish, and the sleepless nights, and the melancholy,* Lena had said. Hadn't I suffered all those too?

"Why didn't you just say, rather than make me decipher your cryptic words? I hated myself for what I'd done." I snapped. "You arrogant bastard."

He closed his eyes. I pushed away the impulse to apologize.

"Both are undeniable," he said after a minute, "although I failed you not from arrogance this time, but because I needed to deny myself the ease of simply asking you to read what I had written at the time. But in punishing myself I punished you too, and for that I am sorry, *mo duíne gràhadh*."

"Can't you ever take the easier path?" I growled. "You and your accursed inclination to self-sacrifice, Cillian. I don't care if you over-water your wine, or eat too little, but when your self-denial hurts others, you have gone too far, regardless of what your god Catilius says."

"Do not lay this at Catilius's hearth," he said. "The fault is mine, and mine only. You are not wrong."

"Not wrong?" I said. "I am fucking well right, and you know it."

We stared at each other for a heartbeat, and another. "I see my vow is no longer needed," he said.

"What? Oh, gods, Cillian, you are annoying." I grabbed the other chair, turning it, and sat down. "No, it isn't. I am past needing protection. And you are avoiding answering. Are you going to admit I am right?"

"Completely."

"Say it. No circumlocution."

"You are right. My tendency — no, my habit — of negating my own desires, of not choosing the easier path has served me well, even in this last year. But I have overlooked its effect, in some cases, on those I love." He ran a hand through his hair. "Will you forgive me?"

"It was I who was to beg forgiveness."

"Unnecessarily." He reached out, touching my fingers with his for a second. The silver bracelet glinted on his wrist. "Sorley, I want you to stay. But in fairness you must know your alternative, or one of them: Ruar would like you to succeed Bhradaín as *scáeli* to Dun Ceànnar."

"He didn't tell me that."

"I persuaded him not to. I thought perhaps I had a prior claim. Was I wrong?"

"I don't know," I said. "I don't know anything, Cillian. I didn't expect you to be here. I came to give Dagney a letter. I'm wet and cold and I wish there were baths."

"There will be, soon. Druisius and Apulo are building them. But the existing bathhouse still has its tubs, and I will wager that Apulo has anticipated the need."

"Druise," I said. Another confusion. "He chose to come?"

"Assigned as bodyguard to me and Ésparias's heir," Cillian said. "But do you really think he would have let Gwenna out of his sight?"

I smiled, wearily. "Not for a moment." As I stood my eyes fell on the *xache* game. Cillian followed my gaze.

"The pieces stand as you and I left them," he said. "It is your move, I believe."

The bath was ready, and afterwards I declined dinner. Exhaustion suffused me. I couldn't face Cillian again, or anyone. Apulo led me to a bedroom.

"What do you need?" he asked. "Soup, maybe?"

"Soup," I agreed, and a little later he brought me soup and *fuisce*. I drank half the soup, and all the *fuisce*, and then I slept.

CHAPTER 58

CHAPTER 58

Hunger woke me halfway through the morning. I dressed and found my way to the kitchen and Isa, who gave me a hug in greeting. "Lord Sorley," she said. "Is it breakfast you want?"

"Yes, please," I said. "Isa, I am not Lord Sorley to you."

"You must be," she said, handing me a cup of tea. "You are a *scáeli* now."

She was right; there were formalities and protocols at a *Ti'ach*. "If I must be the Lord Sorley, what do you call Cillian? Is he Lord Cillian now?"

"Ah, you always did like to tease," she said, smiling broadly. "He is *Comiádh*, is he not?"

Comiádh? I put down the tea. "Where is he?" I asked.

"In his library. But drink your tea while I make your porridge."

"Later," I said. "I'll come back for it."

The door to the library stood open. He looked up as I entered. "When were you going to tell me, *Comiádh*?" I asked.

"Had you not been so sure you could not stay, I would have told you last night," Cillian said. "But it seemed inappropriate, given your anger. Your entirely legitimate anger, I would add. To mention it then would have appeared I was attempting to distract you."

"But how? You are a prince of Ésparias, and their senior diplomat."

"I am not a prince here. That was one of my conditions, when Ruar made the offer. I am only the *Comiádh*, here by the grace of the *Princip* and the generosity of the *Teannasach*. An arrangement that suited them both."

"And suits you and Lena, too, and Dagney must be so pleased. It was what you wanted. I am happy for you, Cillian." I said, meaning it.

He didn't smile. "I had one other condition for Ruar," he said. "Dagney wishes to retire soon. I told you yesterday I want you to stay, Sorley. The letter you brought confirms your appointment here, to teach music and oversee the *torp*. If you wish, of course."

If I wished? *Scáeli* to the *Ti'ach na Perras*. But no, I realized. The *Ti'ach na Cillian*. A lifetime at his side. All I had ever dreamt of, once.

"What does Lena say?"

He did smile, then. "She will be somewhere around the house," he said. "Go ask her. She won't take her secca to you."

I found her in the kitchen, feeding Gwenna milk and oatcakes. I'd forgotten how much a baby grew over a winter; Gwenna had dark eyes, and a cloud of dark hair. I received a doubtful frown, and her thumb went to her mouth.

"Don't take it personally," Lena said. She'd given me a level look, nothing more, when I came in. "She's forgotten you." She offered her daughter another piece of oatcake. Gwenna took it in her chubby hand, and then, with her father's radiant smile, held it out to me.

I took the piece of biscuit. I turned it in my fingers, then gave it back to her. She giggled. I thought I saw a tiny softening around Lena's eyes.

"Will you talk to me?" I asked quietly.

Her lips tightened. "In our rooms. If you must."

"Let the Lord Sorley have his porridge, my lady," Isa protested. She put a bowl down in front of me.

I ate the porridge gratefully. "Gwenna is beautiful," I said, between spoonfuls.

"Of course she is," she said. "She looks exactly like Cillian. She is also willful and obstinate, more so every day."

"It is just her age, my lady," Isa said. "All mine were the same."

"Likely," Lena said. "But her first word was 'no'." She helped Gwenna finish her milk. "Are you done?" she asked me. "Then come."

I barely recognized what had been Perras's workroom. The table still stood near the fireplace, but most of the shelves and books had gone to the library in the annex, and without them there was room for more chairs, and a sideboard, nearly recreating their sitting room at Wall's End. Lena put Gwenna down on the floor, handing her the silver rattle. "You had it out with Cillian, I understand?"

"Gods," I said, flushing. "Lena, I swore at him. Everything was so sudden. I had planned to see you both at Wall's End, to explain, and beg forgiveness, before I went away again," I said. "Then finding you here — it was all too much. And now — *Comiádh*?"

"And you as *scáeli*, when Dagney retires. That is the plan."

"Maybe," I said. "Lena, can you…allow it? Will you forgive me?"

"You hurt him, Sorley, although he will deny it, and until Druise returned there was only Apulo and me to deal with the effects of that. It will take me a while to completely forgive you, but I must."

"Because Cillian wants you to?"

"No." Again, a softening around her eyes. "Or not only. Because angry or not, I find myself relieved you are safe."

"Thank you," I murmured.

"But beyond even that," she said, "we need you if we are to make an alliance among Ésparias and Linrathe and Varsland. Which is what we are working towards, is it not?"

You are a prince of Ésparias, and their senior diplomat, I had said. His answer had been precise: *I am not a prince here.*

"Lena," I said. "Should you speak of it?"

"No. Nor will I again. But that is why Ruar sent you north, isn't it?"

"He told you that?"

"He told Cillian. What he had sent you to do, and why, and also that he was grateful Cillian had made the suggestions of a marriage alliance ten years earlier. And then he offered to make him *Comiádh*." Her lips twitched, just a little. "Now I have seen Cillian speechless twice."

"Ruar is already an impressive *Teannasach*," I said. We fell silent, watching Gwenna, or at least Lena was. I studied her, seeing how thin her face was, and the lines between her eyes. My fault. I took a deep breath. "Did you know what Cillian had done?"

"No." She didn't look up. "But it explains his reaction to hearing Linrathe had fallen to the Marai. You remember he said it was his doing? He saw, I think, his work for Liam as shaping that outcome, and maybe he is not entirely wrong."

"Maybe. We cannot know." Gwenna dropped her rattle, and grasping the low table in front of her, pulled herself up to bang on its surface with one hand.

"It explains something else, too," Lena said, her voice unemotional. "In the first days of our exile, I told Cillian about Maya, before I asked him his preferences. Women, he said, and one man, a relationship unexplored. When we met you and Turlo on the river, and I realized you were that man, I asked him why he had rejected you when you were eighteen."

"What did he say?"

"That he would have torn your heart out. I thought then he was referring only to his self-denial and his melancholy. But he would have insisted on telling you about his broken oath, and why, and he was right, wasn't he? It would have been more than you could have accepted."

"It almost was now," I said, "and I am ten years older. He protected me, Lena, in more than one way. That was his vow to me, an oath to replace the one he had broken."

"He showed me what he'd written." She shook her head slightly. "By the time he made a similar vow to me, he'd matured enough to understand protection isn't possible." She did look up then. "Shelter is, though."

"He has you to shelter him," I said.

"As best I can," she said. "That is all we can ask: that in our different ways, through our different loves, we shelter each other."

"Even me?"

"Even you," she said. "Because with all we have been to each other, and the love there is among us all—if we can't accept each other's faults and mistakes and needs, then how can we ask as much from our countries? So in time, yes, I will forgive you." She met my eyes now. "But not quickly."

Among us all. There was another difficult conversation to be had, before I could decide if I could stay.

"Da!" Gwenna said loudly. "Da! Da!"

"Soon," Lena said. "She wants Cillian," she explained. "Gwenna has four words. 'No,' and 'da' for Cillian. Can you guess the others?"

"Ma, surely? And maybe something for Druisius?"

"'Du', yes. And 'ma', but," she smiled ruefully, "she uses it indiscriminately for me and for Mhairi. But she will be a child of the *Ti'ach*, won't she? Just as in Tirvan, she would have been a child of the village, although here she will know her father."

"Fortunate girl," I said.

"And will you be her music teacher, Sorley?" She sounded just a little less tense, I thought.

"I will tell you soon," I said. "I would like to be. But Druise and I haven't talked, and we must. Except for last night, I haven't seen him for almost a year, you realize." I hesitated. "Does he know?"

"Yes. Cillian told him. He was unsurprised."

I had guessed long since what Druise and Cillian had spoken of, in the days and nights it had taken to rid Cillian of his dependence on the drug. Druise had heard more than one secret, and learning that Cillian had chosen to act would not have been a surprise at all.

"I'll go look for him" I said. I stood, then bent to pick up Gwenna's rattle. I handed it to her, to be rewarded again with her smile. I smiled back before I turned to leave.

"Sorley."

I stopped at the door, looked back. "You will need time with Cillian, private time, if you stay," Lena said. "I know that. Don't let my anger stop you."

"You don't hate me, then?" I asked, with a faint smile. In her eyes I saw the flicker of memory; a conversation on a ship, two summers past.

"Cillian loves you," she said. "How can I hate anyone he loves?"

Chapter 59

I FOUND DRUISE AT the weapons store, a new use for the outbuilding
that had been the mews. The falcons had gone in the war; now blades and
bows hung on the walls. He was examining a sword when I came in.

"The blade is loose," he said. "We need a smith."

"An hour's ride north," I said. "But I expect you know that."

He grinned. "Of course." He put the sword in its place, and to my utter
surprise, opened his arms. "Come." He hugged me, long and hard. "I was
happy to see you safe," he said, when he let me go.

"And I you, Druise," I replied. "Can we talk, for a little while?"

"I am free, so yes. About what?"

"There is work for me here, a position. I cannot say yes unless you will
be comfortable with me being here." Best to be blunt, I thought.

"Comfortable? In what way?"

"We were lovers, Druise. But things have changed, haven't they? Life
will be different here."

He chuckled. "We have been here nearly three months, yes? We have
talked much, me and Lena and Cillian. I understand all the ways life will
be different."

"And?"

"I am here as bodyguard, yes? So I have been exploring, as a bodyguard
must. In the annex, on the top floor, there are three rooms behind a door,
bedrooms and a sitting room. A private place. If you like."

"If I like?" It took me moment to realize what he was asking. "Are you
saying — ? Still?"

He propped one leg up against the wall. "This is not a land friendly to men like us," he said. "Cillian has warned me, and Dagney. I am still young, and you are too. We are *congruus*, yes? In music and in bed." He grinned. "And it is cold here. I want a bedmate."

"But — " I began.

"I know you may be gone sometimes," he interrupted. "But not often, if what Cillian says is right. That is fine. Just as I will go to Wall's End occasionally."

"Maybe," I said slowly. "Druise, I have to think about this."

He shrugged. "Did I say you had to tell me now? But if you say yes, you must keep to the agreement we made once."

That would only be fair, and not difficult, here. A thought struck me. "What about Isa? She cannot know, Druise."

"You think I am an *idióta*?" he asked, grinning. "Apulo takes care of Cillian's rooms in the annex. He would do ours too. I have already asked him."

We ate a leisurely mid-day meal around the long table in the hall. There were no students yet: the first would arrive in a few weeks, Cillian told me. He did not press me for an answer. Nor did we talk of politics, but of the progress of the baths, and the need for better horses for the *torpari* patrol. Cillian had refused any guard other than Druisius, I discovered, except that which the *torp* could provide. Druise was training them, both in weaponry and in scouting.

"We need beacon fires laid on the hilltops," Druise said, "and bells at cottages and on the tracks."

"That seems excessive," Lena said.

"You disagree, Captain?" he said seriously.

She grinned at him. "Just consider if you would suggest them if you were only guarding Cillian, Captain."

"Captain?" I said, looking from one to the other.

"Both of us," Lena replied. "My remit is to teach weaponry, another of the *Teannasach's* decrees, and Druise is captain of the guard here. But his promotion is a little newer, so I am senior captain, if that distinction is ever needed."

Dagney pushed her chair back. "I have your *ladhar*, Sorley. I have kept it tuned and played; it is a lovely instrument. Will you come and get it?"

I followed her to her teaching rooms. My instrument hung on the wall. In the daylight, the carnelians were a dull pink; they needed firelight to glow. "Can I just leave it there a little longer?" I asked.

"You are staying, Sorley?" she asked.

"I think so. There are still things I need to consider, and things I must say to Cillian."

"Do not tell me," she said firmly. "Better I do not know. I will not be here, to see this plan come to fruition or failure."

"This plan?"

"I have been at the *Ti'ach* a very long time, Sorley, and Perras taught or advised both Donnalch and his father. The *Teannasach* of Linrathe and the *Princip* of Ésparias agreed, or perhaps conspired, to make Cillian *Comiádh* here, and find roles for Lena and Druisius, and you. Whatever the excuse around Cillian's safety or his health, or the Governor's growing displeasure with him, there is something more behind it. But I do not want to know," she repeated.

"But you are glad they are here."

The smile transformed her face. "I could hardly be happier. It was all Perras wanted. Cillian is a born teacher, and Lena is proving an apt student."

"Finding the words of the common people in the *danta*?" I said, remembering.

"A novel approach," Dagney said. "One you could assist with, my dear."

"If I stay. If I do, Dagney, there are rooms in the annex I might like." I explained.

"They were meant for visiting dignitaries," she said. "But you may have them, if you wish." She sat down, indicating I should do the same. "I want to tell you something," she said, "something I have already told Cillian and Lena. The proprieties of the *Ti'ach* require no expression of affection between them in public, and for you and Druisius there could be no hint of anything beyond friendship, of course. It is a strain to remember this, and always be on your guard. But you can do it. Perras and I did for most of our time here together."

It took me a moment. "You were lovers?"

"We were. From a few months after we both arrived."

"I had no idea."

"No one did, except Isa."

"Why didn't you marry?"

"Because it is forbidden for female *scáeli'en* to marry. Did you not know that? As a wife my freedom would be curtailed, and that is not appropriate for a *scáeli*, is it? But we were together, and then we had Cillian to care for, and that was enough."

"More than enough sometimes, I would guess," I said, grinning.

"Sometimes," she agreed. "But now you are both here, Perras's hoped-for heir, and mine. Our world has changed, irrevocably, but here in this tiny corner, things are close to being what I wished they could be, and I may have a few years to enjoy them."

"Not just a few, I hope," I said, before her words sunk in. "I was your chosen successor?"

"You were, and are. Just as you will be head of the council someday, I predict. A man of influence."

CHAPTER 60

I WALKED OUT THE kitchen door and along the stream that ran behind the *Ti'ach*, crossing it at the bridge. The long meadow lay ahead of me, rising at its far end to one of the hills where Druise wanted a beacon fire. Yesterday's rain had been followed by a day of sunshine and gentle breeze. Skylarks sang in the clear sky, and the first lambs leapt and butted with the joy of life.

I turned to look back at the hall. I could see Apulo and Druise and another man working on the new bath house, and Mhairi hanging washing — diapers, I guessed — from a line in the kitchen dooryard. Home? I had no other now. I was wanted here. I wanted to stay.

"Wipe your feet," Mhairi said to me, as I approached the door. The kitchen smelled of stew, tonight's meal. I crossed the empty hall to the annex, and Cillian's study.

He was at his desk. "Am I disturbing you?" I asked.

"Never." He stretched. "I am preparing lessons: the first students will be here at mid-summer, and Ruar perhaps earlier, or so he said in his letter."

"You did that for fifteen years," I said, entering the room. "How much preparation do you need to do?" I closed the door.

"I have not taught for three."

"And you have forgotten? Why do I doubt that?" He looked up at me, his smile lighting his eyes. "You seem very happy," I added.

"I am," he answered. "How could I not be? To be *Comiádh* after Perras was all I ever let myself dream of, although I told no one. That Perras too wanted it, I never knew."

"I wish I'd been there, to see your face when Ruar told you," I said.

"I was speechless," he said. "Ask Lena. I would have been content to be an additional teacher here, and continue my studies."

I snorted. "Lena might believe that. I don't."

He laughed. "Sorley, *mo duíne gràhadh,* you know me too well."

My beloved man. I wanted to hold him, to feel his hands on my back and his lips on my hair. I took a deep breath. "Cillian. I did not just run away from you, from what I saw as a betrayal."

"It was a betrayal," he said. "But go on."

"I had made Ruar a promise, just after the Taiva, that I would help him regain Sorham. When he asked me to go north, to find out certain things, I could not say no. And I wanted to go home, Cillian. To Gundarstorp."

"Older loves," he said. "Older loyalties."

"Yes, in a way. But my father is dead, and I have given Gundarstorp to Roghan — I never went there; it was too dangerous for him and his family. And Ruar will not ask me to go north again. But if I stay; if I take this position, am I still working to free Sorham?"

"Do you think I would I ask you to forgo that?" Cillian asked. "Ruar marrying into Varsland is a beginning. It was in his note to me," he added. "But I envision more than that. We spoke of it once. Private plans, I said. Do I need to remind you?"

"No. It is still sedition, Cillian."

"It is. And because of that, only I can know all of it. I will keep the vows I made to shelter and protect, in this context."

"Then there is something you should know. Unless Ruar told you this, too? About Bjørn?"

"Bjørn? No. Who is he?"

"My *torpari*-born son," I said, watching his face, seeing the doubt. "Or that is what the world has been told. I brought him south with me, and he is at the *Ti'ach na Asgaill.* He is nine years old, Ásmund and Irmgard's youngest son, sent to Linrathe for his safety, and only I and Ruar, and now you, know who he really is."

Cillian sat back. "Is the older boy alive?"

"Yes." I told him of the earls, and the meeting at Dugarstorp, of the plan to declare a regency in Bryngyl's name. "I gave the names to Ruar," I said. "Everything I knew." I grinned. "I put them all to music, to remember them. I had to sing the songs to myself as I wrote them down, to remember."

"There is more than one way to train a memory," Cillian said. "Well done. What will you tell Druisius?"

"Blood runs high in young men," I said. "Girls were part of my — investigations. I would not have needed to explore much further for there to be a child among our *torpari*."

He nodded. "Lena will be told the same. I understand now why Ruar plans to arrive earlier than he had originally said. Will you be here, my lord Sorley, to join those discussions?"

All I had ever wanted, once, was to be a *scáeli*, and to be at Cillian's side. I hadn't counted — hadn't realized, in my innocence — the cost. The danger of uncharted ways. "How can I say yes?" I asked. His hand clenched, the knuckles white.

"What is stopping you?"

"You have not welcomed me, Cillian, not properly."

He laughed, deep in his throat, and pushed himself upright. He held out his arms. I went into them, feeling his hands tight on my back. He was too thin, fragile again after the winter's pain. One hand went to the back of my head before his kissed me, his lips moving from mine to my hair. I didn't try to stop the tears.

A few weeks later, I returned from riding the lands, evaluating flocks and the conditions of pasture with Anndra, who had been managing the *torp* competently. He also knew — as I did not — the exact boundaries, pointing out the standing stones and trees that defined them. We had more land than I had expected: a challenge to Druise and his *torpari* men to patrol.

At the stables, I heard Druise giving instructions. "Three horses, ready at dark." He'd learned basic Linrathan quickly, as he had Ésparian. I left my horse to walk up to the hall with him. "I am riding patrol tonight," he told me. "There is no moon, so the most dangerous time, and the men are not yet experienced. I will be gone until dawn."

"I see," I said. "Is there really a threat, Druise?"

He shrugged. "I do not know. But I have my orders." He touched my shoulder, an innocuous gesture. "You could play *xache* tonight. Cillian has been very patient.”

He was with Lena and Gwenna, in what was their living room when he wasn't teaching. I poured myself tea from the pot on the table, but I didn't sit. I still had work to do, and I was still unsure of my welcome from Lena.

“So-lee,” Gwenna said from the floor where she played at Cillian's feet. She pulled herself up, using my leg, and leaned her face against my knee.

“Fickle child,” Cillian said. I laughed. Lena stood.

“She needs changing. I'll take her to the nursery.” Gwenna slept with Mhairi, on the girls' bedroom floor. She picked Gwenna up, to a wail of protest, and carried her out.

“Does Anndra mind that you are overseeing the *torp* now?” Cillian asked.

“No. He says he's relieved; it was getting too much for him. And I need his advice and his knowledge. There is much to learn.”

“And to teach?” A tentative note in his voice. “The game is unfinished.”

“If you are not in too much pain, we could play tonight,” I said.

“A little cannabium and willow-bark will ensure I can,” he said. “After this winter…well, there are times they are appropriate, so that,” he grinned, “my inclination to self-sacrifice does not hurt the ones I love. Druisius will not mind?”

“He rides patrol all night, training the *torpari*. He made sure I knew. But Lena?”

“She was angry because you left me. Why would she now object to our time together? Did she not tell you that?”

“She did,” I said. She had meant it, I thought. “Tonight, then.” I put the cup down. “But I must go. I have accounts to review and a leaky barn to inspect. Anndra will be wondering where I am.” I bent to kiss his forehead. “Until dinner,” I said.

“Until dinner. And later, *Somhairle*.”

CHAPTER 61

15 YEARS AFTER THE BATTLE OF THE TAIVA

WE WALKED ALONG THE clifftop the next morning, Gwenna and Druise and I, looking down at the waves breaking on the rocks visible only at low tide. Seals basked, stomachs turned upward to the sun. Seabirds cried overhead, and black-and-white sea-pies fed among the rocks visible at low tide.

"It is so lovely here," Gwenna said again.

"But also cruel," I said. "Those rocks have taken more than one boat, and they killed my father."

"How?"

"He had waded out to try to help a fishing boat. A gale had blown up, out of nowhere, Roghan tells me, and the tide was rising. The boat had run onto one of the rocks and was sinking. My father was a big man, and strong, but a wave knocked him over. It is thought he must have hit his head, because he didn't come up again. They found his body on the beach the next day." Broken and torn by the force of the waves on the rocks, Roghan had said, but I didn't want to tell Gwenna that.

"Oh," she breathed. She slipped a hand into mine, to my surprise. A shout came from the hillside above us. Hairle waved in greeting from the back of his horse, then continued riding out of sight. "Where is he going?" Gwenna asked.

"To Pietarstorp, to discuss the price offered for wool this year."

"He's trusted with that?"

"Gundarstorp will be his one day," I said. "And Hairle is a man, in Sorham's eyes. I was doing the same at his age."

"A man," she said. She glanced up the hill again, to where Hairle had been. "This all should have been yours."

"I gave it to my brother," I said.

"But you still love it here." She shook her head in frustration. "That's not right. More than love, but I don't know how to say it."

"*Dùthcas.*" She looked up at me quizzically. "I can't translate it," I said. "Belonging is close. But more than that. I carry this place deep inside me, and I hear it calling to me, always. Cianalas, we say."

"Always?" I nodded. "Does my father know that?"

"He does."

"Did he, when you were sixteen?"

Had he, the wanderer with no ties of blood and memory to field and fell and sea? *You are home to him*, Lena had said once. Not all knowing was of the mind. "Yes," I said.

"He broke his oath so you could stay here. But you didn't."

"He kept me safe," I said. "I wasn't disowned. Leaving was my choice."

"To be with him."

"Yes."

"Druise said he isn't a hero. But he was trying to be, wasn't he? He thought he could keep you safe, and Linrathe, even though he was supposed to be working for Liam."

"That," I said with a grin, "sums up Cillian extremely well, Gwenna. A concerning tendency to self-sacrifice, I told his father once."

She smiled. "*Mathàir* would say it is Catilius's fault." She glanced up at me, and I felt her hand tighten, just a little. "Sorley, are you and my father lovers?"

I had waited for this the entire summer, and now, with no warning, the moment was here. I heard Cillian's voice: *Do not mislead her*. I took a breath.

"Yes," I said, for the third time.

Her body tensed. From the corner of my eye, I saw Druise move a step or two closer. If she ran, he could reach her. Her eyes, wide, worried, were on me. "Always?" she demanded.

"No. Since the year you were born."

Chapter 62

14 Years Earlier

I SHOULD HAVE TURNED left from my room, to reach the first exit from the building. But I didn't. I let my feet take me right, and right again to the corridor where Cillian's study was. Light flickered under the door. I stopped. My head pounded in time with my heart. No, I told myself. You are too angry. Keep walking. I continued down the corridor, toward the door that would take me out into the night.

Then I turned. At Cillian's door I knocked, my quick triple tap.

"Come," he called, just loud enough. I went in. He was contemplating the *xache* board, studying the game we had left unfinished. "Sorley," he said. "Have you come back to finish the game? It was your move."

I picked up a piece almost at random, moving it the requisite spaces.

"Are you sure?"

"Does it matter?"

He frowned a little. "You are still upset."

"Yes," I said.

He sat back. "Will you pour us both wine?" I did as he asked, but I didn't sit. "How do I make amends?" he asked. "I was dismissive, I admit."

I drank a little wine, for courage, although it would not help my head. "Before Druise left," I said, "he came to talk to you. About me. I overheard much of that conversation."

"I see," he said. "I believe I remember the conversation to which you refer. What do you think you heard?"

"That in your eyes I am still a boy," Anger blossomed again. "That I don't know you, and that I need to be treated carefully. Still, Cillian? After

Casil, after your illness, after trusting me with your plans? How dare you treat me as if I am a child?" I had never spoken to him like this. I could feel myself trembling.

The lamplight flickered. He picked up a *xache* piece, turning it in his fingers, his eyes hooded. I waited. His fingers tightened around the gamepiece. Deliberately, carefully, he put it down, spreading his fingers wide as he did. "You misunderstand," he said.

"Then use your vaunted skill with words to enlighten me," I replied.

"Will you help me up?"

I couldn't refuse. I put my wine down, moving around the table to offer him my arm. He gripped it with one hand, the other grasping my shoulder as he rose, the action pulling me towards him. My arms went around him, instinctively; he mustn't fall. Under my hands his breathing was shallow, rapid, as if he were in pain. Regardless, anger still seethed, behind the reflexive concern. Did he think an embrace, words of regret, were going to placate me? I stepped back a little, to say as much.

What I saw on his face stopped me. Not pity, or remorse, but something not revealed — not allowed, I understood somehow — since a spring night so many years before. Desire.

Anger became confusion, and then disbelief. He brushed the hair from my eyes with one hand, the beginnings of a smile on his lips. His hand moved to cup my cheek. I turned my head, joy and need rising. I kissed his palm, hearing his taken breath. "*Somhairle,*" he whispered, before his lips found mine, gently at first, and then not, not at all. His hand tightened on the nape of my neck. I moaned, my hands travelling to his hips, pulling him closer. His lips moved to my throat, making me shudder. "Do you understand now?"

I couldn't find words. "But… you cannot… Lena."

He laughed, softly. "Ésparias is not Linrathe. She is fully aware this moment might come, and she sees nothing wrong in it, although it has taken her some time to convince me she truly means what she says."

I fought for clarity. "How can I believe…" *If he decides the way I think he will, it is with my blessing.* "She told me too, but I didn't understand."

"It is for you to decide," he said. "To resolve, *mo duíne gràhadh.*"

"Why?"

"Because I have chosen twice for us, once at Gundarstorp, once at the *Ti'ach*. The third time decides the path: that is the saying. Or have I waited too long?"

I was not Gundarstorp's young heir, nor the student of music newly come to the *Ti'ach*, not now. I was innocent of my desires and my needs no longer, and what might have been between us once was only a dream. But that did not mean all paths were closed. I could not stop the trembling that had begun in my limbs. "No," I whispered. "Not too long."

His hand moved on my back. "I am," he said, "not capable of rugs by fires, now. Will you find the treatment bed…inappropriate?"

I shook my head. Words were beyond me. In the adjoining room, he indicated the door to where Apulo slept. "Lock that." He was lighting lamps. I pulled off my shirt, helped him with his, my fingers exploring the skin of his chest. He covered my hand with his. "You do realize, my lord Surley," he said, "you will have to teach me what to do?"

Spent, still not quite believing what had happened, I lay beside him, my hand on his chest, his arm around me, sensation still resonating. He hadn't needed much teaching. He kissed my hair, and I opened my eyes, smiling. I traced his lips with one finger. "I love you," I said.

"I have been so unfair to you," he murmured.

"No," I said. "It had to be this way, Cillian. Or you would not have Lena, or Gwenna, and I could not ask that."

"Nor I. She is as necessary to me as breathing."

"Your greatest love," I said, remembering. "She said…Cillian, she said she was afraid, a little, of…this. What might happen, as a result. But it won't, will it? You would never hurt her."

"Not even for you, no."

"This is just the once, isn't it? A memory to hold." A memory of tenderness and laughter, and a singing joy. He kissed my fingers, not replying. Loss and gratitude twisted inside me.

"Oraiáphon convinced the god to give his love back," Cillian said, almost inaudibly. "In all the stories, none said what was expected of her, in return for her life."

"An offering, then?" I said. No surprise, and no hurt; only an encompassing peace.

"An offering. A thanksgiving, too, and an atonement, *mo Somhairle gràhadh*," My beloved Sorley. I closed my eyes, breathing in his scent, willing myself to hold on to this moment. He spoke again. "But surely the god will need to be propitiated more than once."

Amusement in his voice. I opened my eyes. "But how can we?"

"How many nights have you kept me company with music or *xache* when I cannot sleep? Why should we not find other ways to enrich those times; not often, but occasionally? A grace note in our lives, you might say, rarely played."

A grace note. I liked that. "Will you tell Lena about tonight?"

"Of course."

"And if she discovers she is angry, or hurt?" I asked.

"She assures me she will not be. But you are suggesting we cannot decide what happens between us, until we are sure of her reaction, now what was only a possibility is real?"

"Yes."

"And Druisius?"

"He meant what he said." All the overheard words made sense now. "Pragmatic Druise. We are good companions, and maybe more, but he stays for you and Lena, and his beloved Kitten now as much as for me."

"Gwenna more than all of us. Druisius has found his higher loyalty in her, perhaps." He stretched, easing his leg. "Understand that I must follow the practices of the women's villages before I return to Lena, and I must be with her, or where she can easily find me, each morning. We reflect each other's vows, as best we can."

"She will always come first. I understand. But the practices?"

"Before a woman returns to her partner, after Festival, the baths are required. She has asked me to do the same." They had talked about this, planned for it. I couldn't imagine those conversations. "That means I must go to them very early. But morning is some hours away."

Chapter 63

15 Years After the Battle of the Taiva

GWENNA'S ARMS WENT AROUND me, hugging me tightly, her face against my chest. "I am so glad," she gasped. "I was afraid. I thought — I thought what I saw last year was something new, and if it was, and other people noticed, we might have to leave the *Ti'ach*. And *Athàir* loves it there, and we are safe."

"We've always been careful," I said. I met Druise's eyes over her back, making a face to reflect my bewilderment. He grinned, shrugging. "Or so I thought. But Gwenna, what did you see? Were we careless in front of you and the other *daltai*?"

"No," she said. "Never then, and I have been watching. Only in front of me and Colm. He won't have noticed," she added. "I did, though, the last time I was home. We'd had lessons, you see, on watching people, looking for what they were hiding, and I was practicing. We were having tea the day I arrived. You went to fetch *Athàir* another cup, and when you gave it to him, your hands touched…it was just how he looked at you, and you at him. I had seen it, between men, at the fort. And there were other times too, once I knew what to look for, but only when we are in our private rooms." She hesitated. "*Mathàir* seemed unhappy, too, watching you. She doesn't *mind*, surely?"

Druise chuckled. "No more than I do," he said. "I would know. Tell Gwenna what Lena said, Sorley."

"The same thing she has been saying for fourteen years," I said, matching Druise's grin. "And she was right, it turns out."

Chapter 64

IT WAS ONLY AN hour or two till dawn. I was fighting sleep now. "Cillian," I murmured. "I had best go back to my room. The guards should not see us together, not at this hour, and you have the baths to go to."

"You are probably right," he said. "For your sake, at the very least. Liam would not approve."

"No." I sat up, bending to pick up my clothes. Cillian watched me dress. "Do you need help?" I asked him.

"With the breeches, yes. I can manage the rest." When he had, I leaned in for a last kiss.

"Breakfast with us," he suggested.

"I can't."

"Why not?"

"For one thing," I said, "I need some sleep. So do you."

"Mid-day, then. In our rooms." His lips quirked. "Are you afraid to face Lena?"

"Yes," I admitted.

"You are shying at shadows, *mo duíne gràhadh*. Mid-day," he said firmly.

I fell asleep as soon as I reached my bed, waking late in the morning to lie in a cloud of incredulous remembrance and joy. My bruised lips and my general languor told me it had not been a dream, but the sense of unreality did not go away as I washed and dressed in fresh clothes. Nor had it gone when I knocked on Cillian and Lena's door.

Lena opened it. Reality returned in a rush. I tried to speak, but nothing came out. From across the room, Cillian said my name.

"Oh, gods," Lena said. "Get in here, Sorley." She tugged on my arm, closing the door behind me. "You cannot look at each other like that in public. Or anywhere you might be seen, and, *kärestan,*" she said, addressing Cillian, "that includes Apulo, and the nursemaid, and the kitchen staff." She sounded both exasperated and amused, and nothing more.

Cillian laughed, and came over to drop a kiss on her head. She leaned into him for a moment, shaking her head slightly, smiling. "Is anyone here?" he asked, as she straightened.

"No."

"Good," he said, and reaching out an arm, pulled me to him to kiss my hair. I felt myself flush.

"I imagine," Lena said drily, "you might be hungry, Sorley?" I still couldn't find words. "Oh, gods," she said again, and came to wrap her arms around me. "Foolish man," she said. "Did I not try to tell you?" She kissed my cheek. "Come and eat."

Chapter 65

15 years after the battle of the Taiva

"DO NOT LOOK AT each other like that," I repeated. How many times had Lena said it, over the years? "Your mother always warned us that we would give ourselves away. It was the only thing that worried her, and the real reason she shows little affection to your father when you and Colm are there. She thought it would remind Cillian and me to do the same."

"Well, she can stop being silly about being affectionate in front of me, and so can you," Gwenna said. "You could have told me at least two years ago, and then I wouldn't have been worried all this past winter. And you lied to me, Sorley, and I had asked you a direct question."

"When?"

"I asked if Apulo would have served my father, if he loved men, and you said he does not love men."

I grinned. "Nor does he," I said. "Only me, ever, Gwenna. You were not precise in your question."

"Oh," she said. "Sorley, that was unfair."

"A diplomat must learn to ask exactly what she wants to know."

"Then," she said, serious again, "answer this. We are not safe at the *Ti'ach*, are we? Not really?"

"In what way?

"There are still secrets, aren't there? *Athàir* is planning something dangerous."

"There are still secrets, yes," I answered slowly. "I can't tell you more, even if you were to ask me directly. I have been forbidden to."

"By *Athàir*?" She didn't wait for my answer. "Am I wrong, about the danger?"

The breeze pushed her dark hair over her face. She swept it off with graceful fingers, waiting for my answer. You are as beautiful as your father, I thought, and perhaps as brilliant, and you are heir to Ésparias. I had sworn an oath. "You are not wrong."

"But he vowed to shelter us, *Mathàir* and Colm and me. He's breaking that vow." Nothing she had heard at the White Fort, then. Her own mind, analysing, reaching conclusions.

"Shelter, Gwenna," I answered gently. "He has not promised to keep you safe, or to always shield you. Only to give you shelter, as best he can."

Her chin came up. She took a breath, and another, her eyes distant, unfocused, until she turned them back to me. "Is he making a mistake, Sorley?"

"I am a musician," I said, "and not a good enough *xache* player to know."

"Am I?" She had been no more than four when he had shown her how to set up the game, the pieces just the right size for her tiny hands. Fostering a skill.

"Not yet," I said. "I'm not saying you are a child, Gwenna. But you have much to learn still of tactics and strategy, and taking the long view."

"Then," she said, "should not *Athàir* teach me?"

"That is not all Lena said to you," Druise commented, back in the privacy of our room.

"No. But I have told Gwenna the rest before, and she'll realize that Cillian and I were lovers when I fled north, Druise."

"Cillian never saw anything to forgive," he recalled. "Lena raged, until he told her to stop. You would go to Gundarstorp, he told her, but you would come back. I asked, once, how he knew. It was how you had signed the letter, he said."

"I broke a promise. One made three times, Druise, and that matters." I picked up my *ladhar*, almost without thinking.

He rolled his eyes. "Linrathan men. Do you ever forgive yourselves? Vows and promises, so important to you."

"These are hard lands," I said. "Linrathe and Sorham, and Varsland too. Perhaps they demand hard oaths, to keep us strong."

"You think? Of the three of you, *amané*, who is strongest? Who has not fled from responsibility, or love, or hidden behind a philosophy, all without these endless vows? One promise only, and always kept, yes?"

"Two," I said, my fingers finding the right notes from the *danta*. "One to her Emperor, and one to Cillian. And yes, she's kept them both."

Chapter 66

"STAY," LENA HAD SAID, when the meal was over, and Cillian had reluctantly returned to work. "Today is a rest day for me. We could go riding?"

Away from the fort, where we could talk privately. "All right."

Up on the high land east of Berge we reined our horses in. Neither of us spoke. I looked north, as I always did, into Linrathe and towards Sorham, far beyond. Lena's eyes had been on the sea, but she turned to follow my gaze.

"Can I say a few things?" I nodded. "Cillian loves you. And not, as you must be sure now," she grinned, "as a friend and brother. I believe he has loved you since you were sixteen. He also loves me. Being a woman of this land, I see no contradiction there, or competition."

"He says you are his greatest love, and his greatest blessing."

"As he is mine." She glanced at me, her face serious. "But even on the river, and in Casil, I saw how different he was when he was with you. You were — you are — home for him, in a way I never will be, no matter how much we love each other. Just as Linrathe will always be home, for him and you, not my land."

"Lena, no."

"Yes. Have I never told you of the time he recited *War in Winter* for me, at the Kurzemë village? He was worrying about the boy who had given him music for his words, he told me."

I blinked, several times. She chuckled. "Don't cry. Once we'd met on the river, he told me more. He was honest about his attraction to you, but until the night before the Taiva, when he asked me if you could live with us, afterwards, I wasn't sure."

"And yet you welcomed me. More than welcomed." I had to ask. "Lena — I didn't understand at the time. But you said you were frightened of what might happen, if — "

"If you became lovers?" she said. "I was, a little. We know, women of this land, that the men who father our children also partner with men, when they are not with us. But for us to live together as we do — it is unprecedented, like so much else now. But what a ridiculous fear, Sorley, compared with the others we have faced together, all of us, and will face, over the years to come."

"It won't be often, Lena. A grace note, he said, rarely played."

"Will that be enough?"

"Enough? It is so much more than I thought there would ever be. Lena, thank you, if that doesn't sound…absurd." I would never fully comprehend her generosity, I knew.

"It is not all for you, you know," she said drily. "And not all for Cillian, either. You said it in Casil: perhaps you and I need each other too. Because he is far from easy, Sorley. You have some idea of that now; you'll have more, over the years." Her eyes rested on me. I saw her lips twitch. "I vowed he would never wake alone again. I did not say it had to be with me."

I laughed, a release of tension as much as anything. "How can you not be upset? You were so scared of wanting a woman's touch in Casil. I told you then the betrayal was not in the desire, but in acting on that desire. Which Cillian and I have done, and yet — "

"Idiot," she said, grinning. "Two reasons. One is what I have just said."

"And the other?"

She shrugged. "What I felt in Casil was casual, a response to a stimulus, in your words. To act on that, with no love behind it, just to escape my fears — that would have been a betrayal of what Cillian and I share."

"Then is Druise a betrayal?" Evan certainly had been, if I judged by Lena's measure.

"No! Gods, Sorley, is your mind completely befuddled by last night? You care for Druise, don't you?"

"Not as I do Cillian."

"That's not what I asked."

"Yes," I admitted. "I do. He is solid. Practical and comforting, and always cheerful."

"And kind. We have all been lucky to have him with us, for different reasons." She smiled, her hazel eyes creasing. We sat on the horses, looking north. A cloud obscured the sun, and the air was suddenly cold.

"You called him back from death," Lena said, her eyes still focused beyond the Wall. "Gnaius says the gods allowed that for a purpose. You know what Cillian believes that purpose is, and we are all part of that, me, and Druise, and yes, perhaps Gwenna, someday. But you — I believe you are bound to him by what you did, and he to you."

There was no amusement in her voice now. A shiver ran under my skin. "He told me once," I said slowly, "that the gods might demand a price from me, for that."

"They may," she said. "They may ask one of us all." I had no answer. Without speaking we turned the horses' heads downhill.

"There is one thing, before we go back," Lena said, before we began to ride. "An expectation you may have to adjust."

"What?" She told me.

"Truly? Cillian, who is so good with words?"

"Nonetheless."

CHAPTER 67

15 YEARS AFTER THE BATTLE OF THE TAIVA

"WHAT HAS MADE YOU smile?" Druise asked.

"Lena. We forget Gwenna is half her, because she looks so much like Cillian, and has his manner. But there's a fierceness in her that comes from her mother."

"Fierceness, yes. But compassion, too. All her concerns have been about her family, not herself."

"Her question wasn't what I expected. How could we have guessed what worried her?"

He grinned. "By remembering who taught her to play *xache*?"

"To think about the implications of actions, not just the actions themselves? You're right, Druise. But I wish she had not carried that fear for a winter, secretly."

"You think?" he asked. "Maybe easier to worry about that than other fears, yes? Will Cillian tell her his plans?"

"I believe he will tell her everything, one day. Someone must carry on after he's gone, and she is the heir." I began to wrap my *ladhar* in its oiled cloth.

"She will need strength," he said. "All Lena has given her."

"And the judgement her father has instilled in her, and your pragmatism, and my — " I shook my head. "I don't know what I've taught her, except a little skill on the *ladhar*."

"How to love."

"What?" The statement was completely out of character.

"*Amané*, everything in your life is about love. Cillian. Your music, your country, your lands. Your brother. The rest of us. Competing loves, sometimes. You find ways to hold them all, when most could not. I have seen that here. Gwenna has too."

"Her parents have taught her that. And you."

"In part. But you more so. So when Cillian tells her all the plans, the ones he does not share with us, she will understand more of why. That it is all to safeguard who and what he loves."

I exhaled, a long breath. "When he betrayed Linrathe to prevent me from being shamed, he vowed to keep me safe. I think everything else — almost everything else — he's done has sprung from that day and that vow."

"He would do that," Druise said simply. "You were his first love, yes?"

"He won't say so." Nor would he ever, I knew. In his silence was the same acknowledgment I made when I gave Lena the first cup of wine every evening. "Only a regret, sometimes, for the years apart. But I could never have been what Lena is to him. She isn't part of the oath-breaking, and she is separate from his atonement, as I am not. She is…" I groped for words, "the music that frees him. I'm content to be a grace note." Or a bell of remembrance, our rare times together both a joy and a reminder of the price paid.

Druise ran a hand down my arm. "As I am content with our duet. It does not bother you, that he does not say?"

"For all Cillian's skill with words, Lena told me once that she could count on one hand the number of times he's actually said he loves her. Endearments, and indirectly, but otherwise, no."

Druise grinned. "That does not surprise me. Some things are too deep for words. Not to you either?"

I shook my head. "Never. Not directly. Little more than you have heard him say."

"It is enough?"

Mo Somhairle gràhadh. "It is," I said. I reached for Druise's hand, turning it over in mine. A hand that wielded a sword for our safety, and made music, and held me close. "Partner," I said. "Lover. Beloved friend. Shall we go home, Druise?"

A Preview of Empire's Heir

Chapter 1: Daughter

"GWENNA." RUAR SAT BACK in his chair. "I can't accept that."

He is your ally, not your adversary, I told myself, facing the *Teannasach* of Linrathe across the table. "The tariff on fleeces must be increased," I said firmly. "Ésparias has no shortage of sheep. We've dropped the fees on timber, after all."

"Timber benefits only some landholders. Fleeces bring money to almost everyone," Ruar countered. Beside him, his young son shifted a little. Bored, perhaps; we'd been renegotiating the border tariffs for two days.

I glanced down at the figures before me. I still had a little room to bargain. "A reduction in the tariff on salt fish would serve the coastal *torps*." I suggested a number. We needed timber, with all the new buildings being constructed, and salt fish for the ships going back and forth to Casil. The coarse wool of the hardy northern sheep was of limited value in the Eastern Empire.

"Is this fair, Daragh?" Ruar asked his son. In the tradition of Linrathe, the boy was there to listen and learn. This wasn't the first question the *Teannasach* had asked him over the last two days.

"I think it is," Daragh said. "If Ésparias does not want our fleeces, Varsland will. We will not lose revenue, *Athàir*."

"Nor will we," his father agreed. "I accept the new tariffs. Fairly done, Gwenna."

"Thank you." Tension seeped from me. My first independent negotiation was over, and I'd got the agreement I'd been directed to produce. Granted, this was a routine process, slight adjustments made every three years, but still—I'd done it. "The agreement will be ready to sign soon, will it not, Sorley?"

"I'll have two copies done in the morning," Sorley said from down the table, where, in his role as *scáeli*, he'd been recording the session. "Will that be soon enough for you, Ruar?"

"It will," the *Teannasach* said. "We'll leave tomorrow. I've still things to discuss with Cillian, but I shouldn't be away from home too long. Nor should we intrude here any longer than we must."

Sorley's lips tightened. "The needs of government go on. Government and Empires."

"And lives." Ruar put a hand on his son's shoulder as he spoke. "Loss comes to us all, and sometimes far too soon." His too would be a house of mourning before long; his wife, Helvi, was dying. She'd been ill for over a year, a wasting illness slowly killing her. An expected death, now, unlike the sudden fever that, just over a week ago, had taken the little sister I had barely known.

We—Sorley and Druise and I—had returned home four summers past from our northern travels to my mother's announcement that she was pregnant. The baby, she told us, was due a few weeks after mid-winter. I'd been—what? Embarrassed, I suppose, although less so than I might have been before that summer and Druise's blunt words to me. He, I remembered, had been delighted.

But I had gone back to cadet school, and the next summer I'd only had two weeks of leave, and how well could one get to know a five-month-old baby? Lianë was sweet enough, her hair not the almost black of mine and Colm's but a reddish-gold, and she gurgled and smiled contentedly in Mhairi's arms.

Except for the requisite three months in the company of my classmates, taking advanced lessons in diplomacy from my father, I'd been home fewer than eight full weeks in the last four years. Not much time to become more than fondly interested in Lianë. In the months of intense study, I hadn't been treated as a member of the family, but as another senior diplomatic cadet from Ésparias. Only in my private seminars with my father was the formality dropped, and we'd had other things to talk about than my baby sister. She hadn't been mentioned more than once or twice, and even then, it was still in the context of our discussions.

Ruar stood. "I'll see you both at dinner," he said. "Come, Daragh; let us find the *Comiádh*, and discover what you are to read and study." Daragh was twelve, and in the usual course of things, he would have become a student of my father's this year. But there would be no students at the *Ti'ach na Cillian* until at least midwinter, because in a very few weeks, mourning a dead child or not, we were travelling to Casil to witness the investiture of Alekos, son of the abdicating Empress Eudekia, as the Emperor of the East. Alekos was twenty-one, and unmarried, and the invitation had been specific. I, heir to the leadership of Ésparias, must be present.

I hadn't needed six years of diplomatic training to decipher the message. Alekos needed a bride, and the Empress thought that bride might well be me.

Paths Untrodden

Sorley's song for Cillian

My true love's eyes are darkly gleaming
In candlelight and music's lure;
One night alone, at spring's fair dawning,
To keep me longing through the years,
To leave my soul bereft and mourning.
You danced that night with grace unfettered,
A glance my way, a touch bestowed.
Your dark hair swept by supple fingers.
Too soon the day, the calling road,
The shaken head when asked to linger.
A long, long path, and distance boundless,
Years of sorrow and empty days
Till chance or fate together brought us,
So far from home, in summer's blaze,
With war behind and war before us.
The gods and time have blessed us both
With love's reward for all our years
Of wandering on lonely ways;
A respite offered for our cares,
A soul to hold ours, all our days.
But candlelight and music's memory,
Dark eyes gleaming over wine

Revive that youthful love and longing
For graceful fingers touching mine
For kisses left at day's first dawning.
My life's companion loves me truly
My heart is his and his is mine,
But older love is not forgotten
There is, by fate, or god's design
A yearning still for paths untrodden
You danced that night with grace unfettered,
A glance my way, a touch bestowed.
Your dark hair swept by supple fingers.
Uncharted ways might be explored,
Still dreams this wistful, loving singer.

Acknowledgments

OF ALL MY BOOKS to date, Oraiáphon and Empire's Reckoning were the hardest to write, for several reasons: voice, structure, and theme. Switching narrators to the musician Sorley meant finding my way into the mind of a new character, after twenty years of listening to Lena, and a male character at that. The two time-line structure also plagued me, and I may or may not have put it together effectively. But theme was by far the hardest: the price of war, personal and political, and the courage we need, as individuals and countries, to move beyond it into reconciliation and new ways of living – and why that courage may look, at first glance, like betrayal.

To Terrence Thomas, who acted as developmental editor, and Bjørn Larssen and Van Waffle, beta/sensitivity readers, my deepest appreciation for pointing out flaws and suggesting solutions. Your honesty, invaluable criticism. and willingness to work with me is so deeply appreciated. Bjørn especially insisted I examine the relationship between Sorley and Druisius more closely, and also told me to stop making Sorley so nice. Any remaining errors, in content or structure, are my own.

I will admit that in the personal story arcs in Reckoning, I wavered on how far I would take the parallels between the political plot and the personal, and to my husband, Brian Rennie, who was adamant that only one outcome was true to my characters, my world, and my theme, I owe a huge thank you for insisting I did not compromise my vision.

Writing may be a solitary pursuit, but it is so much easier with support. For that support, thank you to other members of the Arboretum Press collective (Terry, I know Aristotle would be throwing up his hands in despair over Reckoning, but your editorial work was still respected and helpful); to the Guelph Genre Group of Vocamus Writers' Community; to the members of the Writing Room at The Bookshelf, and to the #WritingCommunity on Twitter: all have provided me with good conversations, good friends, and hours of procrastination.

Special thanks to my cover designer, Anthony O'Brien, who always creates a cover that looks exactly like what I had in mind.

And of course, thank you to you who buy my books, both those who asked for Sorley's story and those who are just discovering the series. That there are people out there who love my world and its characters as much as I do remains a source of wonder and delight.

Guelph, February 2022

Other Books by Marian L Thorpe

Empire's Legacy:
The Complete Trilogy
Empire's Daughter
Empire's Hostage
Empire's Exile
Empire's Heir

 Empire's Passing

Empress & Soldier

Social Media Links

Visit my website:
www.marianlthorpe.com

ABOUT THE AUTHOR

NOT CONTENT WITH TWO careers as a research scientist and an educator, Marian L Thorpe decided to go back to what she'd always wanted to do and be a writer. Describing her books as 'historical fiction of another world', Marian also has published short stories and poetry. Her life-long interest in Roman and post-Roman European history informs her novels, while her avocations of landscape archaeology and birding provide background to her settings. Marian lives in a small city in Canada with her husband and (currently) one cat.

www.ingramcontent.com/pod-product-compliance
Lightning Source LLC
Chambersburg PA
CBHW050844210726
48290CB00004B/1071